ANGEL
STATION

Other Tor Books by Walter Jon Williams

Ambassador of Progress
Hardwired
Knight Moves
Voice of the Whirlwind
Divertimenti: *The Crown Jewels*
House of Shards

ANGEL STATION

Walter Jon Williams

A TOM DOHERTY ASSOCIATES BOOK
NEW YORK

ANGEL STATION

Copyright © 1989 by Walter Jon Williams

A TOR BOOK
Published by Tom Doherty Associates, Inc.
49 West 24 Street
New York, NY 10010

First edition: July 1989
0 9 8 7 6 5 4 3 2 1

CHAPTER

1

WHEN THEIR FATHER KILLED HIMSELF HE RECORDED THE EVENT, just as he recorded everything else of importance in his sad, ill-organized life. "I know what's coming," he said. "I know I can't stop it. Can't change. I'm sorry."

When it happened *Runaway* was in deep space, drifting between singularity shots. Pasco, their father, hung in the air, weightless, in the computer compartment. Fat, ineffectual, his long grey hair and beard uncontained and floating out around him, he looked like a weeping Father Christmas. Behind him, outside monitors showed a random, slowly rotating field of stars.

"We can't survive," he said. "Not the way we're going." He swallowed, hard. His hands were shaking as they drifted weightlessly by his sides. He was surrounded by his junk: old computer consoles, malfunctioning holo cameras, tangles of optic wire, battered microscopes, microsurgery and gene-splicing equipment, an old autowomb. All the stuff he'd gathered over the years, gathered as part of a superstition almost, as if all the little bits of equipment, the programs he'd stitched together and run, the sperm and ova he'd tinkered with, the incessant recordings of himself that he'd made, hours on hours, would somehow add up to a whole, would re-create the universe in a way that made sense to him. Would magic him away from the slow death which he, his children, his ship, were facing.

"I'm not adaptable enough," he said. "Look. I've made you smart. You're fast. Maybe you can figure a way out of this. I'd just be in your way." A fastlearn cartridge, unnoticed, hung by his foot, making slow-motion pirouettes in the whispering stream of recirculated air.

"If I stay around, I'll fail." He shook his shaggy head. "I'll go down, and you'll just go down with me. I'm not strong enough. Not any more." He was drifting closer to the camera now. His children could see the pouched eyes, the broken veins on his nose and cheeks, the saliva that clung to his lower lip. Eyes that were dilated and mad. A stream of red pills, unnoticed, was trailing out of a pocket, spinning into the compartment like drops of blood. "I'm going to get out of your way. An overdose. It won't hurt. Kick my bod out the airlock when I'm gone." He began to cry. "Take care of Kitten," he wept. "I know she loves me."

His children waited for him to say more but he just hung there, crying. His massive, rounded shoulders shook as he rotated slowly. His tears hovered in the compartment like jewels. One of the teardrops drifted to the camera lens and adhered to it, refracting motion, colors, a smear of bleeding madness. Their father gasped. "I'm sorry," he said again, his voice a husky whisper, and around the splatter on the lens they could see him reaching for the camera to shut it off.

The screen went black. Ubu reached for the controls with his upper left hand, hesitated, looked at his sister. "You want to see it again?" he asked.

She looked at him with her wide, deep-space eyes. She stroked Maxim, the white cat in her lap, without looking at him. The cat's purr seemed louder than her voice. "Erase it," she said.

Ubu hesitated for a moment, his finger hovering above the Erase button. He wanted the message to contain something worth remembering, some knowledge that would be of use, a final dying piece of wisdom that would help put his father into place, into some synthesis in which his life, their lives, his dying could all be understood.

There was nothing. Nothing but the final sad crumbling of a mind run out of choices and no longer sane, backed into a corner it couldn't see a way out of. That and the inane request about Kitten. Ubu understood this. But his longing made him hesitate.

There was an ache in his throat. He pressed the button. The little electric memory died without resistance, without a sound. The ache didn't fade.

Beautiful Maria looked at him. "It wasn't unexpected," she said. She chewed a lip. "We knew he wouldn't last. That . . . *something* . . . was going to happen with him." She stood, gathered the cat's four dangling limbs. Her long blue-black hair fell forward, shrouded her face. "I'm going to my compartment," she said.

Ubu was still staring at the screen, his brows knit. Wanting the wisdom to come. He turned to his sister.

"Do you want company?"

She shook her head. "Later, maybe."

"Shall I call you? When I . . . put him out?"

Beautiful Maria's hair shimmered like dark rain. "Yes. Please."

Ubu watched as she slipped out of the command cage. Then he turned back to the comm board again.

A distant shudder came up from the floor, up the chair's single metal pillar, through Ubu's spine. A little misalignment in the ship's centrifuge, the huge bearings burning slowly, metal being shorn away slice by slice. Not critical, not yet. There were years to go before he'd have to really worry about it.

The fuge droned around him. He'd have to fire his father out the airlock before the next singularity shoot.

He stood and walked to his cabin, a humming metal shell on the second level of the fuge. The walls and ceiling were covered, every inch, with pictures he'd pasted up. Holo star charts that brought constellations to within an inch of his nose, pictures of nebulae, of black holes, of ships. People suited for vacuum, combat, exploration. Phil Mendoza looking gallant; Michiko Tanaka holding a sizer guitar in one hand, a pistol in the other. Hype-people with painted eyes and lips like drops of bloody dew, gazing into the distance with unreachable longing. Alien creatures imagined or real. Pictures of death, of faceplates spattered with blood, of eyes gazing out in horror. Pictures of his father.

Ubu sat on his rack and stared up at the ceiling, at the chaos of fading plastic, the images that had once had meaning for him and now seemed pointless, a ridiculous, childish display of fantasy and longing, no longer a mirror of his mind.

Suddenly his father was by him, sitting in a chair in the center of the compartment. Pasco was younger, his hair and beard neatly trimmed. Confident, fit. Like the father in the pictures Ubu had pasted to the ceiling.

"Is something bothering you, son?" his father asked. "Is there anything I can help you with?"

Ubu looked at his father and narrowed his eyes. "Get lost, Pop," he said. "You killed yourself, asshole."

Pasco looked at him sadly for a moment. "I just wanted you to know that I'll be around," he said.

"Fuck that." Ubu reached for the control panel and turned off the holo display. His father vanished. So did his chair.

Ubu's skin felt hot. He stood on his rack and began tearing at the pictures on the ceiling. They were glued on thoroughly and he scarred them white with the tracks of his fingernails. A rain of plastic fell, a drifting snow of curling white foam. Sobs tried to break out of his chest. With difficulty he kept them down.

At the end he stood amid piles of ruined chaff. Captain of the *Runaway*, he thought. Maria didn't want the job; it was his by default. Bossrider. Singularity shooter número uno. Captain of all I survey.

Quietly, he began to laugh.

"I have a plan."

Beautiful Maria looked up at him, seeing his pale skin and fair hair spattered with flecks of foam. She and Ubu were in computer central, the brass nozzles and long black tubes of tempafoam sprayers in their hands. Two months after their father's death, they had finally nerved themselves to deal with his belongings. They collected all the rubble, lashed it together, covered it with tempafoam until they could sell it for spare parts at Ascención, their next port of call. Probably the only thing that would bring money would be all the cameras that Pasco had set up throughout the ship to record his activities.

Maria hooked a stray strand of hair behind one ear. The rest of her black river of hair had been tied back until they returned to the fuge's gravity.

"What plan?" she said.

Ubu grinned. "You know Dig Angel? The Long Reach subsidiary? They've got an open advert on the Ascención Station board wanting contracts for Kanto-compatible miners and comps for their new operation in Angelica."

"Be wanting to shoot for whoever's gonna pick up the contract?"

"Better than that, Maria. Better."

Beautiful Maria rotated gently in midair, hooked one hand around a padded castoff bar on the command cage, then caught the battered old autowomb with her nimble feet. She drew it close, then let go of the bar and rotated, using the tension on the tempafoam hose as a pivot point. She pressed the trigger. The turbines of the portable compressor whined and foam spattered the clear plastic womb where Maria's heart had taken its first beat, where her developing eyes first turned away from the light.

Burying her past in foam, she thought. A distant sense of loss hummed in her mind. This wasn't just Pasco's gear, this was a part of her life as well. Artifacts of her existence were disappearing, smothering in layers of foam, dying.

"We pick up the contract ourselves," Ubu said. His voice was insistent. "We get a loan, buy the miners from the Kanto rep, deliver them in our own holds. Our profit be increased at least a hundred percent."

Beads of foam swelled over the womb's control panel. Maria blinked bits of the stuff from her eyes. "Why isn't Long Reach supplying their own operation?"

"Be too successful, that's why. I checked the price of Long Reach stock. They're expanding so far ahead of their programmed growth that they're running short of supplies out here on the Edge."

"It's still funny." Maria wiped sweat from her forehead. She looked at Ubu thoughtfully. "And who's gonna give us a loan, anyway?"

"OttoBanque."

"OttoBanque." She repeated the word slowly, knowing what Ubu wanted. A new tension rose in her body, armored her against Ubu's idea.

He looked at her defiantly. "We've got the miners for collateral. And the contract's just *sitting* there."

"I don't like it."

"Look at the figures."

She looked away. She didn't want to think about it. "What if it goes wrong?"

"What if it goes *right?*" He kicked off from the black padded shutters that they'd closed over the computer readouts while they were playing with the foam, came to her, took her shoulders in his upper set of hands.

Maria's knuckles were white as they clutched the hose and sprayer. "I don't know if I want to do this."

"Let me show you the figures."

She shook her head. A river of sorrow opened in her heart. Are we really this desperate? she thought. "Okay," she said. "I'll look."

"You may not have to. They may give us the loan anyway."

"Yeah. Maybe." Not believing it.

Knowing she couldn't resist much longer.

"Words?" Ubu looked at his sister.

Her eyes reflected the light of the monitor, a cold gray glaze, like the glaze in Pasco's eyes when Ubu had reached out to close them. She raised a hand to her throat. "He was old," she said. "He tried hard and couldn't make it. We didn't know how to help him. He died." She shrugged. "I can't think of anything else."

A good father? Ubu wanted to ask. He made us out of frozen sperm and ova that he'd bought somewhere, stitched together in a secondhand splicer he'd bought as junk. No genes in common, neither with ourselves nor Pasco, not a real brother and sister and father, just people living together. Gave us talents we're not sure we know how to use. Jacked our growth with hormone boosters and fastlearn cartridges, machine maturity to go with prematurely adult bodies. He thought we had something to give him, something he was desperate for. We were looking to him for answers, and all the time it was Pasco who wanted the answers from us.

Ubu looked at the monitor, the heavy body zipped into its plastic tote bag. Good father or not, now a dead thing.

Ubu had put Pasco in an airlock, not in the trash ejector, wanting him to go like a person and not a piece of garbage. He touched the ship systems board, gave it an order. The hardwired safety codes tagged off alarms, red lights. Ubu overrode them. The lock door blew open, and in a blurred instant Pasco was gone, a plastic-wrapped projectile falling down a long cold curve toward galactic center. A harsh metallic alarm was his last epitaph. Ubu closed the lock and the alarm faded. Red lights changed to green. Tears fell down Beautiful Maria's cheeks. She stood and turned away.

"I want to take us through the next shoot," she said. Ubu could barely hear her soft voice. "Okay?"

"If you want."

"I'll set it up in the computer. I'll let you know when it's time." She walked away. She was naked, the way they often were in the ship, and Ubu watched the way her long hair molded itself to the curve of her spine, a river of black contrasting with the warm milk-white skin. Warmth fluttered in his nerves, his stomach.

Why do I care more about that than Pasco? he wondered. Does it matter that I don't care more than I do?

Ubu stared at the monitor for a moment, the gray flickering image of the empty airlock. He stood up, left the control cage, pulled open the door of a maintenance locker.

Time to deal with Kitten.

Two months after picking up the Dig Angel contract, *Runaway* whiteholed out of the Now within a few thousand kilometers of optimal, a week out of Angelica Station. After their radio signal reached the station and returned, Ubu discovered they were in trouble.

He sat bolt upright and looked at the newsfax coming in. Maxim, disturbed, leaped from his lap. "Dig Angel," he said. "Gone under. Long Reach crashed."

"We had a contract," Beautiful Maria said. Her voice was jagged with the aftereffects of the singularity shoot, the pulse of the Now. The dreamy quality of it sent a pale blue color into Ubu's head, contrasting with his own blazing frustration.

Ubu clenched his teeth. Anger poured up his spine. This was all his fault.

He cast a look at Beautiful Maria. She wasn't looking at him, didn't want to say *I told you so*.

"We'll be on the tail end of a long list of creditors," Ubu said. "We won't get our money in years."

"Another buyer?"

"No other small companies in this system. We're way the hell out on the Edge—there's only one big city on the planet, and the rest is mining in the asteroids. We'll have to sell to a speculator. Maybe a rep from another mining company in another system, if we can find one." Ubu glared at the newsfax and ran sums in his head. "If we can get docking charges and transport, we can be happy."

Beautiful Maria licked her lips as if trying to taste their options. "Maybe we can pick up a cargo to tide us over. Drugs or something, that doesn't take up space in the cargo bay."

"Better than dying right in Angelica." He began flicking through the newsfax. "Let's see who's buying." He felt sweat trickling down his nape. Data flickered on the screen. There had to be a buyer somewhere onstation. Had to be.

If there wasn't, Angelica was the end.

The sound of finger exercises came from the upper lounge. Beautiful Maria was warming up on her sizer keyboard. Ubu walked along the smooth green centrifuge carpet and opened the screen. Maria looked up.

"Do you remember Cole Redwing?" Ubu said.

"Vaguely. He was on the *Roland*, yes?" Her fingers moved precisely over the keys.

"Used to be. Been watching the newsfax coming out of Angel. He killed his family, then himself."

Maria looked at him in shock. Her left hand hung on one chord, shooting a bright yellow flare into Ubu's mind. "When?" she said.

"Fifteen standard ago. Infix Station. The bank had just confiscated his drive."

Maria looked down at her hand. The chord burned on.

Though Ubu and Redwing had only met once or twice, Ubu's mind could sketch him perfectly. Black hair, pebble eyes, soft voice, large hands. He'd used a hamier, the newsfax said. Ubu thought aboqt a hammer in those big hands.

"It used to be years before you'd ever hear of a murder on a shooter ship," Ubu said. "Remamber? And nkw there's two or three a year.-'

"Killed his family."

And for a mkment they looked away from one ankther while the sizer chord shimmered on, each thinking about Pasco, aboqt how maybe they were lucky he'd chosen his particular form of self-destructive despair when his time ran out.

Maria lifted her hand from the keyboard and looked at it as if she'd never seen it before. "Get your guitar," she said, "and play with me."

"Yeah." He opened the instrument locker and took out his old black Alfredo with the plastic triangular body and the genuine hardwood neck.

His mind was already buzzing, hard angry chords to call up Redwing and lay him to rest.

Wherever there were shooters and systers, wherever people lived in the Now, there lived also the zone with which they lived in symbiosis, where they were both fed and eaten. The neighborhood had many names: on Masquerade it was called the Road; on Bezel it was Port Town; here on Angelica Station, it was called the Fringe.

The Fringe lived in perpetual twilight. It curved gently upward from where Maria and Ubu stood, dark storefronts full of bustle, holograms moving in explosive colors, a population in perpetual transit.

The main street had no name, being the only one, the long metal road that circled the rim of wheel-shaped Angelica Station. Crowded against it were the small operators that made their living from the commerce of shooters and systers: margin banks, trading companies, gene banks, small casinos, hotels, bars, hookshops, missions for Jesus Rice or the Mahayana Buddha, eateries, cosmetic surgeries, pawnshops . . . the usual bright, noisy gamut of shops, most facing the street, some turned into little dark side-alleys that curled off the main road, like appendices off some primitive intestine.

Ubu and Beautiful Maria walked the length of the Fringe, savoring the bright colors, the smells, the exotic flavor of the traffic. Maria bought some chips and fried chicken from a vendor. Ubu bought a recyclable plastic bulb of Kolodny beer.

Maria had two arms and two legs, not entirely the norm for full-time tide riders. Ubu had an extra pair of arms. Their father had bred them for adaptability, not specialization. Ubu was thirteen years old and six feet four inches tall. The prevailing fashion was for androgyny and he dressed against it, wearing cutoff jeans, sandals, a silver vest hacked out of an old piece of reflec and held together with orange tape. His fair hair was shaggy over his ears. His upper body, massive with overlapping arm muscle, was powerful, a shooter typicality. He moved fast when he wanted to.

Beautiful Maria was eleven years old and an inch shorter than her brother. She wore a long robe of the same smoky color as her eyes. Her pale face glowed, like cream poured in sable glass, from its soft aureole of blue-black hair. Her voice was soft, her hands moved white in the air like doves. The long hair was unusual in a shooter, but appropriate on Maria. Her name was not inappropriate, either.

A four-armed shooter, a mutanto, slid by on his easicart, waved an arm that rotated on a hip socket. There was pain in his eyes, distorting a seamless face unworn by gravity. A desperate man, Maria knew, to come all the way to the rim to do business, when he could stay at the hub where his weight wouldn't crush him and do his business through the phone.

Desperate. Like the crew of the *Runaway*.

At least, she thought, she and Ubu had more choices. If the mutanto lost his livelihood, he'd have little choice but a long-term indentureship to some company like Biagra-Exeter. A contract on their terms, the mutanto being a beggar.

Maria swallowed a piece of chicken, cayenne pepper burning her palate, then took a shot of Ubu's beer. Saw the edge of the Fringe ahead, where the twilight turned into the bright white corridors of the

Outside Life. A coldness touched her. "Uniquip," she said. "It's gone. Look. The Fringe's got smaller."

"Jesus Rice. It's only been a few months." He licked his lips. "Where we gonna sell our cargo? Hiliners won't want it."

There wasn't a line drawn at the edge of the Fringe, or a sheet of transparent glass set up where the Fringe turned away from the Now, toward the Outside, but there might as well have been. The Fringe was dark, crowded, alive with the pulse of people cutting deals, the whisper of small commerce, the sharp smell of sweat and adrenaline from those who were operating on the margin. Beyond the twilight the metal street had been paved with razor-thin slices of the marble encased in plastic and laid down in big rolls, like toilet tissue. Along the bright street were the big companies, the concerns that stretched all the way across human space, operating their fleets of haulers, stations, liners, their centers of finance and investment . . . the Outsiders who had the ear of the Multi-Pollies in the center of human space, who wanted the entire universe to be nothing but a succession of white humming corridors, filled with orderly humanity busy accumulating capital, making investments in the safest places, giving it to the Outsiders to finance the Multi-Pollies' policy of Consolidation, denying the Edge, the margin, expansion.

Ubu hawked and spat, his saliva arcing out of the twilight, toward the cold fluorescent life of Outside humanity. "Fuck that," he said.

"It's smaller," Maria said again. Sadly.

"Maybe they'll keep part of the Fringe open," Ubu said. "Clean it up a little, then keep it as a place for Mudville tourists. So they can get drunk and gamble away their souls to the Hiline companies."

"*Consolidation*," said Beautiful Maria. It was the foulest word she could think of.

Ubu turned away from the Mainstream. A whore's metallic laughter floated toward him from the Fringe.

"Let's go," he said. "We've gotta do some business."

Ubu heard the locker close behind him. His right hands held a charged silver glitch rod, two feet in length. There were faded red warning labels pasted on it. A red LED blinked urgently by his hand, telling him it was armed. His finger was near its trigger.

He felt his arms tremble. His tool chest banged against his left knee. His breath was quick. He paused outside Pasco's door and wiped imaginary sweat from his forehead.

He stepped in. The front half of the compartment was empty. Full of disordered junk, fastlearn cartridges tossed on furniture, pictures of the family Pasco had lost in the airlock explosion, printouts lying under a light tracing of dust, unlooked at for years, computer consoles pulled apart and never put back together . . . all levels of Pasco's madness, receding into the years, awaiting excavation like some old desert mound on Earth. Ubu put down the tool chest. His heart pounded. He wiped his face again, stretched out his left lower arm, opened the door into the bedroom.

It isn't murder, he told himself.

The android sex toy was sitting on Pasco's rack. She looked up at Ubu as he came in. Ubu knew he would remember that forever, the toss of the short blond curls, the flash of the silver-and-lapis stud in her left nostril, the look in the wide green eyes. Seeing the glitch rod, and knowing. Kitten was naked, as Ubu had more or less expected, wearing only the jewelry that Pasco, in his senile passion, had given her. Rings flickered on her fingers, bangles danced from her wrists. A sapphire hung between her breasts.

Ubu stopped in the doorway. Just go in and do it, he told himself.

"Pop's dead," he said.

"I know," said Kitten. Her eyes glittered with artificial tears. "He left me a message. He said he loved me."

"He would." The glitch rod at the end of his upper right arm seemed to weigh a hundred pounds. He shifted it to the other right hand.

Kitten had been three years on the ship. Pasco had kept her in his cabin for a week before Ubu found out about her. He'd heard her tinkling, idiot laugh from his father's double cabin as he passed by, then heard his father's answering laughter. Somehow he'd known it wasn't a hype.

He had just got his growth then, shooting up a foot in the space of a year, and the spurt had left him clumsy. His muscles ached from the onset of mones that stressed him like stellar tides. Passions swept through him like fever: hatred, resentment, lust, fury . . . He worked like a demon to exorcise them and did his best to avoid Pasco and Maria, spending his onstation time alone, a solo shooter.

At the sound of the laughter Ubu stopped in the corridor, turned . . . and somehow his feet got tangled and he had to throw out his four arms for balance. Unknowing laughter mocked him, leaving a scattering burnt-orange color in his mind, a sour taste on his tongue. Anger rose unbidden. He opened Pasco's door.

Kitten stood on a small table, her arms raised, her legs apart for balance. Little-girl laughter tinkled from her throat. Her green eyes looked into his. The laughter continued.

Pasco was crouched in front of her among a scatter of pills, black and red. His slack furry body was marked with blue and ochre. He was painting her, the spray gun in his hand. Violent colors gleamed wetly across her body. The room smelled of sex. There was something in Pasco's laughter Ubu had never heard, something that made sharp metallic colors dance in his skull.

Pasco made a sound in his throat and rose from his crouch. He put his arms around her, pressing himself to her color, smearing himself against her. He reached a hand up behind her back to grasp her hair, pulling her head back as he pressed his head between her breasts. Her laughter never stopped, never changed its tone. Ubu could see the programmed puppet-sounds vibrating in her taut throat.

Her eyes never left him. Even as he closed the door he could see her watching him through slitted lids. He stared at the face of the closed door, wishing it were possible to forget.

Kitten's eyes were open now, watching Ubu standing in the door with the glitch rod in his hands. Tears ran down her face. "I loved him, Ubu," she said. "I'm programmed that way. Programmed to love what my partner loves, a kind of feedback."

Did he teach you to cry? Ubu wondered. Or did that come in standard programming? "I know," he said.

He knew she was an idiot by most standards, a puppet. Good enough for sex, if your taste went that way, useless for anything else. Even conversation was highly limited, mostly parroting what she'd been told, that and the laughter that sprayed from her whenever her small mind told her the time might be appropriate. A parasite on the ship, unable to contribute even to her small upkeep. Pasco had bought a rich man's toy and put *Runaway* in hock to do it.

She was smart enough, though, to want to survive. Kitten gazed up at him. Licked her lips.

Do it, Ubu thought. It's not killing.

"I could learn to love someone else," she said. "It's an easy operation. You don't have to . . . use *that* for it. Just a little adjustment. I could be whatever you want."

And have me senile by the time I'm fifteen, Ubu thought. Dancing on the end of her robot's strings while she laughs her idiot laugh. He stepped forward, shifted the rod to his upper set of hands. Kitten flinched back against the wall.

He pushed the rod out. Remembered paint gleaming on her synthetic flesh, the smell of sex, the sound of Pasco's laughter.

"You don't have to do that," she said quickly. "I'll stay out of your way." Her voice rose to a wail. "*Why don't you* like me?"

Ubu closed his eyes, not wanting to see. A fist seemed to tighten in his throat. He pushed the glitch rod forward blindly, swept it left and right with his finger on the trigger.

A crack of electricity. The fall of something heavy onto pillows. The smell of burning.

Ubu opened his eyes. Kitten lay crumpled on the rack, a scorch mark on her flank where the glitch rod had touched. She was wiped, her programming erased. Her eyes were open. There was a tremor in her thigh. Her fingers twitched randomly. Already the scorch mark on the synthetic skin was beginning to heal.

If he'd had the oral codes that controlled her, he wouldn't have had to do it this way. But only Pasco had the codes. He hadn't trusted anyone else around his blonde obsession.

Ubu dropped the rod to the padded floor. He turned and went back to the front compartment for his toolbox. Brought it in, put it on the rack, opened it.

The smell of burning was still in his throat, unforgettable. He reached out to Kitten's shoulder, feeling the warm touch of perfect skin. He turned her over. Her limbs splayed over the rack. Ubu took out a knife, cut the skin between the shoulder blades, parted it before it healed. Revealed the control switch. He inserted a screwdriver and shut off the android's automatic systems.

"Ubu." Maria's voice, grating in the ship intercom. "Fifteen minutes to shoot."

Ubu took the jewelry from the cooling body. Turned the head, pulled the silver stud from the nose, felt the flesh resist and then tear, knew the small brutal act would be in his mind forever—far longer than the wound he'd just made, which would heal when Kitten was reconnected.

He put the jewelry in a pillowcase. Sell this stuff, he thought. It would look nice on Maria, but he didn't want to see it again.

The sheet under Kitten's head was turning wet. Her tear reservoir, draining.

Ubu knew that he was not going to be able to forget this, that he would relive it, the smell, the anger, that final electric *snap* and the draining of ionized tears . . . it would come back to him. He stood up and walked blindly out of the compartment to find another plastic bag. Stuff her in, he thought, sell her once we reach Caliban Station.

He was trying hard not to feel like a murderer.

"Your play?" The bouncer leered at Beautiful Maria from behind his window of glass. Teeth gleamed below a mustache sharp as an icepick. Black eyes stared stonily from behind the perfect round metal frames of a black-ribboned pince-nez.

Beautiful Maria gazed at the double reflections of herself. "Blackhole," she said. Red Nine was moving through her veins. Her nerves jittered, flared.

"Stakes? You got, or just looking?" The steel smile came again. "Mudviller inside, looking for a shooter femme, maybe. Has that yearning gaze anyway. You could be his good luck."

"Ten-twenty," Maria said. She held up a black credit counter. The smile broadened.

"Be my guest, shooter femme. Take my word. Tide riders be lucky at blackhole."

Especially me, Maria thought. There was an electric buzz as the bolt locked back. She pressed the doorplate and it swung in. The door sighed shut behind her, the lock snapping closed.

The place was called Stellar City, a deliberately old-fashioned name, a self-mockery. It was on the third level of a ramshackle collection of eateries, a cheap hotel, a used-clothing boutique. Maria had to climb a narrow foam ramp to get here. The walls were made of tempafoam: the place had recently moved from somewhere else on the Fringe, would probably move again before long. The casino was dark, spotlights picking out the active tables. Fringe people, systers, shooters. The room was silent with concentration, sweat, and thought.

The Mudviller was obvious, overdressed like he was expecting weather here, a middle-aged man staring hopelessly at the naked brown breasts of the woman who was dealing vingt-et-un. Beautiful Maria grinned. Nobody was going to be *his* luck tonight, not as long as he kept gazing at the distractions the house was throwing in his face.

Red Nine pulsed in her nerves. The people in the room seemed to move through the smoky room in slow motion. Maria moved to the back, to the blackhole booth. She stepped inside, closed the transparent door. When she sat on the padded chair, the long metal projectors, each topped by a delicate web of stimulus antennae, eased out of the walls with a slow hiss, each pointed at her head. She put the credit counter in the slot. Pressed the button. Black diamond space exploded in her head, filled with burning singularities, the radio cry of dying matter.

Maria was in a silver metal sphere called a pinball. She floated in the dark vacuum. Distantly, unspeakable gravities tugged at her. The object of the game was to navigate from place to place by dipping into the singularities' gravity wells, flinging the pinball in and out of the black holes' embrace. There was a time limit to provide a sense of urgency, and the computer would try to glitch up the ride, introducing random variations: making singularities appear in the path of the pinball after it had accelerated too fast to avoid them, running variations on the stars' densities, causing fuel shortages, announcing shutdowns of various parts of her navigation aids and simulation screens. She could opt for an easy ride or a hard one, the payoff rising with the difficulty. It was enough like a regular singularity shoot to produce a sense of familiarity, but enough unlike one so that she couldn't trust her shooter's reflexes.

Red Nine burned at her, urging her to choose the maximum. She overrode the impulse and chose a medium level, deciding to stretch her nerves a little first. She placed her bet.

Numbers spun in the lower right corner of her field of vision, the seconds ticking away. There were cash bonuses if she made her ride in less than seventy-five percent of her allotted time. A destination star glowed briefly, along with the number of black holes she would have to play tag with along the way.

"Okay," she murmured, and began her acceleration. Red Nine fired her neurotransmitters and sparked in her brain as she chose a path, as she felt a gravity well reaching out to touch her. She looked into the black negation before her. Smiled. And felt the pinball moan, torn by the tides of gravity.

Reflex handled the pinball, its burns and course corrections, its dives into the pulsing wells of gravity. Another part of her mind plotted strategy. And, as she played, as the time counters ran in the lower corner of her vision and the pinball spun along its track, she felt another level of awareness arise, slow and sure, a sense of the electronic world that was the complex computer simulation . . . an intuition of the bits of energy that flew at the speed of light and formed the illusion of space, interacted with the decisions that flickered from her mind. The electron world hovered at the back of her awareness, a constant presence.

Beautiful Maria finished her run in sixty percent of the time allotted. Credit was added to her counter. The illusion of space faded from her mind and she found herself in the close-smelling booth. The sense of the subatomic world was nearer now, without the distractions of the game. She leaned her head back and found it swirling around her. She raised a finger, tracing its patterns in the control panel in front of her . . . it seemed almost tangible.

Red Nine was still urging her. She lowered her finger and pressed the button.

She felt the pulse through the electron world before the simulation appeared in her optical centers. There was space, filled with bottomless wells. She laughed, placed her bet, and asked the machine for maximum odds.

Maria would have to orbit each of the singularities at least once, and do it all in the scant space of time allocated . . . no room for mistakes. She used the full time allowed for plotting her strategies, the way the pinball would weave its way between stars, then, alarms whooping in her mind, she pushed the pinball forward, maximum acceleration . . .

The pinball flattened, stretched, was plucked by fingers of tidal energy. Maria burned fuel, whipped around a singularity, dove for another dark sun. She could feel the electron world surrounding her, and somehow sensed from its pattern that the singularity toward which she was heading would increase its gravity . . . she plotted a wider orbit, felt gravity slam down hard, put in a burst of power, burst free, true on the course she wanted . . . the computer's attacks were supposed to be random, but they weren't, as no machine's behavior is truly random, just a part of a large, complex pattern, too vast and too swift, supposedly, for human comprehension.

The pinball moaned with tidal stresses. Maria was burning fuel at a fantastic rate, cutting down on her margin of safety. Singularities spun by, tried to snatch her. She could feel an alteration in the electronic pattern that meant something about to happen, a singularity about to appear, too close to her path. Fire shot through her veins. She threw her head back, her teeth clenched, thrust up her hands, waved, the tension making her arms tremble . . .

She felt her glitch take shape, fly from her fingertips. The pattern altered. The singularity appeared a half second late, after her pinball had already passed.

She finished in seventy-three percent of her allotted time. The machine paid off at more than thirty-to-one.

Maria gasped for breath, her heart racing. She could taste sweat on her upper lip.

She asked the machine for another ride. She laid her bet down. It was the most the law allowed for a game of this type. She was left with her original stake and about half her winnings. She picked maximum odds. She felt the electron world, once again, welling up around her, filled with the black flame of invisible stars.

Pasco's hologram walked across the room confidently. He appeared to be lecturing one of the wall monitors. "Expansion. Contraction. Inflation. Deflation. A flexible subject, describing metals subjected to variation in temperature, wave phenomena subjected to variation in energy, economic systems subject to variation in wealth."

"Shut up, Pop," Ubu said. "I'm trying to plot the next shoot." He was hunched over a terminal and a set of keyboards he'd folded out of the green metal wall of the upper lounge. Holographic models flickered in front of his face. He tapped on keyboards with both sets of ambidextrous hands.

"It is the latter phenomenon which we are addressing," Pasco continued, unperturbed. "Observe." The plot Ubu was working on disappeared, replaced by a complex three-dimensional model. A globe of stars, varying colors, burned before his eyes.

"Pop," Ubu said, "I'm trying to—" He remembered this was a recording and clamped his mouth shut.

A red LED glowed on the terminal, signifying that Ubu's plot was being automatically saved into nav memory.

"Human space," Pasco said. He was still speaking to the wall monitor. He approached it, walking through a chair, his holographic image blurring as it encountered matter. Movement began in the hologram, brightness shifting. "In the model, wealth is represented by brightness in the pattern. The brighter, the richer. Notice that the wealth distributes itself through the model as a wave front. Brightness moving toward the center. Observe the action at the center of the model when random sources of wealth are created at the borders of the model, propagating toward the core. Chaos, right?" Pasco's voice was smug. "The chaos at the center grows even worse if the model is allowed to expand its perimeters. The waves form a muddle. The economic seas are choppy, to use a nautical metaphor with which you are probably unfamiliar."

Grief clawed at Ubu's throat. He shook his head wearily. "Go away," he said dully. "You're dead. You killed yourself."

"People invest in sources of wealth," Pasco said. He put his weight back on one leg and threw his shoulders back, declaiming like a ham actor. He was still delivering his lines to the wall. "What becomes of their investment when a new, larger source of wealth is discovered and floods the market like a spring tide? Their own investment loses its value. Destroyed by inflation." He cocked an eye at the monitor.

"The classical example—"

"Kiddyshit."

"—is Europe following Spain's conquest of the New World. Importation to Europe of enormous quantities of American bullion resulted in the inflation of all European currencies. The inflation spread through Europe, beginning with Iberia, then spreading to the east like a wave, eventually causing a fiscal crisis in Poland, the Ukraine, and the Near East fifty years later. Peasants found themselves without the means to buy bread, or land. The pennies they'd been hoarding had lost their value. The result was a century of religious wars that killed millions of people, destroyed the vigor of the Spanish empire, ended the ideal of Christendom as a unifying European concept, and almost plunged Europe into a new dark age."

Ubu's mind swam. "What's Iberia?" he asked. "What's Christendom? And which new world are you talking about?" He wanted to bang his head on the metal wall. "When are you gonna start making sense? Jesus Rice." He began tapping the keys of the computer deck again. His holograph plot was in there somewhere— he'd seen the computer save it—all he had to do was find out where Pasco's raider program had hidden it.

"A similar time of troubles has been plaguing human economies in the last century," Pasco went on, "albeit with less drastic results. No one has to worry about buying bread these days. But the unlimited expansion of human space via the simple means of singularity mechanics has nevertheless had an unpredictable result upon core economies. Waves of wealth generated at the frontier were impacting on the center of human space with a suddenness and force that had been undreamt-of in previous centuries."

Pasco threw out his arms. "Billions thrown out of work! Lives disrupted! Investments made worthless overnight!" He waggled his finger at the monitor. "And what did all those unhappy people want?"

"They wanted to eat shit and die," said Ubu.

Pasco slammed a fist into his palm. It made no sound. "That's right!" he said, grinning. "They wanted stability. Continuity. *Consolidation.*"

Ubu looked up sharply from his keyboard. "Yeah?" he said.

"Not an end to expansion, mind you," Pasco said. "Just an end to the uncontrolled growth that was wrecking their lives. A *planned* expansion, guaranteed not to stress the system. Those at the center of the human sphere outnumbered the population of the frontier by tens of billions. Eventually their weight told, and the Multiparty-Politicals heard them." He turned to Ubu, peering at him owlishly, and a chill brushed up Ubu's bare back. This is just a *recording*, he told himself.

Pasco's voice had lost its rhetorical tone. "But what did Consolidation do to the Edge economies, when they were based on unlimited growth? When the best economic units for carrying out what growth was permitted were the large stable corporate haulers rather than the small entrepreneurial shooter families?"

"Who cares? I thought you were gonna make sense there for a minute."

Pasco straightened. There was sadness in his eyes. Ubu felt a brush of fear touching his nerves. "We die," Pasco said. "We die a slow death." Suddenly he seemed older. His image began to deresolve, interference patterns running through it.

"Where's Kitten?" he asked in a trembling voice. "I miss Kitten."

"Go away, Pop." Kitten had been sold, two months ago, to a hookshop owner at Caliban. The money had gone into Ubu's gamble, the mining equipment destined for Dig Angel.

"Kitten? Where are you, girl?" He began walking across the worn grey carpet. His footsteps made no sound. Ubu kept his eyes on his keyboard. His eyes smarted. He swallowed hard.

His father deresolved with a hissing interference pattern. The navigation plot reappeared. Ubu stared into it hopelessly, grief tearing at his heart with tempered steel claws.

The Mudviller was still playing vingt-et-un, still wearing that strange glassy smile. Still losing and telling himself he was having a good time. Maria took a breath of smoky air, then another. She leaned back against the blackhole booth. Her legs didn't want to support her.

She'd made two runs at maximum odds, winning both at odds of over forty-to-one. The machine had thrown half a dozen obstacles at her the second time, and each time she'd felt its decision in time to react, alter the flow, and guarantee a win. But the interaction with the electron world had drained her. The Red Nine was still crackling along her nerves, urging her back into the booth; but her mind was revolving among a world of phantoms, electrons rocketing along their courses, throbbing in her mind like a strange weighty light . . . her concentration was gone, tangled up in the layers of her perception.

Beautiful Maria took a breath, reached into the pocket of her gown. Took a pair of Blue Seven capsules, the kind called "Blue Heaven," and swallowed them dry. They'd suppress the Red Nine jitters.

It was time for someplace cool and quiet. She retrieved her credit counter and walked through the spotlit tables. Electric spikes jabbed her from every table.

The bouncer turned his head as she neared the door, looking at her over the fussy pince-nez. "Bad luck, shooter femme?" he said, misreading her shaky walk. "Need some credit? I buy you dinner, introduce you to some friends. Tourists. I know they like you, shooter femme."

"I won," Maria said, pressed the doorplate.

The bouncer flashed his metal teeth. "I tell you, hey? Shooters be lucky at blackhole. You want dinner, hey?"

"Pimp." Maria pushed out of Stellar City, bare feet tramping down the nonstick surface of the narrow foam ramp. As her feet struck the street she smelled vat-grown lamb cooking on a skewer, heard a cry of striff music as the door to a nearby bar swung open. Red Nine ran up and down her spine. Colors seemed to swim on the peripherals of her vision. She bought some of the lamb from the kiosk, wrapped it in a chapati, ate it as she walked down the long dark metal ribbon street . . .

An hour later, the Blue Seven soothing her, she was sitting in a bar drinking pomegranate juice that had been spiked with electrolyte replacement while she listened to a glassy-eyed shooter play lick piano with the aid of an extra pair of arms. The man wasn't bad, but his interpretations were too conventional for Maria's taste, too safe. Maria found her fingers itching to touch the keyboards.

"Buy you a drink?"

He was a shooter, she figured, or a syster who dressed like one.

He didn't have the angular, sharp-edged look of someone who had grown up on mones; he seemed a little softer. Two arms and two legs. Two inches shorter than she. Olive skin, curly dark hair cut short. Fifteen, maybe, or sixteen, if he wasn't moned. A bottle of Lark in his hand.

"I don't drink alcohol much," she said.

"Compounds, then?"

Maria lolled her head back and laughed. He got the message: already high.

"Whatever it is you're drinking?"

"I got. But you can talk to me if you like."

The lick piano was wandering off into a pair of interpretations meant to be daring, a harmony line played on each keyboard that was supposed to complement the melody line the sizer memory was repeating, but the result was a jaw-clenching mess that made Maria want to throw something. She could do better than this with just one pair of hands.

The shooter took the stool next to her. She looked at him.

"You a de Suarez?"

"Yeah. Name's Christopher, off the *Abrazo*. How'd you know?"

"You have the look. It's an inbred line. They call you Chris?"

"My friends call me Kit." He frowned. "Mostly the family calls me 'boy.'"

Maria sipped her juice. "Is there a reason for that?" she asked. "Or do they just enjoy insulting family?"

He seemed a little taken aback. "I haven't bossed a shoot yet," he said. "In my family we don't reckon you're grown till you do."

"Jesus Rice," said Maria. "I've been riding tides since I was seven."

"You're moned."

"That doesn't make any difference. You can fastlearn it in a few weeks." She looked at him, speculating. "Unless you're just not good at it."

"I'm good enough in the simulations. My family just . . ." He shrugged. "We do it by generations. I'm the youngest of my generation. I don't do anything important till Marco dies, then we all move up a notch."

"Marco is the big daddy?"

The lick player staggered back, all four hands, into the melody line. Maria wanted to cry out in relief. Some drunks in the back of the room began to bang their hands together loudly.

Kit nodded and took a drink of his Lark. "Marco's my great-uncle. Bossrider of the *Abrazo*, head of the family." He stared at his reflection in the forcebulb. "My father be Second on the *Familia*. I wish I was with him. But Marco needed a new apprentice."

"Marco's not planning on dying anytime soon, right?"

"He'll live forever. He's got this deal with God, I think." He gave an apologetic grin. "He's a serious Old Catholic. Got a shrine to Our Lady in the fuge, next to his office. He's in there a lot, cutting deals with the angels." Kit sipped his Lark again. His dark eyes rose uncertainly to hers. "I heard about your father. I'm sorry."

"The best thing," she said. "I guess."

"Marco says he was a genius who could never finish anything."

Sorrow wafted through her on waves of Blue Heaven. "I suppose he was." Kit finished his Lark and signaled for another.

An idea occurred to Maria. "I haven't met you, have I?" she asked. "How did you know who I was?"

Kit looked at her carefully. "Marco has us study the other shooters. He's got files and things. He says he wants us to know the competition."

Maria felt the waves of sorrow increase and steepen. Once, before Consolidation had taken hold, shooters were something like a huge, promiscuous family. "It's come to that, has it?" she asked.

His eyes reflected her sorrow. "Yeah," he said. "Looks like it has."

Pasco had reached late middle age before his paternal instincts began to reassert themselves, the first of any number of suppressed urges to do so. When he decided to become a father he assembled his children out of bits and pieces purchased at a geneware storehouse, assigned each an assortment of talents and abilities he was, at that moment, interested in. In addition to high intelligence, Pasco gave Ubu a number of traits he felt that he, himself, personally lacked. Insofar as he was slow, fat, and more forgetful than he wanted to be, he gave Ubu fast reflexes, a hard body, and the kind of eidetic memory associated with acute senses and synaesthesia. The extra arms were an afterthought.

When he decided to augment his family, Pasco was more ambitious. He'd just had his fortune told by a professional psychic on Carter's Rim, and some of it had come true. His fastlearn cartridge on genetics informed him that the following genes, in the following locations, have been thought, by a minority of specialists, to be associated with precognition, telekinesis, and extrasensory abilities in general. His assemblage of Beautiful Maria was marked by a kind of overkill: he jammed every ESP-related gene into place on the helix with the intention of producing a genuine witch.

By the time Maria's abilities began to emerge, Pasco had lost interest in extrasensory phenomena. Repeat visits to the Carter's Rim psychic had proved disappointing. That Maria was incredibly successful at electronic games had just been put down to fast reflexes, and that she proved surprisingly good at field repair of equipment was put down to good memory retention. It wasn't until she began running through singularity shots on the simulator, and a substantial percentage of the difficulties that Pasco had programmed for her either failed to appear or suffered mysterious delay, that Pasco began to realize something was up.

He remained interested, this time, for a couple months, which by then was as long as his dwindling attention span could keep him interested in anything. He devised a number of tests to gauge her ability, then a number of exercises to expand it and make it more reliable. By the time his interest faded, Maria and Ubu were able to expand on his ideas and make her abilities more reliable.

By the time Pasco killed himself, Maria's ability was keeping *Runaway* alive.

Marco de Suarez was strapped to his table, floating weightless while he drank espresso from a forcebulb. The pale rose light of the mutanto bar softened the lines in his gaunt face. He seemed oblivious to the complex interweave of mutanto dancers rocketing off the walls in time to the striff band just behind him, a five-piece mutanto group who poured out a white-hot assault that sounded like armies of robots engaged in hand-to-hand combat. Marco was an old man, his elbows standing out like knots in his thin, fleshless arms. His white hair was cropped to half an inch, his cheeks bristled with a three-day stubble. He wore platinum earrings, sandals, an old white cotton jacket that hung to mid-thigh with the sigil of De Suarez Expressways, Ltd., on its shoulder. There was a silver crucifix around his neck on a tight thong. Ubu hated him.

"Bossrider," he said.

The old man's deep eyes turned up to him. Marco raised his bulb, fired espresso past his lips. Making a production of it.

"Bossrider," he said finally. "Ubu Roy. Sit."

"Maybe we can help each other," Ubu said.

"I don't think that's very likely."

Marco was a tyrant—even his own family admitted that. De Suarez Expressways, his trading company, had been molded in his own peculiar image, much as *Runaway*'s had in Pasco's. De Suarez femmes were permitted to have only male children. Marco thought things were easier if each ship had only an all-male cadre, a family united not only by genetics but by sexual attitudes. All women on de Suarez ships came originally from the outside.

Ubu thought Marco was probably as crazy as Pasco, just not as disorganized.

Still, there was no one else to turn to. Ubu had been up and down Angel's rim all day, looking for buyers for *Runaway*'s hold full of mining equipment. "See Marco" was all he'd been told. "Marco's the only one who's got mining contracts since Long Reach folded. Marco's made a deal with PDK. He's running Kompanie supplies to Seven Systems Mining on Trincheras. Marco's in a zero-gee bar in the hub. Called the Bahía. Doing business with a mutanto family."

Yeah, okay, Ubu thought. Might as well give in to the inevitable. Long Reach was locked in an extended self-destruction ceremony, tangled up with creditors, revenue agents, confused lines of corporate responsibility, half-completed contracts and takeover attempts. Half the board of directors had scattered for parts unknown, the Navy had to mount a rescue mission to starving citizens in one of Long Reach's new settlements, and a lot of company records were missing. The only thing that was clear at this point was that no one was getting paid.

There were no buyers in the Angelica market. Besides the

defunct Long Reach operation, only Biagra-Exeter was involved in Angelica System, and Biagra planned years in advance for this sort of thing: they were a self-contained company, keeping major supply purchases entirely in-house, and weren't interested in picking up independent contracts even at a profit.

Ubu avoided filing a claim against Dig Angel for the present: that would have made his difficulty part of the public record, let everyone onstation know that *Runaway* was in trouble and that he was desperate for a sale. So Beautiful Maria was sent off to earn some credit in a Fringe casino, and Ubu took his act up to the hub.

He didn't want to deal with Marco. He wanted either a fellow shooter, who could be trusted to sympathize, or maybe a disinterested Hiliner rep who collected a nice salary whether or not he squeezed the competition. He didn't trust an in-between like Marco, not someone who was shooter enough to understand Ubu's difficulties and Hiliner enough to take advantage of them.

But Marco it was. De Suarez Expressways, Ltd., owned five ships and quite possibly had the capital to take on a venture of this sort, and if they didn't have capital they had access to PDK's. On his way to the Bahía, Ubu fired up some neurotransmitter multiplier, Red Eight, more for superstitious reasons than for any real belief it would do him any good. If you didn't have the smarts to be a bossrider in the first place, he'd always figured, messing with your brain chemistry wasn't going to help.

"Maybe we can't help each other that much," Ubu said, strapping himself to the table opposite the old man. "But let's talk anyway."

Marco inclined his head. Pale rose highlights shone off his white hair. "Be listening, Ubu Roy."

Behind him, the mutanto guitarist, playing with his upper arms while hanging by his lower from a castoff bar, was attacking each note as if it was personally responsible for the death of his way of life. Every striff cry was a marching tune; the question was where this particular parade was headed.

Ubu stared into Marco's deep yellow eyes. "You have a contract with Seven Systems," he said. "I've got some of Dig Angel's equipment in my hold. I'd like to lay off some of Dig Angel's debts. Maybe you'd like to buy it for resale."

The old man sniffed. Ubu could see a shine of green mucus smearing Marco's upper lip: he'd been sitting in his corner of the bar all day, doing his deals, inhaling so much neurobooster the stuff was running out his nostrils.

Marco looked at Ubu from out of his death's head. "Why not take it outsystem and sell it to Seven Systems yourself?"

"I've got a contract to pick up a hold full of pharmaceuticals at China Light for delivery to Salvador and Ascención. China Light doesn't need mining equipment. I'd hate to pay storage or let the contract go just to make a run to Seven Systems, not when I could sell to Seven Systems by selling to you."

All of which was a lie, though Ubu figured Marco would have no way to know for sure. The truth was he'd only got the OttoBanque loan in the first place because he'd talked Maria into glitching their system. The loan was coming due in less than a week and the only way to extend it was to glitch the OttoBanque here, doubling the chance the bank's comps would notice the fact they'd been fiddled with.

Unless he could sell his cargo, Ubu wouldn't be able to pay the new taxes and docking charges here at Angel Station, charges raised by the Multi-Pollies as part of their Consolidation policy.

Ubu looked coolly into Marco's whiskered face and gave him his best shot. "Besides," he said, "I hear you've got an exclusive contract with PDK and Seven Systems. I don't know what kind of terms you have with them, but PDK might reconsider the deal if I sold to them direct and they realized they could get another supplier out here."

The striff cry came to an end in a rolling barrage of percussion and broken guitar arpeggios. Mutantos banged four hands, cheered.

Marco's expression didn't change, but he reached down to his lap, came up with a chak of neurotransmitter juice, and fired one round up each nostril. Which meant he was thinking real hard.

Behind his expressionless face, Ubu smiled.

The hype was called *Renewal*. It was made on a planet where people spoke mostly Mandarin, but there were subtitles in Melange as well as the new-style ideograms for those who spoke other Asian dialects.

Before the story was very old, Ubu was thankful he couldn't hear what the people were saying.

The hype had been widely praised, and the story was supposedly true. It was about dispossessed shooters, people who through their irresponsibility and fecklessness had lost everything, and how a brave few were rehabilitated and turned to useful work by the caring people of a groundling community.

The story didn't mention how the shooters had lost their livelihood. It said nothing about how the groundlings had voted for a government who had sent Multi-Pollies to the human core who then in turn decided to implement Consolidation and destroy a way of life.

Whoever made it had probably never met any shooters, never been out of a planetary well in their life. The hype's shooter life was wildly exaggerated, all madness and drug-induced brutality, though among all the decadence were a few pure-hearted young people longing for a better way of life.

There was so much missing, Ubu thought. The sense of community, the ways families actually work out here. The music: not a musical instrument to be seen.

"Fuck them," Ubu said, and reached for the holo controls. He knew already how it was going to end. The hero was going to rehabilitate himself and end up with the farm girl; the hero's best friend would die tragically as a result of his chronic drug use; the six-year-old blond orphan girl would be rescued from her brute of a father; and every remaining shooter over the age of sixteen would go to hell by the shortest possible route.

As far as Ubu could see, hell seemed the way to go.

He hammered at the controls. The hype's sudden disappearance from the lounge's threedee screen seemed to leave a yawning gap in Ubu's heart. *Is that how they really see us?* he wondered.

Anger rattled through him aimlessly, like stones thrown in a bucket. Billions had seen the hype. Billions now knew that the shooter families were dying because of their own inherent character flaws, and were confident that civilization could no longer afford such barbarians on its fringes. What the hell could Ubu possibly do to change their minds?

He pulled the lounge control board in front of him, called up the hype directory, scanned the list of available recordings. Nothing he came up with seemed to fit his particular mood of aggressive longing.

A title scrolled past. He stopped the scrolling, reversed, gave a grin.

His theme hype. He hadn't seen it in years.

He'd come across it by accident six or seven years ago, just scrolling through the list looking for something to do. The hype had been in computer memory since its installation a century before, one of a whole series of lectures and classic hype given away free with the old Torvald. Most weren't interesting to Ubu, though Pasco had watched a lot of them, but for some reason—maybe the weird title—Ubu had found one of them interesting enough to sample it.

The hype was animated, but the animation looked as if it had been done by a brain-damaged six-year-old armed with crayons: crude figures with big heads that never seemed to stay the same shape, backgrounds sketched in lightly if at all, objects appearing and disappearing without rhyme or reason. Even day and night seemed to change from moment to moment, without any break in the scene—though Ubu, whose concept of day and night was entirely the result of seeing hypes set in Mudville, didn't even consider this odd until he stopped to think about it. The main character was a potbellied little king who wore a crown shaped like a jagged mountain range and clutched in his hand what looked like a toilet brush. He careened about the story at breakneck velocity, stealing money, gobbling food, chopping off heads, and running away from battles.

Ubu loved it. It was as if the little king were some mainline to the primal Id, a creature of pure undirected impulse. The madcap, bloody anarchy of it rang in his mind for days.

Ubu, whom Pasco had originally named Xavier, decided to change his name to that of the crazed king. The mutable terrain depicted, with all its crudity and weird variability, seemed somehow navigable to him, seemed to make more sense than the human interface with which he was normally expected to interact. Certainly, even with all the violence, it seemed more safe.

He tapped the computer deck and called the hype from the

files. The king roared in and began barking out his plots. Heads started falling left and right with sounds like bladders breaking wind.

He thought of the people who made *Renewal*, and wished he could unleash King Ubu on them all.

Enclosed in the silken curtains of Blue Heaven, Beautiful Maria felt she wanted to be in motion. She took Kit's hand and glided down the rim, her feet almost weightless. A thorny plant with pink blossoms, planted in the street's centerline, gave off a sweet pheromone smell. She laughed.

"You want to go dancing?" Kit asked.

"Maybe later. Right now I'd like to walk." She skimmed over the surface, walked through a hologram advertising custom genetics, saw green laser burn holo helixes on her skin. Electronic awareness hummed in the back of her head.

She looked at Kit. "Your family won't let you shoot, right?" she asked.

He looked at the floor with a stubborn frown. "Yeah. I said."

"You want some experience? We can apprentice you to *Runaway*."

Kit stopped moving in surprise, hung on to her fingertips. The green hologram turned orange as it crossed his features. "I—yeah, I'd like that."

"For a consideration," Maria said. "Your family would have to pay for your training."

He swallowed. "I don't know if they'd go along with that."

"It's something to think about. You'd be more valuable to them. On *Runaway* you'd get experience handling cargo, station approach, everything."

The hologram moved down the street. "I'd like that," Kit said again.

Maria tugged him down the rim. She felt as if she was floating, with only Kit holding her to the alloy floor. She passed a male-model android toy dancing under blue lights in a window, a Fringe barker with a synthetic smile running a game on a pair of Mudville tourists. "Sure it's real," he said. Maria felt a wave of uneasiness. The android had a male body, but Kitten's face. She tried to shrug the feeling away.

"How'd you like to pimp for androids?" Maria asked Kit. "Jesus Rice."

"Mudvillers don't know the difference."

"I guess you'd get to keep a hundred percent of the take," Maria said, still dubious about the idea.

"I like your hair. Can I touch it?"

She tossed her head, smiled. "If you like."

Kit moved his grip on her fingers from his left hand to his right, began to stroke her hair with his left hand. She could feel his gentle touch on her spine, her neck. As caressing as Blue Heaven. The flurried electronic traffic of the rim flickered on the edge of her perceptions. Maria steered down an alley. Twilight bordered onto night. She turned and kissed him. A touch, chemical or possibly Kit, trickled down her ribs. A sad dolores ballad moaned distantly from a bar. He raised a hand to lift a long silk riverlet of her hair, and his head dipped to burrow between it and her neck. His lips brushed her throat.

"Let's go someplace," Maria said.

"Too many people on *Abrazo*." Warm breath fluttered against her skin. "How about *Runaway*?"

She thought about Pasco, his holographic ghost frozen somehow in the macroatomic heart of *Runaway*'s main computer. She shook her head. "Same problem." She felt a hand touching her moned breast. Warmth filled her heart. She kissed his ear. "How about a hotel? I've earned some credit today."

He stepped back for a moment, looked at her with solemn eyes. "I'd like it to be in a nice place. You know. Not just a shacktube."

Beautiful Maria smiled at him. His dark skin seemed to reflect her glow. "Yeah," she said. "I know. Don't worry. I've got enough."

Ubu swam out of the Bahía on a growing wave of adrenaline and fear. He'd cut as close a deal with Marco as he dared, and he was still far from out of debt. If he couldn't find some outbound cargo in a few days OttoBanque was going to foreclose on him and Beautiful Maria, sell *Runaway*'s singularity drive to clear the debt, and leave them high and dry on Angel Station. Without its drive *Runaway* was only useful as scrap—hundred-year-old spare parts weren't worth much on today's market. If they were lucky they'd find work as riggers on a syster ship, confined forever to the reaches of this one system. If not—Mudville.

The computers were what had soiled the deal. Dig Angel had been starting operations in this system and had wanted everything, mining robots, tools, parts, and the custom-tooled Kanto computers to control them. Any established mining op, like Seven Systems, would already have enough comp capacity to run their operations. Marco had only bought the robots and parts.

His mind numb, Ubu dropped to the rim, where there was gravity. The bright lights of the Outside Life gleamed around him. The holographic deity in front of the Laughing God Casino boomed out his hearty amusement. People dressed in grey and brown glanced at him as he strode up the pale marble deck, their eyes lingering a shade too long, just long enough to let him know he was out of place. People in Hiliner uniforms refused even to look at him.

He went to station central and filed his claim against Dig Angel and Long Reach. Maybe OttoBanque would extend the loan, with the Dig Angel claim as collateral.

Maybe Mudvillers would learn how to fly. Ubu figured the odds were about the same.

CHAPTER

2

KIT AND BEAUTIFUL MARIA SAT CROSS-LEGGED ON THEIR HOTEL BED. On the bed between them was curried something-or-other, robot room-service food, eaten off recycled white metal trays with disposable alloy forks lighter than plastic. The Hotel Susperides was on the edge of the Fringe, where it could attract minor bureaucrats from the Outside Life and tourists eager to have the Fringe element take their money.

"Not in years," Kit said. He was talking about his mother. "She and my father were always fighting. Finally she left the ship at Masquerade Station. That was six years ago."

"Sorry," said Maria.

"She got a job in a casino, but the place went under. I think she went to Mudville. I haven't heard from her in three years."

Beautiful Maria sighed. "Must be hard."

A stray memory bobbed disconnectedly to the surface of Kit's mind. "She kept cockatoos," he said. He hadn't thought about the big white birds in years.

Maria took a shot of her lemonade. "I'd like to show you

34

Runaway. But before you go there, you should know—sometimes my pop is there."

Kit looked at her with surprise. "I—I thought . . ."

"He's dead. Yes. But before he died he made hundreds of recordings of himself giving lectures on all sorts of topics. He buried them in our old Torvald and programmed them to appear at random. He's a random glitch—hard to find. We were afraid to wipe him because something important might go with him."

Kit frowned and took a hit from his bulb of Lark. "How does he . . . make himself known?"

Maria grinned. "A holographic projection. Sometimes it's an old one, sometimes more recent. Sometimes he babbles, sometimes he just stands there. Sometimes he almost seems able to have a conversation." She reached out to take his hand. "I didn't want to take you to *Runaway.* Figured you'd freak if you saw him."

He looked at her. His fingers tightened around hers. "I might have," he said. "A computer ghost. Jesus."

"We try to turn off all the holographic projectors we can. But they're in use all the time. We can't disable them all."

"No." He fired up beer again. "One of my cousins is a genius programmer. I could talk to him about it."

"Not if it'll end up in your uncle's files." She looked at him. "Please," she said.

He licked his lips. "Okay. I won't tell anyone."

She leaned forward and kissed him, citrus and curry. Her breast brushed his arm. Then she laughed.

"The only haunted ship in the universe, and I'm on it. I mean, who else?"

He looked down at the bulb in his hand. "I don't know that it's so bad. At least you can turn your relatives off if you have to."

"Poor boy." Her white, even teeth closed on the lobe of his ear. Fingernails whispered down his spine as he felt her breath on his nape. He propped the bulb against his knee and turned to her. Put his hands around her, felt the play of flesh over ribs. Her kisses slid over his throat, lodged in a place between clavicle and larynx that made him gasp. She shifted her weight forward, slid her long legs around his waist, adjusted herself in his lap. Her long hair caressed his chest like black smoke. The phone rang.

Maria lifted her head. "Who is it?" she asked. Kit kissed her throat.

"It's me." Ubu's voice came louder than life from the room speaker. "I got your message about where you are. Are you alone?"

"No." She could feel the muscles in Kit's thighs trembling. She grinned.

"We gotta talk in private. It's important."

She arched back in his lap and looked at Kit with her head cocked to one side. His fingertips touched her breasts, tracing the outlines of the nipples. He was getting very hard against her. "Okay," she said.

"Now."

Maria smiled a little ironic smile. "Now," she said. "Bye." She looked at Kit. "Sorry. Maybe later."

"I understand." He was still pressing against her.

Maria dismounted by kicking one leg up over his head and then slid smoothly off the sheets. She held her grey robe up over her head. Kit watched the play of her milkwhite skin over the knobs of her spine. The sight of her sleek hormone-fed body made him feel clumsy. Fat, sweaty, absurdly tumescent. Maria twisted her shoulders and the robe fell and draped her to her calves. She looked over her shoulder.

"Meet somewhere tonight?"

He pulled the sheet over his lap. "Sure. Where?"

"You'd better let me call you."

He looked up at her quickly. "Not at the *Abrazo*, okay? Use the station message board."

Beautiful Maria shrugged. "Whatever."

"I've got a couple days till we start loading. How about you?"

"Maybe that's what I'm meeting with Ubu about."

Kit slid out of bed and put his arms around her. She drifted gently against him, brushing against his body while she smiled absently and gazed off over his head, into space. In spite of the fact he knew her mind was elsewhere, Kit felt his nerves go warm. He thought about an engagement in a freefall chamber near the station's hub, picturing a slow, gentle loving going on forever, the two of them spiraling toward one another as their own miniature gravities called to one another. She kissed his damp forehead and extracted herself from his arms.

"Sorry. Gotta go. Tonight. Okay?"

"Station board. Let me know."

Maria padded from the room on bare feet, throwing him a farewell smile with a quick turn of her shoulders that transmitted itself into a long undulating ripple that swept through her hair. The door irised closed. Kit looked after her for a long moment, then returned to the bed and finished the curry and beer.

He showered, shaved with the hotel razor, and put on his shorts, vest, and battered grey sneakers. He walked through the lobby of the Hotel Susperides without attracting a look from the clerk, then stepped out onto the metal of the rim.

"Hey! Little Brother!"

Kit winced at the sound of his cousin Ridge's voice. He looked deeper into the twilight of the rim and saw Ridge swaggering up the alloy path with a couple riggers he hadn't seen before.

Ridge was a couple years older, Marco's only grandson. He was proud of his torso, and above the waist he wore only jewelry. "Little Brother!" he said again, grinning. Kit could tell he was drunk.

"Riders," Kit said politely. Ridge came up to him and threw an arm around his shoulders, catching his neck uncomfortably between a steel forearm and a rock-hard biceps. The family embrace, Kit thought. Masculine and painful and forever. Smelling of spilled wine and careless brutality.

"These aren't riders, Little Brother. These are Capra and Tuck, a couple syster pilots I know," Ridge said. The insystem haulers nodded hello. Ridge looked at the Susperides lights. "Coming out of the hotel, huh? Get lucky with some Mudviller tourist?"

"Something like that."

"Better hope you didn't get lice. You bring lice on board, you're gonna be sorry."

"No lice."

"Thought for a second there I'd take you with us. We're gonna go up to a hookshop I know in the hub and get some frog ladies. They can do some amazing things with those extra arms they got 'stead of legs. But that tourist lady of yours probably got you all tired, right?"

"Yeah. Tired."

Ridge pinched him in the crook of his arm again. "Yeah. Tired," he mocked. He looked up at the two men with him. "The boy does all right with girls, even if he don't look like much. But getting him to talk about it is like pulling teeth. Why's that, boy?"

Kit looked up at him, at the handsome, leering face. He hadn't lived with Ridge for so many years without learning how to handle him at least part of the time. "I don't want to show you up in front of your friends," he said.

Ridge whooped with laughter and punched Kit in the chest with his free hand. Kit tried not to look like it hurt.

"Don't worry about that, boy," Ridge said. "I be figuring I show these systers here a thing or two in a few minutes. You tell me about this tourist cooze, okay?"

Kit nodded and tried to think of someone as far removed from Beautiful Maria as possible. "Blonde," he said. "Short hair. About my age. Diamond implants in her cheekbones, like some of them wear. She was here with her mother, who came up to gamble."

Kit saw the spreading grin on Ridge's face and knew he'd made a mistake. "Her mother?" Ridge asked. He laughed. "You wanna introduce me to Mamma, boy. I figure the whole family ought to get the benefit of de Suarez talent, right?"

"They're going down the well on the next shuttle. Sorry you missed 'em."

Ridge tightened his grip on Kit's neck. "The little bastard's lying," he said. "He wants the whole family for himself, the fucker."

"It's true," Kit grated. He could feel Ridge's forearm cutting his artery. Blue stars spun in the corner of his vision.

"Yeah? What are their names? I'll check the manifests, asshole."

Kit fought for breath. The blue stars were going nova. "Crystal something," he said. "Check it, for Rice sake!"

The pressure eased on his windpipe. Kit gratefully dragged in air. He realized he should have told Ridge that his girl's mother had her boyfriend with her.

"Yeah. Fuck. I wanna go to the hookshop anyway. See you later, Little Brother."

"Cousin. Systers." The sarcasm in Kit's voice could have been taken for a result of the bruise on his larynx. He blinked splashes of stellar color from his eyes and watched the three heading for the belt conveyor, a reverse quicksilver waterfall, that would take them to the hub. Laughter cascaded from them as they walked. Kit rubbed his throat and turned away from them.

He was de Suarez; he had accepted that. The family was everything, all that mattered in the war of de Suarez against all: that was the de Suarez way. Kit had accepted that, too, with certain reservations. He owed the family his duty, his labor, his talent. As long as he gave them this, whatever else he did was his own affair: this was the quiet deal he had cut with himself. A treasonous deal, by de Suarez standards. Kit knew this, knew also that it couldn't be any other way.

Beautiful Maria was going to stay his secret, one of the few things he didn't have to share with his uncles, aunts, and cousins on his crowded ship. A small, private détente in the war De Suarez Expressways, Ltd., was fighting with the human race. Here, on Angel Station, a few moments of peace.

Ubu reclined on a padded couch in the command cage. He'd called up a dross tune from the comm board, and cool spectra shifted through his mind as the audolin bent notes on the harmony line, each a catfooted glissando along Ubu's nerves. Maxim sat on Ubu's bare chest, feet tucked under him, his forehead butting up against Ubu's chin. With all four hands, Ubu stroked the cat fore-and-aft in time to the percussion. Maxim's purr grated in pleasant disharmony. White hair floated in the light station gravity.

Our symmetry is broken, and our time, chanted the lyrics, *Our hope is a token, and a crime*. A song by Fetnab and Sanjay Gupta, who had been shooters once, before abandoning the life for success elsewhere.

A shooter lyric, an early one. Maybe no one else would understand it.

Ubu's nape prickled, the brief equalization in pressure that meant Maria entering through the station tube. Maxim's ears flicked back at the same instant. Ubu reached to the keyboard on the couch arm and snapped off the music.

Maria began to descend the ladder, the white high arches and taut Achilles tendons followed by the drifting grey cloud of her gown. Her long hair rebounded as she dropped to the deck, a slow blueblack wave rising and falling. She turned, bent over him, kissed him gravely. Her lips had the taste of lemon. Maria began scratching Maxim's neck. The cat put out one foot for balance against the pressure that the new pleasure was exerting on him. Ubu felt the prick of claws against his skin.

"Our shit is weak," Ubu said. "Marco de Suarez bought the miners, but not their brains."

"How much do we still owe?"

Ubu pointed with his chin. "It's on comp. Take a look."

She turned, triggered the display, bit her lip as she saw the figures. She shook her head. "Not good."

Ubu sat up and lowered the cat to the floor. Maxim scratched his ear with a rear foot. "How much did you win at blackhole?"

"Not enough. The stakes aren't high enough in blackhole. It'd take me weeks at this rate. Or I could lose everything, if I get tired or careless."

"We could get into a tourist club with what you won. Play rouge-et-noir."

Her face was turned away from him. "I've never played that." Her voice vanished into the hiss of recirculated air.

"If you lose, we haven't lost much."

"It's a tough game. Totally abstract. Not easy for me."

"Maria."

She was silent. Ubu could see her body outlined in the greygreen glow of the holo display. He waited.

"Okay," she said. Her voice was smaller than before. Ubu had the feeling he was hearing her with TP, that his ears couldn't possibly have picked up that tiny whisper.

"What else can we do?" he asked.

"Nothing."

He came up behind her and put his arms around her, pressed his cheek against the warmth of her ear. He could feel the tension in her. "Want to rest first? We've got a few days."

"I'm rested. Maybe a couple hours under the alpha trodes, though."

"Whatever you want. I'll find the rules to rouge-et-noir somewhere. Let you study them."

Her dark eyes were looking a thousand yards away, not seeing him. Ubu's hackles rose as he realized what she was looking at: a place where there were no choices left, a place filled with litter like *Runaway*, like the Long Reach colonies, like Pasco dying, rotating amid his rubbish. Ubu dropped his arms, turned away, picked up the cat. Maxim purred loudly against his chest.

"I wish . . ." Maria's voice.

"Yes?"

"Nothing." She rubbed her forehead with her thumb. "Maybe I should get some rest, after all."

"Whatever you want."

Maria brushed past him and went up the ladder slowly, like she hoped Ubu would call her back, tell her she didn't have to do it. He didn't say anything, just stood with the cat in his arms and a knot in his stomach and let her go.

He didn't understand it, but he wanted to cry.

Maria had four hours under the trodes, then called the station board and left a note for Kit to meet her on *Runaway* at zero-thirty. She figured it would be over by then, one way or the other.

She and Ubu left the Fringe at twenty-two hundred, stepping from the fever-filled twilight to the brightly lit high-commerce zone. They walked slowly over the marble floor, arm in arm as if they had all the time in the world. They were trying to get a sense of the place. The casino's façade was a long three-level-high hologram, just bright shifting colors, like a planetary aurora. It was a new building, built of permanent materials, not tempafoam, constructed in the last three years as the Angelica System's economy began to develop enough wealth to support high-stakes gambling outside Angelica's gravity well.

"It's called the Monte Carlo," Ubu said. He looked odd in the mascara he'd put on to look like the Hiline crowd. "Funny they named a casino after a statistical methodology. You figure it's a clue to how to win?"

Ubu and Maria were dressed in dark grip shoes and dark socks, grey pipestem pants, light shirts, dark jackets that were almost but-not-quite uniforms. Ubu had his lower arms crossed behind his back, hiding them under the jacket—his modifications weren't precisely unknown outside shooter culture, but they were rarer. Beautiful Maria had surrounded her eyes with kohl, dusted glitter on her cheekbones, put a handful of Red Nine in one jacket pocket and Blue Heaven in the other. She felt like an impostor: her nerves crackled as she walked past the casino's auroral façade and into the arching lobby. She tried not to look at the doormen, knowing that if she made the wrong move they'd stop her and ask her what she was doing here, if she had credit. But their eyes passed over her without stopping, and Ubu followed her in and gave a little laugh as he realized he was past the guards. All they had to do now was win a lot of money.

The casino was on their left. Looking at the gaming tables, Maria was surprised by how quiet it was—instead of the constant barrage of arcade noise in the Fringe clubs, here there was only a low murmur of conversation. This impressed her more than anything else: there was the sense that serious money was being won and lost here.

Ubu was waiting for her to say something.

"The bar first," she said. "I've got to give the Red Nine a chance to work."

She'd taken pills rather than used an inhaler. She didn't know if a chak would be accepted here. The compound rolled up her nerves like an incoming tide. She could feel the electron world buzzing in her ears.

The bar had a lick piano and a view of the casino. The rouge-et-noir tables were on the far side of the room and Maria didn't want to look at them. She sipped slowly at her drink and waited. She didn't want to talk, and Ubu must have sensed that, because he just waited, not saying anything but downing three drinks in the time it took her to finish one.

She was trying to get a sense of the place. She closed her eyes and tried to let the casino speak to her.

White noise. Too much input. She would have to get closer.

Maria stood up. "Gotta go," she said. Ubu followed her. She let her long legs carry her through the casino at a pace that was close to panic. The quiet in the place was frightening. Hiliners and Mudvillers gathered intent around tables, eyes focused on their play. Sometimes Maria heard a laugh from somewhere, a sound that floated over the crowd like a bird, but Maria could never see anyone laughing. She clutched her credit counter in her white hand. Her scalp was prickling with sweat. This wasn't her world.

A rouge-et-noir table glittered in front of her. Colored lights played on the faces of the three players, two women and a man, the light shining up from below, making them look sinister. The tourneur was a small pale-skinned man with a large white forehead and a surprising amount of black hair on the backs of his hands. He watched the play with emotionless eyes set beneath perfectly even brows.

Red Nine told Beautiful Maria to play. She dug her nails into her palms and told herself it wasn't time yet. She stepped up to the table and watched. The woman on her left had the bank: her skin was black, her hair platinum, and diamonds had been implanted on her shoulders and breasts. She wasn't dressed like a Hiliner, and she didn't have the body of someone from Mudville: maybe she was a shooter turned professional gambler. Beautiful Maria didn't want to think how much money she'd paid for the bank.

The other bettors were nondescript. The man was in a dark blue uniform jacket and the woman in a bright, expensive sheath. Her face was painted in fluorescent stripes.

Ubu spoke, and Maria jumped. She turned to him with wild eyes.

"What you say?"

"Do you want to bet?"

She clenched her teeth. Her heart beat madly in her throat. "In a minute."

"You need betting chips. Shall I get you some chips?"

There was an insistent, hectoring tone in his voice she didn't like. "Yes," she said. She wanted him to get away from her.

"I'll need your counter, then." He held out a hand. Maria slapped it into his palm and turned back to the table. The black woman was looking at her. A roar of anger went through Maria and she clamped it down, realizing this was the drug. She twisted her hands together below the level of the table and watched the play.

Rouge-et-noir was an electronic game, run by the Monte Carlo's computer. It was based on an old Earth game called roulette, a popular game until small computers were developed that could judge the tiny biases of the wheel and the tourneur, which forced the game to go electronic. Since no artificial intelligence could produce truly random play, the random factors were added by the players, who could press keys from 1 to 36 in hopes of influencing the outcome. Each bettor had to press at least one key during the fifteen seconds of play or her bet would be confiscated.

The tourneur called out in antique French. Beautiful Maria watched the play, saw how the bettors put their chips on the squares, the way the numbers began to progress, lighting up from beneath. The numbers moved faster and faster. Bets piled on the table as fingers stabbed at keys. The black squares glowed gold when they were lit. Reflected colors flashed in the tourneur's impassive eyes. The green border of the layout flashed three times, and the tourneur said, *"Rien ne va plus."* Maria watched the bettors, all of them leaning over the table, eagerness and hope in their eyes, and then the tourneur said, *"Un, rouge, manque, impair,"* and the banker smiled as the tourneur pushed chips toward her with his stick. She began stacking her winnings. Beautiful Maria looked at the losers. Their eagerness was gone, but their hope remained.

"Faites vos jeux, mesdames et messieurs." It began again. Maria looked at the table, touched her teeth with her tongue. Red and gold gleamed briefly on the table's surface and faded. Numbers flashed. There was an awareness in Maria's fingertips that hadn't been there before. The banker stabbed her key and Maria felt a jolt deep in her heart. The green flashing border dazzled her. There was a whisper in her mind that came an instant before the tourneur's call.

Twelve . . .

"Douze . . ."

Red, low, even . . .

". . . rouge, manque, pair."

Maria felt a laugh rising in her throat and quelled it. She looked up at the players, saw the banker's ambiguous smile. She had broken even on this one. The man had bet red at the last second and made some money. The woman bettor was shaking her head, counting her few remaining chips. Trying to decide whether to play it safe or wager everything on a last gamble.

"*Faites vos jeux.*" Maria looked at the table as the numbers started to glow. Colors blazed in her mind. Players pressed keys. The woman player bit her lip and played *à cheval* on two numbers, 21 and 24. Maria's nerves were afire. Her heart thundered in time to the flashing digits, to the electron world buried beneath the table. She closed her eyes, clenched her teeth. She could detect green light flashing on the outside of her lids, heard the tourneur call, "*Rien ne va plus.*" *Now*, she thought, and her body jerked as she felt the power snap from her spine like an arrow from a bow.

"*Vingt et un. Rouge, passe, impair.*"

The woman bettor gave a soft cry of relief. Maria opened her eyes, saw the tourneur moving chips from the bank to the player. A *cheval* paid seventeen-to-one. The banker's dark eyes were turned inward. Maria could see the pulse beating in her throat.

"Your chips." Ubu's voice. Beautiful Maria held out a blind hand and Ubu carefully put a pile of chips in her palm. She placed them on the table without looking at them.

Careful at first, Maria thought, and put three chips on PASSE. She thought she could probably influence high-or-low more easily than anything else. The banker's eyes flicked to her once, then turned away. Red Nine screamed in her head. Her fingers closed around her remaining chips and she felt them cool against her skin. Colored lights began to flow, responding to changes in the electron stream. Maria tasted sweat on her upper lip. She pressed a key blindly, uninterested in the outcome—so far as she could tell the keys added a random factor without helping the player in any way. They were for idiots.

The colored lights began moving faster. Maria held a hand over the layout, felt the beat of electricity against her skin, saw the resolution, and flung her charge into the system as she shoved forward a stack of five chips, placing her bet *à cheval* on 25 and 26—she couldn't quite tell which would be the result.

"*Rien ne va plus.*" Colors pulsed on the table. Maria wiped sweat from her eyes.

"Twenty-five," she whispered, knowing the outcome.

"*Vingt-cinq.*"

"Red, high, odd."

"*Rouge, passe, impair.*"

Ubu's voice broke in. "Good. Good. Look at the *odds!*"

Blind rage roared up Maria's spine. She spun toward her brother. "*Get away!*" she whispered. "*Get away from me!*"

Shock showed in his eyes. He raised his upper hands, said nothing, backed away. Beautiful Maria turned back to the table, saw the banker looking at her as the tourneur pushed chips toward her place. "*Faites vos jeux, mesdames et messieurs.*" Maria ordered her chips in two stacks, then played one stack *à cheval* on 11 and 12.

She pressed a key as the lights began to cascade. Her breath rasped in her throat. The banker was intently pressing keys. Maria stared at the tourneur's hair-backed hands. Her body wrenched as the play came to an end, and she cried out as she realized her glitch had gone wrong, that the winning number was 10. She should have played more conservatively, bet *transversale pleine* on 10, 11, and 12.

Maria licked her lips as the tourneur moved her bet to the bank. Ubu had broken her concentration: now she had only half her winnings to play with. She put half her chips on MANQUE and decided to play it safe for now.

Red and gold swam up and down the table. Sweat blinded her but it didn't matter. It seemed to Maria as if she could see below the table, see hidden veins and arteries coursing with electrons. She pressed one key, then pressed another because it felt right. Things were lining up: she could see the resolution. Red Nine urged her to increase the bet. She resisted the temptation and cried out as the final number came up: the one she had anticipated. If she had bet the number she would have won thirty-five to one. She reached over the table, thumped a fist down, laughed as the chips moved toward her. She had the table beaten now.

Maria put half her money on MANQUE again. She felt as if her heart were pumping electrons. The numbers cascaded, the glitch formed in Maria's body, she pushed out all her remaining money on nine. Her sweat pattered on the table.

"*Neuf. Rouge, manque, impair.*"

Beautiful Maria shrieked and jumped in the air. The woman

bettor looked daggers at her: she'd stayed even the last two rounds, but had bet everything on *milieu douzaine* and lost it all.

The banker was looking at her, too. She reached into a pocket and came up with a chak, fired one round up each nostril. Chaks *were* allowed here, Maria thought.

She could feel the power coiling in her. She put a handful of chips on PASSE: she couldn't even tell how much. The game began. She saw the resolution, pushed another stack out, won again. Won another time. She was nearly blind with sweat, but that didn't matter: she could feel the pulses under the table and could push chips where the electrons led her. The other players had withdrawn: Maria and the banker were playing against one another. A crowd had gathered: she could hear their noise, but she ignored it. Energy danced on her skin. She knew every move before it was made. She laughed and tossed her hair and pushed chips on the table. Then, suddenly, the energies died. Maria gave a cry of surprise. She blinked sweat away and looked at the banker.

The black woman returned the gaze, her look strangely soft. She raised her hands. *"Elle vient de faire sauter la banque,"* she said, and turned away. She looked left and right, as if she didn't know quite where she wanted to go, and then she stepped into the crowd. Maria blinked after her. She saw that the woman's steps were unsteady.

Maria could hear cheering. Arms were put around her; she realized they were Ubu's. "You just broke the bank," he said. He said it again, shouting. *"The bank is broken!"* He picked her up and swung her around. Her mind reeled. Ubu put her down and she tossed her hair out of her face.

"I want a drink," she said. The people around her cheered, as if she'd said something witty.

"If you will come with me." This was the tourneur. Maria stared at him. "If you will come with me," the man said again, "we will cash your chips." She looked at his furry hands: they carried a small basket with her chips in it. "We will have to go to the casino office," the man said. "The cashiers aren't authorized to pay out this much at once."

She followed Ubu and the tourneur through the crowd. People laughed, clapped, offered to buy them drinks. Maria turned her head, saw the banker walking toward the exit alone. It was *her* money,

Maria realized. It wasn't the Monte Carlo's money they'd won: the money was all the banker's. A wave of remorse dizzied Maria. Why hadn't she realized this before? The house was probably playing banker at most of the tables; she could have robbed the institution with a far clearer conscience.

The door to a side office dilated open in front of the tourneur. He handed the basket to a man inside and stepped back to allow Ubu and Maria to pass. The door irised shut behind them.

The room was small and simply furnished: straight metal chairs with minimal padding, a desk, a video, a comp. A plump woman sat behind the desk, sucking on a cigaret. Maria tried not to show her disgust at the filthy Mudville addiction. The woman's dark hair was cut short and she wore a grey jacket. Her lips were painted bright orange. Two men stood to either side of her. They were both big men in dark clothes. The woman gave a close smile as she looked at the basket of chips on her desk.

"It isn't every day we have such big winners. Sit down. My name is Jamison."

"It isn't every day we win this big," Ubu said. He sat down and bounced his lower set of hands on the arms of his chair.

Maria looked down at her chair. Red Nine was wailing in her body and she didn't want to sit down.

Maria made herself sit. She reached into her pocket for some Blue Seven and put the pill to her mouth. "Could I have a glass of water?" she asked.

"No," Jamison said crisply. "You may not."

The blow knocked Maria sideways in her chair. The pill flew from her lips, struck a wall, fell to the dark green carpet. Red Nine turned Maria's fingers to claws and sent her snarling at the man who had struck her, not even thinking about it; but he slapped her twice more across the face and dropped her back to the chair. Maria heard a thud as the other man's fist punched into Ubu's solar plexus, doubling him over.

Beautiful Maria looked up at Jamison. She could feel her face reddening where she'd been struck. Ubu's panting breaths sounded loud in her ear. Jamison was looking at Maria intently with her orange lips pursed.

"Tell us how you did it," Jamison said. Her voice was perfectly ordinary in tone, as if she were asking the time of day and hadn't just seen two acts of violence. Maria just stared at her. The man by her chair slapped her again, lightly this time. The shock was the same.

"Answer," he said.

Maria could taste blood in her mouth. Red Nine blazed in her nerves. Her vision was filmed with red.

"How did you do it?" Jamison said. "Our tables are built so as to prevent interference. You set off every alarm in the house, so obviously you got past our safeguards somehow. How did you do it?"

"I—" Maria began. But Ubu sprang out of his chair, charging head-down for the man before him, and caught the guard by surprise, driving him back into the wall. He grappled the man's arms with his lower hands, punched wildly with the upper, his head still down. The man managed to avoid the wild swings and brought a knee into Ubu's face, then dropped him with a vicious punch to the neck. Maria's nerves jumped at the horribly solid sound of Ubu's body hitting the carpet. She could feel something liquid running from the corner of her mouth and she wiped it away. The back of her hand came away red.

Her glitching the systems had worked in the smaller Fringe joints, she thought. But maybe they couldn't afford the safeguards the big casinos could. She and Ubu hadn't thought of that.

The man that had dropped Ubu had unclipped a scanner from his belt, was passing it over Ubu's body. "What is it?" Jamison asked. Her tone of voice hadn't changed, was still perfectly ordinary. She sucked on her cigaret. "Some kind of implant induction device? Which of you has it? What is the range?" Her voice changed, became suggestive. "If we can have the device, we might let you keep some of the money."

Maria looked at her, tried to form words in her bruised mouth. "You're not . . . going to give the money back to the banker?"

"To Colette? Hardly. When you buy the bank, there's always a chance you'll lose it. It's a safer form of gambling, but it's still gambling. She knew the risks."

The scanner was passing over Maria now. The operator looked at the readouts, frowned, looked at Jamison and shook his head.

Jamison leaned forward. "Tell us," she said. "If it's a good system, we might let you keep all you won." She shrugged. "It's pocket change to us. We can win it back in twenty minutes on a good night." She stubbed out her cigaret, then broke it in half and dropped the halves on the desk. They made a clattering sound. "Of course you'll never be allowed in any gaming house again," she said. "Here or on the Fringe, which I'd guess is more your style. Your stats will be transmitted everywhere."

Maria looked at Ubu. He was moving feebly on the floor, and his face was webbed with blood. Pain beat in Maria's chest. Her hands clenched.

She looked at Jamison. "The truth is," she said, "I'm a witch."

Jamison leaned back in her chair and sighed. "The answer," she said, "is unsatisfactory."

The man slapped Maria again, hard. Tears spilled from her eyes. "It's *true!*" she wailed.

The next blow drove her off the chair, to her knees. Red and blue pills tumbled from her pockets. Blood dropped scarlet amid the scattered colors.

"Start with number two," Jamison said. "If they don't answer, you may continue to number three."

CHAPTER

3

UBU TRIED TO MOVE, AND INSTANTLY HIS BACK AND ABDOMEN WENT into seizure. Agony tore at his body. He couldn't find the strength to cry for help.

He'd already screamed his throat out. After the beating hadn't produced the desired results, the guards had employed glitch rods. Ubu could still smell his burned flesh.

He waited for the spasms to end, then took a ragged, shaky breath, trying not to choke on the blood that had pooled in his mouth. His lips, smashed over and over against his teeth, had been badly torn.

The place where he was lying was hard. A cool breeze dried the blood on his skin. His eyes were swollen shut and he couldn't see.

Ubu tried to move again. Claws of pain tore at his belly. This time he passed out.

He awoke to feel Beautiful Maria's hair falling like down on his face. Ubu managed to open a single eye and saw Maria crouched over him. Dried blood smeared her unrecognizable face. At the sight a softer anguish filled Ubu's heart. He wanted to close his eye and weep.

"Can you stand?" Maria asked. Ubu couldn't answer. He tilted his head to let congealing blood run out of his mouth, then tried to get to his hands and knees. Maria's cool hands helped him. The guards had given him the boot more than once, and Ubu's scrotum shrieked in remembered pain. Somehow the spasms didn't take him away again.

Ubu squinted through his one eye, saw waffle-patterned metal flooring, harsh fluorescent lights, color-coded pipes that hugged the walls and ceiling. The Monte Carlo hadn't wanted to sully its main entrance by throwing two bleeding gamblers into the street. Instead Ubu and Maria had been dumped in one of the utility tunnels running along the outer rim of Angelica Station. Ubu's brain reeled as he tried to remember whether he wanted to go spinward or anti-spinward to get to *Runaway*, but Maria had already chosen the direction.

At first Ubu crawled, Maria's hand on one arm to hold him steady and offer encouragement. The pain from his groin sent a wave of vomit into his throat, but he bit it back. After he had more confidence in his body doing what he asked it to, he tottered to his feet. Pain stunned him, made him bend over with racking coughs.

Maria dragged him on, holding his hand. Her grey jacket was gone; one of her feet was bare; there were burn marks and bloodstains on her torn shirt. It was his plan that had done this to her, Ubu realized. Guilt clutched at his throat. He took a sobbing breath and staggered on. Pain eddied listlessly through his body, then turned sharp as a hammer struck his kidneys. He stifled a scream.

A blast of heat rose through the patterned metal grate. A compressor roared in the depths below Ubu's feet.

"I'm sorry," Ubu said. Beautiful Maria gave no sign that she heard.

There was the soft hiss of a pressure lock, and they crawled under a narrow lintel into twilight. Music hummed in the distance. They were home, on the Fringe.

They looked like a pair of Mudville tourists who'd got themselves pounded by locals, and snickers followed them to the beltway conveyor. The fading gravity lessened Ubu's pain. He clutched Maria's hand and took the lead as they stumbled over the low-gee surface to *Runaway*'s entry port.

Once inside the ship they headed straight for the sick bay. It was very well equipped, and both Ubu and Maria had fastlearned emergency medicine. Ubu took a cup from the chest and tore away the plastic sanitary envelope. He rinsed out his bloody mouth, swallowed endorphin analogs, a pill to reduce swelling, Blue Heaven. Maxim, distressed, stood in the doorway, lashed his tail and yowled.

Beautiful Maria took a cup in her trembling hands, tried to swallow a pill, gagged it up. She clutched the sink. Clumsily Ubu tried to caress her matted hair. Maria fell to her knees, sobbing. There was nothing left in her, he realized: she'd got him here on the last of her Red Nine and now she was done. He took a sterile cloth from the emergency kit, knelt by her side, and washed her bloody face. She submitted, clenching her teeth in pain.

Ubu coaxed her to her feet and began to take off her clothes. His teeth ground in anger. Breath went out of him in a cold hiss. The bastard with the glitch rod had paid particular attention to her breasts. Tears poured down Maria's swollen face. Ubu started a warm shower and helped Maria into the cubicle. Her mouth opened in a silent cry at the stinging impact of the water. Ubu turned on the soap tap, and foam boiled white on her shoulders. He followed her into the wide cubicle without bothering to take off his clothes.

He washed her carefully, cleaning the cuts, then dropped his own clothes to the bottom of the cubicle and washed himself. Soapy water pooled around their ankles as Ubu's clothing blocked the drains. Ubu turned off the soap tap and rinsed in clean water. Quiet sobs rose from Maria's throat.

Ubu wished he would be able to forget this, the blows, the cries, Maria's torn body and ceaseless tears. Other people's memories faded with time, but never Ubu's: Pasco had wired him for permanency and he recalled everything, every sight, sound, his life coded indelibly in his brain to rise from the past like Pasco's hologram parading the corridors of his ship.

He looked over her carefully. She could stand and walk: no leg or pelvic bones broken. "How are your ribs?" he asked, then saw she was carrying her hand carefully. "Let me see." He took her hand. "Here? These two fingers?"

"Hurt. The wrist, too."

He X-rayed the hand and wrist on the portable machine and kicked in the analysis program. Ubu was informed that the fingers were just sprained, but that Maria had chipped one of her wrist bones. The injury was not critical, but might hamper free movement in the future. He gave her a hypo of a hormone that was supposed to help knit bones.

Maxim called from the doorway as Ubu led Maria from the shower and loaded a pair of chaks with medication, stuff to hype the immune system plus everything he'd given himself. He fired it all up her nostrils. He took the emergency kit in one hand and led Maria to her bed with the other. Blue Seven was beginning its lazy swim through his mind. His hands moving carefully in the first tentative touch of the drug, Ubu disinfected Maria's cuts again, then sprayed neuflesh over them. Maria's eyes fluttered shut. Breath eased through her bruised lips. "I'm sorry," Ubu said, and kissed her temple where the soft hair rose from the pale warm skin, the unmarked interface between black and white.

Leaving a trail of water on the deck, Ubu dragged himself to his new sleeping cabin—the old one was still littered with clawed confetti—and fell into the rack. Maxim hopped into the rack and settled between his knees, purring in a purely defiant way, tail still lashing. Ubu's body warmed with sleep.

"I'm in a great mood today!" Pasco said brightly. Ubu opened his eye. Pasco stood naked in front of the bed, grinning and scratching himself. The recording had been made at least eight or nine years ago—the figure in the hologram was clean-shaven.

"Do you know why?" Pasco asked. "I'll tell you."

Shut up, Pop, Ubu thought.

"Because I've figured out something, that's why." Pasco's smile was brilliant. "We can make ourselves a fortune!"

Ubu decided that it would hurt too much to lean out of the rack and turn off the holo projector. He shut his eye and tried not to listen.

"I've just figured out what Beautiful Maria can do! She really *is* a witch!" Pasco laughed. "Once I've trained her abilities to their full potential—" He snapped his fingers. "The money will just fall into our hands! We can't lose."

"Oh, Jesus Rice," Ubu said.

"We just have to find the proper *applications*, that's all. This Consolidation business was beginning to worry me, but not any more. If we can just hold out a few more years, the money will start rolling in!"

Pasco began to sing, a chirpy sentimental ballad called "Today My Dreams Come True." Pasco couldn't remember all the lyrics and filled in the blanks with nonsense words. Ubu hoped he wouldn't attempt the instrumental break, but he did, doing a bad imitation of a sizer guitar.

Sadness rose in Ubu's chest like a welling pool of blood. He wished he could cut himself off from sorrow, just touch a switch and cease feeling, the same way he could turn off Pasco's hologram. Instead he listened to the off-key singing and hoped Blue Heaven would turn it into a brainless swaddling dream, all harmless fluff like the lyrics of the song, preserve him from the bite of his memory, his own certainty that Angel Station was the place where all dreams died.

CHAPTER
4

THE ELECTRON MUSIC SOOTHED MARIA, BUFFERED HER PAIN. THE
touch of the current wasn't as sharp and dangerous as when she was
flaming on Red Nine, or as immediate; instead the distant background hum built lovely architectures that patterned across the ship,
an invisible electronic skeleton, a lovely lacework continually trans-
forming itself across Maria's perceptions.

She was drugged lightly: Blue Three, to keep the pain at bay,
not as potent as Blue Seven. Clothing hurt, so she lay naked in her
rack or pillowed on the couch in the crew lounge, Maxim her only
company, happy the station gravity was almost nonexistent this close
to the hub. Sometimes she played keyboards or watched holo
hype, more interested in the patterns of electrons in her mind
than the music or in the hype-people inflicting violence on one
another.

Ubu moved distantly, busily through the pattern of Maria's
perceptions, limping from place to place on torn leg muscles. She
sensed the alterations he was making in the electron flow. He was
calling up information, working out figures on the comp.

Ubu was working on a plan. Another plan.

The plan would involve her, of course. Maria knew well enough how his mind worked.

Maria swallowed another Blue Three, concentrated on the electron pattern.

She knew that Ubu, his plan, and her pain were all tinged with inevitability. But she wanted to keep them outside the pattern for as long as possible.

"I don't want to ask you again," Ubu said. "But I don't see a way around it."

Beautiful Maria, her fingers striking random chords on the sizer keyboard, said nothing.

"Another day," said Ubu. "That's our limit. Then we have to deal with OttoBanque."

"Think of something else." Spoken through cracked lips. Maria held one chord with the left hand while she dabbed at her lower lip with the other, looked passively at the dot of blood. The chord filled the room, strained the silence.

"I wish I *could!*" Ubu shouted, the long chord burning red in his brain. Frustration seized his throat in a taloned fist and his fury died. He turned away and limped to the door. He didn't want to look at her naked body any more, see what his last plan had done to it. Maria's features were a puffy discolored mask, incapable of expression. The bruises were bigger now, blooming beneath her translucent skin like bright disfiguring blossoms. The burn marks on her back and breasts were the furious bites of an animal. He couldn't see his sister in that skin any longer.

He leaned against the doorframe of the lounge, his back to her. Chords touched his mind with violent colors, colors like flesh under assault. "I don't want to start out my life as a loser," he said. "This is the first chance we have to make it. The only chance. If we lose, luck gets made for us from this point on. We won't have much to say about it."

Maria's voice was weary. Even Maxim's purr was louder. "Talk to me tomorrow," she said.

Ubu turned and left. The old ship's joints crackled as he moved down the corridor. Facts crowded his mind. Production statistics. Effects of Consolidation policy. Bankruptcy statistics. Current prices for captured singularities. Prices on Angelica Station for heavy magnets. The facts warred with memories, with scents and sounds: Pasco weeping while red pills trailed out of his pockets; Marco de Suarez looking out at him from his skull-like face, the shine of neurojuice on his upper lip; the sharp smell of Kitten's plastic skin as it burned; Beautiful Maria's endless, soft cry as the glitch rod snapped against her flesh . . .

Restlessness tugged at him. He needed to get off the ship. Even if there was no money to spend, even if people laughed at his swelling and bruises. He went to his cabin, threw a caftan over his head, belted it, considered shaving, decided against it. He moved to the airlock with his practiced low-gee skip. Ubu went through the lock, down the docking tube, cycled through the lock on the other side.

As the hatch cracked open, the sounds of Angel Hub commerce flowed through: shouts, blatting horns, carryalls whining as they moved cargo. The hatch swung fully open and revealed a boy standing outside. His soft unmoned face wore a startled expression, perhaps at the door opening unexpectedly, perhaps at the sight of Ubu's damaged face. The boy wore grip shoes, a pastel green blouse with gold metal threads—real stitching, not fake—a pair of shorts with lots of pockets. The de Suarez cast of features was plain. Ubu suppressed irritation.

"Bossrider," the boy said.

"Shooter." Giving him the benefit of the doubt.

"I'm—"

"Christopher de Suarez. I know."

The boy looked at him curiously. "Have we met?"

"Years ago. A shooter meeting called to protest the Consolidation policy." One of many. Nothing had come of any of them.

"I don't remember," the de Suarez said.

"Wasn't very memorable." Ubu's lips twisted in a knowing smile, then belated pain stabbed him from lips and jaw and neck. He winced. "What you need, shooter man?"

"I'd like to see Beautiful Maria." Ubu already knew this: the boy had been leaving messages for Maria all over *Runaway*'s computer. *This*, he thought, was what Maria had been shacking with?

"She's not well," Ubu said. He didn't want a de Suarez aboard his ship, in a position to report to Marco on its shabby condition, its battered crew and empty holds.

"Oh." The boy fidgeted. "Is it serious?"

"Depends on what you call serious."

"I'd like to see her."

The de Suarez seemed to be getting stubborn. Ubu pressed the button that would cycle the hatch shut in his face. "I'll call her," he said through the narrowing crack. "Wait here."

He considered not calling Maria, just telling the de Suarez she wasn't able to see him, but he was irritated, not so much by the thought of lying as by the pointlessness of lying about something so trivial. He pressed the intercom button.

"There's a Christopher de Suarez here to see you," he said. There was a short silence before Maria answered. Her voice had lost some of its weariness.

"Kit. I know him. You can let him in."

Annoyance sparked in Ubu's nerves. He suppressed it. "You sure you want a de Suarez in our ship? I don't want Marco knowing things."

"Kit *hates* Marco. He wouldn't tell him anything."

Ubu was dubious. "Okay," he said. "It's your shoot." Kit, he thought. What a stupid name.

He opened the hatch again and walked out, making the de Suarez step aside. "The centrifuge is locked down," he said. "Don't bother with the climb to the ship's hub, you can open the double hatch and walk in. Maria's in the crew lounge, second on the right past the command cage."

The de Suarez gave a hesitant smile. "Thanks, bossrider."

"My pleasure, Kit." Grinning insolently.

Kit, Ubu thought again as he skipped away. What a stupid name.

Sitting on the cracked old couch in the lounge, Beautiful Maria leaned her bare back against Kit's warm shoulder and took his hand in her own. Turned away from him this way, she didn't have to watch the continued disturbance in his eyes as he looked at her disfigured face. The cat hopped from the sizer keyboard to her lap, then sprawled across her thighs. A distant wave of Blue Three eddied through her.

She gave him the agreed-upon explanation, that she and Ubu had won big in the Monte Carlo, then been beaten and robbed by a bunch of downside thugs.

"Have you talked to the cops?" he asked.

"Sure." The lie came easily. "Haven't heard from them since."

"The groundlice probably paid them off. Angel Station's that kind of place. So long as no one bothers Biagra-Exeter personnel they don't care what happens to anyone else. I didn't even see it in the station newsfax." He squeezed her hand. "I wish I could touch you. Really touch you. But it would hurt you, wouldn't it?"

"I wouldn't be comfortable. I'm sorry."

"I wish I could help somehow. But *Abrazo*'s leaving in just a few weeks. We're waiting for one more shipment to arrive, then we're gone."

Maria felt a long throb of sorrow and was surprised at its strength. She turned her head, saw Kit with his eyes turned stubbornly away, and she touched his cheek with her fingers. "I wish you didn't have to leave. Have you thought about the apprenticeship thing?"

Kit gave a heavy sigh. "I don't think Marco would go for it. And if he did, he'd want constant reports on what you and your brother were doing, what kind of deals you were cutting. And then he'd use the information to try to undermine you."

She shook her head. Blue Three made it more difficult than usual to comprehend Marco's behavior. "He's so awful," she said.

"We're surviving. We're even making a good profit. I just wish he wouldn't do it this way."

Beautiful Maria closed her eyes and let the unfocused sadness drift through her. Kit would desert her. It wasn't his fault, but he would. And then it would be Maria and Ubu again, together and alone and fighting alone against Consolidation again, a fight as constant and as hopeless as that of a ship caught in the coils of a singularity, the shooters trying every maneuver they knew but falling ever nearer, ending as a last forlorn burst of radiation crying from the heart of a lightless sun . . .

"Maria," Kit said. "Maybe there's a way."

"A way to do what?"

"You can come with me. Aboard *Abrazo*. We could live together."

Delight brightened in her mind at the realization that Kit was capable of such a flattering surprise. She turned her head to give him a joyful look. His eyes flinched from her features, then gazed at her steadily. She kissed him.

"Marco would allow that?" she asked.

"Probably. I think he would." Kit's tone was defensive. "I can talk him into it," he said, as if to clarify things. "We're allowed to have our choice of partners. I'm not a shooter yet, but I think I could get him to agree."

Unexpected Blue Three laughter bubbled to Maria's lips. Kit flushed and looked away. Maria kissed him again.

"I wasn't laughing at you, Kit. Just at how sudden this is. We've only known each other one day."

"Long enough to know what I want." Defiantly. "People will make fun of me, but I don't care."

"That's brave of you."

Kit looked surprised. He started to say something, then changed his mind. "It'll work out," he said.

"I can't picture living on a ship with so many people."

"Most ships have whole families. Some more than one family. You an exception."

Maria nestled against his shoulder again. "My father's brothers and sisters died in an accident. A hatch blew or something, back on Atocha Station. Years before I was born."

"It must have been lonely, growing up with only three of you. And now only two."

"No. Not really. I don't think I've ever been lonely for long." She chucked sleepy Maxim under the chin. The cat twisted his body, the forward half coiling back to present the chin for easier access. Warm fur brushed against her bare legs. She stroked the cat's buzzing throat and thought lazily about *Abrazo*, about life as part of De Suarez Expressways, Ltd. "I wonder," she said, "if it's possible to be lonely on the *Abrazo*."

"It's . . ." He raised his hands and let them fall. They dropped slowly in the light gravity. "Complex. The thing is, you have to consider everybody in everything you do. All the thoughts and actions of the others can sort of overwhelm you." There was a dark silence. "But you can be lonely there. You can."

"You're not making it sound attractive."

"Well." He kissed her neck. "With two of us, it would be better. And you're a shooter—you'd be more important than me." He shifted on the couch so that he could put his other arm around her waist. Maria's nerves fluttered as his fingers brushed her belly. "I would really like to touch you," Kit said. Maria continued to stroke Maxim's throat.

"What about Ubu?" she asked.

"I—he—" Another silence, and then Kit sighed, conceded reality. "It won't be possible," he said. "We have too many shooters as it is. Marco would accept you as my woman, but he wouldn't take any shooters just because they were shooters."

"Ubu and I go together, Kit."

There was a long silence. "I'm sorry," he said.

"Not your fault." She wouldn't have to say the other, that she didn't want to be a de Suarez, her presence tolerated only because she was Kit's acknowledged possession. The Kitten in Kit's life.

Still, regret trailed listless fingers through her mind. There had been pleasure in the brief fantasy, to leave *Runaway*, to have someone to care for her. She wished she could have basked in the fantasy a little longer. Tomorrow, she knew, life was going to turn real, and with a vengeance.

"I won't ask you to glitch anything again. But we need it this one time."

His warm hand closed on hers. Maria closed her eyes. A reflection of the electron world, the computer terminal built into the table, tingled in her spine.

"Please," he said.

"We extend the loan," Maria said. "We get another hundred twenty standard to pay it off. Then what?"

"We won't be here when it falls due."

"Where else would we be? We don't have enough to pay

docking fees. OttoBanque won't lend us anything more—we'd have to go through a human supervisor for that, and he'd turn us down."

"I've got it worked out."

The electron stream rose slowly up her neck, brightened in her mind. She could almost touch it. Ubu's voice seemed to come from far away.

"Your stake from blackhole be gone, okay? But we still got the money from the sale of the miners. We take that money, we buy magnetic grapples and a lot of provisions, we go hunting singularities. I checked station stores. There's an old pair of grapples we could buy."

Electrons sang through Maria's brain. She could see the patterns, feel them caress her. "That takes years," she said. "That's why it's all done by robot probes."

"People have done it before." Defensively. "Sometimes they come back rich." He offered her a tattered grin. "We find a black hole, we clear our debts. Pay our fines. Then we go on finding more singularities if we have to. Your talent might make it easy. Maybe you could see them from far off."

Ubu's absurd hope echoed distantly in Maria's heart. She could taste electricity on her tongue. "We still can't pay docking fees," she said.

"We don't pay them. We run for it."

The electric pattern broke up. Maria leaned forward, touched her forehead to the table. Sighed.

"Illegal," she said. "Jesus Rice. You'll put us in prison."

"I'm the bossrider. I'll take the heat." There was a pause. "I've got it worked out. We blow out third shift, when everyone's asleep. The Navy's got a patrol ship here, but it isn't really equipped to stop us, and we can get enough room between us and the station for a short shoot before they can catch us."

"You're going to wreck us."

"I'm desperate. Our shit is weak. I admit that. If you have any ideas, I want to hear them."

Maria pressed her forehead to the cool table, seeking a pattern, an answer. Ubu's insistent voice jabbed at her like a circling prizefighter.

"Do you know what happens if we go down out here? *Runaway* gets sold for our debts, and we don't get anything. If we're lucky, we might get an indentureship contract with a Hiliner; but most likely we'll be split up, maybe never see each other again. Maybe we can get work as systers, but we'd be stuck in the Angelica System for the rest of our lives, and all our shooter talents go to waste. We never get our brains into the Now again.

"If that doesn't work out, maybe we can get work for Biagra-Exeter as miners. Is that your idea of a future, digging rocks out of asteroids? The pay is shit, you get to live in foam bunkers all your life, and the only time you get to see the Fringe is when you get leave for a few weeks to spend your accumulated pay."

"Ubu," Maria said, "I know all this."

"Most likely no one will want us. Then we'll be sent downside to Mudville. Down there we're not even of legal age—they don't care about our mones, our fastlearn skills—*we'll be minors!* The colony will use us to do the jobs no real citizen wants to do. And it's not even a developed colony—things down on Angelica are primitive."

Ubu's voice broke. Maria blindly gave his hand a reassuring squeeze. "The sky isn't *right* down there, Maria," he said. "It changes colors, black to blue or red or something, and you can only see the stars part of the time, and they don't shine, they're all distorted. They *twinkle*. We won't have access to freefall when we want it, we'll be stuck in full gravity all the time. We couldn't keep clean—there'll be *dirt* everywhere. They'll make us grow *plants* in the *mud* to *eat*."

Ubu spat out the foreign-sounding words. His hand was trembling. He took a long breath. "How is prison any different, Maria?" he asked. There was pain in his voice. "How can it be any worse than being stuck forever on some mudball in space?"

Maria thought about Red Nine, about the world alive with electric fire. Fast, dangerous, full of tidal eddies like a game of blackhole. Her mind quailed.

"Isn't there some other way?" she said.

"I can't think of one." There was a silence. His grip on her hand was lax, defeated. "Look, if it goes wrong, we're not any worse off. If we can't find a singularity, if it gets to the point where we just can't stand the search any longer and we're beginning to hate each other—well, then there's no point in going on anyway, right? So we find a developed world somewhere, not like Angelica but a place that's been settled for a hundred years or something, a place with civilization like Bezel or China Light, and we shoot insystem and turn ourselves in. We'd get condemned to Mudville, but at least it wouldn't be *Angelica*."

Maria jumped as his lower hands began to stroke her hair. "We could give up," he said. "We could do it if that's what you want." His words had lost all passion now, were just a pointless, dull recital of fact. "I'll do anything you say, Maria. I wouldn't go against you."

Pain stung Maria's throat. "I know," she said.

"I would never have taken you to the Monte Carlo if I had any idea what would happen."

"I know."

"I love you." His palm burnished her hair.

"I know." Sorrow beat slowly in her heart. "I know." Her resistance was at an end, defeated by his love. She would follow him, follow the plan, follow until the last pattern flashed on the table, and the stakes were swept from the board.

Ubu stood behind Maria as she sat in the cubicle at OttoBanque. Harsh light filled the cubicle as he closed the door. In the reflective screen of the bank terminal in front of her, Maria could see her eyes glittering like impact diamonds. Red Nine danced along her nerves, spread gooseflesh on her shoulders. Every bruise, every swollen muscle seemed lit up, alive with heat and pain. She shaded her eyes with a hand. A sick headache throbbed behind her eyes.

"God, I wish I didn't have to do this," she said.

"The last time."

Maria's nerves crackled with pain. She swallowed bile and wondered if Ubu was actually as naive as he sounded. Probably he meant what he said.

Not that it mattered anyway.

A flash of pain ran through her. Her mouth was dry. She hated this.

The Red Nine might not have been necessary, because she could be in physical contact with the terminal, and that made it easier. But she'd only get one try; and she had to be certain.

Ubu reached over her shoulder with both upper arms, tapped in *Runaway*'s ID number, and called for the loan file. Data flickered into existence on the terminal. Snarling electric current surged into Beautiful Maria's perceptions.

"How should we do this?" Ubu asked. "Ask for the extension first? Or just try to change the file?"

"I'll do it," Maria said. She took a breath and gazed at her reflection in the terminal, the outlines of her image broken by cold lines of fluorescent numbers. She reached one hand to the screen, pressed it over the reflection of her face. One dilated eye stared back, alone and terrified, pupil dark as carbon ice. The flow built in her hand, her arm. With her other hand Maria touched keys, asked for the extension, waited while the bank's central computer considered the request.

She saw the answer coming, knew the denial was under her hand. Her heart crashed in her chest. The glitch seemed to form in her palm, sprang through transparent glass into the screen, then into the electronic array. Phosphors swarmed like fireflies behind Maria's eyes. She felt close to passing out.

Maria took a breath, raised her hand. Amber letters ran beneath her hand.

APPROVED.

"Good," Ubu said, and Maria jumped. His voice seemed incredibly loud.

"You can go back to the ship," he said. "I'll take care of the rest."

Electric chaos buzzed in Maria's mind. "Blue Heaven," she said, reaching into her pocket for a chak. "Now."

A pair of huge superconducting electromagnets had been lashed down in *Runaway*'s cargo space, the bright curved talons of a dismembered insect. Cable dangled from huge alloy spools. Hardware shackles gleamed in the dim floodlit bay.

On the other end of the bay was a tumble of battered tempafoam containers, all of Pasco's junk that Ubu hadn't been able to sell—the obsolete autowomb, out-of-date fastlearn equipment, bits of hardware that Pasco had been tinkering with and that hadn't even been identified yet. Kit looked at the stuff in confusion.

"You're going *prospecting?*" he said. His disbelieving voice echoed in the long metal space.

Maria floated high in front of him, her grey robe billowing in the insignificant gravity, the smooth muscle of her legs a flashing white contrast to the dark fabric. "As soon as we finish our provisioning," she said. She spun slowly to face him. Her hands danced in front of his eyes. There was laughter on her chiseled face. "And as soon as we've said our goodbyes."

Desire performed a sweaty dance through Kit's body. He pushed off, floated toward her. "You could be gone years," he said. "A lot of prospectors never find anything."

There were still yellow bruises on her cheeks, surrounding her eyes. But drugs had reduced the tissue damage. A pneumatic bandage encased her broken wrist. Her chiseled features had risen from the swelling, and now he could look at her face without wanting to clench his fists and smash whoever had done this to her.

She gave a throaty laugh as she reached for him, took his collar, began the slow fall to the bare metal surface of the cargo bay. He realized she was high. They landed on their feet, bounced lightly. Her hair rebounded and settled like a black cloud. He put his arms around her waist, the sacral hollows beneath his palms. Hormone-sculptured muscle flexed under his hands.

"Kit, I'm going to miss you," she said.

Yearning filled the painful, throbbing hollow in his chest. He had never desired anything more than to lose himself entirely in the cloud of black hair, the sleek white body, the dark and somber eyes. He kissed her, tasted spice on her lips, the chile sauce they'd had on their dinner. Kit kissed the bruises on her cheeks, the corners of her eyes. Her hands slid up inside his shirt, traced the spine beneath his skin.

"I've wanted you for a long time," she said. "It just would have hurt too much, is all." She smiled. "I think the light gravity will help."

He held her close and jumped, rising high in the big empty

cargo space. Maria laughed as she threw her head back. Kit kissed the hollow of her throat, felt the tremor of her laughter against his lips. He pulled her gown over her head, threw it over his shoulder, bent to kiss the yellow bruise on one white, sharp shoulder. She threw her head forward to nuzzle his ear. Her hair drifted warmly down his back. Her body was an interplay of light and shade, shadowed ribs, pale skin, dark hollows, bruises descending the ladder of her ribs like indigo paint running down a tilted palette.

They touched the floor again, sprang aloft. Maria peeled his trousers from his legs, drew out the piece of elastic strapping he'd doubled around himself to use as a belt, threw the trousers away. His erection strained against her thigh. She passed the elastic around them both, cinched it so they wouldn't accidentally drift apart. Her long legs coiled around him. Coarse pubic hair grated against the underside of his shaft. He tasted the spicy warmth of her tongue.

Touchdown. His bare feet skated lightly over metal. Maria reached between their bodies, circled him with finger and thumb. Sharp teeth glistened in the periphery of his vision as she laughed at the preposterous warm eagerness pressed against her palm. Her hips rose, thrust down. There was a mutual, humid gasp as she absorbed his glans. Heat patterned Kit's skin at the touch of her fluttering breath. He leaped.

Kit cupped her hips in his hands, tried to drive himself far into her; but he was weightless, floating in a tangle of her hair and limbs and his own blazing desire, and his lunge went nowhere. Maria kept him at bay, her pelvis stirring lightly, maddening him. The air in his lungs turned to fire. She leaned back, holding his body firmly between her thighs. The improvised harness bit into his flesh. He could see the pulse beating in her throat. The cargo bay began to turn lazy, gentle circles.

The floor rose, touched Maria gently on the shoulders and the back of her supple neck. Maria giggled in stoned amusement. Kit reached out with his hands and pushed against the deck, turning the two of them upright; he kicked out again and launched them upward. Maria leaned back again and gasped in air. Her hair streamed behind her, blue highlights on black. The ceiling came up very fast.

Kit reached up and absorbed the shock on the palms of his

hands. They began to ease floorward. Maria's look was concentrated, intent. The muscles of her thighs flexed as she rocked gently, their relative positions changing only by one or two slow, infuriating millimeters.

A drop of sweat seemed to take hours to ease down the back of Kit's neck. His feet touched metal. Even in the near-zero gravity his knees were trembling. Kit sprang again. His control was long gone and they went into a slow sideways tumble along the length of the bay. Bright laughter sparkled from Maria's throat.

They touched, rebounded, and fell, their momentum gently absorbed by a stack of waffle-patterned plastic fenders intended for padding cargo and now strapped to the floor. Maria's eyes were glazed, the corners of her full mouth tilted in a smile. Strands of hair draped her face. Kit took a fistful of the plastic in each hand and used the leverage to drive himself into her. Her hips rose to meet him. Beautiful Maria tilted her head back, the catlike smile still on her face. The plastic matting began to slip from Kit's hands. Her fingers stroked over his ribs.

Kit lost his grip on the plastic and the two began to bounce erratically in the light gravity. He brushed hair from her face and kissed her. Her eyes were focused inward. Kit's entire epidermis seemed engorged with blood. She clutched his buttocks, took careful sips of air. Her breasts were flushing pink. Within moments Kit and Maria were screaming, bouncing madly in a tumbling, purposeful confusion of limbs and bodies and swooning nerve endings. They finished inverted, miraculously balanced, Beautiful Maria's head and neck absorbing their combined, insignificant weight.

Maria popped her neck, straightening her spine. They lofted slowly upward, turned, came down on Kit's head. He let himself fall on his back, the plastic matting pressing lightly against his flesh. Kit wiped sweat from his eye sockets with the back of a hand. Maria's laugh burbled against his neck.

"Gonna do that again," she said.

Kit gasped for breath. "Not anytime soon, shooter femme."

She palmed her hair back over her shoulder, revealed an unfocused grin. "We got hormones on this ship, lover. Drive you *crazy*, Maria promise. We do it till we so sore we can't keep on, then

I find us something for the pain." She looked down at him and giggled. "If I got to be gone for years, I'm gonna have fun while I can."

"Yeah." Glassy-eyed. "Right."

She undid his elastic strap, rubbed the red line over her hips where it had marked her. "Ow." His hands brushed her ribs, touched her breasts. A river of desperation poured through his heart at the thought that he would lose her. Each infusion of Maria left him wanting more, only seemed to make a point of how lonely he had been before. He thought of *Abrazo*, of the close crew quarters filled with relatives all sharpening their knives for total war against the universe, and he realized how pointless he would be without her, without her presence.

"Come with me," he said. "I love you." He didn't get it all out. Maria's palm pressed his mouth at the word *love*, and the words died. Her dark eyes were solemn.

She leaned forward, pressing her cheek to his. "Shooters always got the Now," she said. "That's all we need."

He closed his eyes. Grief stung his throat. He inhaled her scent, caressed her back with his hands. She lifted her head to look at him. Her hair covered them like a tent, provided the illusion they were alone in their dark world.

"This be more than Mudvillers get," Maria said. "That's why they come up the gravity well to have their fun."

"Yeah," he said. "I suppose so." He wrapped her in his arms, pressed her to him.

He wanted her to drive the wind from him, to manifest a comforting solidity that would leave some impression of permanence. He found instead to his sorrow that her weight was no more than that of a kitten.

The ventilation of the shacktube was intermittent, and the room was hot and smelled of garlic chicken and sex. Amy Santines, shooter femme, glanced over her head at the cold fluorescent numbers that announced station time. "Should go," she said. "The ship's loading in forty."

"That gives us forty, yes?" said Ubu. He propped himself up on the left set of arms and reached for his drink with the other.

"We stay another few minutes, we pay for a whole hour."
Sensibly.

"Right," said Ubu.

"Besides, it's too stuffy in here."

She took her drink, gathered her clothes, and crawled to the door. There wasn't room in the tube to stand. She was a tall moned femme, all flex and wiry muscle. Her skin was smooth like Beautiful Maria's, but her hair was brown and short, her eyes light. She and Ubu were old shackmates, had known each other for a long time, since the first onrush of shooter mones had driven them both together.

Amy scratched behind her neck with the elongated, prehensile toes of her right foot, then popped the tube's hatch and kicked her legs out. Fresh air brushed Ubu's skin. He took a drink from his forcebulb, discovered that a pressure leak had made his Kolodny go flat. He gathered his clothing, threw the foodplates into the recycle bin, and followed Amy.

They dropped to the catwalk outside with their clothing bundled in their hands, startling a pair of overdressed tourists on the catwalk opposite. Amy leered at them and licked her lips suggestively. They almost ran to their tube, whispering fiercely.

"What's *wrong* with those people, I wonder," Amy said as she pulled on her shorts.

"Who cares?" Ubu donned his shorts and caftan. He put an arm around Amy and kissed her. They walked to the end of the catwalk and dropped down the belt conveyor to the lobby. Ubu retrieved his counter, their amount of time automatically deducted, and he and Amy stepped out into the rim.

Amy grinned at him. "I get pregnant, you want the kid?"

"I'm protected," he said.

She laughed. "Just kidding," she said. "So am I."

Ubu raised his forcebulb to his lips again, put it down without firing. "Just a second," he said. "I want to buy another beer."

Amy followed him into a bar raucous with Fringe life. He dumped the bulb's contents and refilled, waved to Amy's brother Sig, who was onstage playing his audolin with a shooter band, mostly Garcias off the *Corsair*. Amy waved with one of her feet. The bartender took his credit counter, plugged it in, deducted the beer.

"I saw Kit de Suarez and your sister together yesterday," Amy said.

"They've been seeing each other some," Ubu said shortly. He collected his counter and fired beer over his palate.

"He's a pretty boy," Amy said. "All right, if you like 'em natural."

"I guess." He frowned, shifted from one foot to the other. "Wanna stay and listen, or move out?"

"Gotta load ship. So does Sigmund, so he better finish his song damn quick."

"I'll go with."

She waved farewell to Sig, then walked out of the bar. Ubu followed. She glanced at him over her shoulder.

"When's your ship loading? You said you were leaving tomorrow."

"We're loaded." Ubu hefted his credit counter. "We're just staying to spend what's left of our money."

"I don't remember *Runaway* being in the loader queue."

"We loaded secretly in the dead of night."

Amy shrugged. "If you say so."

He put his left arms around her waist and shoulder. The electromagnets had actually been loaded by shuttle, through *Runaway*'s rear cargo hatch. With a full cargo, requiring many loads, that would have been ruinously expensive; but the superconductors only occupied part of the cargo hold and had been loaded in a single shuttle run, in the end much cheaper than waiting in line for the station autoloaders.

He'd also been telling everyone he was planning on leaving tomorrow. *Runaway*'s actual departure date was third shift tonight.

They rode the conveyor to the hub, then said goodbye at the loading gate. "See you next station, bossrider," Amy said. She kissed him and pinched a buttock.

See you next lifetime, Ubu almost said; but he just forced a grin and said, "Yeah. Next Now, shooter femme."

Taking shots of beer, Ubu headed back to the bar where they'd left Sig. Sig would be leaving; maybe Ubu could fill in on audolin for a while.

Crackling dross filled the air as he entered. Dancers obscured his view of the band. He stood by the bar and finished his beer while waiting for the song to end, cleaned the bulb and refilled it with Sharps, then sidled up to Sig and asked if he could borrow the audolin when he left to load ship. Sig looked up at him in surprise, shaking copper-colored bangs out of his eyes.

"Shit. I forgot about the loading."

"Good thing I told you. Amy was planning on being pissed."

Sig jumped up from his seat, handed Ubu the audolin and bow, and left in a hurry. Ubu examined the audolin, turned off the robot autotuner, and started tuning by hand. The guitarist, an older shooter with short-cropped dark hair and faded tattoos on his forearms, was looking at him. Nestor Garcia, bossrider of the *Corsair*. Ubu grinned.

"Hi, Nestor."

"Bossrider." Nestor scowled. "You gonna get weird on us, Pasco's Ubu?"

"Weird? Not me, Nestor."

Ubu plucked notes with the upper right hand, his left fingers bending each with experimental touches on the neck slides. His fingers were awkward; he hadn't played in weeks.

"None of that half-tone shit you do. This is a band. We play together."

"Be so. Whatever you say."

The Garcias were serious about their music and earned spare credit playing during their layovers. They were as professional as shooter bands ever got without actually abandoning the Now to live in the Outside Life, the way the Guptas or Evel Krupp had.

Ubu ran the alloy bow over metal strings. Colors shimmered up his spine in a reverse waterfall of pleasure.

Nestor looked at his daughter, Sara, who sat behind a row of keyboards. "*A la Luna*," he said. Sara nodded and rolled her fingers experimentally over the sizer boards, produced a booming percussive thunder. Then she dropped into a crouch over the boards, counted aloud to Nestor, then slammed into rhythm as everyone dove into the song. Antony, the vocalist, yowled into his headset mic, his hands working belt controls to alter his timbre and occasionally harmonize with himself. By the end Sara was playing a third board with her prehensile toes, one knee cranked up to her ear while she balanced on the other leg. Sara had only two arms, but she had ambidextrous genes wired into her chromosomes, handy when playing dolores styles where there were at least two patterns going on at once.

Ubu concentrated mainly on keeping up. He was too rusty to do anything adventurous—he wasn't technically a very accomplished player anyway—and the way the dolores ballad's rhythms kept falling away, shifting, then returning in odd ways required his full attention.

When he was little he'd fastlearned keyboard synthesizers, but he found them unsatisfactory. Sizers were always on pitch, without the odd stray harmonics that Ubu found the most interesting aspect of natural tuning—there were programs you could feed into your sizer that were supposed to imitate the effect, but Ubu could always tell when people were using them.

He switched to stringed instruments, first guitar and then audolin. He enjoyed the ability to bend his notes, to brighten the spectrum of his perception with new, subtler tonalities. Most of the people he played with seemed immune to the effects he was after, but their brains weren't wired the same way and Ubu learned not to expect their approval or understanding.

After the dolores came a dross song, all flash and forte, a universe brought to submission with every crashing chord. Ubu's fingers were slowly waking up to the task; he concentrated on not letting the thunder overwhelm him, on his attack, and on the little bursts of color and taste burned through his mind by the lowered thirds and sevenths.

After the dross was over he looked at Nestor. "Mind if I use your spare hollow-body?" he asked. "I'd like something to do with my lower set."

Nestor looked at him for a cold half second, then nodded.

The guitar was about a century old, a Sandman with the trademark pink plastic Q-shaped body instead of the usual triangular style. Ubu had inherited an imitation Sandman from the grandfather he'd never met, the guitar found in a locker on board *Runaway* next to other instruments abandoned there when Pasco's family all died on Atocha. The Sandman's neck had staggered frets to give strong harmonics with every chord and a ROM-controlled smart capo to keep the strings on pitch. Ubu disabled the capo and tuned with the pegs, then made sure the guitar's transmitter was being picked up by the Garcias' mixer.

The next number exploded into existence like a nova, blazing colors sharpened in Ubu's mind by the guitar's formidable sonics. The harmonics were so powerful they could easily overwhelm the rest of the band; Ubu saw right away he had to be careful. He concentrated entirely on technique, on his left-hand glissandi and right-hand attack, the rest strokes and careful finger hooks. With the audolin he produced a harmony line that drew a tart thread, like a burst of lemon, along the back of his tongue. At the end he hauled the neck of the guitar in a long seesaw motion to produce a chorus vibrato that sent little waves of burning metal into his perceptions, like a strobe flashing off boiling, dancing quicksilver.

Nestor gave him an over-the-shoulder glance. Not disapproving, just letting Ubu know he'd heard. Ubu grinned back, then reached for his bulb and fired Sharps over his palate. Fire flamed down his throat and he gave a laugh as he waited for Nestor to kick off the band.

Ubu played furiously for several more numbers, lost in the sound, the polychrome patterns mounting in his mind. He dosed himself with Sharps during each break. Then, in the middle of a song, he saw that Nestor and the other guitarist were looking at him, Nestor as if he'd just seen his worst fears confirmed, and that Antony was giving him sharp glances, too, whenever he could spare them . . . Ubu's fingers almost froze at the cold realization that he'd run off on a strong guitar harmonic and that the whole band had followed along without quite realizing it, that the guitar's soaring sonics had drawn everyone into a melody line about half an octave too high . . . Antony's vocal cords were twisting themselves into scraps of bleeding meat trying to stay with the band, and no one knew what to do.

Ubu glanced at Antony and gave him an encouraging smile, about all he could think of at the moment. The smile froze to his face as he counted ahead to the end of the phrase, seeking a way out as his fingers worked automatically. The phrase came to an end before he was quite ready, but he took a deep breath and chopped the last note short with a series of three chords that dropped the guitar back into Antony's range.

Fortunately everyone followed. Ubu gave another, more confident smile to Nestor, then confined himself to playing careful backup till the end of the song.

His fingers were turning numb. Time to end it anyway.

"Thanks, bossrider." He turned off the guitar and returned it to its rack. "Sorry about that last."

"It happens." Nestor seemed more forgiving now that Ubu had actually found a way back out of the disaster he'd almost created.

"Thanks again."

"It was fun." This from Sara. Ubu gave her a grin and stepped off the stage.

He returned the audolin to Sig by the autoloaders and then bounced down a connecting tube to *Runaway*'s dock. It was the middle of the second shift, almost time to power-up the ship and blow station.

Ubu bounced one level down a connecting tube to *Runaway*'s dock. He finished his beer and put the bulb in his pocket. As he keyed the lock on *Runaway*'s docking tube he wondered if Kit de Suarez was with Beautiful Maria. He'd been spending most days on board, then going home to sleep on the *Abrazo*, apparently because he didn't want any of his family to know he was seeing Maria. All of this, especially the fact Kit wasn't sleeping on the ship, was fine with Ubu.

Ubu ghosted through the tube, opened the inner lock door, and bounced forward as the lock door slid upward. He cried out in alarm, but too late. Hands seized a pair of his wrists. Ubu caught a glimpse of green uniforms, yellow belts and collar tabs. Terror dashed headlong through his nerves. Programmed metal-and-plastic serpents coiled around his wrists. Strong arms dragged him upright. Ubu stood stunned, all four hands shackled.

"Ubu Roy." The cop was middle-aged, mustached. His two assistants were younger and more muscular. The older cop handed Ubu a printout.

"You're under arrest. Larceny, bank fraud, data tampering. *Runaway* and its contents are seized by OttoBanque in lieu of payment for the tampered loan."

Ubu stared at him. "Where's my sister?"

"You'll see her in a little while. We picked her up this afternoon."

"I don't understand this." Insistently.

"Read the writ, bossrider." The cop was weary. He'd done this many times before. "I'm just a messenger boy, Ubu Roy," he said. "You want an explanation, find yourself an attorney. They're paid to understand this. I'm not."

Ubu let them drag him away. He thought about Mudville, life as a juvenile on Angelica.

He thought about his sister. The pain took his breath away.

CHAPTER
5

BEAUTIFUL MARIA STEPPED TO THE SHACKTUBE DOOR, PRESSED THE Open button. Bending low, she stepped inside.

Ubu was watching a holohype, his upper set of hands clasped behind his head. Space pirates, led by Phil Mendoza, were perpetrating rape and massacre in the air before his face. There were empty beer bottles in the trash. Carnitas lay uneaten in a cardboard container set on the floor by his rack.

"Be going for a walk," Maria said. "Wanna come?"

Ubu's attention drifted toward her. "Guess not," he said.

She crouched by his side. "You ought to get out of here."

Holographic gore exploded across the space between them. "I don't think so," he said. "No place to go, right?"

Maria looked at him. "It's your shoot."

"Don't remind me," he said. His attention returned to the hype.

Sadness poured through Maria's heart. Ubu had barely moved since his arrest, barely spoken. He didn't want to step out onto the rim, didn't want to see anyone.

Maria turned and left the tube. Kit de Suarez, fidgeting, waited on the catwalk. "He's not coming," she said, and closed the shacktube door.

Kit seemed relieved. "Too bad," he said. He put his arm around her.

"I want to help him," she said. "He thinks it's all his fault, and it isn't."

"He'll get over it." There was no conviction in Kit's voice.

Maria said nothing. She was thinking hard.

Being under arrest had proved surprisingly painless: after Maria and Ubu had given the station their finger and retinal prints, the procureur looked at their records, yawned, and concluded they were nonviolent. Rather than take up the resources of the tiny jail, the station put them up in a pair of shacktubes. Four times each day they were required to press their thumbprints to the scanners set in their comm units and prove they hadn't jumped station.

Runaway was sealed, its access codes altered. Its formal condemnation by the Admiralty Court was only a matter of time.

Maxim was the only member of the crew still on the run. The station cops had pursued the cat through the ship but failed to catch him. Maxim could live for another few months on the contents of the ship's automated food and water dispensers, but before then *Runaway* would almost certainly be broken up and its singularity drive sold. The cops were currently taking under advisement Maria's offer to fetch the cat herself. Apparently they needed to know if OttoBanque considered the cat part of *Runaway*'s assets.

From the Angelica news service, Maria had learned how they had been detected. The Monte Carlo had put their names on the station comp on a security alert, and when Ubu reapplied for the loan with OttoBanque, the bank's computers automatically referenced the security file, found Ubu's name, and alerted a human supervisor. The supervisor had taken a few days before bothering to look over the loan; then when he'd seen it, he'd first checked his core programming to see if it had been tampered with, then called the cops.

Maria had the impression the bank really wanted to know how it had been done. Until they either offered money or dropped the charges, however, OttoBanque could just go on wondering. Until then Maria was sticking to her story: if she got the loan extended, it had to be some kind of glitch in the program. She hadn't expected the application to be successful: she'd been surprised herself when it was.

Things were awaiting further definition.

"Hey. You Beautiful Maria, right? I'm Oswald."

"Go away."

"Hey. Just want to talk, shooter femme. Maybe I can help with your problem."

Oswald was tall and had a supple moned body. His voice was surprisingly soft and wonderfully plausible. Maybe he'd been a shooter once, gone bankrupt on the Edge, and found himself in a new line of work.

He wasn't particularly good at it, Maria reflected. Most of the other pimps had begun appearing within two hours of her arrest.

"Get away from me," Maria said. She moved closer to Kit, put her arm around him as they started walking down the street. The man followed them, his white manicured hands fluttering in emphasis to his words.

"Your problem's money, right? Gotta pay the lawyer, pay the bills. And this place is full of people with money. All you gotta do is find someone to perform the proper introductions."

Kit turned toward him. "Leave or die," he said.

Oswald looked skeptical. He shrugged, looked at Maria. "Talk to you another time," he said. His eyes flicked back to Kit. "*You* I'll see later, maybe."

"Anytime."

Maria and Kit continued their walk. "You didn't have to do that," Maria said. "He would have left."

"His threats don't impress me," Kit said. Belligerence crackled in his voice. "Compared to my family, the guy's gotta be an amateur. I'd have taken him apart."

Laughter bubbled to Maria's lips. "*Leave or die.* Jesus Rice. You sounded like some guy on a hype."

"Yeah. Guess I did." He joined in the laughter. "First time I've ever done that."

"Lucky it was somebody like Oswald."

Kit laughed again. "Yeah. Guess it was." He looked at her, the laughter fading from his face. "I'm worried about you," he said.

"I'll be okay."

"You may go to jail."

"Probably not, the lawyer says. They have no evidence against me. I'll probably just get deported down to the planet as an undesirable."

"That's bad enough."

"Ubu's the bossrider. It'll go harder with him."

"Water falls right out of the *air* down there."

She looked at him. "I'll watch out for the water, Kit," she said.

He shrugged, accepted the reproach. "I'm still worried, though. I wish you could come with us when we clear station tomorrow."

"I'm under arrest."

"We come back." Hopefully. "We stop in Angel every six months or so."

"Maybe I'll see you then." Maria tossed her head. "Let's get lunch."

"Right."

They had spiced lamb in garlic sauce, wrapped in chapatis. Under the table, Kit kicked off his sandals and ran his bare feet up Maria's legs. Maria grinned and wiped juice from her lips.

"How long before *Abrazo* leaves?"

"*San Pablo* shot in yesterday with our shipment. They're only three days out. We'll jump station as soon as we transfer cargo from the *Pablo*."

"What kind of shipment? You never said."

Kit hesitated, then offered an embarrassed grin. "Reflex," he said. "Marco's been drilling me all my life never to say anything about the business."

Maria shrugged. "I don't really care about the shipment, Kit. I was just making conversation."

"It's a new ore crusher." Stubbornly. "Made by Seven Systems for the Biagra-Exeter operation on a big asteroid they've shifted to Cold Harbor." Maria smiled at the defiance in Kit's words. Perhaps he'd never broken one of Marco's taboos so openly before.

"Thank you, Kit," Maria said. "I'll give you ten percent when I sell the information."

Kit looked startled, then grinned.

Maria raised her glass of lemonade to her lips. Sadness drifted through her as she thought about what she might have to do, how Kit might be used. She didn't want to hurt him.

But he was necessary.

"I'm worried about my cat." It was better, Maria thought, if the idea came from Kit. "But they've got a guard on the tube."

Angelica's rim, its brightness and noise, faded below them. They were in one of the station's smaller spokes now. Maria's voice echoed in the conveyor's confining metal tube. "I hope Maxim's okay. The cops couldn't catch him."

Painted numbers were flaking away on the interior of the tube. The metal gave a series of popping noises as it adjusted to heat stresses. Kit had his arms around her from behind, standing close on the small platform. "He'll be all right. He gets food and water."

"They're going to condemn the ship and tear it apart."

"All we have to do is find the right person to ask."

The hub's fifth level drifted past, then the fourth. *Runaway* was on the third level: they stepped out of the conveyor, drifted slowly to the metal deck, touched down. The sound of the docks, metal and horns and hammering, blossomed around them.

Maria looked for *Runaway*, saw the big matte-black station cargo doors crossed by yellow plastic ribbons—police seals—that looked as if they'd been taken by mistake from somebody's birthday party. There were more seals on the personnel lock, and before it a lanky uniformed woman who sat on a folding chair and turned the plastic facsimile pages of a magazine.

An unexpected sorrow pulsed through Maria's heart. *Runaway* waited behind those locks, the ship powered down now, controls dark, life-support silent, the centrifuge locked down. She had a vision of Maxim padding through the empty corridors, Pasco's sad ghost walking alongside. Nonsense, she thought, they'd probably shut the computer down with everything else. For some reason that thought increased her sadness. Tears stung her eyes.

Kit touched her arm. "You okay?"

Maria shook her head and fought off the sadness. She pointed at the guard. "Damn," she lied. "I've met that one. She wouldn't let me in yesterday."

"I'll ask her."

"No good." She frowned. "If I had access to a vac suit I'd be able to get in through an outside airlock."

"Haven't they changed the codes?"

"There are trapdoors in our system. I could beat any new codes easy."

"I see." Suddenly his tones changed. "Oh. It's Marco."

Maria turned and saw Marco and one of the younger de Suarezes leaving the Bahía, moving toward their conveyor. Marco's deep yellow eyes were already fixed on Maria and Kit. He bounced once, landed, came to a stop in front of Maria. The other de Suarez followed, flexing his shoulder muscles. Maria could sense the tension in Kit's body, the masklike quality of his expression.

"Bossrider," Beautiful Maria said. "Shooter."

"Bossrider," said Kit. "Elder Brother." He turned to Maria. "This is Ridge, my cousin."

"Nice," said Ridge, looking at her. This was not, Maria decided, short for "Nice to meet you."

"Heard of your trouble," Marco said, not bothering with formal politeness. "Too bad you got to pay for your pop's mistakes."

Maria fidgeted with the brace on her wrist as she looked down at the shorter man. "It's something everyone does," she said. Marco's eyes hardened.

"Some people overcome it. The rest just learn how to fail." Marco turned to Kit and pointed at him with the horned middle finger of his right hand. "See you at eighteen hundred."

"I didn't know I had duty," Kit said.

Marco scowled at him. "Do now. Beats hanging around with losers."

"Bossrider," Kit said.

Marco bounced toward the conveyor. Ridge looked at Maria again, then turned to Kit.

"Hope you're not paying much," he said. "Members of that family should be going cheap about now."

Kit looked at him. "I'm not paying anything at all," he said.

Ridge laughed and clapped him on the shoulder. Kit staggered. "Good boy," he said. "You'll have to tell me all about it." He turned to Maria, laughed again, and jumped high over Maria's head on his way to the conveyor.

Kit stood still, his jaw working. He turned to Maria. "Sorry," he said.

Maria took his arm. "Is he always like that?"

"Just about. Ever since he started taking the hormones." He frowned. "He's the bossrider's favorite. He's learned all Marco's lessons." He thought for a moment. "That was a lesson we just had, by the way. The proper way to deal with losers."

"I suppose I'll have to get used to it."

Kit took a long breath. Maria sensed resolution in him. "I'll help you," he said.

"Help me how?"

"Help you get aboard *Runaway*. I'll take you over tonight, if you like. Third shift."

Beautiful Maria leaned toward him and kissed his cheek. "Thank you," she said. She had forgotten that she'd been aiming him at this.

Maria was glad Kit wasn't just doing this for her any more, that his defiance now had a personal dimension. She didn't seem to be using him now, not as much as once it had.

A pair of soldiers were making love. Outside their window, an entire world was dying in bursts of red and yellow fire.

The hype possessed at least the possibility of being erotic, poetic. It was neither; it was both incompetent and numbing. Ubu didn't mind. He wanted to be numb.

He watched the hype for hours at a time. People were shot, stabbed, blasted out of airlocks. Hurried acts of sex appeared between ships being decompressed or exploded or riddled with shrapnel. An apocalypse occurred every fifteen minutes. Whole galaxies spiraled down in flames.

It all passed across Ubu's vision without making much of an impression. At least he didn't have to worry about Pasco showing up, not here on this holograph projector that was filled with nothing but pointless excursions into violence, motion, and rut.

For the first time in his life Ubu had nothing to do, nothing to learn, nothing to worry about. The future was in the hands of the procureur and the judge.

Bright blades flashed across a dark vacuum. In absolute silence a man died, his vac suit ruptured along with his abdomen. Air vented, turned to sugar-crystal. There were bright close-ups of intestines just in case anyone desired details. Ubu looked at the room's chronometer. It was almost time to press his thumb to the scanner again and let justice know it was being done.

His door hissed open. Maria came in, approached him.

Sadness chimed through him. He knew that soon they might be separated, that he'd never see her again, and that he should be spending time with her. But he couldn't face it, couldn't face the reminders of pain and sorrow, the reproaches that would remain unspoken but that he knew were deserved.

"Hi," Ubu said. "Thought you were with that de Suarez."

"Marco assigned him duty. Didn't want him hanging out with losers."

The swords were shining in the vacuum again. Clashing in immaculate silence. Ubu watched them. Maria watched him for a moment, then spoke.

"Ubu," she said. "I've got a plan."

CHAPTER
6

SILVER BLADES CLASHED IN SILENCE. SUITED FIGURES CONTINUED to spin and tumble in the weightless night. Beautiful Maria reached out to take Ubu's hand. "I have a plan," she repeated.

Pain eddied in Ubu's chest. Mere inches away, holographic faces screamed in noiseless agony. "I don't want to hear this," he said.

"You just plan on lying here. Letting the proc and the judge do what they want."

"They have my best interests at heart. That's what they tell me."

"Listen to me, Ubu." She snapped off the holo unit. Her hand took his chin, turned his head to force him to look at her. Ubu wanted to shrink from the determination he saw in her face.

"We steal *Runaway*," Maria said. "We run off past the Edge and find ourselves a black hole. We capture it and we come back. Then we pay our fines and penalties and go on doing what we have to do." She shrugged. "It's all your plan, basically. Except the first part."

Ubu could feel her warm breath on his face. He closed his eyes. "We'd get caught. We always get caught."

"Even if we are caught, how worse off could it be?"

"I don't want to find out."

She drew back, tilted her head, and looked at him meditatively. "I could do it myself."

Ubu's reply was sharp. "How?"

"Kit de Suarez said he would let us—let me—use one of *Abrazo*'s vac suits to get around the guard on station and enter through one of *Runaway*'s exterior hatches. He thinks we want to take off Maxim, some data and personal belongings. I can glitch one of the outside locks—that'll be easy—and once I get aboard, I power-up the ship and blow station."

A trembling bubble of sadness rose in Ubu's mind. The whole plan seemed a path already too well trodden, laden with familiar hope and despair. "Oh, Maria," he said.

Her eyes challenged him. "Why won't it work?"

Heat flared in Ubu. "The other de Suarezes will find out. Your glitch will be detected. You won't be able to power-up without someone noticing." He waved his upper set of arms as his voice became a shout. "That Navy cruiser will blow *Runaway* apart. You won't find a black hole for years. You'll have an accident or get sick and you'll die alone. All sorts of things can happen."

"I'm going to go through with it," said Beautiful Maria. "I'm going to take the ship and blow station. If you want to stop me, you know how to contact the proc's office."

"I don't—"

Maria's words were bitter. "Prove Marco right if you want. Give yourself a loser certificate."

Rage roared through Ubu like a nova flame. He bit it off. "I said I wouldn't make you use your talent again," he said.

"You're not *making* me do anything. Are you?"

"You'll get hurt." The words poured from him without thought. "You'll get hurt, Maria. I don't want to see that again."

For the first time she looked away. Her voice was small. "It won't be your fault. It never has been. Okay?"

Ubu said nothing. His anger had faded; there was a bitter pain in his throat. "I don't want to lose you," he said.

"Then come with." She turned away, leaving him to his decision. Terror eddied through him. Another loss, he thought, another defeat.

"Yes," he said, hopeless. "Yes."

Two hundred hours. The second-level docking bay was silent, echoing distantly to the hum of autoloaders moving on the loading dock below. Kit, alone in the broad brightly lit space, shivered. By family standards at least, he was about to commit an act of treason.

There was a modulation in the light from the direction of the belt conveyor: someone stepping off. Kit cast an anxious glance and saw it was Ubu. He relaxed only slightly.

Beautiful Maria stepped off the conveyor just after her brother. Both wore shorts and t-shirts, their feet bare, small cases in their hands. The two approached.

"Bossrider," he said. "Shooter."

"Shooter."

"Kit." Maria had braided her hair into a single long braid that dropped down her back. Kit admired the revealed curve of her bare neck, her graceful ears. Dumb longing wrung his heart. He'd never seen anything so lovely.

"We'll have to be quiet. The whole crew's on board."

Ubu's look was sharp. "Anyone standing watch?"

"Not third shift. Not unless we're loading. But just be quiet. Don't want to wake anyone."

Maria stepped close, squeezed his hand, kissed his cheek. Her lips were cool. "Thanks, Kit."

Kit shrugged. "It's okay."

He turned and hopped to the personnel airlock. The others drifted floorward behind him as he tapped code. The lock opened with a slight hiss, as if it didn't approve of what they were about to do.

Kit led Ubu and Maria through the accordion-walled docking tube and into the trunk airlock. From there it was a short skip past the steel-walled software locker, past storerooms, then into one of the cargo bays. The big room smelled of lubricant. Metal cargo containers, their enamel chipped, lay snugged down on alloy pallets, held by silver alloy straps and cushioned by plastic mats. An intermittently functioning red hologram fizzled in a corner, marking the crew lock. Kit headed for it.

The flickering red light seemed to spatter Ubu and Maria with blood. Kit punched the polished steel panel that opened the lock hatch. The hologram turned green as the hatch swung open, and Ubu and Maria moved like pale ghosts into the lock.

"Here are some vac suits I stashed," Kit said. He looked at Ubu. "You'll have to fold your lower arms on your chest; we don't have any suits configured for you."

Ubu nodded. "I'm used to it."

Kit went to one of the suits and handed it to Ubu. "I let the chest out as far as I could."

Ubu smiled. "Thanks, Kit. You did good." Kit felt his anxiety diminish slightly. For some reason, even though he didn't like Ubu, the boy's approval somehow mattered.

"I figure we should keep radio silence out there," Ubu said. "Someone might hear us. It's a small chance, but they might."

The suits were lightweight and went on easily. Peroxide hissed through nozzles as attitudinal jets were tested. Kit pressed the button to cycle the airlock. Air pumps began to throb. Kit bit his lip: would the sound of the cycling lock carry through the ship to where his people were sleeping? Marco was a notoriously light sleeper. If he recognized the sound he'd wonder at the noise being made at this hour.

The light over the outside hatch turned green. Kit rolled it open, then drifted through it. Sunlight stabbed at his eyes like thrusting daggers. He dialed up the polarity of his visor and the sun dimmed.

Kit's pulse beat a fast pattern over the gentle hiss of the air supply. He gulped, tried to calm his nerves. *Runaway* was on the hub level above him. He spun in place, trying to recognize it through the helmet's tunnel vision. *Runaway* rolled into sight, a shining, irregular assemblage of bright pitted metal. Kit headed for it, peroxide jets tugging gently at his suited form. Sweat trickled into his eyes.

One of the rotating station's spokes eclipsed the sun, then the stabbing brightness returned.

Runaway grew larger. Yellow police seals had been placed on all the locks.

Maria flew past him to an airlock, braked, drifted against the skin of the ship. She peeled the police seal away from the lock mechanism and contemptuously flung it into space. Kit felt his heart lurch as the wadded plastic tumbled brightly away. It hadn't really occurred to him that, besides going against Marco, he was about to break the law. He could actually get into trouble for this.

Too late, he decided, to worry about it now.

Ubu, one hand clasped around a castoff bar by the lock, watched as Maria floated over the lock mechanism. Cool suspense hummed in his nerves. He did not quite dare to hope this would work.

Maria placed her gloved hand over the lock, closed her eyes in concentration. Kit craned his neck inside his helmet but saw nothing: the glitch was invisible and fired in a fragment of a second. Maria drifted back from the lock, a distant smile on her face. Through his hand and the bar, Ubu could hear the throb of air pumps. He gave a startled laugh. They were in.

The lock hatch began rolling open. There was surprise on Kit's face: he didn't know how easily Maria could crash the lock. Ubu held his breath as he swung himself off the castoff bar into the airlock.

The airlock cycled; the inner hatch opened. Ubu cracked the seal on his helmet. Maria brushed past him and pushed open the inner hatch.

The air in *Runaway* was hot and close: the coolers and circulators had been shut down and Angelica's sun had played on the ship for days. But still the scents and sights and textures were those of home, striking Ubu's senses like a blow. It was *real:* they were past the guards and wards, back where they belonged. Ubu laughed again and shook out his long hair, then stripped off the vac suit and freed his lower arms. Stretching his cramped shoulder muscles, he stepped into the ship. Hope bubbled in him, a low boil. He didn't dare believe in it.

They were aft of the fuge, in the thick trunk housing used for storage of food supplies, medical equipment, and personal inventory. Ubu turned to Maria.

"Why don't you and Kit run off and have some fun?" he said. "We need to power-up some fuel cells to get our computer up and unload some data, but I can handle that by myself." He gave a grin. "I'd sort of like to be by myself for a while anyway."

Maria looked at Kit, held out a hand. "Sure," she said. "Thanks."

Kit seemed surprised. "Thanks, bossrider," he said. He took Maria's hand and the two of them moved aft.

"As long as we're here," Maria said, "let's find some of my favorite hormones." She led him into the medical bay.

Ubu turned and launched himself into the corridor leading to the centrifuge hub. Warm air brushed his skin, his hair. He was home and in motion.

He dropped from the hub to the bottom floor of the centrifuge, stepped into the command cage, sat down in the padded couch.

The ship systems board sat beneath a light scatter of grit, flaking paint fallen from the decaying polymerized inner walls of the fuge. Rows of red lights stared at him vacantly. Ubu reached forward with all four hands, touched controls, began fuel-cell initialization.

The trick was to power-up the ship without draining so much from the station power coupling that the heavy usage might call someone's attention to the ship: that meant a slow and deliberate self-contained power-up, from the fuel cells to the maneuvering system pressurization, the singularity drive, and ultimately the reaction drive, reawakening necessary shipboard systems on the way, chiefly the computer and life-support.

Fuel cells came online. Ubu powered-up the inertial measurement and navigation unit and the Torvald main computer, then loaded primary maneuvering software. He enabled the radio and station communication coupling and listened for a long moment. He heard no alarms. He sat back and waited in the growing silence.

There was a yowl of complaint from the hub, and he looked up to see Maxim launch himself from the hub ladder, forepaws aimed directly at Ubu's chest. Ubu grinned, his heart lightening, and braced himself for impact.

His reflex was based on living for too many days in one gravity: Maxim's paws struck with the unexpected lightness of a feather. A pale cloud of stray hair rose from the collision like debris scattered by an explosion, and the cat rebounded. Clumsily, laughing, Ubu retrieved him. Maxim stood on his chest and leaned forward, eyes shut, and butted Ubu's forehead, his purr thundering. The cat settled on Ubu's chest while Ubu used his lower arms to stroke along the cat's length. Ubu moved his seat forward on its tracks, his upper arms moving over the ship systems board, continuing his power-up.

It seemed possible, at last, to hope. He wanted to shout his pleasure aloud. His crew was together, his power-up was going unnoticed, and soon, within hours, he was going to have his ship back. The ship was coming alive, and he was coming alive along with it.

Maria bounded upward in the light gravity and drew on her shorts. Kit, swaying in her rack, reached toward one of the blower nozzles and directed a stream of cool air onto his humid skin.

"Ubu's got life-support up," he said. "He's gotta have a lot of power systems online."

"Holding at ten minutes."

Ubu's voice came smoothly from the speakers. Maria tossed her braid back, looked at Kit. Regret eased slowly into her heart. The time had come.

She drifted to the rack, sat, kissed him. The bed swung gently on its gimbals.

"Time to go," she said.

He propped himself up on one elbow. "Don't you need to pick up some of your stuff?"

She brushed his face with her fingers. Sorrow touched her throat, almost froze her voice. "Ubu and I aren't leaving," she said.

Kit's eyes widened. Slowly he sat upright. "You're—" he said haltingly.

"We're taking *Runaway* out. To another Now."

She tried to keep her voice calm, matter-of-fact. Kit stared at her for a long moment, his skin flushing. When he spoke his voice was thick. "You didn't tell me."

It was getting hard to watch him. "I'm sorry."

"You . . . lied." The word was reluctant.

Maria turned away, looked at her hand. "Yes. We didn't want anyone to know."

His body stiffened as another realization struck him. "I could go to jail for this!"

"We'd tell them you didn't know." She paused, looked at him. Kit swung his legs out of the rack, reached for his clothes, moving fast. One leg into his shorts, he straightened as if he'd remembered something. "What about Marco?" he demanded. He wasn't looking at her. "Jesus Rice. If he found out about this, he might leave me in fucking Angelica Station forever."

Maria reached up, touched his arm. "I don't want to hurt you, Kit."

He drew away from her. "I'm not gonna have anything to do with this. You and your damned brother are going to prison."

Kit finished dressing, slid open the partition, and stepped into the second level of the fuge. The floor curved downward from him. He dropped to the nearest ladder, then began the climb to the hub. Beautiful Maria followed.

"You're not going to tell anyone, are you?"

Kit spoke through clenched teeth as he maneuvered to the airlock. "I'm not going to send *myself* to jail."

Regret cut her like a broken, whipping cable. This wasn't the ending she'd anticipated. "Kit," she said. He ignored her, shot down the length of the hub, through the trunk corridor at the far end. He opened the inner lock door and stepped inside. The three vac suits lay empty around his feet.

Maria paused outside the lock door. Kit, breathing hard, was drawing on his suit. Pain beat in her throat.

"Kit," she said. "You could come with us."

His movements slowed. For a moment Maria felt a flicker of hope.

He turned away. He could barely speak. Maybe he was crying. "Come with you to *prison!*" His voice turned to a shout. "You *used* me!"

"I care for you. I didn't want to hurt you." Sorrow stung her eyes.

"All you care about," Kit took a deep breath, "is your family and your ship."

"Not true."

He turned to her. His face was blotchy and his voice was ragged. "You're the same as Marco," he said. "The only difference is that he's honest about what he wants." He pressed the CLOSE HATCH plate.

Beautiful Maria watched the hatch roll shut, helpless to appease his anger.

"I'm sorry, Kit," she said. For some reason she thought of the black woman in the casino, Colette, walking with broken tread away from the rouge-et-noir table.

The hatch sealed, shutting her off from humanity.

Kit finished drawing on his vac suit, his fingers fumbling with the straps. In his frustration he kicked one of the spare helmets across the lock. It struck the padded outer hatch, rebounded, and went right for his face. Kit warded it off with an arm and kicked the other helmet.

After the suit was closed it seemed to take forever to cycle the lock. Kit bundled the two empty vac suits awkwardly in his arms. When the hatch finally opened he hurled himself through it. He didn't bother closing the hatch behind him, just located *Abrazo* on the great wheel of the station's hub and then jetted toward it.

Anger rushed aimlessly over his body, prickling the hair on his skin. His arms trembled as he stripped off the vac suit in *Abrazo's* lock. At least, he thought, when *Runaway* bolted the station, no one would connect him with it.

The lights went green. He pressed the plate to open the inner hatch.

His blood went cold.

Marco waited quietly just inside the hatch, eyes glowing softly in their deep sockets.

CHAPTER
7

"RECOMMENCE COUNTDOWN." MARIA'S VOICE CAME SOBERLY FROM the intercom. Ubu frowned at a red light—the trunk airlock outer hatch was still open—but started the countdown anyway. The lock could be closed later from the systems board.

A few minutes later Beautiful Maria drifted down the ladder, then came into the cage and strapped herself into the shooter's seat. Ubu glanced at her. Her face was colorless.

"You okay?"

"Had a fight with Kit."

"Sorry." Ubu restrained a grin.

"I wish I hadn't lied to him."

Ubu shrugged. "It was necessary." He frowned at her. "You rather I boss the shoot?"

Maria shook her head. "I'll be all right."

"Okay." Ubu turned back to his panel. His initial course was plotted and loaded in the computer; the hydraulic pumps were up and online; he gimballed the main engine and smiled as more green lights blinked on.

Maria was silent. Ubu looked at her. "You sure it's okay?"

"I really like him."

Ubu reluctantly thought about this for a moment. "He's all right," he said.

"I wish things were different."

There was nothing to say to that. Ubu turned back to his board. "Three minutes," he said.

Kit stared for a long, appalling moment into Marco's deep eyes. Marco was wearing only a g-string. Skin draped his ancient bones in grey folds. He said nothing.

"I was outside," Kit said.

Marco waited a moment before speaking. "I can see that. I heard the lock cycle and wondered."

"I just went out for a while."

There was another silence. Kit wondered whether or not to leave the lock. Marco dropped his eyes to the floor of the lock. "You went out," he said. "With three vac suits."

Kit took a breath. Panic throbbed in his chest. "The other two were here before," Kit said. "I mean, I left them here. When I was here before."

Marco looked at him steadily. Kit's words trailed away. Kit bent to gather up the vac suits.

"Come here, boy. Leave the suits." Marco's voice was soft. Kit let the suits fall to the floor and stepped out of the airlock.

Marco stepped close to Kit, put a hand on Kit's shoulder. Kit tried not to flinch from the contact. There was a cold smile on Marco's unshaven face.

"I shouldn't have to tell you that I don't believe you. You know that." Marco leaned closer. His breath touched Kit's cheek. His words were calm, measured. "I have limited energy, boy. I don't want to waste any of it turning your life into shit, though I will if I have to. All I want to know is where you've been, and who was with you. Understand?"

Fear fluttered in Kit's limbs. He licked his lips. "I was out with some girls," he said.

"What are their names? Where are they from?"

"Tourists. They wanted to go out in the vacuum. One of them

sort of panicked when she got into freefall and I had to take her into one of the station airlocks. I was just taking the suits back."

"Fine." Kit's heart beat time to another long moment of silence. "That doesn't answer my question. What are their names? And if I wanted to talk to them, where would I look?"

"I don't know where they're staying. Some hotel, I guess."

"I don't believe you." Marco stepped forward, his face within inches of Kit's. His eyes were rimmed in red. "You were with Pasco's Maria and her brother, weren't you?" Spittle touched Kit's upper lip.

Even though they stood in light gravity, Marco's arm on Kit's shoulder seemed to weigh tons. There was a bright pain behind Kit's eyes. At least, he thought, Marco never lied to me. Never told me he was something he wasn't.

Stumbling over his words, Kit told the man what he wanted to know.

"Hatch sealed. Pressurization test complete." Flame drew burning paths along Ubu's nerves. He recited the checklist purely as a way of keeping himself calm. "Personnel tube withdrawn. Pressurization test complete." He reached to the one red light remaining on the board and closed the outer lock hatch that Kit had left open. "Trunk lock closed. Pressurization test complete."

His bare feet kicked out at the floor, moved his tracked couch to the pilot's station. Ubu could feel sweat trickling slowly down his nape. Now was the moment. He held the countdown at minus ten seconds, toggled the comm unit, and aimed an antenna at the Angelica's control station.

"Angelica Control, this is Biagra Salvage personnel aboard singularity ship *Runaway*, cargo bay C-15. Request permission to undock from the hub for the purpose of testing ship maneuvering systems. Over."

There was a moment's pause. Angelica's voice, when it came, was young, hesitant, and female.

"Angel Control to *Runaway*. Identify self again, please."

Ubu took a deep breath. "Jock's Castro of Biagra Salvage. We are evaluating ship systems at the request of shipowners Otto-Banque."

Jock's Castro was a real person, Biagra Salvage a small division of Biagra-Exeter. A small amount of research in the Angelica directory had provided the necessary information.

There was another pause. Ubu blinked sweat from his eyes.

"Angel to *Runaway*. Is your flight plan on file?"

Ubu only realized he'd been holding his breath when he let it out and discovered that taking another breath felt wonderful. He grinned. Angelica Control had apparently concluded that she was in fact talking to Jock's Castro.

"Filing plan now, Angel Control." He touched a control that transmitted his phony plan. "The plan's filed, Angel Control."

"Angel to *Runaway*. Do you need shifting to Station COM?" The Center of Mass was where *Runaway* could be launched without the added complication of compensating for the station's rotation.

"Negative, Angel Control. We can launch from Station C-15."

There was another pause. "Plan evaluation positive, *Runaway*. Permission granted for station departure and independent scheduled maneuvers."

Ubu restrained an urge to laugh. "Thank you, Angel Control. Departure in ten seconds."

He touched the countdown toggle. In the corner of one eye, a holographic -*10* became a holographic -*9*, then a holographic -*8*.

Station power coupling disengaged.

-*7*. -*6*.

Electromagnets released Angel's ferrous docking strips.

-*5*. -*4*.

Bolts shot back from *Runaway*'s docking module. *Runaway* floated free in the docking bay.

-*3*. -*2*.

Ubu pictured the guard sitting in front of the armored station doors, reading her magazine, unaware that the ship just behind the doors was leaving without her.

-*1*. *0*.

Maneuvering jets hissed gently. Ubu felt a gentle tug on his harness straps as the station's rotation threw the ship on a looping path into space. The command cage swung lightly on its gimbals. *Runaway* was free.

* * *

"No percentage in it. OttoBanque's gratitude is limited. AIs aren't programmed to say thanks."

Kit watched as Marco put the neurojuice inhaler to each nostril and pressed the trigger. Marco sniffed and swiped at his nose with the back of a knotty forefinger. He took a bulb of grapefruit juice from the folding galley table and sipped at it.

"They might offer a reward after the ship's stolen. You don't know where Pasco's Ubu is going, do you?"

Kit shook his head. Marco hadn't even bothered to look at him when he asked his question. Kit felt empty, drained of weight and substance, and numbly wondered why he wasn't floating randomly across *Abrazo*'s galley like a Brownian particle.

Marco toyed with his inhaler, thinking hard. "No glory, no money. Shit. *I* don't give a damn if Ubu wants to go over the Edge. He won't survive, but it's none of *my* fucking business." His eyes turned to Kit, and Kit's nerves turned cold.

"You got off cheap, boy," Marco said. "You learned something, and it didn't cost the family a thing."

"Yes, bossrider."

"People are going to want to use you, Kit." Patiently. "They're going to take a profit percentage from every weakness you've got. Got that?"

"Yes, bossrider."

"You know how you got used?"

"Yes, bossrider."

Marco gave Kit a slow smile. "Tell me."

Kit felt very alone standing on the cool tile of the galley floor. "I—" he started, then faded. Marco's smile turned to stone.

"Pasco's Maria got you to break the law for her. You put yourself in danger without even thinking about it, and that's because you thought that she gave a damn about you just because she let you fuck yourself blind. Have I got that right?"

Kit closed his eyes. Warm fires burned brightly behind his lids. "Yes, bossrider." It might well be true. He thought there might be more to it, but he really couldn't tell any more and Marco's version of events might be correct as far as things went. He just wanted the night to end.

"I've already given you all the shit jobs on the ship," Marco said. His tone was conversational. "So there's not much more I can inflict on you to show you how you shouldn't make these kinds of mistakes. So we'll just have you do the shit jobs for a longer period of time, right?"

Kit opened his eyes. He realized he was swaying back and forth as he stood. "Fine, bossrider," he said. "Whatever you say."

"Go to sleep."

"Yes, bossrider."

Kit moved numbly to his rack, fell slowly toward it, touched once, bounced, settled again. He thought about Maria and wondered if she and Ubu were making their escape. All his anger was gone, burned away by Marco's venom. The yearning and the sense of his own incompleteness remained.

He wished he was on the *Runaway*. Leaving everything behind, looking for something new.

Ubu looked at the radar and transponder displays. No ships nearby, no one within range to be cooked by the particle torch.

"Ten seconds to torch ignition. Mark."

Ubu triggered the countdown. Another set of holographic numbers began flashing. Nozzles gimballed to a new attitude. Matter poured into the singularity, creating huge energies confined only by the magnetic fields.

The fields transformed, allowing plasma to pour through the engine nozzles. A deep hum moved through the frame of the ship. Ubu felt it in his bones. Acceleration built gently, the ship's enormous mass moving not to a sudden kick but to a slowly building impetus. The control cage swung on its gimbals, reorienting to the direction of thrust.

The flight plan he'd filed with Angelica Control featured this burn, a turn around Angelica's largest moon followed by a deceleration and a return to Angel Station. Ubu planned instead to use the moon to slingshot him toward deep space, then make the first shoot as soon as he was a safe distance away from Angelica's mass. If he kept the moon between himself and Angelica, Control might not even notice the deviation from the flight plan until its remote sensors on the far side of the moon picked up the burst of radiation from the singularity shot.

Acceleration built, climbing past one gee. Maxim growled deep in his throat and crouched uneasily on Ubu's stomach, his ears flattening. Ubu looked at Beautiful Maria. She lay on the shooter's couch with her eyes closed, the stimulus antennae forming a delicate lattice about her head. He could see her eyes moving under the lids: she was monitoring the ship's progress through the stim antennae.

"You okay?" he said.

"Just resting."

"Got your shoot planned?"

The corners of her mouth turned up in a strained smile. "Easiest I've ever conned. We're not going anywhere in particular, right?"

Ubu grinned. "I guess not."

"We're just going Out. I'll shoot us as far as I can, then we can figure out where we are once we get there."

"Right."

Ubu turned back to his board. Two gravities sat on his chest. *Runaway* was still accelerating. He almost missed Maria's words.

"I wish we hadn't lied to him."

Ubu frowned at his control board. "We did what we had to do."

Her voice was weary. "That's all Marco's ever done. *What he had to do*. How does that make us any better?"

Anger twisted in Ubu. "We're not Marco, Maria."

"I don't know."

"We're not." Insistently.

"What about Colette?"

He had no answer to that.

Two and a half gees. Maxim's weight bored into Ubu's stomach. The cat was ship-bred and knew better than to try to move now.

"Don't talk about it, then," said Ubu.

Sadness pooled in Maria's heart. Spacetime analogs moved slowly in her head. Projected onto her optical centers was the Angelica System as an electron might perceive it, a pattern of cold gravity sinks locked in their courses, bright magnetic streams, thermal configurations moving and flaring on Angelica itself. The vision, anticipating the Now, failed to divert her.

She had used Kit, taken advantage of his trust and friendship, and hadn't even realized she was doing it. It had all seemed so natural.

The moon swung past, a cold well in spacetime speckled with low-intensity radio emissions from mining sites. Maria floated free in her harness as the torch cut out for a few seconds while the nozzles realigned; her heart beat madly and she took a few fast, unburdened breaths. Then she was pushed back into her couch again as the control cage swung and the ship began to accelerate on its new course, keeping the moon between itself and Angelica Station. *Runaway* was riding on the lip of the moon's gravity well.

Matter poured into the ship's singularity. Radiant brightness flared on the edge of its terrible gravity, its tides constrained by magnetic fields. The ship was poised a hair's breadth from annihilation. Shooters learned early to take full advantage of the breadth of that hair.

Beautiful Maria thought about Kit. Gravity sat on her chest like sorrow.

"Maria. A problem."

She opened her eyes, turned them toward Ubu. The control station superimposed itself on her view of the electron world.

"Angel Control has figured out something's wrong. I'm getting queries."

"You didn't come around the moon as scheduled."

"The controller must have been suspicious. Why's she even paying attention to us?"

"Tell her you'll respond in a minute. You've got attitude control problems. You're trying to overcome them with a forced acceleration."

"Right. Good idea. Tell me how soon you can shoot."

Maria returned her attention to the stim analog. Massive bodies too close to a shoot complicated the equations and made the result problematical; there was also the problem of the burst of radiation that accompanied a shoot, and which could burn anyone too close to *Runaway*'s exit from the real.

"No," Ubu was saying, "I do not wish to declare an emergency. We'll be back to you, Angel Control."

Approaches to the shoot spun out in Maria's mind. The mining sites on the moon were only lightly shielded against radiation and there were even more lightly armored spacecraft hopping around. Patterns and trajectories blazed across the display, the minimum safety distance displayed as an ever-moving green globe centered on *Runaway*.

"At this acceleration we've got four minutes to shoot," Maria said. With a push of her mind she began the countdown.

"Jesus Rice. I don't believe this. She's ordering us to shut down the torch and stand by for the Navy cutter."

"We'll be in another Now before the Navy even gets their captain out of bed."

Ubu's annoyance was unalloyed. "What if they shoot a missile at us? They'll make us *pay* for it."

Maria laughed. "We're gonna be able to *buy* Angel Station when we get back, right? That's the plan, right?"

"Why don't they leave us alone?"

"Strap in and give me the shoot."

Maria opened her eyes just in time to see Ubu turn off the radio with a stab from one finger. "There," he said. "Shut the femme licebag up."

"Stop being so agitated. We've got away with it, okay?"

"Yeah." Grudgingly. "Okay." He touched another control. "The command's yours."

Another level of awareness flooded Beautiful Maria's perceptions. She felt the power of the torch, the matter seared by its near-escape from the black hole at *Runaway*'s heart.

The singularity burned in Maria's thoughts, its dark weight poised in magnetic harness. Ever-changing calculations sped through the jump computer at speeds too rapid for Maria to comprehend. Displays flickered, making minor changes in course and trajectory. Maria couldn't affect things at this level: her business would begin after the countdown ended.

Runaway crossed the safety line: no one nearby was going to get fried during the shoot. Seconds were left in the countdown.

The torch died. Maria drifted free in her harness. Warning lights were blinking; a soft tone poured from speakers.

The countdown ended. The powerful magnetic fields that confined the singularity opened a small but carefully calculated pathway.

Within the merest fragment of a second, the black hole that lived at the heart of the ship devoured *Runaway* and all in her.

Maria was in the Now.

The ship itself had vanished from her vision. She accelerated down the center of a crying radiant tunnel, poured down tightly confined magnetic fields onto the surface of a lightless sun. Above her, the universe spun past in accelerating brightness, its white light become shattering rainbows. The keen of dying matter sounded in her ears.

The Now was actually advanced in time, a jump up the *T* axis. The shoot computer was composed of row upon row of macroatoms, each transferring data faster than light, each a step ahead in time. Maria was experiencing *Runaway*'s dive into the singularity before it actually happened, while there was still time to alter the pattern.

Falling into the star, the ship was—would be—accelerated to relativistic speeds: the insignificant fraction of a picosecond in which the magnetic bonds of *Runaway*'s singularity were loosed and the ship devoured was experienced by Maria as the better part of an hour.

It was an hour in which she was very busy. On this microlevel of existence, the constitution of the singularity was not uniform—flares burst forth from the singularity's null heart, scattering radiation, only to be swallowed by gravity and buffered by magnetic walls. Tidal eddies created wide variation in gravitation and velocity. All of this was reflected in wild uncertainty in the outcome of the shoot: ships could end a shot hundreds of thousands of miles—light-years even—from the plotted destination.

The taste of the Now on her tongue, Maria rode the ship into the eye of the gravitational storm, fought to overcome the random elements introduced into the shoot by the star's variation. It was like riding the pinball in a game of blackhole, with the payoff expressed in distance crossed rather than cash won. *Runaway* lurched, staggering in a confused cross-chop of gravity waves, and Maria altered the configuration of the magnetic bottle by a push of her mind, compensating for the star's variation.

Now . . .

She sensed a change ahead, a fluctuation in the singularity's mass: she cut a slightly wider orbit, accelerating, and when the fluctuation came it served only to draw *Runaway* back onto its optimal course. Navigation aids burned their configurations into her senses. A flare patterned her belly with radiation, was compensated for by an alteration in the magnetic bottle. Her awareness skimmed closer to the singularity. Her fingers were outstretched to touch stinging bands of radiation. Magnetic storms howled in her throat. Relativistic effects increased.

Now . . .

Electron awareness poured into her body. She was dealing with events on the quantum level now, and her talents leaped into play, glitches pouring from her without conscious volition—she inhibited the probability of a flare warping the magnetic bottle, let it burst out behind so that its force would increase *Runaway*'s acceleration. No other shooter in existence could do this: no one else operated at this level. Her navigational aids lagged behind reality, unable to comprehend events on this scale; she worked from instinct alone, distorting gravity waves, dampening mutability, fighting tooth and claw against the furious, unforgiving mathematics of the singularity . . . animal noises grated from her throat as she ripped at the fabric of quantum existence, fought to the last moment in order to keep from being overwhelmed by sensation, by gravity.

The battle was lost before she began it. When gravity finally overcame her, when the singularity finally swallowed her awareness in its coils, she gave a cry of defiance before throwing wide her arms and embracing the annihilation of her senses, her being . . .

Whitehole.

The universe leaped intact into Maria's mind. Expanding from the singularity, a radio cry burned outward toward dull stars that sat in their distant wells.

Runaway had leaped from the Angelica System and was drifting in deep space, light-years from any pursuit.

CHAPTER
8

"JESUS RICE." UBU'S VOICE CAME DIMLY TO MARIA'S AWARENESS. "Longest shoot we've ever made."

The stim antennae withdrew and the electron world faded from Maria's mind. Still she felt an urgency, gravity's claws rising to embrace her. She opened her eyes. The control room came into bright, focused existence. Sharp-edged, hyper-real.

"Damage control reports no damage, no leakage, no shifting of cargo. Maneuvering systems operational and on standby. Positioning software running—be getting us an exact fix on where we are."

Maria moved experimentally in her webbing. Pain loaded her joints. Sweat trickled down her face, slicked her body.

"Centrifuge engaged. Building to one gee."

Gravity and motion tugged at her belly, her ear. The fuge gave a long shudder, a moan. That bearing wearing away. Maria released her harness and sat up. The movement bounced her a few inches from her couch; increasing gravity drew her back. She brushed sweat-dampened hair from her face and looked at Ubu.

Her brother was sitting up, Maxim on his lap. He looked unbelievably fresh, alert. His four arms hovered over the control panel, waiting for something that needed doing. He glanced at her.

"That looked like a tough one. You okay?"

"Yeah." She pulled her t-shirt over her head and used it to wipe sweat from her face. Her joints protested the return of gravity. The fuge groaned again.

"Gotta hit the rack," she said. She smiled weakly. "Be tired."

Ubu was still looking at her. "You want a massage or something? You were fighting that shot with every muscle in your body."

Maria swung her legs off the couch. "Sleep's all I want." The surging gravity almost brought her to her knees.

Ubu was off his couch and steadying her in an instant. Maxim, sleepy-eyed and stretching, complained at his abrupt removal from Ubu's lap. Ubu's arms around her, Maria staggered to her quarters. She dropped her shirt to the deck and fell into the rack. She looked up at her brother.

"Thank you."

He took her hand, gave her a look meant to be encouraging. "We did it," he said.

"Yeah. We did it."

"Thank you. For everything."

She gave him a weary smile. "That's okay."

He looked at her for a long moment. "I never thought you'd get hurt."

"I—" She shook her head. "I know that."

He shrugged. There was longing in his look, longing and a lasting, accepted sadness. "I'm glad you're with me," he said.

"Yeah. I'm glad, too." He squeezed her hand, then stepped back to the cabin door. He touched the light control and slid the screen shut.

Maria could see the electron world, faint and in motion, a silent presence in the darkness.

Gravity dragged her into sleep.

Maria woke hearing the soft sounds of the ship: the crackle of joints, whisper of the vents, the soft hum and occasional moan of the centrifuge. The electron world had faded beyond her awareness. She showered and dressed and stepped out of the cabin.

The command center was empty. She glanced at the boards and saw that the positioning software had got a fix on their location, recording a jump of ten point seven light-years. Ubu, she saw, had loaded the navigation software and been working on their next shoot. He had picked a target star another thirty light-years distant, called Montoya 81. Long-distance scans had shown that the star possessed planets. It was sufficiently distant from the frontiers of human space that automated singularity seekers wouldn't yet have been sent to it.

Runaway hummed around her. Ten point seven light-years, she thought. Suddenly the air seemed cold. She shivered.

She found Ubu asleep in his rack, lying on his back with his upper arms pillowing his head, the others thrown wide. *All you care about*, Kit had accused, *is your family and your ship*, as he looked at her with Colette's stricken eyes.

Well, she thought. Family's all I have now.

Ubu started, his arms jerking, and then he looked at her wildly. "Anything wrong?" he said.

"Nothing. Just wanted to see where you were." Silly, she thought. Where would he go?

His posture relaxed. "Just a nap."

She drifted closer to him. "Sorry I woke you."

"That's okay. Time to wake up anyway." He looked at her again, and concern entered his eyes. "Are you all right?"

"Yeah. Just a little lonely."

She sat on the edge of his rack. He put one of his lower arms around her. "I'm scared, too," he said.

She smiled. "I guess we didn't have time to be scared before."

"I guess not."

Maria stretched out beside him, pillowed her cheek on his muscled shoulder. Ubu kissed her and put his arms around her. She couldn't think of any reason to stop him.

Ubu was what she had left.

Beautiful Maria slept, her white body asprawl under a dark blanket of hair. Ubu kissed her pale cheek and slid out of the rack. He stepped to the galley and charged a bulb with beer. Maxim appeared, stretched, brushed Ubu's legs with his warmth, then moved amid a cloud of floating hair to his automated food dispenser. Ubu sipped his beer and walked back to his cabin door. Maria's body glowed softly in the darkness. At the sight a drifting sadness eased into his heart.

He had never ceased adoring her. The booster hormones, burning in their veins, had first driven them together, locked them in a scalding intricacy of legs and arms, cries and weightless yearning. Ubu hungered for her, wanted to tangle himself in the lithe white limbs and fall endlessly into the dark singularities of her eyes. He wanted to lose himself within her, find a home for himself within her skin, her breath, her heart. He wanted a manifest apocalypse, an annihilation of himself at her soft, innocent hands.

The fiery longing burned on. Something stood between them, kept him from merging himself into his sister, scattering himself into the storm of love and oblivion he desired. Beautiful Maria never seemed more out of reach than when he held her in his arms, when he caressed the formless stormcloud hair and kissed her translucent eyelids, when he felt her shudder beneath him and heard the bright birdlike colors that were her cries of bliss.

The mones drove him to her; the mones drove him away. Ubu, then Maria, sought other partners. Manipulated by other, less accomplished, less caring hands, he found a greater satisfaction.

Still, the longing never died. Sometimes he would watch Maria and something would bring it all back: the toss of her head, the careless shift of a shoulder blade, the pearly rustle of her nails as she scratched a reddened itch on a milk-white arm . . . It wasn't even necessary for Maria to be there, sometimes there was just a sound, a taste in the air, a remembered inflection overheard in a bar, in a song, on a hype. And there it was, a catch in the rhythm of his heart, a shining merciless blade twisting inside him . . .

Ubu fired aromatic beer over his palate and looked at Maria lying in the darkness of his cabin and wondered what it was he'd missed, how he could have the femme and lover he'd always wanted and still have so little.

Maria shifted on the bed, sighed, drowsily opened her eyes. Memory stabbed Ubu to the heart.

Desire rose among the desolation. Knowing fully the hopelessness of it all, he put the forcebulb in a bracket and stepped toward her, his hand reaching blindly to draw aside the dark screen of her hair . . .

A few hours later they made another shoot of a little over eight light-years, Ubu riding this time, spiraling into the singularity that dwelled in his mind. He was a brilliant tide rider, his accuracy and precision a reflection of the perfection of his memory. He never forgot a shoot, a simulation. A tidal perturbation and the correct response, once locked into his mind, remained in his reservoir of options forever, and once presented with a similar situation he knew with perfect confidence how to respond. Only when confronted with something unprecedented would he have to make his best guess and plow on, and that happened with increasing rarity.

But as a shooter he did not achieve Maria's brilliance. He could respond to what happened within the black hole, but he could not alter its reality as Maria could. He always left to her the final jump into a system, the leap that would put them as close to their goal as possible.

Precision wasn't necessary now, but still Maria and Ubu strove for it. For the sake of practice, if nothing else.

Progress was made in a series of staggers. After more shoots, each shorter and more precise than the last, Maria whiteholed *Runaway* into Montoya 81's twelve-planet system. There were four gas giants, planets large enough to have captured miniature black holes that might have existed since the universe itself had whiteholed its way into existence. The system was so far from human-inhabited space that the navigation software, correlating known stars, took almost six hours to fix their position. A short burn placed the ship on course for the outermost of the set, a brilliantly striped red-orange ringed god among planets. The giant was christened King Ubu. Detectors were set to strain the sky for the radio cry of invisible singularities. Three days of vac suit work fixed the superconducting magnets on the exterior of the hull, claws ready to come to grips with the first black hole wailing on the detectors.

Another burn, and *Runaway* was in orbit, far enough away from the planet to avoid its dull but constant radiation. King Ubu's rings lay edge-on like the sharpened blade of a knife. *Runaway* circled, waited for the telltale sound of dying matter.

Waited in vain.

Ubu had the pink Q-bodied guitar in his lower arms, the triangular Alfredo in his upper. His bare buttocks were sweating as they rested against the plastic fold-down lounge seat. He'd tuned the strings of the Alfredo about an eighth of a tone off the other guitar and was playing the same sad dolores ballad on each, one of innumerable laments for the state of one's heart. The strange little interference beats that sounded when the off-tuned strings were played simultaneously made little bright spots in his mind, layers of colors like far-off phosphors flashing on the night side of an open habitat.

This was precisely the kind of odd musical behavior that made other people reluctant to play with him.

Ubu played on, the beats building chroma in his brain.

Maria slid open the door screen and stepped in. She was wearing a blue-striped t-shirt and nothing else, and holding in her hand a piece of raw meat on a recycled green plastic waste sheet.

"The pork's off," she said.

Ubu struck a pair of final chords, one on the upper guitar, one on the lower. Interference beats hung resonantly in the air like the scent of a different season.

"How off?" he asked.

She stepped toward him and pushed the piece of pork in his face. Black, hard tumors dotted the meat like malevolent currants. There was a bad smell.

"Shit," he said, averting his eyes. He didn't want to have this memory stuck in his brain forever.

They had pork loin cells in the freezer, enough to clone a new batch, but he'd have to clean out the pork locker, disinfect everything to make sure the tumors' runamuck genetics were destroyed, before he could fill the locker with nutrient gel and let the new meat grow. It was a long and messy job.

"I'll get to it after dinner," Ubu said.

"I'm reheating last night's curry."

"You wanna get out your sizer and play? I feel like lamenting the condition of my corazón."

She looked at him in a speculative way. "Something wrong with it?"

"I can be sad if I want to." Aggressively.

"I got a right to know if you're sad for a reason."

He sighed. The guitars' fading resonance seemed to beat off key in his heart. "Pasco was here," he said.

"Oh." Maria looked at the corrupted meat in her hand.

"He was going on about Kitten. About how she understood him." He shook his head. Inside him was a hollowness that longed to be filled with pain. "Jesus Rice," he said. "I don't understand it. Him and her."

Her dark eyes turned carefully to his. "He was trying to protect us, Ubu."

He glanced up bewildered, his eyes burning. "Say again?"

"Think about it. About when Kitten came on board. We were just starting our moning, remember?"

"I guess."

"Think about what it was like. We were crazy. We were in heat all the time. We couldn't stop ourselves."

"So?"

"So think what it must have been like for him, with two people on board who would fuck anything that walked, and him not having any partners for weeks and months at a time."

Bile touched Ubu's tongue. He swallowed convulsively. "I don't want to know about this," he said.

Her voice was kind. "He was trying to protect us, Ubu. And then once he had her . . ." She turned away. "He was falling apart anyway. It would have happened without Kitten. She was just a focus for it, is all."

Ubu touched the guitar strings, felt them hum distantly like guy wires in a wind. The saddest song in the human sphere couldn't adequately describe how he felt.

He put the guitars away and went to burn the tumorous meat.

After two months *Runaway* shifted, moved to the next planet sunward, trading the red-and-orange giant for cobalt-and-green, King Ubu for Maria the Fair. The ship waited.

The spectra from the sensors demonstrated an endless, predictable symmetry. The radio squawks and the ripples of gravity perturbation, the latter recorded as they resonated with *Runaway*'s own singularity, showed nothing out of the ordinary. *Runaway*'s detectors were not as sensitive as those on one of the autodrones sent to find singularities, and now *Runaway* was paying the price of being asked to do something it wasn't designed for.

Ubu gazed at a terminal in *Runaway*'s machine shop, looking at holograms of sensor schematics. Another holo system displayed a vastly magnified picture of the work at hand. He was trying to build a more sensitive system, using microscopic waldoes to manipulate circuits.

The schematics swam before Ubu's eyes. He shook his head, looked from the schematics to the work and back again, and realized it no longer made any sense to him. He turned off the holo and ordered his waldoes to cover the half-built circuit with a sterile, protective plastic, one he could dissolve when he wanted to work on the assembly again.

He watched the waldoes complete their task and shut themselves down, then stepped out of the workshop and went down a ladder to the second level of the centrifuge. Gravity increased with each step.

Beautiful Maria sat in the lounge, Maxim on her lap, a stim headset circling her brow. The four-dimensional spiderweave of a puzzle game, projected by holograph, filled the rest of the room. A silver ball leaped from one location to another as digit counters ran down the game's remaining seconds.

Ubu looked through the grid at Maria's naked body, her flushed concentration. Despair beat slow time in his heart.

A tone sounded. Time had run out.

The four-dimensional grid vanished. Maria looked up at Ubu and grinned. "I'm trying not to cheat. It's hard when you want something to happen."

He joined her on the couch. The surface molded itself to his bare buttocks. Maxim's purr was loud in the ship's silence. She took one of his hands between her own, held it on her thigh. "Finished?" she asked.

"Half done."

"There's tomorrow."

"Yeah." Closing his eyes. "One thing we've got is time."

She gave a brief laugh. Her thigh was warm against the back of his hand. "I don't ever remember things being this way," she said. "We've always been in such a hurry before."

"Yes."

Conversation trailed away. They had run out of things to say days before. Maxim purred on.

Ubu opened his eyes. "I should drop into the rack."

She looked at him. "You want some company?"

He shook his head. "No." He turned to her, saw a concerned frown on her face. He kissed her. "I . . . need to be alone for a while."

"Yes. If you want." She brushed his bare shoulder with her cheek. He kissed her again, then walked away.

Ubu dropped into his rack, turned off the light, stared hopelessly at the ceiling. A long, distant pain twisted inside him, became more acute, became despair.

Beautiful Maria had come to him out of loneliness, he knew that. Now his own impossible loneliness was driving him away from her. He had wanted his own annihilation in her arms, the obliteration of his incessant burden of percipient selfhood, of constant awareness, of his impossible, weighty memory; instead he received only a shining revival of old memories, old agonies, all of them confirmed, brightened, by recent superimpositions . . . by the way the heat rose to Maria's skin at the most casual caress, the teasing brush of her hair on his belly, the burbling laugh that transformed in his mind to darting kites, bright blues and crimson, ribboned tails dancing against the stippled night sky of some ponderous, rotating habitat. It was all familiar anguish, familiar despair . . . a heightening and confirmation of his own perception, the knowledge of his own ultimate isolation.

He had to bring an end to it.

"I think I've got it hacked." Pasco's voice was loud in the darkness. His image, appearing after this announcement in midair, dazzled with sharp, radiant brightness.

"Go away," Ubu said. Another moment of grief, he thought, he would never forget.

Pasco was youngish, fit, and genial. Glee sparkled in his eyes. "First shift tomorrow I'm gonna put my print on a contract," he said. "We'll be moving cargo on a regular consignment run from the Pan-Development Kompanie at Trincheras to the new mining facility at Masquerade." Ubu shaded his eyes and looked in surprise at the glaring image of his father. Rainbow interference waves burned through Pasco's body, stabbed Ubu's eyes. The image gave a laugh. "I was getting worried, with Consolidation setting in. But now we'll have a long contract. Years. Lots of money." He laughed again. "Looks like our worries are over."

The recording must have been made years ago, when Ubu was a child. He hadn't heard of any deal with PDK, not even one that had fallen through. Ubu searched Pasco's image for a sign of what had gone wrong. He wondered whether this was all some delusion of Pasco's, something that he'd misunderstood or misinterpreted or invented out of whole cloth.

"I'm gonna celebrate," Pasco said. He fumbled in a pocket for a chak, fired a round up each nostril. "I'm gonna head for the Rostov Restaurant and have a party with my friends." He grinned, sniffed, and rubbed his nose with a knuckle. "Worries are over," he repeated, and reached forward, out of the hologram, to shut himself off.

Pasco's laser afterimage painted itself on the sudden velvet darkness. Ubu blinked and succeeded only in multiplying the image. What the hell had all that been about?

He dropped back onto his pillow and felt Pasco's image burn itself into his mind as it faded from his vision. Sadness flooded him. Tears rose. Another of Pasco's lost opportunities, this, another somber ghost haunting the humming corridors of *Runaway*, leading at the last to the weightless auxiliary control in the center of the ship, to the weeping man whose tears, like Ubu's, drifted through space much as he drifted through life, forever dying.

Beautiful Maria started her spiderweave puzzle again. The giant silver ball bearing jumped from lodge to lodge, her mind making trial leaps amid the gentle hyperbolic folds of the fourth dimension as she sought the key to the puzzle. In the end it all fell apart. She couldn't keep her mind on the subject.

Maria shut down the game and heard Pasco's voice ringing distantly through the fuge. It rose to a climax, was followed by long whispering silence. She sat for some minutes listening to the ship, and suddenly she didn't want to be alone. She scooped Maxim off her lap, rose, placed the cat in the dimple she left in the couch. Maxim, appearing faintly surprised by this intrusion, rose to a sitting position and yawned, then settled back down and, with an air of determination, shut his eyes. His purr continued unabated.

Maria stepped into the corridor and moved toward Ubu's quarters, her bare feet moving over nonskid green carpet worn smooth by time. She stopped, hesitated. Her brother's door was shut. He hadn't slid his door shut in a long while, not since Pasco died.

She gazed at the door, breath fluttering in her throat, and wondered if the door was closed forever. Sudden fear leaped in her heart.

She turned and walked to the control center, sat at the controls, told the computer, for lack of anything else to tell it, to rerun the last few hours of recorded sensor spectra.

Had she used Ubu, she wondered, as she had used Kit? Was there something heartless in the way she had gone to him that first night, something knowing in the way she had used his desire for her own comfort? She knew he wanted her, known as well that he needed her with a far greater intensity than she had ever needed him, or anyone.

Spectra fast-motioned past Maria's eyes, all smooth predictable curves. Strange, she thought. All she had done was try to give Ubu whatever it was that he wanted. Could she blame herself for the fact he hadn't got it?

Had she used him badly? Doubt wavered in her mind like a shimmer of rising heat.

She didn't want to be alone.

A spike appeared amid the spectra, the track of a rocket rising and falling. The peak was right off the scale.

Electricity hummed in her mind. She leaned forward, tongue tapping her front teeth in a fast pattern of concentration. She ran the spectra back, saw the sudden burst of hard radiation followed by a continuing busy little resonance pattern in the surface of *Runaway*'s singularity.

Hard radiation, gravity waves. There was a triumphant singing in Maria's nerves. This might be the real thing.

Carefully she examined the spectra. The first burst of radiation was followed within minutes by a rise, then a steady leveling off. Her heart sank. It was all too familiar.

There was a singularity all right. The black hole was inside a ship.

Runaway was no longer alone.

Maria plotted the ship's arrival point and turned the outside scopes on it. There it was, a bright burning stream of plasma, the torch of a ship heading for Maria the Fair at a constant two-gee acceleration. Predicted arrival time: five to eight days, depending on when the crew tired of pulling heavy gees and shut down the reaction drive.

It was definitely a ship, not a robot singularity hunter. It was too large to be anything else.

The important question was whether or not the people on the ship knew *Runaway* was fleeing from the law.

Maria looked at the data again, then at the hologram, the viscous streak of mother-of-pearl drawn across gaping blackness. The ship couldn't be hunting them—no one on *Runaway* had known where they were going, let alone anyone back on Angelica Station. The ship was probably in a situation similar to that of *Runaway*, driven by desperation into the business of singularity hunting.

She stood and moved spinward toward Ubu's cabin. He wouldn't mind being interrupted once he knew what it was about.

Runaway tracked the ship for the next three days. The two-gee acceleration, save for pauses before and after a surprisingly large number of correction burns, continued unabated. The crew had to be composed of supermen, but their navigation software apparently left something to be desired. Ubu wondered if the ship was military, if the Navy had in some highly improbable secret fashion managed to follow *Runaway*'s purposeless leaps into the unknown. If so, there was little *Runaway* could do about it—he and Maria couldn't stand that kind of prolonged acceleration.

The ship, to Ubu's relief, proved not to be military. As it grew closer, *Runaway*'s scopes were able to perceive its dim silhouette against the fluorescent wash of plasma, a silhouette crowned with the projecting horns of the magnets used to catch black holes. The ship was a prospector, after all. And a big one, approximately half again the size of *Runaway*.

The ship burned on past its logical turnaround point and Ubu wondered if it was just going to run on, accelerate clean past Maria the Fair, perhaps to use the blue-and-green-striped globe to slingshot them in another direction. But no, half a day later, the ship rotated about its center of gravity and commenced a brutal three-and-a-half-gee deceleration burn. It evidently intended on settling into an orbit similar to *Runaway*'s.

"Jesus Rice," Maria commented. "The crew's got to be as flat as chapatis by now." She sat in a chair in the control cage, her bare feet propped on the comm board in front of her. She was dressed in a thin robe with a gentle geometrical motif, all based on the shadows cast by four-dimensional objects. Ubu was in his usual pair of shorts, his muscular shoulders bare. Above the console the control room videos and holos all showed the same phenomenon: jetting plasma directed toward *Runaway*, a bright burning light at the center surrounded by a fluttering ghostlike penumbra, the whole obscuring *Runaway*'s view of the intruder.

"They're getting here a couple days early," Ubu said. "What's their hurry?"

"Maybe it's a robot prospector."

"Be too big."

Maria's toes wriggled below the multiple images. "Maybe whoever owns it can afford to maintain a ship that size."

Ubu thought about that. "If it's a robot, we could steal it," he said. "Match orbits, then you can glitch us inside and we can use their ship to find our singularity. Then return it to its original programming once we're done."

Maria shrugged. "I guess we could."

Ubu frowned, leaned toward the console. Three of his hands

tapped swift instructions to the outside scopes. As the big ship swung past, still moving very fast about ten thousand kilometers outside *Runaway*'s own orbit, the telescopes and other sensors would track the intruder and give Ubu and Maria a clearer view.

Minutes hummed by. The multiple images of the plasma jets grew larger, brighter.

"Here we go," said Ubu. He pushed the chair back, stood, and looked upward into the largest video display.

The picture's angle shifted abruptly and the ship tore past, the scopes holding fast on its racing form, its silhouette picked out by the glowing light of its own torch, the backdrop a swift blur of rushing stars . . .

The hair on Ubu's arms rose as if he'd been brushed by a current of phantom electricity. A fountain of pure adrenaline staggered him. As he stared at the vids he heard a sharp cry of wonder and awe from Maria, followed by the slap of her astounded bare feet on the deck.

The intruder's skin was dark, but some of the structures on its surface fluoresced in the hot glow of the plasma, flickering spectral images that danced like a planetary aurora, pale green, bright blue, blood-crimson. The ship was as round and rough as a walnut, one end pouring a white plasma stream, the magnetic grapples set on the other. Antennae and what might have been the skeletons of cargo cranes dotted its surface, outlined by bright ionized flow and by the leaping auroral ghosts. Bulges—atmosphere craft, possibly—clung like limpets to the vessel's surface, placed apparently at random.

No human had ever built that ship. That much was obvious from the first instant.

Ubu's nerves burned with white-hot fire. Lightning calculations jagged through his mind.

The intruder swung past, became a dark silhouette against the alpine glow of its torch. Ubu reached blindly to the systems board to make certain that the alien passage had been recorded.

Ubu turned toward Beautiful Maria. Her grey eyes still gazed in awe at the receding image on the video display. Ubu laughed, and Maria looked at him in surprise.

"Maria," he said. "This is our big score." He laughed again, raised all four arms toward the dark ovoid superimposed on the flaring plasma light.

"Shooter femme," he laughed. "We've just jumped into the big time!"

She was staring at him.

"First thing we do," he said, "we get them to sign a contract."

CHAPTER
9

GENERAL VOLITIONAL TWELVE FELT THE PALE LATTICED RESIN soften around him. The nutrient supply increased to his body and brain, and the special gel cells that cushioned his mind and memory surrendered up their buffering liquids, shrank and permitted enhanced neural connection and the swelling of brain matter. While subcellular repair units flooded his nervous system, knit frayed or worn nerve endings, and built chemical transmitters, other tailored units cleaned capillaries, revived muscle tissue. Twelve's pain centers were shut down during this procedure, but he still felt an eerie sense that a message was trying to get through to him, and stray twinges of agony crackled in his limbs and mind, the pain rerouted through another part of his brain and experienced secondhand.

Twelve's resinous high-gee tethers were disintegrating, leaving him wafting to and fro in the gravity-free compartment. As his vision returned he could see others hanging in the room with him, three general volitionals, a pair of navigator volitionals, two giant cargo movers, and some general-purpose nonvolitionals. One of the navigators hung lifeless, his feeding system having failed during transport.

Twelve opened his mouth and his taste palps flickered outward to sample the environment. A blast of warm, fragrant air began blowing the liquid remains of the resin toward the screens that would collect it and save it for further use. Tiny nonvolitionals crawled over Twelve's body, cleaning his flesh with grating, lapping tongues, chirping at their discovery of food.

The air spoke. "Come to Beloved," it said. "Come to fusion." A surge of pleasure rose up Twelve's spine. Taste palps trembled on the verge of ecstasy. He thrashed against his few remaining tethers as he tried to free himself.

Frothy nutrient liquid burst from the mouth of General Volitional Eight. His lungs inflated and he screamed, limbs flailing. Something had gone wrong. The pain blockers had failed early. His umbilicus snapped and he drifted about the compartment, kicking wildly, the umbilicus stump bleeding. "Beloved!" shrieked Eight's voder. Twelve raised an arm to fend Eight off. Eight clawed for the door and with a convulsive spasm managed to propel himself into the corridor outside.

Eight was followed by the larger nonvolitionals. The cargo movers detached the dead navigator and rumbled away toward the dissolution chambers. Twelve's last tether snapped, gnawed at by his sharp, pointed inner fingers. He drifted in the honeycomb chamber, connected by the umbilicus only and impatient for the process to complete itself. Subcellular repair units finished their task and dissolved into component strings of protein, flushing out of his body through the umbilicus. His chest heaved as he pumped liquid from his lungs. He gasped for air, alveoli inflating with a series of crackles and pops. He felt the flood of nutrients tapering off as his umbilicus began to constrict. It pinched itself off and released him. A few weightless drops of blood floated free from the dissolving bond. Two small nonvolitionals leaped for the blood, sucked it avidly. Twelve climbed the umbilicus to its root and reversed himself, placed splayed, long-toed feet on the surface, and pushed off for the entrance. The surviving navigator followed.

The corridor outside was oval in cross-section, lit by cold fluorescent strips. Tympani beat compelling rhythms in the walls. Twelve drifted easily down its length, passing General Volitional

Eight en route. Eight was in shock, curled in a foetal shape, arms and legs still stirring feebly as he drifted about the corridor. "Beloved," he whimpered. Twelve avoided him, his forward set of eyes fixed resolutely forward. Eight was obviously fated for dissolution.

Other mobiles, sentients and semisentients, filled the corridors. Twelve's hearts raced. He had never seen so many of his fellow inhabitants alive and awake at once. Something serious must have happened for so many to be mobilized. Was it war? he wondered, and then hot pain stabbed his joints and drove thought from his mind: the pain blockers were being metabolized.

Humid warmth flowed over Twelve's skin. His palps tingled. He was nearing presence of Beloved.

"Glory," he sang, "glory."

Beloved occupied several chambers in the center of the ship, and her translucent flesh covered the walls of several others. Twelve sped to one of these chambers, a fusion chamber equipped with a large tympanum that beat out an urgent rhythm, several pulsing hearts, a cluster of neural umbilici that waved in the air like a spidery anemone, swaying gently with the rhythm of Beloved's respiration— for one of Beloved's nostrils was here, inhaling the scents of her dutiful children, expelling the hormones that conveyed the ineffable essence of Beloved's glorious, eternal, and transcendent self.

Several of Beloved's children already hung in the room, each attached to an umbilicus. Eagerly, General Volitional Twelve seized one of the umbilici in his blunt outer fingers and attached it to the locus at the base of his skull. The umbilicus gripped his flesh and clung, and Beloved's microscopic neurons, drill-tipped with purified carbon, penetrated his skin along with a hushed wave of anaesthetic. "Glory, glory," Twelve chanted as he hung weightless at the end of his elastic tether. Others among Beloved's children—movers, build- ers, scavengers, volitionals and nonvolitionals alike—jostled him as they sought other umbilical connections. "Glory, glory," they all reported.

Twelve's body convulsed in ecstasy as Beloved's nerves achieved union with his own. His personality melted. Pleasure centers whimpered and cooed in ultimate bliss.

Stand by, stand by, broadcast Beloved.

A pair of general-purpose nonvolitionals appeared with the still-stirring body of General Volitional Eight. Eight was held to an umbilicus until attached, then allowed to flop listlessly at the end of the tether. "Glory," he whimpered. Spittle and blood bubbled from his mouth.

Stand by.

The others fused with Beloved. Small nonvolitionals crawled over Beloved's flesh, lovingly cleaning and grooming her with their diligent tongues, chirping their joy. One hopped from the wall and attached itself to Twelve.

Children, said Beloved, *I inform you of opportunity.*

Twelve gave a shout of joy. Dimly the shouts of the others reached his ears.

Opportunity. It had been a long time since Twelve had heard anything smacking of good fortune.

Beloved had been having a run of bad luck.

Twelve's last mission for Beloved had been to sell Beloved's sole remaining child. For years, after the disappearance of First Child and her ship, things had got worse and worse, and the children conceived in happier, more optimistic days had been scattered up and down the course of Beloved's travels, conveyed as cold barter into alien and unsympathetic hands. At first the prices had been good, the trades at least for something useful: new-model servants, freshly grown hardware for the ship, volumes of coded knowledge etched in chains of living genetic matter. Then, as core economies collapsed and the whole business of trade had become progressively more precarious, Beloved's children had been traded more and more for the means of simple survival.

That final, sad child, entombed in its six-foot resinous shell, contained within its dormant genetic matter the potential for another Beloved and all her servants, another ship the size of Beloved's. Twelve, his hearts overwhelmed with sorrow, had with the other two members of his delegation carried the child forth from Beloved's ship and into the foreign domain of Clan Lattice, a huge spherical trading station that orbited the pale amber gas giant, Lattice 4007.

The intelligence at the center of Station 4007 was not of the

Lattice race, but rather a captive entity, once a child bartered away to the Lattice Clan just as Beloved's own child would be bartered. While still in her shell, Entity 4007 had been injected with Lattice hormones and Lattice genetics, her original inbred loyalties subverted at the subcellular level until she became an obedient chemical slave of Clan Lattice. Lattice Station 4007 was exposed to the gene-damaging radiation of the gas giant, and Clan Lattice did not wish to risk their own precious plasm in such a perilous environment: the purchased slave served their purpose well.

Twelve and his comrades whimpered with sadness as they carried the shell from Beloved's vessel into the enormous alien sphere. Entity 4007's tympani beat urgent rhythms, foreign to Twelve's vocoder. Twelve's skin prickled at the presence of outsiders. Lattice Station 4007 was filled with commerce, not only members of Clan Lattice but those from other clans who had business here. Cargo haulers worked double shifts moving containers from ship to ship, ship to warehouse. Hard-shelled atmosphere miners, their bodies worn by colossal gravity stresses, returned to the station in scoopships they had driven deep into the gas giant's lethal atmosphere in search of exotic gases and long-chain organics. The giant's moons were being mined for less precious materials by other servants of Clan Lattice, and slugs of precious ore were carried from the gaping mouths of intersystem transports by latest-model near-sentients.

With unfelt dignity, General Volitional Twelve, seconded by General Volitionals Eight and Nineteen, carried the child from the busy cargo area to the executive levels of the station. Here the tympani beat a less urgent cadence. Hurried volitionals, nearly all from Clan Lattice, swept through the gently curving corridors and sneered at the cowed outsiders. Twelve's taste palps were tormented by the overwhelming presence of Lattice, a scent echoed and re-echoed by all Lattice's children; but as Twelve neared the station's heart he thought that he could detect something else, an alien flavor the Lattice programming had been unable to entirely subvert: the distant and forlorn suggestion of what Entity 4007 had once been, the hopeful offspring of a now-fallen clan. The reminder of the child's fate drove a wedge of diamond sorrow through Twelve.

Probably Beloved's child would become a Clan Lattice cargo hauler rather than anything so grand as a station. Would she still have the scent of Beloved about her, lost and forlorn among the crippling alien odors?

The Lattice delegate to the meeting was a very young general volitional, four-armed and bred to zero gravity, his skin a brilliant scarlet. Twelve had not encountered him during the earlier negotiations. He awaited them in the chamber prepared for Beloved's child. The room featured a thick umbilicus, one tipped with a chemical synthesizer that would produce a solvent to dissolve the child's shell and permit the rape of her mind and heritage.

The Lattice delegate sketched a brief salute. His palps flickered at Beloved's alien odor. "The representatives of Clan Lustre will deposit their seed here," he said.

Twelve adopted a motionless, dignified posture and refused to acknowledge the other's contemptuous greeting. He fixed his two forward eyes on the Lattice delegate. "We expected a larger reception," he said.

The delegate's lower hands twitched. "This-individual has been fully accredited and is capable of dealing with this-matter," he said. "This-individual needs merely to receive your seed and inventory, and give agreed value-in-exchange."

Twelve's palps could taste the indignation radiating from the other delegates. He forced himself to remain calm, his sharp inner fingers digging into his palms. "We nevertheless expect a reception commensurate with the honor we do Clan Lattice," he said. One of his rear eyes could not help but see Entity 4007's umbilicus groping for the child, its sensitive olfactory buds alerted by the alien scent in the room.

The scarlet delegate remained motionless. "Clan Lattice individuals are engaged in many important tasks," he said. "They cannot be spared for minor matters. This-individual is prepared to accept the agreed-upon exchange. If not, this-individual has other responsibilities."

Anger flushed Twelve's skin. He wanted to launch himself for the Lattice delegate, throttle and decapitate him, take his head in triumph to Beloved. He fought the anger down. There was no choice in any of this. "Due to Clan Lustre's regard for Clan Lattice," he said, "Clan Lustre will complete the arrangements, but protests you-individual's lack of courtesy."

"The protest is noted." Coolly. "Please hand this-individual the inventory."

The delegate held out a hand. General Volitional Nineteen, behind Twelve, gave a hiss of fury. Twelve drifted toward the Lattice delegate and handed him a tablet containing complete information of the contents of the child's genetic makeup, an inventory of Beloved and all her possible servants. In return, the delegate offered Twelve a deed-tablet that made Beloved owner of a set of magnetic prospecting grapples and a genetic culture that would permit Beloved to grow a nonvolitional sentient capable of detecting singularities and operating the equipment to capture them. This nonvolitional was an obsolete model, one offered at a discount; but he was all Beloved had been able to afford in exchange for the full inventory of her own capabilities.

His mind burning with anger and humiliation, Twelve led his delegation out of the chamber before he witnessed the ultimate agony of Beloved's child being possessed by the groping umbilicus. General Volitional Nineteen gave a cry of anguish as he followed Twelve down the corridor. "Blasphemy!" he cried. "That-individual should be condemned to dissolution!"

"Be calm," said Twelve. "We are Clan Lustre. We are serving our Beloved."

"Woe!" Nineteen moaned.

"Silence!" Twelve shouted. His rear set of eyes fixed Nineteen in a furious glare. Eight gave Nineteen an angry shove with one hand. Nineteen trembled, but kept silent.

Twelve, as he descended into the dock area, felt a renewed flood of despair. He could see how the polished bodies of the cargo haulers reflected the latest bioengineering techniques, that the enlarged brain cases of the navigators showed increased capacity for multilevel calculation, and observe how the Lattice Station's very newness seemed to demonstrate the obsolescence of his own Beloved. Even the nonvolitionals that cleaned detritus from the walls were newly grown models.

Nineteen shuddered as the delegation drifted across the huge cargo space. His eyes rotated independently, not focusing on anything. He gave a long sigh, voided his bladder, and then curled in a ball. Nonvolitionals detected the urine with their advanced sensors and leaped to intercept.

Twelve and Eight batted the nonvolitionals away, took hold of their malfunctioning comrade, and carried him Home. Other sentients looked after them with mingled horror and contempt.

Nineteen showed no sign of recovery even after his return to Beloved. He remained catatonic, and Beloved ordered his dissolution.

As he helped carry Nineteen to the dissolution chambers, Twelve braced himself for a dissolution command for himself and Eight. Beloved might conclude that their mission had been too traumatic and that their stability and future usefulness had been compromised.

The dissolution command did not come. After a short, ecstatic fusion, Beloved had ordered them into stasis, their bodies cushioned and supported against the shocks of high-gee acceleration by resinous webbing.

Now Eight was gone, his reawakening a failure. Only Twelve's mind still held the horrors of that last trip, the remembered agony of delivering Beloved's offspring into the cold hands of an indifferent clan.

Only Twelve's mind. And Beloved's.

Opportunity. Joy danced like sparks in Twelve's blazing mind. And then the knowledge came, and all joy was blotted out.

Strangers! Invaders! Kill! Twelve screamed and waved clenched fists at the stunning knowledge of strangers more foreign than those of any hostile clan. Madness bubbled in his brain. Half Beloved's servants were glassy-eyed with shock.

Opportunity, soothed Beloved.

Kill!

Opportunity. Beloved's gentle voice was insistent.

Not-us. Plaintively. *Not-Lustre. Foreign beyond all foreignness.*

Opportunity. We are secure. We are generating a company of warriors should Our safety come into question.

Beyond his own baffled complaints, beyond the glory and ecstasy that was Beloved, Twelve detected the reactions of Beloved's other servants, dim cries of protest and mounting lunacy. The shock had driven some of Beloved's servants into numb catatonia, others into bleached and fervid madness. With diligent care, Beloved's drill-tipped nervons drove into the minds of her dysfunctional servants, severed cortical connections, allowed the madness to rave on in disconnected, solipsistic fashion while Beloved appropriated the calculating capacity of the victims' brains.

Opportunity, opportunity. Beloved's voice soothed as the raving, violent chorus from her servants diminished under her surgical assault. *Explanation follows.*

Glory, glory, Twelve whimpered, his protest subdued.

Beloved, with slow patience, explained her plan to her remaining sentients. The whole awesome dimension of the scheme swelled in Twelve's mind. He hung from the umbilicus in limpid astonishment. *Glory,* he cried, *glory.* Others, slower to comprehend, began to join in Twelve's chant. Bodies twitched as pleasure centers flamed.

Now we shall begin, said Beloved.

Deliberately, with careful precision, the thoughts of strangers fell upon Twelve's mind in resonant, shattering layers.

Twelve spent a long timeless moment in trance, alien concepts sizzling through his mind. Beloved had wakened all her children, even the nonsentients, in order to make use of their brain tissue; she had fused the whole community into a massive organic whole dedicated to the concept of decoding the alien signals. The general volitionals directed the scope of the project and managed the flow of information; nonvolitional sentients worked diligently on individual parts of the puzzle; nonsentients loaned their limited calculating capacity to piecework.

Many of Beloved's servants died, their bodies withering while their brains burned in service to Beloved. Though ordered to maintain themselves, they were so overwhelmed by the terrifying thoughts of the strangers and the scale of their assigned task that Beloved's careful instructions slipped their minds. Twelve managed to remember his assigned tasks, but could not count the times he de-fused from Beloved, fed, excreted, and re-fused, all in a half-focused daze, the strangers' madness roiling through his mind. At one point he realized that he was eating Eight's umbles, chewing mechanically while Eight's head, by now severed from the body, mouthed silently at the end of its tether. Beloved's ship became tainted with the scent of decay. The nonvolitionals who cleaned the ship were falling behind in their task.

The foreigners were deranged, that much was clear. Twelve's universe was One, symbolized by the ultimate, transcendent fusion with Beloved; but the foreigners were Two, living in a schizophrenic duality: Mother-Father, Man-Woman, their loyalties hopelessly confused, hopelessly tangled. Even the *purpose* of a male seemed rank blasphemy, and the notion that his function was the diffusion of gene plasm rather than its careful conservation was not only unwholesome but absurd.

The shattering of the ultimate One had resulted in a splintering so terrifying, so obscene, that Twelve dared not contemplate its full dimensions. The alien creatures were alone, living in an isolation so total as to constitute blasphemy. *As alone*, he thought, *as Beloved*, but that realization was so frightening he immediately let it spin away from his mind.

Twelve began to realize what a risk Beloved was running. Many of her servants had been driven to madness, and Beloved herself was in danger of having her sacred mind polluted by alien thought. Twelve perceived only a small part of the awesome communication; Beloved of a necessity perceived it all. Twelve was terrified she would crack under the strain. Even in the ecstasy of fusion, Twelve perceived Beloved's increasing stress, the growing brittleness of her mind. Should Beloved shatter under the thrust of alien concepts, all would be lost.

But Beloved did not shatter. The project continued. The warriors, sentient and semisentient, that Beloved had grown for her defense were added to the network. Beloved absorbed all into her glory, and Twelve could not but gape in awe.

And then the grand fusion came to an end. Beloved's servants were dismissed and returned to their tasks. Twelve remained in fusion and helped Beloved to direct her servants, assigned brood chambers to grow replacements for those who had faded, died, gone mad. In the end only Twelve remained in fusion, alone in the room filled with Beloved's heartbeat, her gentle and sustaining breath.

For My servant General Volitional Twelve, I have high praise.

Twelve shouted in happiness. Beloved's soothing voice continued. *For My servant I have another task.*

This-individual wishes only to serve my Beloved, answered Twelve.

You have served Me well and in difficult circumstances. Because you have demonstrated flexibility in dealing with outsiders, I desire that you serve Me as chief negotiator with the foreigners.

Part of Twelve's mind quailed beneath the responsibility, the necessity of dealing with loathsome alien species and their contaminant madness. But still his mind leaped, as it must, in fevered assent. *Glory, glory,* he chanted.

A corridor is being prepared, sealed off from the rest of Home. When the time comes, you will isolate yourself there, in order that foreign pollutants should not contaminate My other servants.

Glory, glory.

Go about your ways.

Glory, Beloved.

Twelve repeated his praises until Beloved's umbilicus withdrew from his spine. His head reeled.

Near him, separating from its umbilicus, was the head of General Volitional Eight, the faithful servant of Beloved, now inert and dying.

Carefully, Twelve took Eight's head in his hands and carried it to the nearest dissolution chamber.

CHAPTER
10

IT WAS LUCKY THAT THEY'D NEVER BEEN ABLE TO SELL ALL OF Pasco's junk. Ubu and Maria headed for the cargo bay, unstrapped a package, dissolved away its tempafoam shell. Inside were the fastlearn cartridges that had given him and Maria the ability to write before their hands could quite coordinate their grip upon a pencil. Maria took the cartridges to computer central, jacked them in, and cracked open the contents, liberating the actual text of the language instruction from the software-to-wetware shell that actually read its contents into the human mind. Ubu found more cartridges— mathematics, spacetime geometry, singularity physics—and took a seat at another terminal.

The intruder in the meantime looped away from Maria the Fair on a long aphelion, swung back, burned again to put itself into a less elongated orbit. By the time the stranger settled into its new orbit, *Runaway* was ready.

Maria lifted Maxim onto her lap as Ubu moved to the comm board. "I hope they use radio," she said. "It's gonna be hard getting their attention if we have to use semaphore flags or something." She gave a laugh. "We wouldn't even know how many flags to wave. They might have eight hands apiece."

"Radio makes sense."

"Who says *they* gotta make sense? Besides," reasonably, "light makes as much sense as radio. Maybe they modulate a laser—"

Ubu looked at her. "We'll deal with it if it happens," he said.

She grinned at him. "Relax. Okay?" Ubu turned back to his board.

"I hope to hell they use high-energy communications, whatever kind. Otherwise the radiation from the planet's gonna fuck up our reception." He turned back to the boards and locked transmission and reception antennae onto the intruder. He prepared the transmitter to fire a series of standard greetings on a wide range of transmission bands, then made the receivers ready to pick up any return signal at all.

Ubu gazed hungrily at the dark silhouette of the intruder ship, the fluorescence gone now that its torch had shut down. Ubu's nerves hummed. There was a knot in his stomach. He suppressed a tremor as he ordered the transmitter to begin.

The signal raced away. Ubu licked his lips, waited. Maxim's purr was suddenly very loud.

Ubu's heart leaped as an answer came back very quickly at 1427.4 megahertz. He looked at the board and saw a response time of less than three seconds between the intruder's reception of the message and its reply. "They use microwave!" he laughed, and then his joy faded. The response time was so fast that the other ship *had* to be automated. But no: the response consisted of several lines of gibberish followed by a repeat of Ubu's initial message.

He looked up at Maria. "We're talking to each other."

Maria jumped from her chair with a cry that sounded in Ubu's mind like burnished silver. Maxim thrashed in her arms in surprised annoyance. Maria danced to Ubu's station, bent over his shoulder. Her hair brushed his shoulder. He laughed. "Better go slow," he said, and began his language lessons, right there on the megahertz band.

MORE. After twelve minutes of slow transmission the single word began to glow on the communications screens. Ubu gave the intruder what it wanted.

The intruder started out fast and got faster, its comprehension span ranging between thirty and fifty times the speed of the average human child. Anxiety gnawed at Ubu. What if the aliens were so smart they wouldn't need anything the humans could give them? But, he thought, if they were so smart, how come they needed all those correction burns to wander into the right orbit?

CONTINUE.

Fast as the intruders were, it took them weeks to absorb what Ubu could send them. The intruder never asked questions, just transmitted short requests for more information.

PLEASE CONTINUE, *RUNAWAY*. Which proved they were absorbing at least some of it.

Maria and Ubu took six-hour shifts on the communications decks, watching the transmissions blaze out, the curt replies come back in answer.

THANK YOU, *RUNAWAY*.

At least they were polite.

Beautiful Maria pointed out that they should be careful in transmitting technical knowledge. The aliens ought to *pay* for that if they wanted it. *Runaway* tried to limit its transmissions to abstract areas of knowledge—mainly math and language—and kept its practical applications to themselves.

Still, Maria was worried. Just the vocabulary they were transmitting would give the intruders a very good idea of human capabilities.

BRILLIANT SHIP REQUESTS YOU PRAY CONTINUE, *RUNAWAY*.

When the message came, Maria called Ubu out of the rack. "Maybe the ship really is automated," she said.

"Why's it so big?"

"Maybe the whole ship's a big AI. Maybe that's why they're processing things so quickly."

"Jesus Rice."

"Maybe that's why they call themselves the *brilliant* ship. Because they're so smart."

Ubu gave up on sleep. From time to time he dozed at the

communications board. There was nothing to watch—the information pulsing out, the brief replies coming back—but he wanted to be ready in case something happened.

MANY THANKS, *RUNAWAY*. SHINING ASSEMBLY REQUESTS CONTINUANCE.

"Shining assembly," Maria said. "Look at that. It *is* a machine."

"We'll see."

How do you figure the angles on a machine? Ubu wondered. How does a machine sign a contract?

Finally there was nothing left, nothing but the technical knowledge they wanted to keep for themselves. "They know a damn sight more about us than we know about them," Ubu said. "Now that we can talk, I want to see them up close."

Maria shrugged. "Let's ask them."

Ubu felt his mouth go dry. Fear flickered in his belly. He couldn't put it off any more.

A memory of Pasco reached up from his mind, his father eating a huge piece of crumb cake while he hunched over the computer, working on a new project, some kind of big four-dimensional economic model that was going to give him a handle on Consolidation, another project he never finished. Ubu wished he had Pasco for this, Pasco's genius and imagination. This was exactly the sort of thing that might have brought Pasco alive again, out of his spiral into death.

Ubu reached for the headset mic, then lowered his hand. Communication with the intruder had, so far, been entirely in terms of written language. If they got a voice transmission they wouldn't know how to interpret it.

If contact continued, Ubu realized, it was going to get tedious to type everything or use the dictation software.

No choice, though. His fingers tapped keys.

RUNAWAY REQUESTS SHIP RENDEZVOUS AND FACE-TO-FACE INTERVIEW BETWEEN OUR REPRESENTATIVES.

The answer was as swift as it had always been, with no more than a second between the reception of *Runaway*'s message and the transmission of the intruder's reply.

RADIANT CLAN AGREES WHOLEHEARTEDLY TO MEETING, *RUNAWAY*.

A shiver ran through Ubu.

"Let's do it," he said.

"*Clan*," said Maria. "Maybe they're not machines, after all."

Runaway seemed more maneuverable than the intruder, so Ubu volunteered to match the other's orbit. *Runaway* made a pair of burns that put the ship within a half kilometer of the intruder.

Maria and Ubu watched as details of the intruder's design became visible on the vid. The intruder's ovoid, symmetric hull was studded with antennae and receptor dishes, and marked by artifacts of commerce: cargo cranes and movers, big hatches meant for bulky objects, smaller rider ships, some of which were winged for descent into atmosphere. There was a kind of symmetry to it all, a similar style and sense of proportion that seemed to mark the entire alien design from the largest feature to the smallest. It was the big singularity grapplers that seemed out of place—they looked as if they'd been tacked on. *Runaway*'s grapplers were tacked on as well, but didn't alter the look of the human ship. *Runaway*'s entire battered design made it look as if it were assembled out of spare parts.

"Maybe they're desperate," said Ubu. "Maybe they bought some grapplers and ran out here for the same reason we did."

"I hope so." Maria squinted at the display. "What's it made of?"

"Something dark."

"Why dark?"

"Be crazy."

"Yeah. Crazy. Guess I'll find out."

Ubu pushed back from the comm board and stood. "I gotta make an adaptation to my vac suit before I can talk to these people." He looked at her. "Watch the boards. I'll let you know when I'm done."

"Right." She grinned at him as she tracked her chair to the comm board. He bent to kiss her. Her taste ran like wildfire through his mind, triggering associations, memories, a storm of desire that burst without warning. Maria looked at him, wide dark eyes startled.

"Ubu," she said.

Ubu realized to his astonishment that the rules had changed. Life didn't equal despair any more.

He kissed her again, tasted the possibilities. He was falling in love with hope.

Beautiful Maria monitored the boards while Ubu took his four-armed vac suit to the weightless workshop aft of the centrifuge. He had to work out a fast way of communicating face-to-face, otherwise it would prove more efficient to continue chattering on the radio.

The suit had a maneuvering unit attached, power jacks, a chest analyzer that would provide readings on atmosphere content and pressure.

From storage Ubu took a portable computer keyboard, one of those with the wide steel keys intended for use outside a ship, when the programmer's fingers would be sheathed in clumsy gloves. He strapped the deck to his vac suit's chest, ran a dictation program into it, jacked in a lead from the helmet mic. He removed one of the two helmet lamps and attached a holo projector to the empty bracket. He leaned over the mic and spoke a few lines, saw a print version of his words parade in bright golden letters over the helmet. He grinned.

That was the easy part.

The helmet had a heads-up display that projected data on the interior of the faceplate—life-support and power information, suit systems and comm unit status, any readouts from attached equipment. Ubu ran the microwave receiver on the helmet through the comp, then reprogrammed the heads-up unit to display any received information. He took a spare suit comm unit from the rack, jacked it into a computer deck, and aimed the antenna at the helmet receiver. He tapped a message, fired it at the helmet.

Nothing.

It took him two more tries before the jury-rigged system worked properly. Then he tested the vidcam unit in the helmet—he wanted to record this—and drifted his suit to the dorsal lock, entered the centrifuge, and dropped to the first level. Maria sat before the comm board. She looked over her shoulder and smiled.

"I'm ready," he said.

*   *   *

LUSTRE SHIP WILL ILLUMINATE THE APPROPRIATE AIRLOCK. OUR AMBASSADOR WILL AWAIT YOU.

The illumination was blinding, the lock outlined by a series of multicolored strobes so bright that Ubu had to dial up the polarization of his helmet. The other ship was taking no chances that Ubu might miss the appropriate hatch.

The outside hatch was open, about eight feet by five. Relief eased through Ubu at the realization that it was human-sized. He rotated, fired attitudinal jets, drifted into the lock, and raised a pair of arms to stop his motion against the far hatch. His own shadow, hard-edged in the light of the strobes, flickered in bursts of bright color against the interior hatch. Ubu triggered his transmitter.

"I have arrived in the airlock." His fingers tapped the broad steel keys. He could see the gold glow of hologram letters above his head.

The door behind him slid smoothly shut. Phosphors, images of the strobes, burned in Ubu's vision, then faded. He dialed down his polarized visor and turned on the video camera. Get some pictures, he thought, of this historical moment.

Fluorescent strips on the walls glowed with bluish light. There was another blue light source, a circular plate that Ubu assumed operated the lock. The corners of the lock were rounded, not angular. Ubu looked at the smooth dark grey surface of the walls, brushed gloved fingers against it, tried to work out what it was made of. It didn't seem to be metal. Possibly it was plastic.

In time he became aware of a world outside his vac suit, that there was now an atmosphere in the lock that transmitted the muted hiss of air coming in, and then, more distantly, a complex drumming sound, a long weighty chain of rhythm.

A wedge of bright blue light spilled into the lock. There was a metallic whirring noise that made Ubu's heart leap. The drumming sound was much louder. The interior hatch had begun to slide open.

Something waited beyond the hatch, outlined in the light. Ubu's pulse beat louder than the clattering door, the sound of the ship's throbbing drums.

It was, at first glance, reassuringly humanoid. About two meters tall, with two long arms and two legs, dark brown in color, a head where a human's would be. It was bent over a football-sized object that it cradled in its arms.

Letters rose crimson on Ubu's heads-up display. GREETINGS, they said. Apparently the other was holding a transmitter.

CLAN LUSTRE BIDS YOU WELCOME.

Ubu's blood ran cold as his eyes adjusted to the brightness and details of the stranger became visible.

The hands and feet were alike in each having three digits and a pair of opposable thumbs. The proportions were alike, the legs just a little thicker. There was not even the hint of a neck. The head was squared-off, almost a cube, eerily equipped with a pair of very human-looking eyes at the upper corners, dark pupils set in white eyeballs that each peered out of a wrinkled vertical slit. As the creature bent over its transmitter, Ubu could see a slight concavity on top of the head.

Drums boomed on, hardly muffled by Ubu's suit. Random noise, possibly, but Ubu thought not—there was a pattern in there somewhere, even if he couldn't quite understand it.

The creature was pointing at the transmitter with a stylus. His movements were slow, careful. At each touch of the stylus a letter jumped onto Ubu's display.

I, THIS-INDIVIDUAL, AM VOLITIONAL TWELVE.

This-individual's mouth was a flattened oval and apparently had no teeth. Something flickered in and out, as if with respiration— Ubu thought at first this was a tongue, then realized there were two of them, a ribbonlike, branchlike construction at the corner of each mouth.

I ABASE MYSELF AT MY CLUMSINESS WITH THIS DEVICE. I AM NOT YET FAMILIAR WITH ITS OPERATION.

The creature—Volitional Twelve—looked up at Ubu. Its pupils were very wide. The branchlike structures flickered in and out of its mouth. There were little bits of purple phosphorescence at the end of each branch.

My turn, Ubu thought. His lips were dry. The steel keys rattled as he tapped them.

"I am honored by your hospitality, Volitional Twelve," he said.

At the appearance of the holo letters over Ubu's head, Twelve's eyes bulged from the corners of its head and focused intently on the bright display. "I am Ubu Roy, bossrider of the human ship *Runaway*. I hope that we—" Volitional Twelve startled him by making quick jerky movements with its hands and feet. Ubu stared, then staggered on. "—that Clan Lustre and I—and *Runaway*—" Ubu halted and caught his breath, wondered what sense, if any, the translation program was making of this. Volitional Twelve continued twitching. "I hope we will have a long and continuing friendship," Ubu said.

Volitional Twelve bent busily over its transmitter. CLAN LUSTRO, spelling badly in his agitation, IOS HONORED BEYONDD ALL MAGNIFICENCE BY THE PRESENCE OF BOSSRIDER UBU'S ROY'S PERSON.

Ubu licked sweat from his upper lip. What the fuck could he say now? Volitional Twelve continued its painfully slow typing.

Ubu's heart gave a lurch as he realized that Volitional Twelve wasn't holding the stylus with his fingers, or at any rate with the fingers Ubu had noticed till now. Volitional Twelve's large, stubby digits each had a delicate, smaller finger curled inside, each nesting in a slot like a blade in a clasp knife. Intended, Ubu concluded, for delicate work.

The tapping continued. A chill ran up Ubu's spine as he watched the little fingers move.

THIS UNWORTHY AMBASSADOR IS UNPREPARED FOR SUCH AN HONOR AS THIS. DOES BOSSRIDER UBU WISH ME, THIS-INDIVIDUAL, TO RETIRE FOR FURTHER INSTRUCTION?

Ubu looked at it hopelessly. "Let's get to know each other first," he said.

Volitional Twelve began twitching again. I PLEAD THAT YOU MAY FOLLOW ME, it typed.

"Lead on," Ubu said.

Volitional Twelve pirouetted and reached out to touch the airlock door, pushed off, and moved out of sight. Ubu followed.

The corridor was oval. One end was blocked near the lock, and there was another dead end about fifteen or twenty meters farther along. Long blue phosphorescent strips were set at apparent random along its length. The walls were the same dark grey color as the ship's exterior. Drums boomed and rattled in the air. There were none of Volitional Twelve's kind in sight.

Ubu looked at his chestpack analyzer. Air pressure 1.87 millibars. Nitrogen 69 percent. Oxygen 26.333 percent. Carbon dioxide less than .1 percent. Insignificant amounts of argon and helium. Ubu could breathe it if he had to.

Methane 3 percent. Ozone .5 percent. Long-chain proteins and complex organics—the analyzer wasn't sensitive enough to report more than that—almost 1 percent. At this Ubu looked up in surprise, and his heart staggered at the sight of Volitional Twelve returning his gaze even though Twelve's back was turned.

Ubu took a deep breath, tried to settle his nerves. Volitional Twelve, he saw, had another pair of eyes set in the rear corners of its head. It could give itself binocular vision forward, aft, left, or right, or probably any combination. Useful, Ubu thought, for a weightless three-dimensional environment. He moved on.

Portals were set in the walls every five or ten feet, cross-corridors. Each of them had a thin, opaque scrim drawn across it—doors, Ubu thought, until the drumming sound grew louder as he passed one of the screens and he saw it vibrate with each beat. The membranes—some of them anyway—were drumheads or amplifiers.

Ubu noticed four darker spots on Volitional Twelve's back, arranged in a vaguely trapezoid pattern. Scales? Ubu wondered. Calluses?

Volitional Twelve checked its movement and touched one of the door screens. The membrane withdrew to the door's rim with galvanic speed, and Volitional Twelve cast itself through it with a push of its arms. Ubu followed.

The room was cube-shaped, about twenty feet in diameter, with rounded-off corners. Fluorescent strips were strewn over its surface. There was no furniture, no equipment, nothing to attract the eye. Ubu wondered if the chamber had always been like this or whether it had been carefully stripped of all it contained. Volitional Twelve spun slowly to face Ubu, the structures in its mouth fluttering rapidly.

Ubu saw four dark trapezoidal spots on Volitional Twelve's chest, the same as had been present on its back. They looked like calluses of some sort, patches of rougher skin. It bent to its transmitter again.

I TREMBLE IN AWE AT YOUR PRESENCE, BOSS-RIDER.

Ubu looked at Twelve. "At ease," he said.

Twelve led the outsider to his room in a haze of terror. Panic flooded him at the horrifying realization that Ubu was the bossrider himself, *Runaway*'s governing entity. He had expected to deal with only a volitional, or volitional-equivalent. The holy presence of an actual intelligence, a full-blown entity whose mind encompassed all history and knowledge, might well overwhelm him. Twelve knew he might be inadequate to deal with the situation, might well be ordered to dissolution either by Ubu or Beloved if he proved unsatisfactory.

Even Beloved, he suspected, might not have anticipated this. An alien intelligence on Beloved's ship! The oily flavor of the stranger, or his suit, came faintly to Twelve's palps. Beneath his fear he felt a rising anger, the urge to hurl himself at the intruding intelligence and destroy it.

Beloved's beat throbbed through him, allowed him to collect his wits. He calmed himself. Beloved had given him this task. He would do his best. And if defense were needed, a company of swiftly grown warriors waited just beyond the thick screens that had isolated him from the rest of the ship's company.

The stranger was looking about from inside his protective shell. His lips moved. As he read the words projected over the human's head, Twelve could vaguely hear sounds muffled by the shell.

"I am curious as to the composition of your vessel," the human said.

The display was a useful knowledge, Twelve thought as he read the bright letters. He would have to acquire this on behalf of Beloved.

Twelve assumed a stiff, prideful stance as he stabbed at his transmitter with his stylus. IT IS COMPOSED OF THE FINEST EXUDATE. He saw the words scroll in reverse across the interior of Ubu's transparent faceplate. The human's answer came back.

"Exudate? I do not entirely understand."

A tremor rolled through Twelve's mind. Could an actual intelligence, a bossrider, not understand these things? The thought was frightening. Could Ubu be mad? Through his agitation Twelve endeavored to frame his answer simply.

IT IS MADE OF RESIN EXUDED BY NON-VOLITIONALS.

The human took a moment to frame his reply. "I believe I understand. Humans build ship hulls primarily out of alloyed metal, though resinous compounds are used elsewhere in construction."

Relief edged cautiously into Twelve's mind. The bossrider was familiar with alternate means of building ships: that did not necessarily make him a lunatic. No doubt, Twelve thought warmly, Beloved also understood how to build metal ships, and chose to use exudate because it was more efficient.

One of the nonvolitionals on the walls leaped for the intruder. Ubu flinched and raised a hand. The nonvolitional fastened itself to his arm. Ubu peered at it.

"What is this?"

A NONVOLITIONAL ORGANISM. ITS FUNCTION IS TO GROOM THE WALLS AND INHABITANTS OF OUR SHIP. IF IT FINDS FOOD IT WILL MAKE A SOUND TO ALERT THE OTHERS TO THE SOURCE OF NOURISH-MENT.

"It is harmless?"

YES. IF YOU DO NOT WISH ITS PRESENCE, YOU MAY REMOVE IT AND THROW IT TO ONE OF THE WALLS.

The human reached for the glistening creature and gingerly removed it from his arm. The nonvolitional coiled to try to clean his fingers, but Ubu flicked it away. It tumbled across the room and struck a wall, adhering. There was a moment of silence.

"I was also curious," Ubu said, "about the drumming sound."

Another odd question. Perhaps the bossrider had other means of communicating with his servants. IT IS AN EXPRESSION OF OUR BELOVED, Twelve replied. A WAY SHE COMMUNI-CATES HER INTENTIONS TO WE-HER-SERVANTS.

"I see."

Twelve made no reply to this self-evident statement. The human's constant use of the first person, all this "I," was growing irritating. Twelve had difficulty using the word himself, even though the human's language allowed little else. It was almost as if they possessed a disgusting defiance in their solitude, their unregenerate apartness.

"I gather from the appearance of your vessel," the bossrider said, "that your ship's function is the discovery and capture of singularities."

Twelve assumed a dignified posture. OUR BELOVED HAS CHOSEN THIS TASK FOR US. BUT IT IS ONLY ONE OF MANY. CLAN LUSTRE, he lied, IS A GIANT APPARATUS WHOSE TRADE ROUTES ARE NUMBERLESS AND WHOSE MEMORY SPANS THE LENGTH OF ALL TIME.

The human absorbed the information as it crossed his display. "You represent a trading company?" he said. "As it happens, so does *Runaway*."

Triumph danced through Twelve's mind. Beloved's divine purpose would be fulfilled, and he would be her instrument!

PERHAPS, he transmitted, THIS MIGHT BE OF BENEFIT.

CHAPTER
11

UBU STEPPED OUT OF THE SHOWER AND TOOK A TOWEL FROM THE bin. He stepped into the corridor and, leaving a trail of water and elation, dried himself as he walked to the upper-level lounge. Beautiful Maria, wearing shorts and a halter, sat on the couch, her chin propped intently on bent knees as she watched the recording of Ubu's journey. Ubu tossed the towel on a chair and sat down next to her. On one of the wall-mounted fold-down tables was a plate of Mongolian beef next to a charged flask of beer. Ubu was ravenous. He bolted the food while, on the giant vid, a nearly life-sized Volitional Twelve floated in his blue glowing suite. Beloved's drumbeats sounded in his head.

Maria looked at him. "Trade," she said. "That sounds great in concept, but what do we have to offer them?"

"We have a hold half full of mining computers."

"The computers are configured to run automated robot miners," Maria said. "Which we *don't* have."

"The computers can do anything we program them to," Ubu said. "They just won't do it as efficiently as they run mining robots."

"Great. So we can sell them on some inefficient computers. What have they got to offer *us*?"

"I don't know."

"Something so valuable it saves us from our legal problems," Maria said. "Something so valuable that we can pay our lawyers and fines and debts."

"They've got it. We've just gotta figure out what it is."

"Maybe their holds are as bare as ours."

"Maybe."

"Who goes prospecting with a hold full of merchandise?" Frowning. "I want to run the recording again." Her fingers tapped instructions to the projector. The flat screen brightened with the three-dimensional image of the alien airlock. Ubu sipped beer as he watched the encounter from start to finish. Remembered the fear and elation that leaped through him, the pulsing rhythms of the alien drumming, the smell of sweat that flooded his suit . . . Other memories tweaked at his mind. The flickering of the branchlike structures in Twelve's mouth, the way its eyes focused and dilated, the odd language of twitches and gestures. If he could learn to read that, he could find an advantage.

Start with the music, he thought. He crossed the dark grey carpeting and opened the padded metal door of the locker where the instruments were stored in foam padding to keep them from being damaged during acceleration runs. Ubu took out the old imitation Sandman Q-shape in its battered plastic case, then dragged out the music sizer under it. He set up the machine and fed Beloved's drumbeats to its computer.

No wonder it had sounded, on first exposure, like random noise. There were three different patterns going on, and none of them were like anything Ubu had ever heard. The first was based on a five-beat measure; the second on a five-beat measure that went on for three measures, then switched to a three-beat measure for two measures, then back to the five-beat measure again; and the third was identical to the second except syncopated in an odd way. Everything fit together somehow, the patterns reinforcing and commenting on one another. The full scope of the drum series was apparent only after the sizer's comp set it all up in musical notation and displayed it on a holographic projection.

Ubu scanned the notation, his mind whirling. What was it supposed to mean?

"Do you believe him?" Maria asked. "Do you think they're the representatives of some huge company?"

"They might be as desperate as we are."

"Do you think they are? It would give us an advantage."

Ubu shrugged. "I can't tell. They could be worse off than we are, they could be the equivalent of a Hiliner company. I can't read his expressions." He thought for a moment. "I'll run the vid again. Note his expression and posture when he's making claims, that he's part of a huge trading combine, that sort of thing. Compare it with what we see later. Maybe I can learn to tell he's lying."

"What are those things on his chest? I can't tell."

"He's got them on his back, too. In the same places."

"Primitive eyes?"

Ubu shuddered at the thought. All Twelve needed was more eyes. "No. More like calluses, or scales. They didn't seem to have any purpose."

"Like male nipples."

He grinned. "Yeah. Male nipples."

"For someone who just learned our language, he had a very formal way of speaking."

"Translating very literally from his own speech."

Maria's eyes narrowed in thought. "You should try to talk like that."

Ubu laughed. "*Nobody* can talk like that."

"*He* does. They're very formal. Keep that in mind."

Ubu thought about it, Twelve's speech patterns scrolling across his mind like words on his heads-up display. He wondered what the formal mode of speaking meant, why Twelve seemed so reluctant to use the first person. There was something there. He'd have to work at it.

"Okay," he said. "I'll tremble in awe from time to time. Compliment Beloved on her fine-looking volitional."

"And who's Beloved?"

Ubu looked at her and grinned. "His girlfriend?"

"She's got a lot of authority."

"Their bossrider, I guess."

"She's got a *name*, Ubu. This one was just Volitional Twelve, but Beloved had a *name*."

"A god?"

Beautiful Maria pursed her lips. "Remember that Twelve almost came apart when you introduced yourself. Maybe names are very important. Maybe he was expecting you to have a number, and when you told him who you were, he realized you outranked him."

Ubu began to smile. "If that's the case, he and I are going to get along real good." He laughed. "I may get a lot of value for those inefficient computers."

Maria was still frowning, her chin still propped on her knees. "He's got to report to Beloved. She's the one we've ultimately got to deal with."

"She may not be on the ship. Assuming she exists at all."

She looked at him with dark, acute eyes. "We're assuming Beloved is female. We might be wrong."

"And we just started calling Twelve 'he.'"

She shrugged. "Narrow hips. No tits. He looks more male in outline than female."

"To us. I didn't see any outward sexual characteristics at all. Twelve could be female, neuter, bisexual—who knows?"

Maria straightened her legs, tossed her head. "Ask him next time. It might tell us something."

"It might . . . spoil the illusion. That I'm his superior."

She grinned at him, reached out, ruffled his wet blond hair. "He'll figure that out anyway."

Maria looked at Twelve's image again. "They evolved on a planet. He's got *feet*, not two sets of hands, even if they are feet with long digits and thumbs."

Ubu leaned back on the sofa, his upper arms pillowing his head. "We're gonna be famous," he said.

She leaned close to him. "We're going to jail if we're not careful."

"Even in jail we'll still be famous." Alien rhythms clattered through his mind. In spite of his weariness he wanted to leap from the couch and dance.

Maria dropped her head on his shoulder. He put his lower arm around her, drew her close. Her warmth and scent capered through his senses. Suddenly everything, every mad wish and triumph, seemed possible.

She gravely accepted his kiss. Ubu held his breath, expecting a knife to turn inside him, but it didn't.

"I missed you," she said.

"I needed to be alone."

"I wish you'd said something."

He shrugged. "Didn't know what to say."

Maria looked up at him. Her eyes were dancing. "Wanna fool around?"

He laughed. "Yes," he said. "Yes, yes, yes."

Twelve gave a cry of ecstasy as joy flooded his pleasure centers. *Glory*, he called. *Glory*. Alien memories were driven from his mind. For a long moment he hung at the end of his umbilicus, his brain and body blazing with rapture.

The pleasure faded. Twelve, his hearts thundering, tried to collect his scattered thoughts.

You have met with the outsider.

It was the bossrider in person, Twelve reported. Anger flared as he thought of an alien entity on Beloved's vessel. *Contamination!* he reported. *A foreign intelligence!*

Be at ease. Beloved's thoughts were soothing. *I have buffered Myself well. And I trust to you as My first line of defense.*

Twelve filled with pride. *Glory!* he cried.

There is little need to feel in awe of the intruders. I have analyzed their language and drawn conclusions concerning their nature. They are inferior entities indeed.

Of course. Loyally.

I have every confidence in your capabilities. You are fully their match. A roar of Beloved-induced pleasure blanketed Twelve's mind.

Glory!

We must proceed carefully.

Glory!

We must never let them know our weakness.

Glory. Glory. Glory.

Tell me everything.

* * *

Ubu hovered in the bare audience chamber, his golden holographic greetings floating above his head. His lips writhed behind his transparent faceplate. "I believe we could be of benefit to one another," reported the golden letters.

Twelve composed his body into an attitude of polite attention. "Clan Lustre desires nothing else."

"As we both represent trading companies, perhaps we might be of use to one another in the matter of trade."

Twelve waved his palps in salute. "I tremble at this revelation of your perspicacity, bossrider."

There was a pause at this. A nonvolitional jumped for Ubu and attached itself to the side of his helmet. Ubu ignored it.

"I do not know what of ours may be of use to you."

Twelve's eyes dilated in pleasure. The bossrider's statement had been unsubtle. To admit ignorance at all was to place oneself at a disadvantage. Ubu continued his message.

"I thought perhaps one of our artificial intelligence systems might prove of use to you."

Twelve referenced the alien concepts in his mind. Computers, primitive nonvolitional brains of inorganic origin. "Of what use could these be to us?" he asked.

"We have some of the finest human computers aboard our vessel, the very fastest models available. They can move data rapidly, perform swift calculations. As, for instance, the speeding of communications between Clan Lustre vessels, or performing the calculations necessary to guide a singularity ship in its leaps from place to place."

"This vessel," said Twelve, "already possesses a navigation intelligence. And our data transmission appears to be faster than yours."

"Our transmission was slowed considerably by the fact that our systems were incompatible. Our AIs may still be . . . of particular use for making interstellar jumps. Our computers allow us to make jumps of up to ten light-years with inaccuracy computed at less than one thousandth of one percent."

This was, Twelve considered, a preposterous amount of candor. Beloved was more than justified in assuming that Twelve was capable of negotiating with these grossly limited beings.

Twelve took a long moment to process Ubu's information into

terms he could understand. He was not a navigator, and he was not entirely at ease with the concepts and terminology employed; but he had participated in negotiations in which Beloved purchased new navigators or modifications for navigators already purchased, and he had a broad idea of the capabilities of those aboard Beloved's ship.

Lightning surprise darted through him. His palps trembled. Twelve took a fevered moment to recheck his calculations.

The figures, if true, were astounding. The human computers possessed greater accuracy than the latest-model navigators by a factor of almost ten. Joy and skepticism warred in his senses.

"This-individual conceives, out of friendship for *Runaway*, we might possess some slight interest in these devices," he reported.

"I am pleased that you might find our devices useful," Ubu said.

"Blessed is Beloved," Twelve agreed.

Ubu contained his laughter. Twelve's hands and feet were twitching, something Ubu had seen before, and he knew Twelve was excited. The intruder ship had made one correction burn after another as it flew to Maria the Fair, and Ubu suspected that if their singularity governors were no more accurate than their other navigation systems, they could probably use even computers configured for mining robots.

Beloved's drumming beat percussive patterns into his skull. His memories told him the drumming was different from the time before, but the pattern was too complex to follow.

Okay, he thought. Now he knew what to offer them. What was he going to get for it all?

Another of the strange little hopping creatures flung itself from the wall to his right, aimed for his helmet, but it missed him by a few inches and tumbled past the faceplate. Apparently its guidance system wasn't any better than Beloved's.

What, he thought, if everything they had to offer was as pathetic as this? He might be dealing with the morons of the Milky Way.

In that case, he thought, get *Runaway* back to civilization and sell the alien trade rights for as much as he could. He cleared his throat.

"Although *Runaway* should be more than pleased to present

the AIs to you out of our enormous regard for Clan Lustre, we nevertheless do not wish to insult Clan Lustre by offering something without valid exchange." Trapped you there, he thought.

"Your wish does you credit."

Glee bounded through Ubu. After he realized the formal nature of Twelve's speech, his mind had busied itself trying to work out a way to offer his deal in an indirect way that couldn't be refused.

Twelve worked busily with his stylus. "We can offer you cultures enabling you to grow a supply of fine nonvolitionals, each adapted to its purpose."

"I thank you for your generous offer," Ubu said, "but we already have devices that fulfill such functions, and there is also the problem of keeping your nonfunctionals alive. We may not have that capability."

Twelve's eyes dilated. His feet trembled. Ubu wondered whether this was in reaction to Ubu's turning down his offer, or to the revelation that their life-forms might not be compatible with the human environment.

"This-individuall," spelling badly again, "is distressd that he can offer little that is not based on our own intrinsic natures."

"I am certain that Beloved's resources are many." Or so he hoped.

"Glory to Beloved."

"Glory," Ubu repeated. Jesus Rice, he realized, these people can't even sell us *curios*. If he came back to civilization with a hold full of weird alien arts and crafts, at least that might be worth *something*. A bunch of little slugs adapted to keeping resinous walls free of dirt were not in high demand back home.

Maybe he could give them the AIs on consignment. Maybe they could shoot back to wherever they came from and trade them for something of value, then hustle back to Maria the Fair while *Runaway* continued its prospecting.

"Maybe we should conclude this meeting," Ubu said. "Perhaps we should give our exchange some further thought."

"The bossrider is wise."

"Glory to Beloved."

It seemed the proper polite response.

* * *

While Ubu shot across the gap between the alien ship and *Runaway*, he pointed a microwave antenna at *Runaway* and, using a frequency other than that he used for communication with the intruders, fired a blip transmission to *Runaway's* receiver dish containing his full recording of the meeting. By the time he'd gone through decontamination, taken off his suit, and showered, Maria had viewed it twice. When Ubu joined her in the lounge, her eyes were dancing.

"We've got something he wants," she said.

"Yes."

"But what do *we* want?"

Ubu grinned. "What do they have?"

She bit her lip. "We don't know. You haven't seen enough of their ship."

"They've got me well insulated. Everything goes through Twelve, and the corridor where we meet is sealed off." Ubu took a flask from the rack and stepped to the bar. Beloved's drumbeats rumbled through his mind, echoed his words.

From the galley's readouts Ubu saw that *Runaway* was running low on veal. He would have to feed the cloned meat some nutrients, generate some more. He charged the flask and joined Maria on the couch. She looked at him. "Those computers won't give the accuracy you're claiming for them. They won't be very efficient at bossing a shoot."

"They're designed for humans. I'll point that out."

"And our stim projectors won't work with them, so they won't get that edge. I assume."

Ubu threw up his hands. "We don't have spare stims anyway, so that's not a problem."

"It could be."

"We'll see."

He took the laptop keyboard from its folding rack and ordered the projector to run the meeting one more time. He needed some ideas.

Glory, glory. General Volitional Twelve chanted his Beloved's praises, waiting for her response to the latest negotiation.

Beloved's voice rang in his mind. *Do you have confidence in this claim?*

Twelve's mind lurched in surprise at the thought that Beloved did not have the answer to so critical a question. She perceived his distress and carefully soothed it. *You are my interpreter*, she said. *To keep my own mind inviolate, I must learn to trust in your impressions.*

Glory. Pride rose in Twelve at the thought of his guarding Beloved from thought contamination.

Carefully he considered the humans' claims. "Artificial intelligence" itself seemed a preposterous contradiction in terms. How could one detach an intelligence from its organic case? *This-individual does not know the answer, Beloved*, he finally confessed. *Though the humans possess a large and specialized vocabulary relating to artificial intelligence, still the claims are without foundation in my limited experience.*

And in mine. Through their neuronic link Twelve could sense the intensity of Beloved's cogitation. The power of her mind was terrifying, and he trembled.

There is a limit to the speed by which chemical means can transmit information, Beloved said. *The human computers claim to exceed this limit.*

Then the claim is nonsense. Pleasure danced in Twelve at the certainty of his answer.

Not necessarily. Consider the nature of human terminology. Artificial *intelligence implies a nonorganic basis.*

Twelve was awed by this conclusion. *This-individual is humbled at your wisdom. My concept of the outsiders' language was insufficient to perceive this.* Twelve was disturbed. That the humans possessed such unnatural abilities was powerfully unsettling.

We must find something that will prove worthy of exchange. We must test the human capability.

Glory.

You are authorized to offer the humans anything short of a child.

Shock reverberated in Twelve at this news. *Anything.* Would Beloved risk so much in pursuit of her plan?

Glory, he repeated.

Opportunity, she repeated, the grandest word of all.

To this there was no possibility of reply.

Drumming throbbed through the alien space, a different rhythm this time, less urgent but more complex. Layered. *Damn* this, Ubu thought. Twelve can receive information from Beloved this way, but I'm isolated here.

Words printed themselves across Ubu's faceplate as Twelve worked with his stylus. Twelve's movements were more assured, Ubu thought. Maybe he'd been practicing.

"Though Beloved is glorious and powerful beyond measure," Twelve reported, "the capabilities of a single Lustre ship are nevertheless limited."

"I have every confidence in the abilities of Beloved," Ubu said.

"Glory." The force of the automatic response was mitigated somewhat by Twelve's stylus-work.

"Glory."

There was a pause. A nonvolitional leaped across the room, stuck to Ubu's chestpack with a wet smacking sound that carried into Ubu's vac suit. It chirped, apparently having found something to eat. A few other nonvolitionals bounded toward him, most missing.

Twelve began to work with his stylus. I'm going to give this guy a keyboard, Ubu thought. This is agony.

"Bossrider Ubu Roy, Beloved's desire is for nothing but an exchange of value."

"Glory to Beloved." Which seemed a safe answer to this promising opening.

"Glory." Ritually. "Beloved wishes not to insult *Runaway* with an offer of insufficient value."

Better and better, Ubu thought.

"Beloved wishes to offer an inventory of her capabilities, that Bossrider Ubu Roy may indicate an appropriate choice."

Delight blazed through Ubu. "I am cognizant of the honor Beloved offers to *Runaway*," he said.

Cognizant, he thought. He'd never in his life used that word in conversation. Here it seemed natural.

Sweat poured down his nape. The circulating air had pushed

Twelve to one wall. Twelve put out a long-fingered foot and stabilized himself, then pushed off gently. He slowly moved across the room as he tapped his communicator. Ubu, with bursts from his maneuvering jets, rotated in place to face him. Twelve used first his forward pair of eyes, then his left pair, to keep Ubu in focus.

"Beloved has the capability to create many servants," Twelve reported. "There is a wide variety of nonvolitionals capable of a large variety of automatic tasks, including the synthesis of habitations and ship hulls. Nonvolitionals can maintain atmosphere, synthesize and prepare foodstuffs, build communications equipment to order, maintain and create ship systems. Photoreceptive nonvolitionals are very efficient generators of electric power. Semisentients include servants capable of handling large loads with great precision, operating ship systems, and certain types useful in war."

War, Ubu thought. So things aren't all rosy in Beloved's home sphere.

Twelve continued as he touched the opposite wall, stabilized, gently pushed off again. "Fully sentient nonvolitionals include navigators and those capable of highly refined sensing activity. Sentient volitionals include general-purpose servants such as myself, navigators for singularity jumps, maneuvering, and small craft, and servants built for war and capable of command."

Ubu considered the list. If nothing else he could return with a holdful of general volitionals and cargo movers and offer them for sale.

But this was *Runaway*'s chance for the big score, and for that Ubu needed to keep the discovery secret. No marching with a battalion of semiautonomous entities into Bezel Station.

"I should add," Twelve said, "that some of Beloved's servants are not at present available. Some of the specialized varieties are carried in embryo only, and though our ship contains some servants intended for war, we possess only the bare minimum necessary for our own defense."

"*Runaway* has no intention of aggression," Ubu said. "We decline with thanks."

"Perhaps the bossrider wishes time to consider."

Ubu thought about the richest cargoes carried by his ships over the years. Drugs were at the top of the list in terms of value-per-tonne. So was heavy, specialized machinery, including construction robots. AI systems. Semiconductor material. Sometimes profit could be made cramming syster ships and atmosphere craft in *Runaway's* cargo holds. Also prebuilt habitats for miners.

Beloved had demonstrated no capability for AI. Any craft she could build would not be configured for humans. She seemed to have scant knowledge of machinery beyond that necessary to move cargo.

In his vac suit Ubu could smell sweat and failure. There had to be something, Ubu thought. Something of value he could find in all this.

"Beloved possesses nonvolitionals capable of maintaining and regenerating the air," Ubu said. "And synthesizing it if necessary," Twelve clarified.

Fairly complex biosynthesis, then, assuming the weird organics floating around in here were considered part of the atmosphere. Ubu felt a stirring of hope.

"Can these nonvolitionals synthesize anything else?"

"We are self-sufficient in all necessary compounds."

"Ahh . . ." Ubu hesitated as he worked at the way he wanted to phrase this idea, and then laughed as his holo projector printed *AHH* in the air above his head. The dictation program wisely refrained from transcribing his laughter.

Beloved's drum pattern rang off Ubu's helmet. He could recognize that five-beat measure again, mixed with the 5-5-5-3-3 pattern, but the third line was different. Was it six?

He looked at Twelve. "If I present you with a substance, could you inform me if you are capable of synthesizing it?"

"Possibly." Twelve's reply seemed hesitant. "Can you give an indication of what manner of substances you might require?"

"Pharmaceutical compounds," Ubu said. "Used to stimulate healing, growth, neural function. Consisting of long-chain proteins, polypeptides, complex and charged molecules."

"It is possible in theory." Ubu's heart leaped. Twelve's reply was not delayed by any internal translation of the specialized terminology. Twelve's stylus tapped his communicator. "I would have to have a clearer comprehension of the structure of these pharmaceuticals before I could make proper reply. Also I grieve to report that my own knowledge of these matters is imperfect."

"I can provide samples," Ubu said.

"That will enable this-individual to provide a more concise answer, bossrider."

"Perhaps we should end this conference. I will return with samples."

Twelve's mouth structures waved bravely in the air. "My, this-individual's, mind is relieved that we will not sully the reputation of Clan Lustre in not offering gift for gift."

"Clan Lustre's reputation can never dim."

"Glory to Beloved, it is so."

Glory to Beloved, Ubu thought, *we're in business*.

CHAPTER

12

DELIGHT BRIGHTENED IN MARIA'S MIND AS SHE CONTEMPLATED A spectrum of dazzling possibilities. General Volitional Twelve, frozen in motion, hung on the flat threedee screen before her. She touched the keyboard and Twelve vanished.

Ubu stepped into the room. Complex muscles moved under his skin as he raised one arm to towel his shaggy hair. Laughing, Beautiful Maria jumped from the couch and flung herself at him.

He dropped the towel and caught her with all four arms. She wrapped her legs around him, pressed herself close. "We did it, shooter man," she cackled.

He swung her through the room in a staggering circle. Bristle scraped her cheek. "Gotta check the pharmacy," he said. "See what compounds we've got."

"Later, shooter man."

He drew back and looked at her. She could see his pulse beating in his throat, the pale, almost translucent lashes around his eyes. "Why later?"

She bent forward, nipped his lower lip with her teeth. "Celebrate first."

He gave a laugh. "Yeah," he said. "We've earned it."

Ubu carried her downspin to his new compartment, past his old abandoned room. There was a light under the old compartment's screen. Maria could hear her father's broken voice raging. "Fuckers!" Pasco roared. "They promised! Fuckers!" There were sobs in his voice.

Ubu slowed. His grip on her turned hard. "We had it all *arranged!*" Pasco cried. "We were gonna *do* it!" Maria watched Ubu's eyes go dull.

Pasco began to cry. Ubu walked out of earshot with stiff machine strides. Maria reached out, gently touched his hair. "That was long ago," she said.

"Yeah."

"What went *wrong?*" Pasco's wail, fading with distance and years.

His face a mask, Ubu walked past his new compartment and stepped into Maria's room. He reached behind with one arm to close the screen against Pasco's indistinct cries. Maria dropped her bare feet to the floor, felt the furze of carpet against her soles. She kissed him lightly.

"Things are different now," she said. "We've solved it. Got it licked."

"Yes." His face working. Trying to let something out.

"I wish he was here," Ubu said.

"Me, too."

"It was despair that killed him. Knowing he couldn't change things."

She pressed her cheek to his. Sadness fluttered in Maria's heart like a torn curtain flying in a cold grey wind. "It's time to stop mourning him, Ubu." Trying to keep her voice kind.

"I wish I could."

"The way he keeps coming in and out can't be making it any easier." She tugged gently on his hair and drew his head back so she could look at him. "I could try to glitch him out of the computers. He was a good programmer, but he can't hide in there forever. Not from me."

His eyes were stubborn. "I don't know. He wanted to be what he is."

"I could try to dump him in a file, keep him there. That way he wouldn't keep surprising us. And if you wanted to see him, you could call him up."

Ubu's hands slid indecisively over her back. "I guess," he said. "You could do that if you wanted to."

Maria kissed him. "In my copious spare time."

"Yeah." His arms coiled around her. Her breath went out of her in a soft rush. She could feel tension ebbing slowly out of his body.

He looked at her. His eyes were grave. "Turn off all the holos," he said.

"Yes," she said. "I will."

This is all they desired?

Duplicate biochemical synthesis. Yes, Beloved.

Their capabilities must be almost nonexistent.

Yes, Beloved.

The humans are crude.

Beloved is wise.

We shall absorb them into Us and be the greater.

Glory to Beloved.

Tell them to delay. I wish to grow an analyzer in your compartment.

"I want to see them myself, shooter man."

"Next time." Ubu attached the first-aid kit to his chestpack.

"Yeah." She tied his hair back with a piece of elastic. "They'll probably think I'm some kind of nonvolitional."

Awkward in his vac suit, Ubu bent to scratch the cat that was padding slow figure-eights around his legs. "I wonder what they'd make of Maxim?"

"He's not a nonvolitional, either."

"Wouldn't take them long to work that out." Ubu stroked the white, uplifted head, then straightened and reached for his helmet. Chestpack readouts reflected in Maria's dancing eyes. He sealed the helmet, stepped into the lock, gave a wave. The inner hatch slid shut.

Suit system readouts and checklists scrolled across his inner faceplate. All green.

The outer hatch opened and he fired his maneuvering jets. Beloved's ship lay like an insect, black chitin and curving mandibles, against the cool green of Maria the Fair. Excitement began to hum through Ubu's nerves.

The air nozzle hissed somewhere under his chin. His heartbeat and respiration were very loud. Somewhere behind the sound, obscured beneath the surge of his blood, there began a distant complex throbbing, the percussion of Beloved rising in his mind. Beating time to his thoughts, making him ready. When Ubu cycled through and the inner hatch rattled upward, Beloved's genuine pulse rose behind Ubu's remembered rhythm, the two climbing together like a pair of twining vines. Ubu gave a laugh. Nothing was going to go wrong today.

To Ubu's surprise, Twelve led him to a different chamber, a spherical room smaller than the first. From the far wall grew a nest of pale grey tethers, each thick around as Ubu's thumb, that waved in the faint breeze like the dangling stingers of a jellyfish in a surging, invisible tide. Another object stood from the wall as if it had grown there, something that looked like a pink, partly opened flower. Twelve drifted across the room to the bloom of tethers, turned, faced Ubu. Some of the tethers moved over Twelve's chest, held him gently in place. Twelve ignored them and picked at his radio with his stylus.

"This-individual will achieve fusion with Beloved. Respected Bossrider Ubu Roy, please place samples of your substances upon Beloved's analysis organ, and I will relay Beloved's conclusions."

Analysis organ, Ubu thought. Right.

He jetted toward the flowerlike object, braked, hovered in front of it. The petals glistened with a shiny coating. Ubu opened the velcro flaps on the first-aid kit and reached for a vial. He glanced at Twelve and froze. One of the grey tethers had attached itself between Twelve's shoulders, was pulsing as if somehow propelling fluid from Twelve to the cluster. A chill hand touched Ubu's neck as he realized that the tether had penetrated Twelve's skin. As the tether twisted, Ubu could see it raising Twelve's dark grey skin as if it was rearranging Twelve's spinal structure to suit itself.

Beloved's rhythmic drumming altered slightly. Twelve's eyes went unfocused, stared in different directions. A glob of drool drifted absently from Twelve's mouth as the branchlike structures hung slack.

Sickness swam in Ubu's belly. He looked away. The sound of the stylus tapping, transmitted faintly through his suit, brought his attention back. Twelve hung at the end of his tether, his eyes focused again, his attention apparently returned.

"This-individual has fused with Beloved. The respected bossrider is requested to offer his samples."

Fused with Beloved. The nest of umbilici was Beloved, then, or a part of her. Ubu fought down nausea.

Ubu looked uncertainly at Twelve, then at the budlike object. He reached into the first-aid kit strapped to his chestpack and withdrew from it what, volume for volume, was probably the most valuable thing aboard *Runaway*.

The vial was tiny and Ubu had difficulty holding it in his gloved fingers. It contained a few ounces of Orange Seventeen, a complex neurohormone the function of which was to stimulate neuronic connections within the forebrain. A full course of treatment could raise intelligence between thirty and forty percent, but the hormone was difficult to synthesize, even more difficult to stabilize, and required continued small maintenance doses in order to maintain elasticity and efficiency within the new neural connections. Both Ubu and Beautiful Maria had taken the treatments, and their dwindling supply of the hormone was a treasured, irreplaceable possession.

Ubu activated the vial, touched its controls, readied a small dose. Twelve eddied in his peripheral vision. Carefully, Ubu reached out toward the budlike object.

The bud uncoiled and, with a silent, efficient movement, reached out for Ubu. Terror seized Ubu as he tried to leap back, succeeded only in thrashing in his suit.

Bile burned in Ubu's throat. His heart thundered louder than Beloved's drums. The budlike structure waited, glistening, its petals extended.

"Analysis organ" was an apt description, he realized: the thing was budlike only in form. It wasn't even of vegetable matter.

The thing was made of flesh. It was alive.

Ubu gasped for air. His suit perceived his panicked state and increased the percentage of oxygen in his environment, preparing him for flight or battle. His mind swam.

Give Beloved what she wants, he thought. He tried to control the trembling in his hand as he pushed the vial forward. A petal offered itself like a wet pink tongue. Ubu touched the vial to the spongy surface and pressed the trigger. A minute amount of neurohormone was deposed on its surface.

The organ-flower silently withdrew into itself, the bud refolding. Ubu fought down his panic. With shaking fingers he managed to stuff the vial back into its pouch.

Slowly his pounding heart eased. Letters rolled across his faceplate as he heard Twelve's tapping stylus.

"Polypeptide. 203 amino acids. Single chain."

Ubu turned to see Twelve floating at the end of his elastic tether. The umbilicus had ceased to pulsate; Twelve's eyes regarded him with cool disinterest. Ubu cleared his throat. Eddies of fear and disgust etched his words with acid.

"Is it the ever-glorious Beloved addressing me?"

"Beloved speaks to me," Twelve reported. "I translate her words for you."

Get this over with, Ubu thought. Then get out of here. "Does Beloved believe she can create this polypeptide?"

Twelve's stylus did not hesitate. "In any quantity."

It took a few moments for the significance of this answer to shoulder its way past Ubu's ebbing haze of fear. In the end he could only repeat Twelve's words. "In any quantity?"

"Given a sufficient source of hydrogen and nitrogen."

Ubu gave a short, disbelieving laugh. "Right, then," he said. "How long to make a tonne?"

"It will require Beloved forty to fifty hours to create the appropriate chemical assembler. Once the assembler is built, a single assembler can create a tonne of this polypeptide in approximately four to six hours." There was a slight hesitation, then Twelve tapped his transmitter again. "This-individual apologizes for the imprecision of his answers. Beloved's projections are uncertain as she cannot predict precisely whether her attention will be needed elsewhere."

Ubu's mind swam. He gazed at Twelve in stunned comprehension. "The estimates will do very well," he said. He reached blindly for the first-aid pack. "I have some other samples."

"Proceed, reverend bossrider." The analysis organ unfolded again. Ubu felt his nape prickle.

Ubu's samples were all compounds in the public domain, all having been marketed for over the last ten standard years. Anyone could manufacture them. His second sample was a complex protein used to speed repair in contractile tissue, a medicine particularly useful in burn cases. Beloved could produce a tonne of it in less than an hour. The third sample was a synethetic messenger RNA used in genetic engineering. The stuff was frighteningly expensive: Ubu had only the residue left in the vial from Pasco's assembly of Maria's genes. Beloved had little difficulty with that one: her minutes per tonne were down to fourteen.

Ubu's fourth sample was Blue Eighteen, a neurotransmitter that resulted in improved brain and nerve function, a more efficient and complex form of the stuff that Marco de Suarez was always firing up his nose. Supposedly there were businessmen in the Hiline companies who sat at their desks all day with Blue Eighteen going into their arms through a permanently implanted intravenous drip. The price, Ubu thought, was going to go down.

He placed the vial on Beloved's extended pink tongue and pressed the trigger. The sampling bud retracted partway, then stopped. Its leaves trembled. Ubu looked up at Twelve. Suddenly Beloved's drumbeat staggered to a halt.

Twelve's body convulsed as if struck by lightning. The stylus went flying. His eyes popped from their corners, his mouth structures flailed wildly. He bent to the transmitter and, with great effort, painfully hammered out a message with a blunt finger.

RUN BACK TO SHIP.

"What's happening?" Ubu said. His words vanished in an onslaught of sound—Beloved's drums were back, thundering a furious message so urgent that Ubu felt it as a kick in the chest. Twelve's last vestige of control vanished. He flailed at the end of his tether, spittle flying from his mouth as he swiped at Ubu with his feet. Twelve's eyes stared, pupils contracted to nothing. Ubu watched in stunned surprise as Twelve reared back with the transmitter and flung it with all his strength. Ubu raised a pair of hands. The transmitter cracked painfully against a forearm and bounded away.

Run back to ship. Right.

Ubu fired directional jets and rocketed from the chamber. Twelve reached for him with clawed hands and feet as Ubu raced past. Ubu avoided him, shot through the doorway, smashed into the wall opposite the opening. He absorbed his momentum with his arms, bounced, fired his jets again. Hammerblow drumbeats crashed against his deafened senses. He arrested his motion before diving into the airlock and saw that the wall near the airlock, the resinous grey material that blocked the passageway, was coming down before a bruising onslaught of Beloved's servants. Through the widening hole he caught a horrifying glimpse of creatures encased in armor like crabs—many arms, slitted furious eyes, weapons waving . . . something resembling a segmented tentacle shot from the cracking wall, reaching for him. There were barbs on the end, each glistening with a drop of liquid, poison or acid. The tentacle wasn't long enough. Ubu powered into the airlock and bounced against the far wall. His teeth rattled with the impact. There was the sound of rapid gunfire from behind him, bullets whining off resinous walls.

Ubu looked desperately for lock controls and saw the circular fluorescent plate he'd seen earlier. He punched it repeatedly and, with a rattle, the inner hatch rolled down. Beloved's drumming grew dimmer. Ubu could hear his trip-hammer heart layered over Beloved's beats. Pumps began to throb.

A blow thudded into the hatch behind him, then a rain of blows. Beloved's soldiers were trying to tear the barrier down as they had the blocked passage. Ubu screamed in fear and knew there was nothing he could do but drift in the airlock until the lock finished its cycle.

Sound faded as air emptied from the chamber. Ubu could hear nothing but his breathing and thundering heart. The hatch vibrated to blow after blow. Somehow the knowledge that the hatch's demolition was proceeding in silence made it even more horrifying.

The outer hatch rolled open. Ubu fired himself through the opening, his jets jammed full on. He clawed at his helmet, found the microwave antenna, pointed it manually at *Runaway*. His words came at a near-shriek.

"Get up maneuvering power. We've gotta get out of here."

"Do we have a problem?" Maria's voice was infuriatingly calm. Ubu wanted to hit something as rage boiled up inside him.

"We're at war, damn it! As soon as I'm in the hatch, fire our ass out of here!"

"Roger, bossrider." Comprehension of the emergency seemed to be dawning.

"Jesus Rice!" Ubu couldn't tell whether his words were prompted by anger, terror, or a sudden onslaught of piety.

Runaway grew larger. Ubu didn't want to decelerate for the hatch, had to force himself to grip the controls and fire the retros.

He wished *Runaway* had weapons aboard. The closest thing was a welding torch.

Runaway swallowed him. The outer hatch rolled down, and sudden gees kicked him hard.

CHAPTER

13

CLAN LUSTRE OFFERS FERVENT APOLOGIES. CLAN LUSTRE BEGS THE FORGIVENESS OF RESPECTED BOSSRIDER UBU ROY.

"They *say* they're sorry," Maria said, looking at the screen.

"Be crazy. Jesus Rice."

CLAN LUSTRE BEGS TO OFFER EXPLANATION. BOSSRIDER UBU ROY'S SAMPLE PEPTIDE IS ONE OF CLAN LUSTRE'S CHEMICAL ATTACK SIGNALS. THE PEPTIDE HAS NOW BEEN METABOLIZED BY OUR BELOVED AND RENDERED HARMLESS. AGAIN WE BEG *RUNAWAY'S* PARDON FOR OUR MISUNDERSTANDING.

Ubu wiped sweat from his eyes. His hand trembled. *"Misunderstanding!* They tried to *kill* me."

Runaway had swung out on a wide orbit, had been programmed into a random evasion pattern. Its strongest search radars were looking for incoming missiles. Ubu and Beautiful Maria were strapped in before the nav and piloting boards, ready for further action.

Beloved's vessel had not altered its position.

168

"Let's look at your recording," said Beautiful Maria.

"It's still in the camera. In the airlock."

"Go get it. I'll watch Beloved on the radars and make sure she doesn't pull any tricks."

CLAN LUSTRE OFFERS SINCEREST REGRETS. PLEASE REPLY.

"*Look* at that." Ubu felt the stridency in his own voice. "They're just trying to get us closer so they can finish us."

CLAN LUSTRE SUGGESTS AN AMENDMENT IN PROCEDURE. BOSSRIDER UBU ROY SHOULD DELIVER SAMPLES AND INSTRUCT VOLITIONAL TWELVE IN THEIR USE. THE BOSSRIDER SHOULD THEN WITHDRAW. IF SAMPLES SHOULD PROVE DANGEROUS, HE WILL NOT BE HARMED.

"Do you *believe* that?" Ubu waved his arms.

PLEASE REPLY, *RUNAWAY*.

Beautiful Maria frowned at the communications board. "I want to see the video."

PLEASE REPLY, *RUNAWAY*.

Maria reached for the keyboard. Ubu stared at her.

"You're not going to answer, are you?"

"Yes." Firmly.

"Jesus Rice!"

Her glance was cold. Determined. "What choice do we have?"

Ubu's furious reply stuck helplessly in his throat. He had no answer to give her.

Runaway asked for further information, which arrived promptly. Beautiful Maria viewed Ubu's video of the meeting and pointed out that nothing on the video showed anything to contradict Clan Lustre's version of events.

"That analysis organ," Maria said. "That's Beloved. So is that nest of tentacles. She *is* the ship."

"I know."

"Or she's infiltrated it. Or built it around herself."

"Same thing."

"Your analysis of the air in there showed all these complex organics floating around in the atmosphere. Part of their communication must be chemical. You hit them with something so strong that not even Beloved could control her reaction. Everyone went berserk."

"I know, I *know*. You don't have to tell me." Ubu jumped from the control cage, took a few angry steps. "You want me to go back, I know."

"I'll do it. You said I could do the next one."

Ubu thought about that. His fingers beat agitated rhythms against his flanks. He realized it was one of Beloved's patterns, and his fingers froze.

"If I didn't go," he said, "it might . . . make them think I didn't trust them."

"You don't."

"We can't deal if we don't trust them. So I'll do this one. You can do the next one."

She looked at him. Her face was masklike. "I don't mind. I'll do it."

Ubu remembered the long barbed tentacle reaching for him, its needles tipped with acid. He thought about it coiling around Maria, piercing her while she screamed, while armored soldiers boiled out of corridors.

The soldiers had been there all along, he realized. He wondered what else might be inside Beloved's hull.

He took a breath.

"I'll go," he said.

Maria's face softened. "Thank you," she said. "I really didn't want to."

"Neither do I. But bossriders gotta take the bad with the good." She smiled. "Lucky for me."

"Maybe I'll find a chemical that will make them love us forever." Grinning. His grin faded as he saw Maria's expression turn serious.

"Do you think we could?" she asked.

Ubu's nerves hummed as he considered the idea. "We'll see," he said.

Ubu took a keyboard from stores, stripped the modular memory out of it so that it could be used only as a dumb terminal, and cabled it to a transmitter he built out of spare parts so that it would broadcast only on 1427.4 megahertz. He stuck the keyboard and transmitter together with adhesive, then added an old battery pack that would last maybe a month before it needed recharging.

Maria found a touch-typing program in *Runaway's* data store. She would broadcast it to Beloved's ship after Ubu delivered the communications unit.

Ubu was sick of the length of time it took Twelve to pick out messages with his stylus.

Beloved's strobes exploded ahead of Ubu, brightening the dark surface of the ship. There was a deep fear in him, moving in Ubu's bowels like the slow wave of a subsonic. His vac suit felt hot, confining. His body itched as nervous twitches were damped by the unwieldy skin of the suit. He kicked up the air cooler, felt a little relief.

Blazing strobes imprinted themselves on his vision as he entered the lock. He pressed the entry plate; the outer hatch dropped. Terror prickled the hair on his arms. He panted for each breath.

Sound returned: Beloved's drums thudding in counterpoint to the beating airpumps. Ubu blinked sweat from his eyes, pictured Beloved's plated soldiers jammed in the hatch in their eagerness to reach him, the swift violence, the scarlet, lonely death . . .

The inner hatch rattled open. In the cold blue light Ubu saw only Twelve, hanging inverted in the corridor while tapping painfully with his stylus.

"My apologies for the circumstances of our last meeting, respected bossrider."

Ubu licked salt from his lips. "S'okay," he said. "Could happen to anyone."

I have completed analysis of the new samples. The humans will be pleased with the results.

Twelve hung from his umbilicus with Ubu's keyboard strapped across his front. Ubu's sample case was in one hand.

Glorious is Beloved, he said.

You must now negotiate for their artificial intelligence.

Glory. Twelve's palps fluttered as Beloved touched his pleasure centers.

We must not only have a human AI for ourselves, we must have others to sell.

Glory, Beloved.

But ours must be better than the others.

Twelve warmed to Beloved's strategy. *Of course, Beloved,* he agreed.

In the meantime, Beloved said, *you will practice your typing.*

Twelve was only mildly surprised when *Runaway* announced that Bossrider Ubu Roy would not be coming to the next meeting, but rather another human called Beautiful Maria. Once the protocols had been established, Twelve reasoned, a general volitional would of course be sent to handle the details. A governing entity such as Ubu would not find the matter worth his time.

Twelve was relieved. Dealing with an independent sentience, even one as limited as Ubu, had kept him forever on the edge of terror. Afraid that the last mistake might destroy him, Twelve worried he would not be as effective at bargaining as might otherwise be the case.

The prospect of meeting Beautiful Maria gave him fewer anxieties. A *maria,* he assumed, was a type of volitional; *beautiful* would be his subclass. He had probably been made "beautiful," whatever that meant in human terms, in order to increase his value as a negotiator—humans who encountered him were doubtless intended to be distracted by his aesthetic qualities, and their concentration would suffer. Twelve had no worries on that score.

Twelve had only one definition of beauty: that which pleased and served Beloved.

In the event, Beautiful Maria looked much like the bossrider: hair and eyes darker, hips wider, and two fewer arms, but otherwise the same nonspecialized human form. Twelve gathered that humans didn't vary much. In any case he didn't find himself moved by his beauty, if that's what it was. Perhaps the beauty was hormonal in nature, and his protective suit masked it.

Negotiations opened formally, precisely. Beautiful Maria offered an artificial intelligence capable of guiding the ship through singularity jumps, and suggested that fifteen hundred tonnes of the first sample would be adequate payment. Twelve began to dicker. And then a disturbing realization swept through him.

Beautiful Maria was *female*.

Twelve was appalled. Femaleness seemed rightly to be a thing reserved for Beloved, for a sentience and near-deity: the idea of a general-purpose female was faintly blasphemous. Even worse was the notion that the female Maria was outranked by the male dominant intelligence. Twelve felt himself begin to tremble. He willed his mind closed, tried to wall off the unsettling realization. Perhaps Beautiful Maria was sterile.

He would try to maintain that comforting notion.

"We find the notion of an artificial intelligence quaint," he typed. "It is possible that we might be able to take other units in order to exploit the curiosity market."

Even though he was a bit clumsy and made frequent mistakes, communication was much faster on his new keyboard. The keys weren't quite sized to his inner fingers, but his dexterity was improving.

Beautiful Maria's mouth moved behind her transparent face-plate. Twelve read the instantaneous print translation above her head. He was glad he did not have to comprehend their speech: reading the translation slowed down the speed of the negotiations, and that allowed him to better compose his thoughts.

"You appreciate, I'm sure, that we've been speaking of hardware only," said Maria.

Apprehension began to flutter in Twelve's mind. He hadn't appreciated this at all.

"Twelve's a chump." Maria, her skin flushed from her shower as she padded through the galley, accepted a plate of pot-stickers from Ubu and lifted the steamer lid to reveal stuffed dumplings. The smell of garlic rose like an airy blessing.

"I let him talk me down to nine hundred tonnes for the first AI. Then I mentioned that the software was extra. He wondered if we have any way to contain the stuff, and of course we don't. Then I mentioned that the software wasn't very useful without instruction. So in exchange for the instruction, Beloved will build containers of the 'finest sterile exudate,' whatever that is, and to our specifications so we can empty them with standard equipment once we get past the Edge. And then, after I pointed out that the software was duplicatable and that they'd only have to buy it once, we worked out two thousand tonnes for the software."

"Tonnes of what?" Ubu asked. He spooned dumplings out of the steamer. Maxim brushed himself hungrily against Ubu's shins.

"Tonnes of anything we want. Except for Blue Eighteen. We don't wanna be around that stuff."

Ubu looked at her. Admiration stirred in him. "A good deal."

"If we stow the cargo properly, our holds will take a little over twenty-eight thousand tonnes." Maria grinned. She dropped Maxim a pot-sticker. "At the price we agreed on for the AIs, they'll end up owing us a couple thousand tonnes they can deliver next time we meet."

"Careful. That's hot."

Maria hastily dropped a dumpling on her plate and sucked a burned finger. "This is gonna be the richest cargo in history. And they're giving it to us for junk. Beloved isn't very smart."

"I wonder if they're saying the same about us?"

She kissed him. Red chiles stung his lips. "Twelve hinted at something. I think he might be trying to work out a way to build delays into the software. Or make their primary more efficient."

"So they'd have an edge over the competition."

"Right."

He picked up a pot-sticker on his fork, stirred it in the chile sauce, bit, smiled. "Point out that on our next exchange we can sell them faster machines."

"You already told them *these* were the fastest computers in existence."

"I told them they were the fastest computers *available*."

"Smart. I didn't notice that."

"Neither did they."

"Okay," Ubu said. He charged a flask of beer. "We capitalize everything with the drugs. Once we've got a few cargoes delivered to civilization, we can start delivering other services. Prebuilt habitats, air-generating systems—maybe even ship hulls grown to order."

"We can't keep it secret that long."

"I've thought about that, and I think we at least have a chance. We get Beloved to grow the stuff for us, then she leaves it in orbit around a certain star. We'll send one of our contractors to pick it up. He won't even *see* Beloved's ship. If he guesses we've made contact with nonhumans, he won't know where to look. In the meantime, he's making a great profit just by keeping his mouth shut."

Maria thought for a moment. "It might work."

"If we play it right."

Carrying plates, Ubu and Maria began walking to the lounge. Maxim, disappointed, trailed in dwindling hope.

Can we trust them?

I cannot say, Beloved. I can only follow your counsel and guidance.

Their claims are beyond Our experience. And they ask for so little in exchange for their apparatus. Yet, if they try to cheat Me, they are preposterously naive in the nature of their attempt.

Perhaps the value of their devices will become self-evident once we acquire them.

Still, the creation of these chemicals will strain our nitrogen reserves. I would prefer that something of value arise from this effort.

There was a moment of silence from Beloved. Twelve acquired the impression of remote, formidable, remorseless thought, rolling through faraway reaches like distant thunder. *I require further information.*

Glory.

You will gain permission to travel on Runaway.

Alarm clamored in Twelve's mind. His hearts lurched. He raised hands and feet in a warding posture.

I am prostrate, Beloved. I am unworthy of this great commission.

You have My trust. You are proven capable of dealing with the outsiders.

Beloved's praise did little to quell the distress that wrung Twelve's bones. He would be separated from Beloved. Cast among predatory intruder species. At the mercy of the independent sentience Ubu. And exposed at every moment to contaminant thought and the unholy disunion of the entire human species.

What if they are hostile, Beloved?

You will die as befits one of My servants.

Glory, glory. He chanted the words, both mentally and aloud, while trying to calm himself. Panic shrieked and shivered in his veins. He wanted to curl into a foetal ball and let the threatened madness come.

You will attempt to discover the size of Runaway's *commercial enterprise. I do not trust the claim that they are part of a greater whole.*

Yes, Beloved.

You will observe the workings of Runaway, *its crew, its artificial intelligences.*

Yes, Beloved.

You will discover whether there are any other humans, other than those aboard Runaway, *with whom I might deal in the future.*

Yes, Beloved.

You will make these observations, and you will report the results to Me.

Glory, glory.

Terror still roiled in his mind. He knew that on his return, he might be so thoroughly infected by humanity that Beloved would order his dissolution in order to protect Home.

He was, he reminded himself, Beloved's instrument. If dissolution was her intent, then his dissolution was just.

Pleasure flooded his senses at this idea. Beloved was rewarding him for the correctness of his uncontaminate thought.

But even as his nerves pranced in galvanic joy, his panic still beat within him, a subdued terror running his mind like a motif through one of Beloved's rhythms, an endless, painful whisper of subdural fear. And behind the ecstatic haze of artificial pleasure, Twelve could sense Beloved's displeasure in his fear; and he could discern also the working of her mind as Beloved plotted the consequences of his fear—and his fate—with cold, patient, and remorseless calculation.

"Agreed. Eight hundred thirty each for all the rest."

"The next shipment to contain more efficient AIs."

"Agreed."

The scarcely noticed words rolled across Beautiful Maria's vision. She had been in her vac suit for over three hours and her vision of Nirvana had narrowed until it encompassed only the ability to scratch thoroughly behind her right knee, beneath her left breast, between her shoulder blades . . .

"Beloved will introduce a navigator into this environment," Twelve reported. "The appropriate attachments will be grown between your computer and the ship's systems. You will instruct the navigator in the use of AI."

"Agreed." Which meant hours, Maria thought, teaching computer systems while confined to a vac suit, using the heavy-duty steel-alloy keyboards designed for airless spaces and gloved fingers . . . At this realization, the itch between her shoulder blades began to glow with a transcendent fury.

More letters paraded across her vision. "This-individual hopes to be able to increase the efficiency of our communication."

Maria licked her lips. The itching was driving her mad. "That would be beneficial," she said.

"Humans use audible speech for personal conversation. So do the servants of Beloved."

A sliver of interest penetrated the gauze of Maria's agony. This was news to her. "I have not heard you speak."

Twelve's little inner fingers busily tapped his keys. "There has not been the necessity."

"It would require a very elaborate programming job to create software capable of translating Melange," Maria said. "We aboard *Runaway* do not possess the necessary capability. Not right now anyway."

Twelve's body was turned slightly in relation to Maria, allowing him to view her with three of his eyes. Maria's own eyes ached as they tried to return his glance, unable to decide which pupil to connect with.

"My species have many different bodily forms," Twelve said. "We cannot communicate using gesture or expression, only sound. Therefore, our sound-generating organ is very flexible, capable of great subtlety and discrimination. I will demonstrate."

Rattling through Maria's vac suit came a high drumming, layering itself on top of Beloved's throbbing. The new sound seemed to be coming from Twelve rather than Beloved. Then it began to vary in tempo, in intensity. The sound of a distant siren added to the mix. The drumming faded and vowel sounds began to form, *ohhhh, ouwww, oieeee*, still with the siren warbling in the background.

Surprise rang through Maria like a bell, and she gave a brief cackle of delight. The sounds weren't coming from Twelve's mouth, she saw, but rather from his head. The slight concavity atop his head was vibrating like the diaphragm in an amplifier, producing the succession of sounds.

Bow! Pai! Keee! Maria thought of comic-strip balloons, the sounds of heroic violence as fist connected to jaw, as fast-homer bullets sizzled off laminate armor. The siren noise ended. *Mmmmaaaah. Mmmmoiii.* Twelve continued typing as the noises bounded from his head.

"I am trying to present an impression of the flexibility of my speech organ." *Zoou. Zohhh.* "Though I do not have complete confidence in my ability to imitate all Melange speech sounds, I believe we can attempt useful approximations for those sounds of which I am incapable." A deeper drumming began, kettledrums rather than snares, the pitch varying. Beneath it there rose a growl like increasing feedback.

Dai. Deeee.

Maria was enchanted by the display. She listened till Twelve finished his demonstration. "Your speech is certainly flexible," she said. "But in order to learn to speak like us, you would have to spend hundreds of hours learning how to pronounce Melange like we do."

"I would wish to spend this time."

"We meet only for a few hours per day. It would take months."

Consciousness began to return to Maria's body. The itch behind her knee was narrowing in focus, increasing in intensity. She bent to scratch herself there—here in a pressurized environment, maneuvering in the vac suit was much easier than it would be if the suit were ballooned in a vacuum—and she managed just barely to drive her fingers deep into the slick nonporous suit material and reach the precise point of burning agony. Bliss exploded beneath her nails. In her concentration on this endeavor Maria almost missed Twelve's message.

"I would like to request permission to move to *Runaway* for the purpose of language instruction, and share your next journey with you."

Maria straightened in surprise. Twelve hung in his blue heaven, regarding her with three eyes. Maria stumbled through her reply. "I—I will have to discuss this with Bossrider Ubu."

"I understand."

"I will bring an answer soon."

"We are agreed."

The itch redoubled in intensity. Maria, sweat dotting her forehead, decided it was time to bring the meeting to a close.

Ubu made ferenc vindaloo for dinner. By the time Maria had showered, covered herself with a blizzard of talc, and brought her dinner into the lounge, Ubu had played the recording to its finish.

"He wants to come with us." Ubu seemed amused by the idea. "You think he'll stand out in the zero-gee habitat at Infix?"

"We'd have to keep him hidden." She settled on a chair, put her bulb of alljuice down on the chair arm.

Ubu tossed up one set of hands. "Where? There are gonna be police and Navy all over the ship, I bet."

"Put him in a closet. Tell him not to move. We can tell everyone he's a special-effects hype robot or something."

Ubu laughed. "Be serious. They'll take one good look at him and—"

"No one's gonna *want* to look too closely at him, Ubu. We can do it."

"Why run the risk?"

Maria raised the vindaloo to her lips, felt intense heat still rising, put down her fork. "Because if we have to," she said, "we can prove that we met an alien species out here. We can prove we didn't steal our cargo, that we came by it legitimately. And we may *have* to prove that, Ubu. We may have to stand a Navy investigation."

He looked at her. "You think?"

"Be knowing, Ubu."

He thought for a moment. "We got another problem. Contamination."

"Yeah."

"One of our chemicals made them berserk, and all by accident. That shows our body chemistry has enough in common so that we might be in some danger. What are our various microfauna going to do to each other? Twelve could give us a plague just by spitting. And he could be allergic to—who knows what? Cat hair, maybe." He grinned. "Maybe cat hair will turn him into a monster. Like in a hype. Maybe he'll kill us all."

"We're gonna have to find out sooner or later."

"I was hoping not to be the experimental animals in this situation."

Maria took a deep breath. "If we're going to expose people to the plague, it's only fair we expose ourselves first."

Ubu scowled. "The *hell* with those other people. You're the one I care about."

There was a moment of silence. Maria stubbornly drove her fork into a piece of ferenc. "I'm volunteering, Ubu."

Ubu didn't answer.

"Did you hear?" Blowing on the ferenc, tasting it. Delicate aerial bones crunched beneath her molars.

"Yeah." Ubu gave a long sigh. "Sure would make things easier not to have to keep in our suits all the time."

Maria smiled and scratched the back of her knee. Talc dusted her fingertips. "I was thinking that."

"Let's bring Twelve over here. Expose him to *our* air first. If he folds up and dies, we'll know we've got problems."

"Sounds fair."

He ran fingers through his shaggy hair. "We're getting deep into this. Real deep."

"Yes."

"And we're gonna get deeper."

She grinned at him. "This the first time this has come to your attention, shooter man?"

Ubu sighed. "Not exactly. I just never expected the big score would involve this much *work*."

"You love it. Admit it."

He smiled. "Yes. Guess I do."

"It's gonna come to an end, though. Someday it's gonna get so complicated we can't hide it all."

He absorbed this, nodded. "I'll be ready."

"I hope so."

"Yeah." His expression turned calculating. "Me, too."

Twelve appeared in *Runaway*'s dorsal airlock in an ill-fitting vac suit that looked as if it had been stitched together by demented mice. He took off the suit and floated for several hours in the cargo bay that contained the AIs, conversing with Beautiful Maria, absorbing her words together with the holographic translation. Neither finished their conversation any the worse.

Ubu and Maria moved the AI and its tackle to Beloved's ship in a series of shifts. Beloved had nonvolitionals aboard that could be programmed to infiltrate the walls of the ship and excrete electric cables of purest gold—inefficient compared to the superconducting glassware on *Runaway*, but sufficient for the human computers' needs. Power was provided through another connector, fitted through a stepdown transformer that altered the voltage to human norms.

While Beloved's nonvolitionals were invisibly spinning their connectors, Maria fitted the AI with a fuel-cell power source and, happy to bound free of her vac suit, was introduced to Navigator Four.

Four was shaped like a tick, broad and flat, with six short arms, no legs, and a smooth, wide, shiny head that fused perfectly with his body. He had two eyes, one on either side of his head, and both were weak. His glossy ebony frame was heavily muscled to withstand high-gee stresses, he had hyperefficient circulatory and respiratory systems, and his upper body as well as his head contained the extra brain matter necessary to perform swift calculation of course and direction. Front and back, Four's body displayed the same four callosities as that of Twelve—more evidence for Maria's male-nipple theory. Four's digestive apparatus was almost nonexistent: he was followed by a nonvolitional, something shaped like a drawstring sack on four legs, who would eat his food for him, digest it, then regurgitate it into Four's mouth. When working, Four was connected through a half dozen umbilici to the ship's singularity and drive systems, the ship's sensors, and Beloved. A nonvolitional would force-feed a pure oxygen diet to his lungs, Beloved would flood his system with neurotransmitters to increase his calculating efficiency, and other nonvolitionals would bathe his upper body in cooling fluids in order to carry off the excess heat generated by all that brainpower.

All of which was hard on navigators—Maria gathered that Four was only half a dozen years old and his nervous system was already beginning to fray under the demands placed upon it. Presumably that was why Beloved was able to spare him; he was nearing the end of his useful life anyway.

Four acquired computer skills quickly: his absorption of information was precise, without flaw, and he only had to do a task once in order to learn it. The only thing that held him back was that his hands were not very precisely adapted to the computers' keyboards.

Four didn't seem to have much personality. Despite his intelligence, he was about as interesting as the tick he so resembled.

Still, Beautiful Maria felt sadness for him after she realized she was making him obsolete. Four's physiology and metabolism had been adapted to make rapid calculations necessary for interstellar flight, calculations that the AI, inefficient as it was for the purpose by human standards, could nevertheless perform much faster than Four, than any organic intelligence. The AI would replace him—all that was necessary to operate it was a fairly intelligent volitional with good typing skills.

What, Maria wondered, did Beloved do with the servants she no longer needed? Was there a retirement home for obsolete or worn-out volitionals somewhere behind the sealed-off sections of Beloved's ship?

Maria thought not. Her sorrow for Navigator Four increased.

Work went on. If Four was sorry for himself, he didn't show it.

Fever burned through Twelve as he hung in fusion. If he was to live aboard *Runaway* he could not be safely webbed with the others into the acceleration chamber's elastic resinous harness during acceleration, maneuvers, and deceleration, but rather must be subject to high-gee stresses. His body had been designed with the possibility that he might have to function in gravity—that was why he had functioning feet instead of another full pair of hands—but Twelve had never personally experienced gravity, and his body was unready.

Hormones poured from the umbilicus into his blood. The crystalline structure of his bones was altered, cell by cell, to handle vertical stresses. Hormones increased the weight and strength of his muscles. His hearts were increased in efficiency and, at the base of his skull, an atrophied organ swelled and blossomed among a web of neurons that connected it to Twelve's brain—an organ of balance, enabling him to control his movements under gravity. He might grow dizzy if he had to move fast while weightless, but the necessity of swift movement did not seem to be high. Twelve's diaphragm grew another layer, the new muscle's grain growing across that of the previous layer, strengthening it, enabling respiration to continue under gravity stresses.

The experience was disorienting. His communication with the humans grew distracted; his attention wandered; his balance and coordination were uncertain. Connected to Beloved while the hormones were pumped into his system, he was aware of Beloved's glee in the reports from Navigator Four, and was aware also of the awesome scope of her activity. Ubu had provided the dimensions of his cargo bays and the sizes of the standardized human connectors, and Beloved ordered her nonvolitionals to begin manufacturing supplies of the drugs as well as standard containers to hold them. Nor did she grow a single volitional for each drug: she grew whole banks of them, an entire wall of each hexaform cargo bay studded with cone-shaped miniature chemical factories, with another wall in each bay devoted to the growth of containers. Biomass reserves went down. So, as soon as the drug factories commenced production, did reserves of nitrogen.

The ship's volitional insystem pilots had, in the meantime, been reawakened. It had been years since they'd been needed: half died during revival and the rest were weakened when they woke. Breeding programs were started for new pilots while the others, even in their weakened condition, united with Beloved's shuttles and atmosphere craft. These detached from the mother ship and shot to the largest of the gas giant's dozen moons, a frozen white striated sphere covered with a dense layer of photochemical haze. One weakened pilot lost control and drove his shuttle into a methane lake, producing a moonquake and a spectacular reaction that glowed on the ship's sensors for hours.

The other pilots succeeded in landing their craft on long plains buried kilometers deep in ammonia ice. Cargo doors swung open. Adapted nonvolitionals rose from the cargo bays, swallowed ice, melted it with their own internal heat, regurgitated it into cargo containers. A few hours later, once the bays were filled, the heavy craft staggered aloft and rejoined Beloved. The ammonia was pumped into a long series of tanks under Home's surface. Heat was gathered from the photoreceptive nonvolitionals that covered the ship's skin, warming the ammonia, which was then injected with millions of tiny nonvolitional processors, each no bigger than a single cell, that would absorb the heat in order to break the ammonia into its constituent hydrogen and nitrogen.

The gases were routed to the chemical processors in the cargo bays, where they were recombined into proteins and polypeptides, the drugs and hormones *Runaway* required in exchange for its artificial intelligence. Tonnes were produced each hour.

In the meantime the pilots returned to the moon for more ammonia. Events were speeded when one atmosphere ship landed on a layer of frozen ammonium cyanate, a compound created in the moon's photochemical sky and precipitated onto its frozen surface. Ammonium cyanate was richer in nitrogen and also contained carbon and oxygen; it was easier to break down, and more useful and varied elements resulted. Beloved could always use more oxygen to fuel her internal processes; and carbon was useful at any time.

The new generation of pilots reached maturity. More craft went down.

The work advanced, speeded up, grew more efficient.

Runaway moved close to Beloved, hovering fifty yards away. Cargo bay doors rolled open. Nonsentient cargo haulers—Beloved understood that sentients might become too disturbed by the alien environs of *Runaway*—moved the containers to *Runaway*'s waiting cargo space and webbed them into place.

AIs, one at a time, moved in the other direction. Twelve knew that one of them would not be sold to other clans. Beloved intended to dissect it and discover its workings.

Runaway's cargo bays began to fill. The exchange was nearing its end.

Beloved's pleasure radiated through her ship, immense, remorseless, as purposeful as all her passions.

CHAPTER
14

HOLOGRAPHIC STARS GLOWED SOFTLY IN UBU'S NAVIGATION DIS-
play. Letters floated alongside the stars, codes that marked systems
with human habitation.

Civilization.

In Ubu's inner ear pulsed a distant whisper of sadness. He was
planning *Runaway*'s journey home. After a few last cargo containers
were stored, Twelve was taken aboard, and the last AI delivered it
would be time to leave Maria the Fair . . .

A red light glowed on the board. The nav comp was saving the
plot automatically.

While Ubu worked on the nav board, Beautiful Maria was on
Beloved's vessel hammering out the contract for the next delivery:
improved AIs and software, some designed for singularity shots,
others for other purposes, all in exchange for another shipment of
pharmaceuticals.

She had also persuaded Beloved to sign a contract, with Twelve
as her agent. If the human authorities demanded to know how
Runaway came by its cargo, they could show a legal, binding

contract, albeit an implausible one. Since what passed for a thumbprint would be decidedly nonhuman, Maria had taken a microcamera with her, intending to get a photo of one of Twelve's retinas. Twelve's eyes were sufficiently human in structure that they might pass, particularly if Maria managed to fuzz some of the details and use computer color enhancements.

Beloved's rhythms beat in Ubu's heart. The bright points of holographic light gleamed in their cube of darkness. Coded numbers referencing Angelica, Bezel, China Light, Salvador, all coded in Ubu's memory as well as the comp, each the location of one defeat or another . . .

He didn't want to go back.

On his return, he knew, everything would change. Ubu didn't want to lose the strange, precarious happiness he had found. The bubble of contentment that had risen in him these last weeks he knew to be fragile, and he feared that it would burst under the strain of living again among others of his predatory, unforgiving species.

He had everything he wanted *now*. All he could do, back in human space, was lose it.

Lose Maria.

A bell rang brightly on the communications board. Maria had concluded her negotiations, and was now sending the recording for Ubu to look at. Ubu saved his piloting plot and stepped to the comm board, where he made sure the record had been received intact.

Out of the corner of his eye, he saw one of the airlock telltales go from green to red. Maria returning.

Ubu began walking to the galley. He was late in making dinner.

Panic whimpered urgently in Twelve's blood, its volume rising at times to a doleful wail of total despair. The human ship, all sharp angles and cold pitted metal, grew larger with every second, closer, more alien and overwhelming. Twelve fought for control, wrestled with the clumsy suit harness, barely stopped his trajectory in time to avoid smashing headfirst into *Runaway*'s silver flank.

Clumsy in his gloves, he manipulated the lock controls, entered the lock, cycled it. The inner door rolled open with sinister, near-silent efficiency. Ubu and Beautiful Maria hovered on the other side, their bodies glowing in ghastly yellow light. They were without vac suits, but each had a portable receiver and a headset that translated their words for broadcast by shoulder-mounted holographic projectors. "Welcome to *Runaway*, Volitional Twelve," Ubu said. "If you will remove your vac suit, we will show you to your quarters."

Twelve tried to remember the sounds for later. He trained one eye on his keyboard and tapped an answer: "I tremble at the honor done me by the reverend bossrider."

He detached the food canister he carried on his back and broke the seal on his suit. *Runaway*'s sterile, comfortless air flooded his senses. The corner of every room and passage was square. His palps searched the air in vain for trace of Beloved, for the airborne signals that marked the solace and glory of her presence. His vocoder failed to detect her drumsong. Panic rose in him again.

He fumbled with the suit harness, dragged the suit off, was shown how to stow it in a locker. Carrying his food canister, he followed Ubu and Maria through an anteroom, down a corridor, into another room. It was large and filled with a distant hum, the whisper of circulating air, glowing lights and displays.

"This is the auxiliary control room," Maria said. "We'll put you here. The room is weightless unless we're under acceleration, and in that case you can use one of the couches."

"I am overwhelmed by the trust of the reverend bossrider, that he would put me in such a critical location."

With a graceful movement of her head, Beautiful Maria tossed her drifting hair out of her eyes. Twelve wondered what precise purpose this "hair" served. The dictionary definition that he'd been fed was precise as to nature, but not function. Possibly hair was intended to enhance her "beauty," whatever in turn that was.

"We have wondered about matters of elimination," Maria said. "There is a toilet cubicle in the corner, but we're uncertain whether or not you are compatible with it."

"I excrete pellets and a small amount of fluid from a valve between my legs," Twelve said. Maria and Ubu looked at each other.

"Sounds familiar," Ubu said. "Guess the toilet'll work."

Twelve received instruction in the zero-gee toilet and the acceleration couches. Beautiful Maria then produced a small boxlike object, a cheerful bright red in color.

"This is a multichannel recorder," she said. "When turned on, it will record any sound in the room. When you want to practice speaking, you can record our speech on one channel and your own speech on the other. You can compare your speech to ours and refine your pronunciation."

Twelve was overwhelmed. "Many thanks, reverend bossrider. I shall treasure the recorder and guard it well."

Twelve took the recorder. The red surface was some kind of soft resinous material, grained like the skin of a nonvolitional loader. Maria demonstrated the machine's use. Twelve practiced briefly, producing sounds from his voder, recording them on Channel One and playing them back. He set the machine to record the rest of this conversation on Channel Two.

Ubu hooked one foot under one of the bars of the command cage. He pointed to each of the five couches. "Each acceleration couch is placed at a different post. Navigation, pilot's station, shooter's station, communications, ship systems . . . We ask you not to use any of the equipment unless you have been instructed and have asked permission."

"Of course, reverend bossrider."

"We would like to show you how to use the communications board. From here you can speak to us if you are in need, or call up music or hype to aid you in learning our language."

"I thank you, reverend bossrider."

Maria gracefully twisted herself in air, planted her feet on a wall, pushed off gently, and caught the padded bar above the comm board. She slid easily through the bars of the command cage and floated above the board. Maria looked at Twelve and showed her white teeth—a "smile," Twelve knew, a gesture which he was slowly learning to think of as reassuring. "Are you familiar with the concept of a hype?" she asked.

"A recorded drama, usually of a sensationalist nature." Twelve's recitation was from memory.

"You understand that a hype is fiction? That it never happened?"

Twelve contemplated this notion—though the word was in his vocabulary, he'd never had to think about it till now—and he restrained a delicate shudder. "It is a recording of a lie, then?"

Ubu and Maria looked at each other, then at Twelve. "Yes," Maria said. "In a sense."

Twelve trembled as two instincts warred in him. He did not wish to pollute his mind with untruth; but neither did he wish to offend his hosts.

"Hypes are dramas about fictional people and—" Beautiful Maria fell silent for a moment, looked at Ubu, looked back. "They're the sort of thing that *can* happen, but usually don't, and they're arranged so as to leave out all the boring parts. All the parts that don't matter."

Twelve gazed at her. Suddenly he was very lonely. "I will consider this, Beautiful Maria."

"*Dramas*," Ubu interjected, his voice loud, "are full of hypothetical action. They are things that might happen, and they explore . . . the ways in which humans might respond to things that . . . might happen to them. Jesus Rice. I'm repeating myself. But—" He looked at Maria and performed a complex gesture that rippled his shoulders.

"We don't want you to take them too seriously," Maria said. "Some of them are very violent, and I don't want you to believe that humans are normally as violent as this. But humans find violence interesting and they dramatize it a lot."

Twelve worked through this slowly. "Hypes are based upon hypothetical action?"

"Yes." Maria's hair drifted before her face and she shook it out of the way. What was it *for*? Twelve wondered. At some appropriate moment he would ask.

"So hypes are instructive in nature?" Twelve asked. "They demonstrate how humans should act in certain circumstances? As with the simulations of singularity shots in your AI?"

"Yes," said Ubu.

"No," said Maria.

Shock exploded in Twelve at the realization that Beautiful Maria had just contradicted the bossrider. A thrill of agony ran through him in anticipation of Ubu Roy's revenge. Would he order her dissolution immediately? Or would he simply kill her now and take her head?

To Twelve's amazement Ubu had no reaction. He just looked at Maria without any discernible expression. "Yes *and* no," Maria corrected. "The range of behavior in hypes is both positive and negative. It demonstrates the range of human behavior rather than any single—rather than what is necessarily correct."

Ubu looked at Twelve. "Maria is right," he said.

Twelve froze in astonishment. The reverend bossrider had not only permitted himself to be contradicted, but had allowed his opinion to be swayed by that of his servant.

Twelve felt weak. He was well out of his depth.

Docilely, he allowed himself to be instructed in the use of the comm board. Ubu and Beautiful Maria took their leave, saying that they had to prepare for *Runaway*'s departure. They would signal him when they were ready for acceleration.

Twelve used the toilet and, without waiting for the signal, webbed himself into the acceleration couch in front of the comm board. His mind was in turmoil.

The air was horribly dry and thick. The yellow light seared his vision. A small white quadruped floated through the door, stared at him for a long moment as it drifted across the room, said nothing, touched the far wall, and sprang out in haste. Twelve's mind wailed for a taste of Beloved. He ordered his recorder to play Channel Two.

"Yes." "No."

Horrible. Evil. Blasphemy.

Yes/No, his mind danced. No/Yes.

They were all mad. They entertained themselves with lies and contradicted their superiors without fear of obliteration. He was trapped here. Panic keened in his veins.

The signal for acceleration came. Was he ready? Maria asked.

Yes/No, he thought. His graceful inner fingers typed an affirmative answer.

The cage gimballed as acceleration came, gentle at first, then with a hideous rumbling intensity. Gravity compressed his flesh, dropped ballast on his hearts. It became hard to breathe. His mind swam. Twelve squeezed his eyes shut and gave himself up to terror, to death.

The horror seemed to go on forever.

Then, suddenly, it was over. The rumbling ceased and Twelve floated free in his webbing. His hearts surged as if to make up for lost time.

Beloved! he wailed.

Yes, he thought. No.

Beautiful Maria's soft hair drifted against Ubu's face, offered a warm blanketing touch. He stroked his cheek against it. Maria leaned closer, kissed his throat, thrust her hips against Ubu, swallowing him.

Ubu was anchored by his upper set of arms from a padded castoff bar set in the ceiling of his compartment. The centrifuge had been locked down prior to acceleration, and he held himself in place by fingertips alone, his lower arms holding Maria's hips, giving her the freedom to move as inspiration took her.

Maria kissed him, tasted his salt skin. He hung motionless as Maria danced against his body. She dusted his smooth muscles with her fingertips, brushed the tips of her breasts against his chest, slowly turned her head from side to side in order to draw her hair's caress across his face and neck.

Ubu released the castoff bar and the two bobbed around the room, their slow trajectory altered in minor ways as their mass reacted to their movements. They finished in Ubu's rack, strapped together in his webbing, Ubu's four arms tangled in the polymer harness, his arm and shoulder muscles flexing as he sought leverage, traction, advantage . . .

Maria's pleasure receded slowly. She stretched herself, infusing her muscles with blood. Her skin seemed a complex organic sensor set to receive radiations of pleasure, striations of happiness, coded signals of joy from the electron world that wove its nets about her, as complicated as the tangle of harness webbing in which she lay . . . She opened her eyes, saw her view obstructed by clouds of drifting hair, pulled it behind her head. Ubu's body hung in the webbing a few heartbeats away. His eyes were distant.

"I wonder what our passenger would think of this," Maria said.

Ubu took a moment to process this comment. "He'd probably think we're fusing. Like him with Beloved."

"That's what we *were* doing."

He grinned. "I think we're a little better than that."

"Probably. It doesn't look like much fun for him."

"I wonder if he knows what fun is."

She drew her hair away again. "Will you braid my hair? Be weightless for a while yet, and it'll just get in my way."

"Sure."

Maria turned over. Ubu sat astride her and held her between the strong muscles of his thighs while his four arms worked the plait with care and precision. He finished and she stretched again, hanging content in the webbing.

"I don't want to go back," Ubu said. The tone in his voice made her look at him over her shoulder.

"I'll be ready," she said. "I'd like to get on Angel's Fringe again." She grinned. "See some old friends. Play some blackhole. It could be fun now the stakes don't matter."

"The Fringe is dying," Ubu said. "We can't stop that. No matter how successful we are." He looked away. "I don't want to have to watch it go."

She frowned at him. Something had changed. "What's the matter? What happened?"

He shrugged. "It occurred to me that right now we're winners. We've got sole knowledge of an alien civilization, a cargo hold worth tens of millions, our freedom . . . and if things go well, all we can do is keep what we've already got. And if things don't go well, we lose it."

We lose each other. That, she knew, was what he meant. She rolled over, faced him.

"There's nothing we can do, right?" she said. "We can't hide out here forever."

"No."

"And we've got our plans. Your plans. Prefabricated ships, stations . . ."

"Yeah." He gave a halfhearted grin. "Lots of plans. But right now we're ahead, and I've never been ahead before, and I just wish we could quit."

She sighed, let herself drift among the polymer straps. "I don't know what you want, Ubu," she said.

"Just what I've got now. Nothing more, not really."

Maria put her arms around his neck, looked level into his eyes. "Hey. Things change."

"Yeah." Suddenly his eyes were hard—brittle chips of blue glass. He reached for the webbing, began taking it down, untangling himself.

Maria's pulse beat a little quicker. "Where are you going?"

"Time to get ready for the shoot." His voice was sharp. He was angry, and Maria couldn't tell why. "And we should show Twelve how to use the fuge elevator before we have to do it under gravity. If he isn't used to the setup he may break something."

Sadness wafted over her. She didn't know how this had started, how to end it, what it meant.

"Okay," she said. "If that's what you want."

After learning how to enter the centrifuge hub and ride the little elevator to the primary control stations on the lower level of the fuge, Twelve returned to auxcontrol and strapped himself into his couch. He remained there during the shoot, frozen with terror. He'd never been conscious during a shoot and was afraid it would be as horrible as the breakaway acceleration from the bluegreen giant. He listened to the automated countdown while his fingers gripped the arms of the chair, and then—there wasn't even a blink in his consciousness—it was over. Amazement flowed through him, then joy. He had survived with body and mind intact.

He opened his food locker, ate, drank water from the tap—no one had shown him how to use the cup dispenser—and then used the toilet. He played with the recorder. "We would like to sshow you how to usze the communicationz board," he repeated, trying to get Maria's inflection right. He kept making accidental, incidental buzzing sounds, and he had a hard time working with the sibilants. "From here you can zbeak to uzz if you are in need, or call up muszic or hype to aid you in learning our language."

Hype. Twelve tried not to think about it.

He ran the recorder forward, repeating the words, fixing them in his mind; but before long the conversation wandered into disturbing areas and Twelve decided not to face the problem of human contradiction just yet.

Twelve listened to the first part of the conversation several times and repeated the words aloud, playing them back, until he could do a presentable imitation of Ubu and Maria, not just their words and inflections but the voices themselves. He tried inventing sentences using these same words in a different order, but the mixture of Ubu's and Maria's voices sounded odd, and for this he had to invent another voice, a kind of modulation of the first two. He worked hard at it.

Time passed. He ate and drank again.

He found himself looking at the comm board.

Hype.

His hearts beat faster. Twelve bent to the comm board, called up the index, chose one title from the hundreds available, and started his recorder.

The title of the chosen hype was *Bloodbath in Building Four*, which suggested to Twelve's hopeful mind that the subject matter might have to do with genetics. Unfortunately the title proved misleading.

The hype's action was complex and left much to ponder. It seemed to concern a struggle for supremacy among a number of human clans. The main character, Ahmad, was an "agent" for one clan, and had somehow been insinuated into another clan for the purpose of discovering their intentions—the precise mechanism of this insertion, which Twelve would have found interesting, was regrettably left unclear. Twelve understood how useful it would be to be able to pass one's own servants off as those of someone else; but Twelve had never heard of any way in which genetic markers could pass undetected. Still, here Ahmad was, operating among his enemies, without their smelling out his origins. Possibly, Twelve noted, Beloved could purchase this ability from the humans and make herself and her servants nearly invincible. Twelve would inquire.

Twelve observed that much of human communication seemed to be transmitted via facial "expression," primarily through the constant motion of "eyebrows," which were forever wigwagging up and down, in and out. Twelve began to categorize these positions but gave up the task as hopeless—there were too many, and he did not yet understand enough context.

Ahmad's task was quite soon complicated by the appearance of an enemy female, Kirstie, whose profession was described as "rughunter," a word not available in Twelve's vocabulary but apparently meaning someone engaged in the detection of the agents of enemy clans. Instead of avoiding Kirstie, Ahmad seemed inexplicably attracted to her. Twelve could not at first understand this perversity, but later deduced that Kirstie's type possessed valuable hereditary traits which Ahmad's clan was anxious to acquire. Kirstie, not surprisingly, was suspicious of his approaches and pressed her mouth and nose to his body frequently in a presumed attempt to detect his alien genetics. Ahmad demonstrated his confidence in his own masking abilities by permitting this.

There were complicated intrigues going on at the same time—in the absence of Kirstie's clan head, who oddly enough was never shown or referred to, various servants conflicted as to the interpretations of clan policy and began killing one another in a perfect frenzy. Kirstie was involved in this slaughter and Ahmad persuaded her to join with the forces of his own clan in restoring order. Though this was not made explicit, it would appear that his price for assistance was possession of Kirstie and her valuable genetics, for after a long combat, in which the forces of Kirstie's clan were almost entirely destroyed, she returned without protest to Ahmad's clan.

Reflecting on the drama afterward, Twelve concluded that despite Maria's insistence that hypes were not necessarily didactic, this particular hype had nevertheless an instructive message, namely that lines of authority had to be firmly established. If Kirstie's clan head, in her absence, had merely indicated which of her servants was to give orders and which to obey, none of the self-destructive attempts to dictate policy would have ever been initiated, and the clan wouldn't have suffered civil disorder and destruction.

Twelve used his recorder to play bits of the dialogue back, and he added to his repertoire of words and phrases. During this process, Beautiful Maria appeared and asked him if he was well. Twelve used his voder in response.

"Got nothing to wrack about," he said, a favorite phrase of Ahmad's.

"Interesting," Maria said, after a pause. She informed Twelve that there would be another shoot within an hour or so, and that after she and Ubu had rested they and Twelve would be able to talk if Twelve so wished. Twelve indicated his readiness.

Maria left and Twelve called up the directory of hypes. He decided to look for something less violent if possible and chose a drama called *The Libation Bearers*, a title that seemed pacific enough. He strapped himself into the chair, turned on his recorder, and waited for enlightenment.

Hours later, after two shoots in a row, Maria found Twelve catatonic in his acceleration couch. He was lying on his left side in a slightly curled posture. His eyes gazed unfocused in four different directions, like carelessly dropped marbles. Mouth branches floated in and out with steady breaths. His keyboard transmitter had slipped its strap and floated over his head.

He would not respond. Beautiful Maria hung on to the castoff bar at the top of Twelve's couch. She hoped Twelve was asleep, that this behavior was something normal. Anxiety skittered under her skin. Twelve's steady breathing continued unabated. Tiny drops of drool were flung by the mouth branches into the weightless room. With a push of her fingers Maria moved to the comm board and called Ubu.

The hype file, she saw, was still up. Maria reversed herself, hooked her feet into the straps beneath the board, and checked the index for any hypes that had been run in the last few hours. *Bloodbath in Building Four*, it said, and *The Libation Bearers*. Both had been played to their conclusion.

Ubu appeared, followed by Maxim, who bounded slowly and gently about the room, interested in the stranger but keeping his distance. Ubu tried to awaken Twelve, first with a call, then by prodding and nudging. He looked at Maria. "What was he doing?"

"Watching a couple of hypes."

"Which ones?"

Maria told him. He frowned. "I saw that first one," he said, then drifted to the comm board and looked up *The Libation Bearers*. "This one's old," he said. "It's been in the comp since the ship was built. 'An adaptation of the classic drama by Aeschylus,' it says. Jesus Rice. No *wonder* I've never looked at it."

"Who's Aeschylus?"

"I'm still working on *libation*." Ubu looked at Twelve, gnawed his lip. "All we can do is keep a watch on him and hope he comes out of it. Don't want to start filling him full of human medication."

"We could watch the hypes. See if we could figure out what set him off."

"It might not *be* the hypes. He might be sick. Maybe we infected him."

"Let's hope it's not mutual."

"Let's." He thought for a moment. "It wasn't the shoot, right? He was okay after the first shoot?"

"I guess. He talked to me. He used some old slang I hadn't heard in years."

Ubu sighed. "I'll bring a sleeping harness up here. One of us should stay with him."

Maxim, bored, drifted away.

Maria looked at Twelve and was startled to see him move, shift slightly in his webbing. Her heart lifted. She waited for his eyes to focus, for his body to come to attention. In vain.

He had made himself a little more comfortable, that was all. It offered at least a little hope that something in there was still responding.

They waited for him to regain consciousness. Waited for hours.

Ubu put the headset down, the final staves of *The Libation Bearers* still ringing through his mind. He had watched it through the stim set rather than risk driving Twelve further into shock by playing the thing out loud again. The drama had been bewildering and frustration flittered in Ubu like the hype's pursuing Furies.

He shook his head. "Weird," he said.

"What was it about?"

"A bunch of old-time people living in Mudville. The mother kills the father before the story starts, so the son and daughter team up with a god to kill the mother and her boyfriend. The whole thing was—I guess it was poetry. And there was this weird . . . bunch of women . . . who wandered through the play, singing and dancing while beating cymbals and drums. And there were demons as well as the god. I *guess* they were demons." He shrugged. Undirected anger shivered through him. "Pretty strange. I don't know what to make of it."

"Have we got a fastlearn on it?"

"I doubt it." His hands started tapping keys. "I don't think the vid is what upset Twelve," he said. "There wasn't even any violence on camera. It all happened somewhere else. *Bloodbath* must have featured five hundred corpses and Twelve went on to watch the next vid." Data flickered in midair. Ubu peered at it. "We don't have a fastlearn, but we've got a recorded lecture on Greek drama. Whatever Greek is."

"On cartridge or in the database?"

"It's in the database. I think the holocomputer came with it and a bunch of other old vids nobody ever watches—I bet nobody's ever used it."

Beautiful Maria looked at him. "Should we check the text?"

Ubu thought for a moment, then shook his head. "I don't see any reason to. I don't think the hype had anything to do with it. I think Twelve's sick."

Maria's look was bleak. "I think you're right."

Ubu took off his lap belt, pushed off the couch, stretched his muscles. The whole thing had been a waste of time. The vid's bizarre choral rhythms keened in his memory. He looked at Twelve, then at Maria. A sudden thought jolted him.

"Hey," he said. "Maybe it was the music in the vid. Maybe the drums were beating the wrong rhythm. What if the vid used the rhythm Beloved uses when she tells Twelve to go to sleep?"

Maria was startled. "You think so?"

"I'll get a sizer. You wait here."

Ubu turned, his feet touched a castoff bar, and he rocketed into the corridor. He returned with the sizer and jacked it into the ship's power source.

Beloved's varied rhythms came drumming into his consciousness. There was one pattern that Beloved had used more than the others during the negotiating sessions. He programmed that one into the synthesizer and triggered it. Drumbeats rattled in the little room.

Ubu watched Twelve. Frustration gnawed him.

The drumbeat went on.

An hour later, Twelve began to stir.

Beloved. Warm reassurance began to whisper in Twelve. Awareness filtered slowly into his mind.

Horror! Blasphemy! The memory came as a shock. His body jolted. *"Warning!"* he found himself shouting aloud. *"Danger to Beloved!"*

"Hey! Wake up! Speak Melange, will you?" An enemy voice, harsh, a clattering language.

"Danger! Danger!" Twelve felt enemy hands upon him and lashed out while crying his warnings. His blows were absorbed by a soft tangle of enemy restraints.

"Hey! Stop that! We're friends, damn it!"

Vision returned. Twelve saw metal walls, chairs, lights that glowed at him like hostile eyes. Twelve realized he was caught in a harness of some sort. He stopped thrashing and tried to focus his mind.

"Help," he said. "Danger to Beloved."

"Look at my holos, Twelve. Read the translation of what I'm saying. Maria, where the fuck's his keyboard?"

Awareness began to turn in Twelve's mind. Ubu floated over him, out of range of Twelve's frantic paws. Maria shot across the room, his keyboard and transmitter in her hands.

A surge of memory left Twelve helpless. "Horrible," he said. He remembered to speak the humans' language. "Danger to Beloved."

"Danger? Where?"

Twelve understood the words before he read the golden graphic rolling over Ubu's head. Twelve pointed a feeble hand at the comm board.

"Pollution. Evil thoughts. Hype." Ubu and Beautiful Maria stared at him. Twelve realized he was speaking his own language again. In a frenzy, Twelve reached through the harness webbing, snatched his deck from Maria's hands, his inner fingers typing furiously beneath his big hands.

"Must protect. *The Libation Bearers* is evil. The hype is thought pollution of the worst type."

The act of forcing his thoughts into the constrictions of an alien language calmed him. Phrases burst from his fingers in torrents. "Insane servants conspire to kill their parent. No one stops them. An evil design." At the very thought of it, Twelve felt himself falling into withdrawal again. With a surge of will he dragged himself from oblivion.

"It was just a hype!" Ubu's voice was loud. "It never happened!"

Twelve banged the keyboard on his knees in a fury of negation. "That doesn't matter! Some thoughts are not permissible!!!!!!!!!" He held down the exclamation key for a long time in frantic emphasis.

Ubu and Beautiful Maria looked at each other. "One of us better use the text," Ubu said.

"You're the one who won't forget it."

Ubu's mouth twitched. "What if I want to?"

"You've seen the hype. I haven't."

Ubu sighed and turned to Twelve. "I'm going to learn something about the play now," he said. "I should be able to answer most of your questions."

Anger and fear burned through Twelve. His inner fingers hammered on keys. "I have asked no questions, reverend bossrider."

Ubu thought about this for a moment. "Maybe I'll be able to answer *my* questions, then." Ubu belted himself into the next couch, put on a headset, tapped keys, leaned back.

Twelve found his anger ebbing slightly under the influence of Beloved's calm, thoughtful drumbeats, and then with a snapping whipcrack realization he remembered that Beloved was far away. He glanced over the room in alarm, focused on the speakers.

"What is that sound?" he demanded.

Maria's voice was soothing. "Ubu programmed an AI to sound like Beloved. He hoped it would help you recover."

After an initial surge of indignation—an artificial Beloved!— Twelve contemplated this notion. It sounded, on further consideration, quite attractive. "Would it be possible for me to learn to use this machine?" he asked.

"Of course."

Twelve warmed at the thought of Beloved's homelike throbbing comforting him in this horrid metal-walled room. "I humbly petition for instruction," he said.

"Use it all you like."

"Thank you, Beautiful Maria."

"No wrack." She gave a sudden laugh. "Where did you learn that expression anyway? I haven't heard it in years."

"I learned the word in the first hype. Was the expression incorrect?"

"No. Just a little out of date."

Ubu sat up in his couch and removed the headset. "Okay," he said. "Now I know who the Greeks were." He rubbed his forehead. "Do you know the word *cybernetic* comes from the old Greek language? It means someone who steers a boat."

Maria looked at him. "What have boats got to do with AIs?"

"I don't know. The database didn't go into that."

"Shows you what the Greeks knew."

Ubu looked at Twelve. "The play that you saw is something called a tragedy. That's a play in which awful things happen."

Twelve's indignation returned. Inner fingers rattled on his keyboard. "Awful and *forbidden* things, reverend bossrider."

"The play was the middle part of a trilogy, Twelve. You didn't watch the first part. Please understand, Twelve, it was terrible that these children killed their mother. But she'd done a terrible thing before, in the earlier play, because she killed her husband."

Twelve thought for a moment. "What was terrible about that?" he asked.

Ubu and Maria looked at each other. "People aren't supposed to kill their relatives," Ubu said.

"She was the procreator, was she not? So it was her right to kill any of her servants."

"Her husband was as much a procreator as she was." Ubu turned to Maria. "Haven't we made this clear?"

Annoyance burned through Twelve. His inner fingers could scarcely keep up with the rush of his passionate thought. "The husband may be the custodian of certain desirable genetic material, reverend bossrider, but that does not detract from the holy character of motherhood. Nor the right of the mother to choose her servants by their appropriate characteristics, or to dispose of others that are no longer useful."

Maria's laughter rang in the room. "Got you there, Ubu," she said. Twelve, annoyed at her disrespect, shifted a pair of eyes to follow her.

"Holy character of motherhood," Ubu repeated. "Right." He thought for a moment. "The children's actions were prompted by a god. By Apollo. He gave a holy character, as you put it, to his orders."

Twelve considered for a moment the notion of godhood. A god, his vocabulary told him, was a superbeing, particularly one conceived as the embodiment of some attribute of reality . . . The word had other definitions, some of which were contradictory.

"Have you ever met a god?" he asked.

Both laughed. Twelve shifted his eyes from one to the other in rising indignation. "Neither of us has met a god," Ubu said. "I don't believe they exist, though many people do. But the writer of the play believed that Apollo existed."

Twelve began to grow agitated again. "Either gods exist, or they don't."

"They do not," Maria interrupted, "in our *experience* exist."

"But if gods order servants to kill their Beloved," Twelve insisted, "then they are evil gods and should be destroyed."

Ubu gave a long sibilant "ahhh" sound which his computer declined to translate. "Kill their Beloved. I see your point." He looked at Maria. "He's worried about Beloved being in danger."

Maria nodded her head, then turned to Twelve. "No god will ever put Beloved in danger. I can say that with certainty."

Twelve thought for a moment. "I am reassured, Beautiful Maria," he wrote. "But cannot Apollo be hunted down and destroyed?"

"No one has seen Apollo in thousands of years," Ubu said. "I don't think he's any danger to anyone."

"His polluting thought remains, reverend bossrider Ubu Roy."

Ubu looked at Maria, then back at Twelve. "Shall I erase the hype, Twelve?"

Twelve's hearts exulted. His hands made fists. "Destroy the contaminating thought! Yes, reverend bossrider!"

"Very well." Ubu turned to the comm board and tapped the keyboard for a moment. He turned back to Twelve.

"I've erased it."

"Thank you, reverend bossrider."

Twelve thought about the hype again and shuddered. He felt triumph that he had participated in erasing such an evil from the world. But still something troubled him.

"Reverend bossrider," he said, "why did the others not prevent this insane act?"

"Which others?"

"The others in the hype. The female humans who sang and beat drums. Were they not akin to the woman who was killed?"

"They were the chorus, Twelve. They do not affect the action, they only offer comment."

Twelve thought about this. "Then they were wicked, too. They should have intervened."

"The—the chorus represents the ordinary people. Ordinary people cannot prevent all the evil in the world."

"The killing occurred right in front of them. They were evil not to try to prevent it."

There was a little silence.

"Twelve," Ubu said, "I think you should not look at hype again."

"Agreed. My thoughts might become contaminated by evil gods."

"Listen to music next time."

"Very well, reverend bossrider. I shall obey your wishes."

They left Twelve to his thoughts. Grim satisfaction filled him at the thought that he had helped to destroy contamination.

Beloved, he felt sure, would be pleased.

"Never thought I'd spend hours arguing with an alien about theology and ethics," Ubu said. "Jesus Rice."

"The holy character of motherhood," Maria said. "I liked that."

Ubu removed his headset and holo projector, stretched his neck and arms. "Now I've got all this data about classical Mudville drama read into my brain. What am I gonna do with stuff like that?"

"At least our passenger hasn't died."

"I want to know what happens if he figures out we've been infected by Apollo's thought. What if he decides our brains are a danger to Beloved?" He finished his climb down the fuge ladder and dropped off onto the blue plastic pad below. A new tear in the plastic scratched his bare foot. He stepped back and rubbed his sole.

"Shit," he said. "Gotta fix that."

Beautiful Maria dropped down the ladder. She reached behind her neck, took her long braid, began undoing it.

Ubu moved toward the command cage. "I'll check our position fix," he said. "Then we should get some sleep before the next shoot."

"No hurry."

Ubu could feel annoyance leaping under his skin. "I wanna get it over with," he said. He walked to the nav station, looked at the plot. *Runaway* was that much closer to civilization.

Maria padded quietly up behind him. He sensed her shaking out her hair and thought about the dark warmth of it spilling over her shoulders, down her back. Maria turned and walked away, toward the lounge.

Things change, he thought. Damn it all anyway.

CHAPTER

15

RUNAWAY'S CARNIVORE SINGULARITY DEVOURED THE LIGHT-YEARS with one ferocious gulp after another. With each swallow of the black hole Ubu felt his own restlessness increase, as if each jump infused him with another dose of angry, undirected hornet energy.

He hardly ever seemed to need sleep. He roamed *Runaway* with a bag of tools, repairing anything that needed it, fixing equipment that hadn't functioned in decades. He patched the broken plastic at the bottom of the fuge ladder, and checked the computer newsfax for lists of successful lawyers in Bezel System. Twice he heard his father's voice ranting from one part of the ship or another. He ignored it.

Runaway was diving deeper into human space this time, leaping past Angelica and the frontier toward the nearest commercial major hub, Bezel. At Bezel Station the compounds could be unloaded at the best price, the legal problems would be settled quickly in a standing Admiralty Court instead of waiting for the circuit judge, and, if everything went wrong, Ubu and Maria would be imprisoned on a Mudville inhabited for a dozen generations rather than on a newly settled, half-civilized place like Angelica.

Ubu didn't spend much time with Twelve, but when passing through the weightless parts of the ship he could hear the sizer beating out different rhythms, different tempos of Beloved's thought and comfort. Sometimes he heard human music as well. Twelve seemed to favor syncopation and a driving rhythm section.

From Beautiful Maria, who spent more time with Twelve, Ubu heard more about their guest. Twelve had wanted to know the cat's function, and on being told Maxim had none, was upset at the idea of the cat's parasitic nature until Maria reconsidered and told him Maxim's function was to provide pleasure to humans, at which Twelve seemed satisfied. Pleasure, Maria gathered, was something Twelve got from someone else, not something he generated himself: Maxim became in Twelve's mind a kind of ambulatory reward that offered itself to humans when they had done something particularly useful.

The food canister that Twelve brought aboard contained a greyish solid mass that smelled like bean curd gone bad and otherwise resembled a particularly revolting soft cheese. Twelve would carve off pieces of it with his inner fingers and then hand them to his mouth structures—sense palps that combined the function of smell and taste—which prodded and stroked the mass into small round balls of digestible size and popped them into Twelve's mouth, where they were apparently swallowed whole. The process, Maria said, was not pleasant to watch.

The odd rough spots on Twelve's chest and back, Maria learned, were a kind of genetic exoskeletal remnant. When Beloved grew soldiers, the callosities developed into armored plating; on other types of volitionals, the callosities remained rudimentary.

Beautiful Maria also discovered that Twelve was genetically a male: he had male genes but no reproductive organs, nothing approximating a sex drive. His male genotype was an accident of his heritage, nothing more: Maria gathered that Twelve had never heard of a functioning male among his own species and thought the idea rather horrifying.

Twelve was learning to speak with remarkable speed. "His memory is almost as good as yours," Maria told Ubu; and this news surfaced in Ubu a layer of sadness as he pictured Twelve floating in auxcontrol, absorbing alien speech, unable to rid himself of any of it. Maybe thought pollution *was*, with Twelve's species, not a metaphor but a reality, a genuine contamination written into the structure of the memory like a phage virus written into human genes, one that could be passed from one individual to another and eliminated only with the destruction of the minds that held it . . .

More light-years flamed and died in *Runaway*'s portable inferno. Ubu had his opening radio messages ready, his lawyers chosen.

His body twitched with suppressed motion. Energy fired his nerves.

Runaway made its insystem leap with Maria, as always, bossing the shoot.

As Maria pushed back the stim antennae, rose groggily from her couch, and mopped sweat from her face, Bezel System sprang into holographic existence on Ubu's navigation displays. *Runaway* was fifteen days out.

Ubu slid his chair to the comm board and fired *Runaway*'s ID number and his messages.

Motes of energy danced in his frame as he waited for the reply.

The legal minuet began the minute Bezel's receptors recorded the ship's entering burst of radiation followed by Ubu's transmissions. OttoBanque filed for confiscation of the ship and its singularity, but before the bank's documents were even transmitted to the court, *Runaway*'s new attorney, C. C. Mahadaji, was in the bank's offices offering settlement, repayment of the loan, double costs, interest, and penalties. Mahadaji was one of Bezel Station's most prominent lawyers, and OttoBanque was inclined to listen. One of Mahadaji's associates was busy meanwhile in the Admiralty Court, bargaining with the deputy judge advocate concerning *Runaway*'s fines for fraud, breaking station, triggering a Navy pursuit, and unauthorized exit of the Angelica System. Another Mahadaji associate began making inquiries concerning possible buyers for large quantities of top-quality pharmaceuticals. *Runaway* applied for a place in the Bezel Station unloading queue.

Within days the legal matters were settled. OttoBanque agreed to the settlement, provided the pharmaceuticals were actually proven to be in *Runaway*'s holds. The deputy judge advocate, in view of the fact that Bossrider Ubu Roy had never before committed any recorded offense, agreed to ask for a heavy fine rather than seek imprisonment.

The drug sale took a little longer. In the end the entire consignment was bought by Portfire Associated Groups, the main pharmaceutical distributor for the area—they wanted to maintain their preeminence, suppress competition, and keep their prices high and their distribution system intact, free from defectors willing to work on the fringes for a discount. *Runaway* placed buy options on advanced navigational AIs.

Ubu watched the zeroes accumulate in his hypothetical bank balance. He was getting a fast lesson in the way things actually worked.

Restlessness still gnawed at him. He had expected more: confrontations, drama, a Navy cutter swooping toward *Runaway* with alarms clanging, boarders armored and waiting in the airlocks, targeting computers reading data to missiles . . . Instead there was nothing but higher and higher figures accumulating in his as-yet-unrealized portfolio and a list of legal charges that would be dismissed as soon as he bothered to appear on Bezel and put his thumbprint on the appropriate documents.

Ubu went to his room and sat under the alpha trodes for an hour, but nothing came to his mind but images of Maria, Pasco, and Marco de Suarez, all involved in some opaque, complex, distasteful relationship and painted in fiery bright colors that danced to the rhythm of Beloved's drums. He removed the foam-padded trodes from his head, pulled the connector from the wall, sat up. Energy still coursed through him.

He was ready for a fight, and everyone had surrendered.

Deceleration stresses tore at Twelve's joints. The dry air burned in his throat as his diaphragm heaved. The synthesizer drummed out Beloved's most soothing rhythm. He had withdrawn his eyes, peering only through slits, and concentrated entirely on suppressing his terror.

Suddenly there was someone else there, appearing in an instant.

A strange human, floating above him. Twelve's fear exploded. He clawed at the webbing.

"Damn it, damn it." A peculiar voice, at once soft and grating. The intruder was a round-bodied male, with flyaway grey-and-black hair on his head and curling on his chest.

"I am sorry, reverend gentleman," Twelve yelped. "Am I occupying your station?"

"I've got it figured out. I know how it happened." The man just floated there. His broad hairy hand swiped his hair back from his eyes.

Maybe he's a hologram, Twelve thought. Maybe a hype got accidentally triggered. He rolled one eye toward the comm board, saw that it was shut down, just as Twelve had left it. Fear began to sing in his nerves.

The human had simply appeared. Out of nowhere.

Twelve's eyes focused on him. "Are you a god?" he asked. He had trouble controlling his speaking organ at the terrible thought; there was a rumble of horror in his speech. "Are you Apollo?"

The man—the god—ignored him. Twelve saw that there was uniformly short hair growing on the intruder's cheeks and chin, that his eyes were rimmed in red.

"Had it all worked out," he said. "Exclusive deal with the Kompanie, shipping from Bezel to Trincheras and Masquerade. Would have kept us going for years."

The intruder's body began to shimmer. Twelve could see rainbow waves running through his body. Superhuman powers, Twelve thought. Helpless, he prepared himself for annihilation.

"But I decided to celebrate. Went to the Rostov and had myself a party. Got high and got . . . careless. Forgot we aren't all friends any more."

The deity's body solidified again. "I told too many people about my good luck. And one of them must have told Marco de Suarez. Maybe I told him myself. Don't remember too clear."

"Reverend sir," Twelve said. "Do not harm me. I am but a servant of my Beloved." He realized he was babbling in his own language. He tried to form the words in Melange but his brain was frozen in terror.

"He must have gone straight to the *Abrazo* and put his proposal together. Explained how, with five ships, he could keep his deliveries on a more flexible schedule than I could with one ship." The god shook his head. "Damn the man anyway." His eyes looked straight at Twelve. "I'm only gonna say this once."

Comprehension dawned in Twelve with the force of a thunderclap. The god was trying to give him vital information! He must never forget any of this.

"I am listening, reverend sir," he said. His hearts beat faster than Beloved's drums.

"I can't blame Marco de Suarez entirely," the god said. "He was working for his people. He's facing Consolidation, same as the rest of us. But you can't trust the other shooters any more, de Suarez especially." The deity pointed at Twelve. "Keep away from Marco and his family. They're treacherous."

"Yes, reverend sir."

"The only people you can trust are aboard *Runaway*. Ubu, Maria, me. That's all."

"I understand, sir."

There was a long pause. Moisture formed in the god's eyes. Twelve had the impression of great weariness. "I wish I'd kept my mouth shut. It's gonna be hard for us. If it weren't for my mistake—we'd be—we'd be—" The god opened and closed his mouth several times without saying anything. His shoulders shook.

Then the god reached toward Twelve. Twelve recoiled, shrinking into the acceleration couch, but the god's hand disappeared in front of Twelve's eyes. The rainbow shimmer ran through the god once more, and then the deity disappeared.

Twelve stared. He looked again at the comm board. No hype had been running.

Beloved's drumbeats urged him to be calm, to think.

The god did not reappear.

Bezel Station rolled slowly through darkness, the cold red light of its star casting a long ruddy smear on its rotating flank. Brighter stars, waiting ships, surrounded the station like points in some complex three-dimensional puzzle. Among them darted flitting silver shuttles.

From the navigator's couch, Beautiful Maria watched as the station grew closer, its video image slowly changing in perspective as Ubu piloted *Runaway* to its assigned loading dock.

Once, when Bezel had been on the frontier of human expansion, its main station had been a torus much like Angelica Station; but under the impact of Fringe commerce the torus had fattened, grown lengthwise, become a wider wheel, then finally a self-enclosed tube. Consolidation had slowed the rate of growth, but by then Bezel System was largely self-sufficient and Bezel Station had become an important transit point for Hiliner profits, Hiliner business.

The place was so busy there wasn't enough docking space in the station itself: modular docking units floated in station space, rendezvoused with ships, unloaded and transferred cargo. When necessary the entire giant module would dock gingerly with the station and move cargo wholesale into the interior.

Displays flickered before Beautiful Maria's eyes. The modular dock was growing closer. In the periphery of her vision she could see Ubu's four hands touch controls lightly, trigger attitudinal jets, call up one primary display after another. *Runaway* was so fully laden that its massive inertia could pose a significant danger even to Bezel itself, let alone the Modular Dock C that awaited them. A moment's inattention could bring disaster. Maria had little function in the process but to scan the displays and certify that Ubu didn't make a careless error.

No error was made. *Runaway*'s fully loaded mass came to a gentle stop within reach of the docking bay's magnetic grapnels. The grapnels fired out and struck home; the huge cables were drawn onto their spools by shrieking engines, and *Runaway*'s Cargo Hold C was pulled to its inevitable meeting with Docking Bay 17A. The ship rang lightly, like a bell, at the module's touch. Maria settled back in her chair.

"Bezel Control," Ubu said, "*Runaway* thanks you." His hands did a rapid dance through the powerdown checklist. "*Runaway* also requests a personnel tube ASAP." The fuge gave a lurch as it began to move. A vibration ran through Maria's bones. Gravity clawed lightly at her ear, her belly.

The powerdown continued. Maria unwebbed, sat up, turned to Ubu.

His hands still ran through the checklist. His eyes were focused, intent. There was a twitch in one jaw muscle.

He'd gone away from her, she thought. She couldn't get close to him now.

The checklist was over. Displays winked out of existence. Gravity grew in the centrifuge.

Ubu was still focused forward as if expecting the displays to return. His hands hung above keyboards.

"What now?" Maria said.

"Our meeting with Mahadaji and OttoBanque's lawyers. And then the Portfire people." His lips skinned back from his teeth. "And the deputy judge advocate. I figure we should go dressed like shooters, right? Dress like who we are."

"And then?"

He looked at her. His intensity seemed to crackle about his shoulders like static. "We fight to keep it all, I guess."

"I meant . . ." She looked down at her feet, pressed long toes into the smoothworn nonskid surface of the deck. "What happens with the two of us?"

His eyes were stone. "Whatever happens. Things change, right? You said it. I believe it."

"That isn't necessarily . . ." She tried and failed to put it in words. That she didn't want either of them hurt, that whatever happened, she hoped it would happen with gentleness.

He unwebbed and stood. "Before you shut down the nav board," he said, "I want you to load the log and erase every trace of where we've been."

She looked up at him in surprise. "That's illegal," she said.

"I don't care. I don't want anyone knowing where we've been or getting any clue to where the next meet is scheduled. The legal matters are all but settled and there's no reason for anyone to subpoena our logs."

Maria bit her lip. Every ship's log was under legal seal, and erasing part of it meant glitching past a hardwired barrier. "Okay."

"I'm gonna check on Twelve. See how he's survived the

deceleration and tell him to stay put till we get back." He stepped past her toward the ladder. She watched him go, felt her last hope of any easy resolution flicker and die.

She turned to the nav boards, called up the log, marked the careful beginning and end of an erasure. A blip on the long-range screen caught her attention.

A new ship had just whiteholed into Bezel System, about two weeks out from the station. The ship's name and owner flickered into existence alongside the new blip, followed by its ID number.

Abrazo, Maria read. *De Suarez Expressways*.

Mahadaji was a small, dark-skinned man with curly black hair and a brief mustache. He wore striped trousers, felt slippers, a long-sleeved t-shirt, glittery mascara, and an embroidered vest with a standing collar. He had a small silver earring in his right ear. His grip shoes anchored him firmly to the surface of Docking Bay 17A.

"Bossrider," he said, bowing. "Shooter." He had to shout to be heard over the resonant grinding of Dock 15A's autoloaders.

Ubu and Maria towered over the smaller man. Ubu wore a pair of shorts, his silver reflec vest, a bracelet on the left lower arm, and a pair of grips on his feet. He looked at Mahadaji and smiled. "Mr. Mahadaji. Pleased to make your acquaintance. You've done good work for us."

Mahadaji waved a hand. "The difficulties were common ones, as were my solutions. What was uncommon was your own good fortune in finding such a cargo."

"Yeah." *And wouldn't you like to know how we got it?* he thought. He looked at Mahadaji's companion, an angular black man in pipestem trousers and a baggy velvet jacket that billowed out about his waist in zero gee and was obviously designed for Mudville. He carried a satchel of equipment for testing the purity of *Runaway's* cargo.

"This is Mr. Cody," Mahadaji said. "He represents OttoBanque in this matter." Contempt twisted in Ubu's belly as he looked at the groundling.

"This is my sister, Beautiful Maria."

"Honored."

Maria was a cool monochrome fantasy, wearing only black

shorts and halter that contrasted with her pale skin. Her hair was pinned back out of her eyes but otherwise drifted free, a free-floating dark halo behind her head. She was barefoot and floated motionless within arm's reach of the personnel lock's castoff bars.

An autoloader horn bleeped down the causeway. "Okay." Ubu grinned at Cody. "Let's get started so we can return Mr. Cody to someplace with gravity before his jacket strangles him."

Mahadaji gave a polite, restrained laugh. Cody's face flushed a shade darker. Ubu reached behind him for a castoff bar, jerked his grips free of the velcro deck patches, and pushed off for the cargo gate. Once there, he gave the code that opened *Runaway*'s cargo hatch, then, when the dock's safety mechanisms showed pressure equalization and gave him a green light, opened the inner hatch.

The colossal container stacks were blood-brown under the intense light of the docking bay. Ubu rotated in the air, looked at Cody. "Check one at random," Ubu said. "Check any or all of 'em."

"Thank you, Mr. Roy." His voice was a generic type, a soft accent acquired in expensive Mudville schools.

Ubu laughed. "Never been called that before."

"Sorry. I thought Roy was your surname."

"Be so. It's the *mister* that's new."

"Sorry. It's bossrider, then, isn't it?"

Amusement rippled through Ubu at the sight of Cody trying to pin down his jacket with one hand while he unstuck his grips and pushed off for the open cargo hatch. He succeeded, but his trajectory was uneven and he began to tumble slowly. The 15A autoloaders rattled silent.

"Bossrider," said Ubu, as Cody rotated past. "Or shooter."

Cody grabbed the hatch coaming, halted himself, pushed off again for the containers. He came up against a container, steadied himself, tried to open his case, and began drifting away from the cargo. One of his hands flailed out, missed the nearest container by half an inch, and the drift into nowhere continued. Ubu's voice was cheerful.

"Bossrider's the title, see, like captain or general or whatever. Shooter's just polite. Like your mister, I suppose."

Ubu was willing to watch the bank official flop about for as long as it lasted, but Maria took pity on him; she kicked off, intercepted

Cody, and carried him to the far hatch coaming. She kicked again, holding Cody by his belt, and brought him up against the stack of cargo. He took a breath.

"Thank you, Miss—Shooter Roy."

"Last name's Maria. First name's Beautiful. Bag be getting away."

Cody snatched the bag, then looked up at her. "Shooter Maria. You and the bossrider had different fathers, then?"

Ubu stifled a laugh. This was the kind of question planet-dwellers always asked. Their social systems, whatever they were, were always stuck firmly in the mud of their little dirtball and they never understood anything about people who lived their lives unencumbered by all the ponderous bureaucratic kiddyshit, all the tax records and education certificates and housing forms and permits even to have people cart your junk away, all the Mudville stuff that weighed them down more than gravity.

Even Maria's patience was wearing thin. Her flat tone indicated her growing annoyance. "Same father," she said, "but we take whatever names we like. Sometimes I'm called Pasco's Maria after my father, and sometimes my brother is Pasco's Ubu. Ubu's given name was Xavier, but he didn't like it and named himself after someone he saw in a hype. His master's certificate is in the name of Ubu Roy, so that makes it official."

"Sounds confusing."

Beautiful Maria looked at him with slitted eyes. "None of *us* are ever confused." Ubu laughed out loud.

Cody didn't say anything after that, just tapped into the first container. Presumably he was satisfied, since he didn't object to what his analyzer was telling him.

"The Admiralty Court is meeting on your case in two days," said Mahadaji. "It would benefit your case if you were to appear in person."

"Fine," said Ubu.

"You also might dress more formally. If the magistrate doesn't like your looks, he might quibble at our settlement."

Ubu considered this. "Okay," he said, his voice doubtful.

"It's Bannerji, otherwise I wouldn't mention it. He's lived

downside all his life, till he got this appointment, and he's very conservative."

Ubu gave an impatient shrug. As soon as he got the payment from Portfire he could buy however many Mudville costumes he needed. Maybe even a uniform like Bannerji's. "Whatever it takes to get this all settled," he said.

The 15A autoloaders kicked in again. Mahadaji winced as the sound of grinding metal rang from the dock's hard alloy surfaces.

"Perhaps you and your sister can join me for luncheon onstation," he said. "We can meet the Portfire people afterward."

"Fine." A wave of the magic wand, Ubu thought, and the hypothetical bank balance would turn real.

"Luncheon is the big meal here. Takes two or three hours. Then tea, then a light supper."

Ubu wasn't interested in any of this, but he smiled at Mahadaji anyway. Ubu knew from the records he'd called up that Mahadaji had done a lot of work with shooters. The lawyer knew his way around, and also knew better than to ask any stupid questions about shooters' names. He'd be useful later.

"We had lunch about five hours ago," Ubu said, "but we're used to flexible schedules."

"Good. It's settled, then. Forgive me for a moment while I call my office."

Cody only examined four of the containers before he got tired of Maria hauling him around the cargo stacks. Maria carried him to the shuttle that took them to Port Town on the station. On the shuttle, Mahadaji and Maria witnessed the signing of the settlement between *Runaway* and OttoBanque. The rest of the journey was made in silence.

Cody was last seen tugging at his jacket, his grips fixed firmly on the velcro surface of the moveway that took him to the planetary shuttle. Ubu waved after him and laughed. Fucking invincible, he thought. I'm invincible. He rolled his shoulders, looked up at the tented metal sky. His body felt as if it were a conduit for energy.

Mahadaji led them down the low-gravity docks to a bullet-shaped gauss shuttle that would take them down the length of the station. They sat down on seats of contoured metal. The smell of electricity snarled in Ubu's sinuses. The shuttle started moving in absolute silence, built up speed. Bright holograms marched overhead, announced the next stop in several different scripts. Apparently people on Bezel spoke a lot of languages.

They stepped out at the third stop. Well-dressed people moved on soft black streets that gave slightly at each step. Some of them stared at Ubu. Ubu stared back, and the others looked suddenly away. He grinned. This was fun.

The ceiling was arched, each radiating beam scalloped and perforated in an intricate baroque design. Mahadaji led them to a building faced sternly in bronze. The floor was laid in some kind of grey stone that must have been shipped up from the planet below. Ubu could feel his grin begin to fade. He'd never been this far into Bezel Station or ever seen a place like this.

The interior of the elevator was plated gold and polished to a mirror finish. Mahadaji pressed his thumbprint to a receptor labeled "Pan-Development Klub" and the elevator began to rise.

PDK, Ubu remembered. The Kompanie. They'd sponsored the first settlements here, built Bezel Station. Still had a lot of say in how things were run.

"My club," Mahadaji said. "I think it has the best food onstation. And the best view."

Ubu's skin shone gold in the perfect mirror of the elevator doors. His energy began to return. He grinned, and the golden god in the mirror grinned back.

The gold-plated room rose forty stories. Gravity grew perceptibly lighter. When the mirrors opened Ubu stepped out into a bright wide room with glass windows and soft white carpets. A string trio played dolores music with a subtle ladino counterpoint laced into its structure. Maria smiled as she dug her bare toes into the shag. Conversation murmured in the background.

"Mr. Mahadaji." A grave copper-skinned man, in a short jacket with bright yellow buttons and a high collar and stock. "Your table is this way."

Overdressed people watched Ubu and Maria as he walked past the bar to Mahadaji's table. The table was set in a cloverleaf-shaped projection cantilevered from the side of the building, bubble-roofed.

* * *

The dolores music followed: great acoustics, Ubu thought, or subtle sonics. He couldn't tell which.

He could look straight up and see stars, the lights of Bezel Station's night side. Looking down, he could see the black absorbent avenues, distant holo adverts, patches of green that looked unnatural against the structured metal geometries of buildings and streets. One of those places, he thought, where they put soil down, grow things, and pretend they're on a planet.

Mahadaji called up the menu. Ubu recognized few of the items, and he and Maria let Mahadaji do the ordering. First there were snacks and a bottle of wine. Then hashish in an ornate brass water pipe—Ubu had always thought smoking a filthy Mudville habit, but he took careful puffs out of politeness, thankful it wasn't something completely disgusting like tobacco. The pipe was followed by sherbet to cleanse the palate. Then some kind of spicy soup. All the dishes were white bone china with the PDK insignia blazoned in gold. Another bottle of wine appeared, with a small animal, native to Bezel, cooked in its shell, which had to be broken open with a special tool. More hashish, more sherbet. Mahadaji explained each course and its preparation in words that skittered over Ubu's consciousness without coming to light. Ubu saw brightly colored birds floating over the dome, and remembered Bezel Station had let them fly loose as a tourist attraction.

The main course was a thick slab of pinkish meat sitting in its own juice, with steamed vegetables on the side. The roast whatever-it-was seemed naked. Ubu waited for the waiter to bring the sauce, saw Mahadaji and Maria begin eating, and decided to cut a piece. He ate it carefully, waiting for the flavor.

"Bland," he said.

Maria looked at him. "It's supposed to be subtle," she said.

Ubu laughed. "Too subtle for me." He looked at Mahadaji. Wine sang a bright melody in his head. "Can I get some chile sauce? Mustard maybe?"

"It's not grown in a vat, see," Maria said. "It's supposed to have a flavor of its own. Not supposed to *need* sauce."

"That's perfectly all right, Shooter Maria," Mahadaji said. "I should have anticipated. My fault." His small dark hands danced in the air as he summoned the waiter.

"I *like* it," Maria said insistently. She cut another piece of meat.

The waiter brought a bottle of chile-and-garlic paste and offered to heat it in a little chromium warmer. Ubu declined and poured the red stuff on the roast and vegetables both. They tasted better after that.

"I have already had inquiries," Mahadaji said, his knife cutting delicate bite-sized pieces of the roast, "concerning the origin of your cargo."

Ubu looked at him. Wine eddied through his veins. "What did you tell them?"

"I told them I did not know, and that all questions should be addressed to you." He touched his mustache with one little finger. "Some of the inquiries," he said, "were from the Navy. Special Investigations Department."

"What's SID's interest?"

"They want to make certain the cargo wasn't hijacked."

Ubu laughed. "If they can find a cargo that big that's been hijacked, they're welcome to try to pin it on me."

Mahadaji looked at Ubu with pebble eyes. Suddenly the air seemed chill. "*Should* I know where the cargo comes from, bossrider? Is it something you can safely tell me?"

Energy flamed through Ubu, burning the wine fumes away. I'm not *that* drunk, he thought.

"It's legitimate. We have contracts: the pharmaceuticals come from an exclusive source. There will be more shipments, perhaps more valuable than this one."

Mahadaji nodded slowly to himself. "You are an extremely fortunate man, bossrider."

"I don't want anyone to know about the future cargoes. Not till we sell this one for the highest possible price."

"There will be a great many inquiries. People will want to know on whose behalf you are working. Perhaps there may be attempts at espionage."

Ubu looked at Maria and grinned. She seemed startled by this thought. "There's nothing they can find out."

"You have taken precautions, then?"

"Yes. There's nothing to discover." Then he thought of Twelve hanging in *Runaway*'s auxiliary control station, and his grin froze on his face. He covered his hesitation by reaching for his wineglass, taking a gulp.

"SID may investigate you whether they have any real evidence or not. Your earlier difficulties have made you the object of suspicion. I think you should both know that you have the right to tell them nothing."

Ubu nodded. "Thank you, Mr. Mahadaji."

"The sudden exploitation of new sources of wealth is . . . against current Multi-Polly doctrine. You know that, of course."

Ubu glanced at Maria, saw her solemn, wide eyes on him. "Yeah," he said softly. "We know."

Suddenly he needed a breath of air. He stood. "Toilet," he said. Mahadaji gave him directions.

In the toilet Ubu could still hear the dolores music. He was surprised to see a small, wizened woman there, handing out towels in exchange for money. He paid for a towel, used a urinal, washed his hands, stepped out into the restaurant again.

The bar and its stools were padded with matching white plastic-covered foam, as if the management was expecting the gravity to disappear at any moment and the customers to start caroming off the furnishings. A black-skinned girl with brilliants floating in her puffball hair looked at him over her shoulder. Ubu walked to the bar and stood next to her. "OxyGen," he said.

He glanced at the girl. She had been lightly moned and it was difficult to be certain of her age—eighteen, he thought, on the outside. She wore silver sandals with straps that went up her calves and a one-piece sleeveless blue dress of some shiny material. She was still looking at him, nodding her head slightly to the beat of the trio. Her earlobes were elongated, almost reaching her shoulders, with big ornate silver plugs in them.

"Never seen a shooter before?" he asked.

She laughed and showed white teeth. "No, I haven't. Not in the real."

He raised his four arms. "Look all you like." Invincible, he thought.

"My name's Magda Desmond."

"Ubu Roy."

The bartender brought Ubu a disposable chak painted in bright red and yellow. OxyGen was an enzyme that would help his body metabolize alcohol. Suddenly he didn't want it. He paid for the inhaler and looked at Magda.

"You live here?"

"I'm here on vacation. Came with a friend, for the gambling."

"From downside?" Remembering not to call it Mudville.

"Yeah. A city called Parbhani."

"Where's your friend?"

Magda grinned. "She's in bed. Bad hangover. A noncheeper." Whatever that meant.

Invincible, Ubu thought. "Wanna come see Port Town later?"

She seemed dubious. "Anything there?"

"Shooter stuff." He laughed. "Don't worry. I'll protect you."

"Can I bring my friend?"

"If you like."

She smiled again. "Okay. Where shall I meet you?"

"Port Town exit on the gauss shuttle. Sixteen hundred, okay?"

"Sure."

"See you then."

"It's a cheeper."

Ubu headed back to Mahadaji's table, then remembered the OxyGen in his hand. Better sober up, he thought, before the meet with the Portfire people. Then have fun after. He swayed slightly as he used the inhaler, alternating nostrils till the contents were gone. He put the empty chak in a disposal labeled "Light Metals" and stepped into the bubble. Maria looked up at him, gave him a tentative smile. A snake crawled with cold, deliberate sloth down Ubu's spine. Ubu thought about Maria and Magda, black skin and white, and sobriety seemed to strike him all at once. He had never felt less drunk in his life.

Get it over with, he thought. It's gonna happen, might as well happen now.

"Mr. Mahadaji was talking about putting security on *Runaway*," Maria said. "He knows some people."

Ubu sat down and reached for the wine bottle. "Fine," he said.

Mahadaji smiled. "I can make the arrangements this afternoon. There can be a guard on your personnel gate by sixteen hundred, and people can install alarms on your outside airlocks."

Ubu drank one glass, then poured a second. "Sounds good," he said. He was aware that Maria was looking at him.

"I think I should set up a meeting with our finance specialist. Especially if there will be more shipments. There's an excess-profits tax, part of Consolidation."

"Excess profits," said Maria. "That's something we've never had to deal with." There was a slight smile on her lips, but her wide dark eyes still watched Ubu.

"The capitalization rules are complex. But there are ways of getting around them."

"Yeah," Ubu said. "Let's do it. Let the Multi-Pollies get their funding someplace else."

Mahadaji touched his mustache with the little finger of his right hand. "They just want things to be predictable."

Ubu scowled. "That's *their* problem."

There were two rounds of dessert, each with a different liqueur, followed by the water pipe and a last dab of sherbet. Ubu was floating again by the end of the meal. He looked in the bar for Magda as they moved on, but she'd gone. Mahadaji led them to the Portfire office, a foam-walled office building near Port Town, just a giant beige room filled with desks and terminals and lit by hanging fluorescents—all that happened here was that data got shuffled from one desk to the next; Portfire moved its actual goods out of a series of warehouses downside and in Port Town.

Ubu signed and printed and was handed an electronic fortune, out of which the Multi-Pollies collected a swashbuckling forty percent as a kind of assurance of further government depredations. OttoBanque was paid off, and Ubu looked in satisfaction at the resulting zeroes.

They said goodbye to Mahadaji after the signing, then headed for a moveway that led to Port Town. Ubu looked at his pocket watch, saw it was fifteen-ten. "I'm gonna have a party," he said.

"We've got people coming by. Guards. Remember?"

"Shit. Forgot."

"If there're actually gonna be groundlice looking into our business, we gotta protect Twelve."

"Yeah. Shit." He touched her on the arm. "Look, you take care of it, okay? I gotta go celebrate."

"We could celebrate tonight."

Anger snapped in Ubu's mind like a whip. "Just do it, okay?" he said. "Be a lousy favor, all right?"

Beautiful Maria looked at him with her dark, depthless eyes. One white hand fluttered to her throat. "Okay," she said. "If that's—"

"How I want it, yeah."

They rode to Port Town in silence. The moveway gave out onto a metal street: no soft black cushion here. Music clattered from bars. Shooters, systers, and dock workers careened by on tiptoe in the negligible gravity. Except for the warehouses, the buildings were all of tempafoam. There was still a shooter life here, and it crackled around Ubu and Maria as the moveway carried them toward the docks.

"Bye," Ubu said, waving to Maria, and he shrugged off her frozen, pursuing glance as he chose a bar at random and dove in. The foam walls were painted a garish blue. There was an autographed photograph of Evel Krupp over the bar. A dozen systers sat onstage hacking at their instruments as they floundered through a dross song. The singers couldn't remember even the chorus; the sitar player was practically asleep. The discordant sounds brought bright, razor-edged colors to Ubu's mind, perfect accompaniment to the brutal energy that seemed to roar through him like the flame of a reaction drive.

Ubu drank some Sharps while the systers staggered through another song. After that he asked if he could sit in on keyboards and played four-handed, giving the systers some direction for their incompetence. His weird synaesthesiac disharmony baffled them. Their drunken staggering around his pounding atonal chords only sharpened his amusement.

He remembered his meeting with Magda at the last minute. He

relinquished the synthesizer to a loud chorus of protest from the other players, who claimed they were just getting the hang of his playing. He bought a chak of Red Four at the bar, sniffed just enough to put a blade-keen edge on his intensity, and headed for the shuttle station.

He grinned as he saw Magda standing by the platform in a red-and-silver cousin to the short skirt she'd worn in the Klub. Her earplugs were red to match, carved impact rubies that must have weighed a quarter kilo each. She carried a shoulder bag. Ubu decided he was going to enjoy being around that skirt in the near-zero gravity. Her friend was a taller, dark-skinned woman of about the same age; her long straight hair was dyed silver. Round smoked glasses, impenetrable as coins, perched on her aquiline nose. She wore a pale silk blouse over knee breeches, silk stockings, and a lot of silver jewelry. Her caste mark was red, her earplugs turquoise. "This is Kamala," Magda said. Kamala looked at him and burst out laughing.

Ubu turned to Magda. "Is there a problem?"

Magda started laughing, too. "We're just in a good mood, is all."

Ubu grinned. "Me, too," he said. He bounced on his toes, turned, landed. Kamala laughed again, bending double. "After you," Ubu said.

The short skirt delivered the news that Magda's underwear was very small and pale blue in color. Magda, arms and legs flailing wildly as she tried to control her inertia, realized her costume's disadvantages early on. Things kept tumbling out of her shoulder bag. When she started to look resentful Ubu took her hand and guided her along.

He led them to a place he knew called the Black Runner, named after a legendary smuggler and featuring scarred black tempafoam walls. There was a crinkled, mirrored ceiling, colored spots, a dance floor with castoff bars set in the ceiling by heavy steel bolts. There were only a few people inside but Ubu knew it would fill up once the shift ended.

Ubu kept drinking Sharps, one little charge after another fired over his palate. Magda ordered something called a sindhu slush, which the bartender had to look up in his computer buzzmaster and which turned out to be thick and red. Kamala sipped cranberry juice and kept bursting out into random laughter at things no one else could see.

Customers came in. Systers mainly, with some shooters and dock workers.

"Can't believe the things up here you can get high on," Magda said.

"Shooters spend months at a time out of range of medical attention," Ubu said, "so we gotta have unrestricted access to the medicine chest."

"Not downside," Magda said. "Half the people are practicing this discipline called—well, the translation from Sanskrit is *Truth and Moderation*, which means basically they don't do anything for fun at all. No gambling, no alcohol, hardly any drugs. Mostly just hashish, and all that does is put me to sleep."

Kamala laughed again. Magda gave her an exasperated look. "Show Ubu your eyes, Kamala," she said.

Kamala removed her spectacles. Her pupils were almost as wide as the lenses of her glasses. Ubu peered at her and she burst out laughing again. Ubu could see her back teeth.

"She's my chaperone, if you can believe it," Magda said. Rotating spots turned the brilliants in her hair gold, then azure. The ruby plugs in her earlobes glowed. "My dad wants her to keep me out of trouble." Kamala, shaking her head at this, put her glasses back on.

"Who's your pop?" Ubu asked.

"Works for PDK. Executive vice-president of downside distribution." Which explained how she got in the Klub: the membership belonged to Daddy. Her lip curled. "I wasn't born here. Dad got transferred to Bezel. Another couple years and we're out."

Kamala stood up, began to reel toward the toilets. Ubu looked after her. "You groundlings gotta get a sense of proportion about drugs," he said. "Shooters are around them all the time and we know—"

"The hell with that. The point is, have you *got* any Blue Heaven or do I have to *buy* some?" Magda banged her drink on the table. The thick red liquid stayed up when the glass came down, falling in a slow motion that curved gently as the station rotated out from beneath it. Magda goggled at it, kept moving the glass to catch it all. When only a last drizzle remained out of the glass Ubu slammed down a hand and kept the stuff from rebounding back out. A few drops of red sleet spattered on the table with the force of his movement. Magda grinned.

"I'm getting to like low grav. It's a dead cheeper."

"There's just enough gravity here," licking sweet red syrup off his palm, "so you know who's on top."

Magda giggled, white teeth flashing in a black face. Ubu looked at her. "Just wish," she said, "I had the right kind of clothing."

"I could tell you how to fit in here."

Her eyes challenged him. "Yeah? How?"

"Take off the dress."

She rolled her eyes. "Appropriate. Sure."

"Look around you."

Her head turned slowly as she scanned the room. Her syrup-colored tongue touched her front teeth in thought. "Maybe I will, later." Her voice was dubious. "Now, would you hop to the bar and get some Blue Heaven? I still don't want to move in this skirt."

"Sure."

She reached in her bag and handed him a credit counter. He went to the bar and bought her pills. When he came back Magda was defiantly stuffing the dress into her shoulder bag. Ubu sat down and watched, as she straightened, the pleasant low-gravity ripples moving through her breasts.

"Rama," she swore. "Might as well. Go slumming, you gotta act—"

Jagged lightning crackled through Ubu's mind. "You think this is a slum?" he demanded.

"Oh." She straightened, looking startled. "Sorry."

"This is a way of life. I could buy and sell your old man." True, he thought, as of fifteen hundred this afternoon.

"Didn't mean to offend." She shivered as if she was cold. "You mind if I wear your vest? I'm not used to this."

"Use the upper set of armholes." He handed her the vest, put the pills on the table. She took two and smiled, then put the vest on, drawing it close around her breasts.

"There," Ubu said. "Now you're almost overdressed."

Kamala returned, carrying in her wake a lanky black-maned shooter off the *Andiron*.

"Shooter Ludovic," Ubu said politely. "I'm Ubu Roy. Bossrider, the *Runaway*."

Ludovic seemed puzzled. "Have we met?"

"Don't think so. I just know who you are."

He seemed doubtful. "Oh. Pleased to meet you anyway, bossrider." He leaned back. A slow smile dawned on his craggy features. "Be rumors about you, Ubu Roy."

"Yeah?"

"You getting famous."

Magda seemed interested. "Yeah? What'd he do?"

Ubu looked at Ludovic. Slum, she said. "It was the aliens. Monsters."

Dawning comprehension danced in Ludovic's eyes. He nodded solemnly. "Right."

Kamala laughed.

Ubu fired Sharps over his tongue. Fire trickled down his throat. "Big things in shells, with lots of hands. Looked like rocks till you got up close. Attacked some asteroid miners off in Terrace Belt."

Ludovic grinned. "Ubu here saved their asses."

Magda didn't seem to know whether or not to be scornful. "No such thing as intelligent life out there. It's *known*."

"Not intelligent," Ubu said. "Just *hungry*. Ate sixteen miners. I hadda go after 'em with this tool I made. Split 'em open so I could get to 'em with a torch."

Magda turned away. "Stop *talking* about it. Sounds awful."

"It *was* awful." Ubu and Ludovic described the awfulness in lively detail till the house band arrived and started to play some expert striff. Ubu and Magda danced till her eyes turned dreamy with Blue Heaven, then he steered her out of the bar to the Port Mansion Hotel, where he rented a shacktube and bought some hormone supplements. Ludovic and Kamala followed and got the tube next door.

Ubu kissed her, tasted sweet sindhu syrup, then took off her remaining clothes. She ghosted inexpertly to the bed while he turned off the light and fired the last bursts of Red Four from his chak. Boiling energy filled his body. Neural white noise hissed somewhere behind his eyes. Dimly, through the beige plastic wall, he heard Kamala's laugh.

He moved on top of Magda, anchored himself to the tubular bedframe with his lower set of arms. She was barely visible in the dim yellow light from the comm unit. As Ubu began to make love she closed her eyes, clasped his lower forearms with her hands. The brilliants in her hair gave off a chromed light in the periphery of his vision. She lifted her hips and thrust herself against him while murmuring someone's name. Her eyes never opened. It took him a while before he fully understood that the name she spoke wasn't his.

He comprehended that well enough. For him, the most important part of this act was that her name wasn't Maria.

CHAPTER
16

A PRESSURE WAVE TOUCHED BEAUTIFUL MARIA'S NAPE WITH COOL, delicate claws. A slow reflexive moment rolled by while she waited to see if there had been decompression on board—there hadn't been and never had; but still time seemed to suspend itself until she was certain, and then life resumed. Intruder alarms didn't start ringing, either. Ubu had therefore returned. She glanced at the green letters of the holo clock above the comm board, saw it was almost noon.

He came down the ladder into the centrifuge and entered the command cage. His eyes were scarlet-rimmed, his hair straggled over his face. He smelled of liquor and expensive perfume.

"Some party," said Maria.

"Yeah. Sorry if I— Maybe I should have called you."

"Maybe." She looked at him steadily. He turned away, scratched the bristles along one jaw.

"I don't think we should both be gone from the ship at the same time," Maria said. "We can't have anyone near Twelve."

"Okay. The guard on the door showed me how the security

system works." The issue didn't seem to interest him. He sat heavily on the nav couch.

"So I get to go out today, right?"

"Uh—I gotta go out later and get a suit made. For our court appearance."

"Tonight, then."

"I made plans." He looked at her, then looked away again. "I'll cancel."

"Good. And we're both appearing in court, remember. I gotta get a suit myself."

"Go now, if you like. Shuttle's leaving for the station in ten."

She turned back to the comm board. "I've been buying new hypes. New games, new music. If there's anything you want, look at the list while I've got it up."

"Okay." He reached out to his board, called up the file. Began moving the cursor, punching in choices.

"I've looked at the money we've got left. Be enough to buy two new singularities and the ships to go with them, even after we buy the AIs. Ships as big as *Runaway*."

He grinned. "Yeah. We can start a transport line. Runaway & Beloved Transport, Ltd."

"Don't forget Consolidation. Things still might come apart."

He looked at her. Red gleams reflected off his eyes from the piloting board, where warning lights showed that cargo bay doors were open and autoloaders were engaged. "Come apart, shit," Ubu said. "We've got nothing but money coming our way. Maybe forever."

"They'll figure it out sooner or later. The Navy investigators have already called, wanting to ask questions."

"What'd you tell them."

"Told 'em to call our lawyer."

Ubu smiled, turned back to the vid list. Punched up another hype.

"They'll find out," Maria said. "We'll lose our monopoly. What do you think is gonna happen to our action when the Multi-Pollies and the Hiliners start jacking their way in? We're just gonna be another shooter line shut out of the real business."

Ubu swung toward her, his face angry. "We could *be* a Hiliner company! You ever figured that?"

"Maybe."

"Shooting's what we know. Shooters are what we *are*! You got any better than the Now?"

"I've been thinking. We could build an excursion ship."

"A what?"

"An excursion ship. Take rich people out to meet aliens. Let them try to talk business with Beloved."

"I don't believe I'm hearing this."

A fiery burning anger crackled in Maria's heart. She sat up. "What's wrong with it?"

Ubu gestured with three arms. "You and me, Maria? Taking a bunch of Mudvillers, rich farmers and Hiline execs and Multi-Pollies and all their stupid children off into something they can't understand, wiping the dirt off their feet, picking off their lice, teaching them how to get into vac suits and shepherding them around in freefall so they don't hit their precious heads and scramble what brains they've got, and serving them bland food, and—"

"We don't have to do it in person, Ubu. We're rich. We just build the ship and own it and take the profit, okay?"

"Jesus Rice."

Anger clawed at Maria's throat. Her words grated out, breath forced through bright steel bars. "We're *rich*, Ubu! If we're gonna *stay* rich we've got to learn how. You wanna be a Hiline company, better find out how Hiliners operate first. Spending our time with other rich people isn't a bad place to start."

He shook his head. "We're into transport. It's what we know."

"Better learn something else. 'Cause we were into transport for years, and all we did was lose."

"Be winning now."

She stood, walked to the ladder, began to climb. Angry energy danced in her body, prickled the colorless hair on her arms. She paused on the ladder and looked down at him. "Things change," she said. "That's you, quoting me."

She looked up a clothing store in the station directory, left Modular Dock C for the station, danced through clamoring Port Town. She bought ginger beef at a tempafoam kiosk and ate it on the gauss shuttle downstation.

The store was called Hong's and was three levels up from the shuttle station, a brightly lit foam-padded place behind black graphite walls. Overdressed people walked by, but didn't seem to find her as worth staring at as the crowd in the Klub had—Maria figured they were more used to shooters on this level. She entered the store and looked at the white-haired Asian man who approached her. She could see herself in his sad black eyes, a tall pale exotic in halter and shorts, her bare feet dirty. She held up her credit counter.

"I need to be in court tomorrow, and I need to look good."

The Asian man cocked his head, considered. "No problem," he said.

Maria smiled.

Fast bright lasers danced over her body, read its contours. Maria chose material and style, and machines in the back of the store sliced fabric, folded, and used expensive stitching on the seams instead of simply melting them together. It took less than an hour.

And all she ended up with, at the end, was The Uniform: short-sleeved light blue shirt with standing dark blue collar, collarless jacket with velcro flaps on the pockets, black velvet slippers, pipestem trousers striped in two shades of grey. Mudville clothing adapted to orbit, with all the zippers and buttonholes taken off so nothing would snag in freefall. She looked at herself in the mirror and flashed on herself walking, in more or less the same clothes, through the door of the Monte Carlo, her nerves humming in terror as her mind fumbled with the rules to rouge-et-noir. Entering a life she'd only seen in hype.

And now she would enter the same world again.

The Asian man seemed disappointed when she decided not to wear the new clothes out of the store. He folded them neatly in a box of pale green recycled plastic.

Beautiful Maria carried the box back to *Runaway*. Twelve was playing dolores music in his room, absorbing Melange lyrics; Ubu, she discovered, was asleep in his cabin. She stored the box under her rack and went to the lounge. Maybe, she thought, she'd watch one of the new hypes.

Abrazo will be here soon, she thought. The memory came

suddenly, without warning. She wondered if Kit was still angry with her.

She called up a hype, began watching it. The characters all lived in Mudville and seemed opaque, and the motivation for their action was obscure. Is it a bad hype, she wondered, or was it that she just didn't understand it?

The phone link gave a beep and Maria told the hype to pause. She reached behind her, swung the control board down from its slot in the wall, accessed the comm, told the link to feed into the lounge holos and speakers.

"Is Ubu there?"

So *that's* what she looks like, Maria thought.

A black woman, long hair drawn back severely behind the head, bushed out behind. Dull eyes. Strange pierced earlobes that looped almost to her shoulders, dangling empty and twisted like loose string. A sullen, pampered look. Clearly displeased that someone other than Ubu had answered.

She was the expensive perfume type, all right. Maybe she didn't even carry lice.

"The bossrider is unavailable right now," Maria said.

"Tell him that Magda called. I remembered the name of the place. It's called the Surat. Can you tell him that?"

"Yes."

"I'll meet him there at sixteen hundred."

"Recorded."

Maria routed the call to Ubu's cabin. He could view it when he woke. She wondered if she'd be spending the night on *Runaway* again, waiting for Ubu's return, waiting for her party.

Laser interference danced in the air. Maria's heart lurched. She turned her eyes away.

"Where's Kitten? Where'd she go?"

Pasco's voice. She knew from his tone that he was close to the end, that the recording had frozen his mind in the final moments of shambling toward its personal precipice.

Hatred exploded deep inside her, rose hot in her throat like bile. Her fists clenched. She looked up at the hesitant, trembling parody of her father.

"You've had it," she said.

He was looking at her with a puzzled expression. "I had something I wanted to say, but I forgot. Have you seen her? I was just looking."

Fury stormed in her mind. "I'm getting rid of you. You're not my pop. I don't give a fuck what Ubu thinks."

She seized the control board and began working.

He had to be in there somewhere.

Working in driven white-lipped anger, Beautiful Maria nailed Pasco after two hours' intense work. Located him, glitched the program that hid and relocated him after each random appearance, unraveled his software like a skein of wool, stuffed him in a file piled high with security. The galaxy's first holographic ghost had been cornered and slammed into a cage.

If Beautiful Maria had anything to say about it, he wasn't coming out again.

In the meantime Ubu went out, came back with a different, more expensive, variant of The Uniform. Surat turned out to be a clothing store. Magda didn't come back with him, nor did the smell of her perfume.

Associating with rich people, she thought. That's what she'd wanted him to do, right?

She dressed for Port Town in a one-piece dark grey leotard with subtle lighter stitches bleached into the fabric by laser, an almost subliminal stripe that started at her right hip and rose diagonally across her left breast to the shoulder. She dusted her cheekbones and shoulders with glitter, put on a pair of fringed mocs, kicked off.

Once in Port Town she bounded down the short metal street that circled the narrow end of Bezel Station like a silver ring set on a finger. She moved from bar to bar, club to club. Ate, danced, sometimes sat in with the usual inept shooter band. Ran into a few old friends and shared their table, their food and drink and raucous hospitality. She shrugged off friendly, faintly envious questions about the origin of *Runaway*'s cargo, shrugged off also a few more direct propositions.

Noise and laughter and shouts boiled up around her. Beautiful Maria drank, danced, laughed on cue, but for some reason her mind was touched with frost. She found her companions just a little strange, a little foreign. Port Town, and other shooter neighborhoods on every other station and habitat, had always seemed like home before. She had drifted through one habitat after another, merging into the boisterous life without thought. But now she was looking at it, at least partly, through someone else's eyes—Twelve's? Mahadaji's? And the shooters looked strange to her: happy, promiscuous, profane, dressed in scraps and rags worn bravely, like flags. Superbly capable at everything they did, so efficient the Multi-Pollies perceived them as a threat and set out to destroy them. Insular, knowing nothing but their own world, their own business, caring nothing about anything outside the burning reality of the Now.

Dying. In another generation, dead.

Because they didn't understand? she wondered. Because they were so confident in their own abilities, the necessity and rightness of their way of life, they never cared to find out why others, the sort who lived and worked in bronze-fronted palaces like the Pan-Development Klub, decided to wipe them away like a sysop erasing an old file he no longer needed. The shooters didn't know why, Maria thought, didn't understand, didn't think it worth their while to find out. Shooting's what we know, Ubu had said. Shooters are what we *are*. You got any better than the Now?

Her heart turned cold. The striff cry seemed raucous, its joy artificial. This was all going to be destroyed, she knew, destroyed as totally as if it were sucked into a singularity on the wrong tangent and crushed into black condensed matter where nothing, not even the tiniest particle, had room to breathe.

She wondered if this was where Pasco had been, if he had looked into that same great swallowing singularity until he could see nothing else, until he had no option but madness . . .

Her drink left the taste of cold iron in her mouth. She stood, excused herself, left the bar for the alloy street outside. Cooking smells and the sound of music rained upon her as she walked the street, circling the station.

She and Ubu would survive, she thought. They had the reserves now, the financial cushion. Almost everything else would disappear or be transformed. The systers would survive longest, shipping raw materials from asteroids or barren moons, living on fringe economies the Hiliners weren't interested in; but they weren't shooters, would never feel the crackling electricity of the Now as they conned a ship into the depthless screaming heart of a black hole and out again . . . Any shooters that survived would be swallowed into Hiline culture, knowing the Now but unable to live it.

Tears blinded her. She staggered off the street, leaned against an upright surface composed of tempafoam recently layered in fresh black paint. Pain twisted in her chest.

Why now? Maria thought. Stupid to mourn now, when you've known all along.

Then she realized it was because she was outside it now. When she and Ubu were dying along with all the rest, it was pointless to mourn. Who mourns their own death? But now *Runaway* was saved, but could not keep its own context alive.

"Live sex show, shooter femme. Twenty. Fucky-fuck, all live. Fifteen for you."

She blinked and brushed her hair back, scanned at head height, then down. The barker was an old mutanto shooter with another set of arms set into his hip sockets, the lower arms folded with the elbows in the upper set of armpits. His knotted fingers splayed on the metal street.

The mutanto was so wasted he couldn't even stand up—the club's management had propped him in the doorway. Whatever he had taken to burn his balance and coordination had messed up his vision as well; he was looking somewhere off to her right.

"Good stuff," he said. "The real thing. Live fucky-fuck." His face assumed a more hopeful expression. "Pills. Real stuff, shooter femme. Blue Heaven, magic Seven. Got it straight, Red Eight. Chaks, tablets, whatever. Hits you fine, number Nine. Cheaper than wholesale."

Beautiful Maria turned and walked away. Sorrow sang a resonant mourning ballad in her head.

So much for the party, she thought.

Days droned by. The Admiralty Court took about ten minutes to dispose of their case. It took a lot longer for Ubu and Maria to get rid of the newsfax reporters who clustered around them as they tried to leave. While they were absent someone tried to gain access to *Runaway*, sneaking past the loaders to enter the ship through the cargo bay access. The intruder must have known right away that he'd set off an alarm, because when the alerted guard jumped from the personnel access into the cargo bay, he met the other leaping out on an opposite trajectory. The guard tried to hit him with an autohomer, but the bullet plowed into a container of Orange Seventeen instead, releasing shimmering transparent balloons of the hormone into the dock's atmosphere. The intelligence of the workers running the autoloaders must have gone up ten points before it was all cleaned up. The intruder got away in a stolen repair capsule he'd parked at a station lock.

A few days later the autoloaders on 17A fell silent as the last of the pharmaceuticals rolled into storage. *Runaway* left the modular dock, hung in its assigned place two miles from Bezel Station with its red warning lights blinking in a personalized coded pattern. A rented warehouse on the station held a growing collection of AIs. Ubu and Beautiful Maria donned vac suits to visit Port Town, traveling alone unless business required them both onstation.

Deposits were placed on the next two black holes to be captured and brought to Bezel. The PDK dockyards, orbiting Bezel a precise sixty degrees in advance of the station, would build ships around the singularities once they were delivered. Big transports, as Ubu wanted. Bigger than Beloved's ship.

Abrazo drew closer to the station, its torch a cold fire in the empty darkness.

Maria never heard of Magda again. Whatever function she'd served for Ubu had been made obsolete. He seemed less edgy now, more relaxed. Whatever it was he did on his excursions to Port Town, he kept to himself.

Maria's visits were quiet, subdued. She was mourning the place. She found a fellow mourner eventually, a gentle, balding older man named Mitaguchi. Just after he'd got his master's certificate, years ago, his shooter family had been broken up, shattered under the first blow of Consolidation, and he'd got a job in a Kompanie transport. He was first officer now, waiting for a vacancy to be promoted captain and finally get a chance to use the master's certificate he'd earned when he was eleven years old. He was married to a shipping executive back in Doranes; they had three children, almost grown.

Mitaguchi still wore shooter clothing when he visited Port Town, looking for old friends, singing old songs. He didn't wear the clothes with much conviction.

Something in his lost quality appealed to Maria—in Port Town the two of them could live in a dream in which neither, any longer, could quite believe. They drifted along the metal ring together, sampling its pleasures, enjoying its rude and bustling life, making grave, balletic love within its tempafoam and laminate walls. She learned about his shooter family, all the memories he treasured. He hadn't seen any of them in years. Two days before he was scheduled to blow station, Mitaguchi convinced himself he was madly in love with her. Eyes burning, he cornered her in their shacktube, spoke in bright, fervid tones of resigning his post, abandoning wife and children and seniority, coming aboard *Runaway* to live with the femme who had returned his life to him, brought back everything he'd lost . . . His weird intensity, the violence of his desperation, stunned her. For a brief moment of claustrophobic horror she was afraid of him. She stared at him for a long, terrified moment; but he saw his answer in her eyes and Mitaguchi seemed to collapse, the steel tension in his limbs melting as if under a fusion torch. He did not argue when Beautiful Maria, sorrow burning in her throat, sent him away.

Mitaguchi sent her a note through the station net just before his ship left, thanking Beautiful Maria for her decision. His courtesy made her feel better about it all.

Abrazo completed its rendezvous with Modular Dock A. For the next few days, in her intermittent journeys around Port Town, Maria felt in her mind a hum of interest, of anticipation. Maybe she'd see Kit. But the days went by and there was no chance meeting, no message on the net. Her anticipation faded.

When the chance meeting finally occurred, it was at the wrong time. Beautiful Maria was in a club called Now and Forever, a tempafoam-over-wire hookshop annex devoted chiefly to efficiently relieving shooters and systers of their money at near light speed. With waiters aggressively pushing drinks at her and whores of both sexes actively soliciting custom, Now and Forever wasn't Maria's sort of place, but she had been taken there by Wu and Pet's Rae, a shooter couple who had been carrying a small shipment for the bar's owner, and who had business there.

Wu and Pet's Rae were friends and contemporaries of Pasco, and they and their family had actually prospered during Consolidation thanks to an exclusive contract with Portfire for delivery of pharmaceuticals from Bezel Station to partly developed Edge systems like Angelica, the same kind of deal De Suarez Expressways had with PDK. Sometimes they passed on extra duties to *Runaway*, and now *Runaway* had probably just given them some more work. Wu and Pet's Rae had known Ubu and Maria since birth, and Ubu and Maria saw them and their five children more often than most other shooters working this part of the arm.

Now and Forever was their fourth stop for the evening. While Pet's Rae propped her gangly brown arms on the bar and talked business with the owner, Wu bought the tray of watery beer shoved at him by the first waiter and handed the bulbs to Maria and his kids. Yawning whores danced under pink and violet spots in the back, their desultory movements bearing little relationship to the furious pounding striff that bounced off the metal floor. Android sex toys would have danced with more conviction, but in the latter days of Consolidation human material was cheaper.

By the time Wu and party finished the first round they were singing along with the striff, much to the annoyance of the hairy-chested waiter. Customers who spent their time singing were not spending money with proper efficiency. While Wu and the waiter negotiated this matter, Maria kicked off toward the toilet, bounded over the next table, landed in the clear, skipped on. She reached over her head to seize a castoff bar and alter her trajectory, and out of the corner of her eye, in the purple reflection of a dancer's spotlight, saw the highlighted cheek and forehead of Kit de Suarez.

Maria's hand reflexively clamped down on the bar. Momentum tugged at her shoulder muscles, bounced her like a ball at the end of an elastic string. Kit was walking toward her. Maria kicked out, dropped lightly to the floor, and in a short bounce hopped next to him.

He gave a start. She said hello and he mumbled a reply. "*Runaway*'s out of trouble," Maria said.

He seemed to be searching the room for someone. Maybe he didn't want to look at her. "I'm not," he said.

"What do you mean?"

"Marco found out." He turned to her for the first time. Frozen anger lay behind his eyes. "Don't ask me for any more favors, okay?"

"Sorry." She ventured a smile. "I'm with some friends. Wanna join us?"

Kit shook his head. "See you around." He turned and kicked off.

"Sorry," Maria called after him. He didn't react. Probably, Maria thought, hadn't heard.

The toilet smelled of sharp disinfectant and the whores' overwhelming perfume. It wasn't until Maria was drying her hands that she looked up at her reflection in the smudged steel mirror and realized that she'd dropped in on Kit as he was leaving the hookshop, that he'd just had a woman back there and probably wasn't very proud of it.

Bad timing.

The waiter's argument with Wu had been cut short by the arrival of a Buddhist missionary, who entered to drop tracts on each table and whose ejection, once he proved to be an expert staff fighter, occupied the full attention of the bar's employees. By the time Maria returned, Wu and family were singing again, their voices defiant, their grins wide.

Shooters could make music whenever they liked.

Maria joined in. Her mind stayed on Kit, his unsettled manner, his cold eyes.

Drumbeats spun a complex rhythm in Twelve's mind. Alien thoughts fought fevered wars in his blood. Floating in auxcontrol, he turned off his recorder and let the hurricane of humanity whirl within him.

Passion. The humans were so improbably passionate, so impetuous in their assertion of the primacy of their emotions. Their entertainments were almost always brassy declarations of passion, usually of love or longing, sometimes of thoughts more complex, but still stated with forthright vehemence.

Some of the music, striff and some dross, was usually fairly straightforward, riding along a thundering avalanche of simple, driving rhythm. These were like the patterns Beloved used for hard labor or combat, simple, overwhelming expressions of urgent necessity. The subject matter was different, but Twelve understood the intent.

Some dross was more complicated, the subject matter less focused, more subtle—more *poetic*, as Twelve gathered. Poetry was a concept that Twelve found, in turns, either hopelessly opaque or vaguely subversive, designed as it was to elicit response by a crafted appeal to levels of awareness that were not in themselves overt or easy to understand . . . Such approaches, Twelve thought, could be used by a cunning intelligence to infect the thought of her enemies.

The worst was the ballad forms used by the dolores music. The tunes were almost always mournful, the subject matter simple and direct—usually love or the loss thereof—but the concentrated human passion was overwhelming, and always laced with poetic terms. This was made far worse when the steady dolores rhythm was contaminated by a style identified by Maria as "ladino," something Twelve was beginning to think of as evil. The patterns were subtle, the rhythm breaking, one pattern infused by another . . . any clear rhythmic statement was subverted before its meaning could be absorbed by the listener. Some of the rhythms were indeed Beloved's, but should she ever transmit such a shattered pattern to her servants, the meaning would never be clear and it would cause only confusion and grief.

And any of Beloved's servants exposed to such a concentrated dose of passion would be driven mad. Twelve himself was only able to distance himself from the process by concentrating on Beloved's instructions to learn, to stay objective and gather data . . . Were he compelled to act within the whirlwind context of humanity instead of simply to witness, he would have been helpless.

The concentration upon passion he found unseemly. The passions themselves were often inappropriate even in what Twelve understood of the human context, and the singers' insistence on the importance of their own emotions was egotistical beyond rationality.

Somewhere in their past, Twelve thought, humanity had been

shattered. Each individual had become a fragment, without a Beloved to arrange their lives to an appropriate pattern. Some humans believed there were gods, others did not. Ubu and Maria had never met one. It was inconceivable that humanity could have arisen to their present level with their lives and emotions in such chaos . . . Had it been their gods who had brought them this far, and then abandoned them for reasons of their own?

The thought struck Twelve like a savage clap of thunder. Would Beloved ever evolve to the point where she would no longer need her servants, then abandon them to stagger along in isolation while she concerned herself with higher matters? Twelve cringed with fear at the thought.

But no. His task was to trust Beloved, to be her witness here on *Runaway*. He must not panic, must not apply his speculations concerning humanity to the holy perfection that was his own heart, his own center.

But the thought of human gods, like a delicate strand of dolores imagery, rose unbidden in his mind. His own visitation had been fraught with difficulties. Though the second part of the god's message had been clear enough, the first part of the message had been confused. Apparently the god assumed that Twelve knew more about humanity than in fact he did.

The god blamed himself for some disaster, that much was clear. The nature of the disaster had been unspecified—there had been talk of "parties" and "shipments"—but the god's warning about the de Suarez family had been intended as a partial remedy.

But perhaps the opacity was deliberate. Perhaps the god's statement had been a kind of poetry, an attempt to speak to Twelve's mind somewhere below his level of conscious awareness. Perhaps, Twelve thought in sudden horror, his mind had been subverted by the crafty human god.

The thought was too disturbing. Twelve let go of his red recorder as if it burned him.

He swam across the room to the sizer, programmed Beloved's most soothing rhythm, then strapped himself into an acceleration couch and withdrew his eyes, concentrating entirely on Beloved's tranquilizing, throbbing statement of defined purpose.

Subliminal human patterns still crept into his awareness. The dry, horrid air still drew moisture from his palps, infected his senses with the scent of humanity.

Human rhythms rattled in his brain like debris falling down a long, dark, endless tunnel.

CHAPTER
17

"YO. YOUNGER BROTHER."

Juan's voice. Kit, his hands and forearms covered in the bright orange grease he was using to lube the centrifuge bearings, looked over his shoulder at the access hatch. Lightly deformed globes of weightless sweat hung tenuously to his forehead, the curves of his nostrils.

"In here."

Juan's head appeared in the hatch, spiky hair glowing red in the dim light of the metal-caged safety bulb above the hatch frame. "Bossrider wants you."

Kit swiped at his forehead with his upper arm, trying not to get grease on his face. The smell of the stuff was sharp in his nostrils. He held up his hands. "I'm not presentable."

Juan's expression was sullen. "Now, Marco said. I'm supposed to finish for you."

Kit reached for a towel. Apprehension sang a wordless, keening song in his thoughts. If Marco wanted him to leave his maintenance work, it was probably because he wanted Kit for something worse.

245

"Okay," he said. "Sounds fair to me. I've finished with the Cantor units, but all the Chingiz still need attention."

"Lazy bastard. Shoulda had half those done by now."

"I knew you wouldn't want to miss all the joy, Elder Brother."

Kit swabbed off as much of the stuff as he could and vaulted feet-first through the hatch. Cooler air touched his grateful skin. The access tunnel was striped with color-coded superconducting glassware cables that carried power and communications to and from the fuge. Kit tugged himself hand over hand in a direction that normally would have been head-downward, reversed himself, kicked out through another access into the personnel level. Cooking smells drifted through the corridor.

Marco was in his office, illuminated from above by a bright naked yellow light. Kit, trying not to get grease on anything, stopped his momentum with an elbow and knee to the doorframe. The mirrored espresso machine behind Marco gave a hiss, as if warning the old man of a hostile approach. Marco's skeletal body, naked except for his silver crucifix, was strapped by a zero-gee harness to his computer terminal. A bulb of espresso was stuck by its velcro tab to his desk. Jesus Rice was nailed in painted agony on the wall behind.

"Bossrider, Juan told me you wanted . . ."

"Yes." The bossrider's eyes were still focused on his terminal. Marco raised an inhaler to his nose, fired, sniffed.

"I'd like to shower, if you have time. I've got grease all over me."

Only then did Marco turn to him. In the strong overhead light it seemed as if his eyes had disappeared into their jaundiced hollow sockets, like the retreating eyes of a skull. Kit tried to stop himself from shrinking away.

"I can talk to you in the shower as well as anyplace," Marco said.

The espresso machine gave another hiss. Marco saved his work on the comp, turned it off, and shrugged off his harness. He left the straps floating at the station, picked up his bulb of espresso, kicked out with a knobbed foot.

Kit's nape prickled as Marco followed him purposefully down the corridor. The smell of cooking onions drifted down from the galley, mingling with the odor of scented candles from the blue-painted shrine to the Virgin. Kit passed the shrine and turned into the cabin he shared with his brother. The walls were covered with hype posters and holographic pornography. Three-dimensional labia, as in a trompe l'oeil, followed him as he moved toward the shower door.

Kit swung it open, flexed to strip off his g-string. He could hear a couple of the younger children laughing next door, their voices louder than the comic hype they were watching. Marco, his muscles hanging slack even in zero gravity, floated into the room and stabilized himself next to Juan's rack.

"*Runaway*'s in station space," Marco said.

Kit felt a cold prickle up his arms and shoulders as he swung himself into the shower.

"I know." Trying to keep his voice level.

"You seen your sweetie?"

"I figured you wouldn't want me to." Kit avoided Marco's gaze as he swung the shower door closed. Dread did a nervous dance in his heart. He started the exhaust fan, then the water. Perfect globes of crystal issued from the black-rimmed plastic nozzles and burst on impact with Kit's skin. Three naked holographic femmes looked at him with appreciative eyes. Marco's shadow appeared on the pebbled glass of the door. His voice carried over the sound of the shower.

"She and her brother settled their troubles with the law. Came in with the richest cargo anyone's seen."

Kit breathed softly through the sieve of his teeth so as not to drown. He reached for the detergent dispenser and pressed the trigger. White soft foam poured into his palm. Kit watched high-impact water drops pockmark its perfect surface before spreading it over his hands and arms. He was glad he didn't have to look in Marco's eyes.

"Twenty-eight thousand tonnes of the highest-class compounds," Marco said. "*Runaway* utilized its entire cargo capacity. When's the last time any of *our* ships did that, hey? And the stuff can't have been stolen, because by now someone would have noticed that much missing." Kit saw Marco's shadow raising a hand to fire espresso into its mouth. When the voice came back it was louder. "You hearing me, boy? I'm not talking for my own edification, here."

"Be hearing!" Kit shouted as loud as he could. Maybe, he

thought, he could make Marco scream at him for the rest of the afternoon.

Marco's voice continued at increased volume. Score one, Kit thought. "The stuff was in standard containers, except the containers were made out of something weird, some kind of resinated compound. People be knowing how to make the stuff for a long time, but why bother? Alloys are cheaper." White foam streaked with orange cascaded from Kit, spiraled down the exhaust. Water droplets were trying to ascend his nose. Expertly he blew them out. Marco shouted over the exhaust's whine.

"And you said they were going out prospecting, yes? They've still got the magnets hooked to their ship. So they probably went out pretty far, right? So they wouldn't hit a system already swept for black holes?"

"I guess so!" Still shouting.

"I figure they ran into somebody out there. Be people saying it was some old Hiliner ship, jumped off course during a bad shoot and somehow everyone died before they could get it back. Ubu and Maria stripped it, may be going back for another load. I don't think so. All *Runaway*'s drugs are products of the last twenty years, all in the public domain. No ship's been lost during that time with that kind of cargo."

"So what is it?" Kit shouted.

"Some people say it might be a lost settlement."

Kit shut off the water and shook drops out of his hair. Tiny jewels exploded from his head, smashed, recombined, were carried down the howling exhaust. Warm air gusted on his body.

Despite the heat, chills rolled up and down Kit's spine. He knew exactly where this was leading.

"How could there be a lost settlement?" he asked. "Sounds a lot less likely than a lost Hiliner."

"Who knows?" Still shouting. "Maybe it's some of us. Shooters. Maybe when Consolidation started pounding us, a group of families went off on their own, built a habitat somewhere. But that doesn't explain how they can come up with twenty-eight thousand tonnes of pharmaceuticals in just a few months' time. Like they were just making the stuff out there, waiting for someone to find them and buy their stuff. But I figured *that* out, boy."

Kit rolled open the shower door and reached for a towel. Certain things, he knew, were inevitable. He would do what his great-uncle asked. He just wanted a fair price for his efforts.

"See, I figure the settlement was exporting the stuff already." Marco realized he was shouting, scowled, then lowered his voice. "They've likely got a few shooter families distributing for them, in smaller amounts, through the human sphere. And when Ubu and Maria stumbled onto them, the settlement bought 'em off. Just gave 'em this giant cargo out of their warehouse and told 'em to forget what they saw. They didn't have enough of *our* containers to hold the stuff, so they had to use their own, the resinous containers they hold their own stuff in. Maybe they'll work *Runaway* into their distribution chain later.

"Ubu's buying AIs, see. The latest model Lahores, meant for shootconning. One's being retrofitted into *Runaway*, the others are meant as cargo. It's like *Runaway*'s gonna outfit an entire fleet. And I figure I know whose fleet. Right, boy?"

Kit finished drying himself and threw the towel into the bin. Marco floated before him, yellow skin, three-day beard, withered grey genitals, sunken chest—a preposterous contrast to the moned, smiling women on the walls. Kit forced himself to stare into Marco's deep eyes.

"You want me to get close to Maria," he said. "Find out where this settlement is."

Marco's lips coiled away from his teeth. "Be getting smart, boy. I want you to play the same game with her that she played with you. Use your famous charm. Maybe once you get yourself in her twat she'll tell you anything you want to know." His bulb hissed as he misted espresso over his palate. "Whatever deal Pasco's Ubu cut with these people, I figure De Suarez Expressways can cut a better. We've got more ships, we can work more efficiently with them, have more flexible scheduling."

"She might not tell me."

"Then you'll have to find out some other way. Get into the ship's log. Do what you have to do."

A tremor ran up Kit's spine. He suppressed it. Marco, he thought, was like some kind of family demon. You couldn't get rid of it, but you could bargain with it sometimes. "I'll do it," he said.

Filling him was a determination that he hadn't quite known he possessed. "But I want something, bossrider," he said.

Marco's liquid black eyes gazed at Kit, as empty of pity as the vacuum that surrounded the ship. He raised a knobby hand, stabbed a finger at Kit. The middle finger, which he always used for pointing. "Don't give me this kiddyshit, boy. I can make life hell for you."

Hate flared in Kit's vitals, gave him the energy to stare into the old man's eyes. "I want shooter status," he said. "On the *Familia*, with my father."

"Huh." Marco appeared to consider this. "You better come back with the information, boy."

When Marco didn't snarl at him instantly, Kit felt a distant surge of hope. Maybe he could get out of here, back to someplace sane. "Is it a deal, bossrider?"

"It's a deal," Marco said. "If you bring me what I need to know. If not, forget it. I don't need shooters who can only fuck up." He reached out to Juan's bunk, turned himself to face the door. "You're off your regular duties," he said as he cast off for the door. "Just concentrate on giving Maria a good time."

Kit watched him go. For some reason he didn't feel like saying thank you.

The thing he had to keep very clear in his mind, he thought, and keep clear every minute, was why he was doing what he intended to do.

"Hi. I just wanted to apologize for the way I acted two days ago."

Beautiful Maria cocked her head as she watched Kit's recording. Had he undergone a course of mones? His face somehow seemed more defined. Grown-up.

Kit fidgeted in his chair. "Marco ordered me not to see you again, and I was afraid somebody would see us together. One of my cousins was there. Maybe you saw him." Maria, thinking back, couldn't remember any other de Suarezes present, but that didn't mean they weren't there.

Kit looked over his shoulder, as if someone might overhear him using the transmitter. "I *would* like to see you, though, if you'd like. I'd just rather not use any public place. Not even a hotel." His voice drifted away. "Maybe I could come to *Runaway*," he said. He looked embarassed. Kit looked into the camera, opened his mouth to say something, then decided against it.

I love you? Maria wondered.

"Leave a message on the station net if you like. I'll be onstation tomorrow morning and the rest of the day."

The message ended. Maria looked at the empty black threedee screen and wondered how Kit had changed. More adult, but also more uncomfortable. Maybe he just didn't know how to phrase his message.

Maxim hopped into Beautiful Maria's lap. At least, Maria thought as she scratched the cat, her relationship with Kit had been simple. He hadn't asked her to bring back a whole lost existence like Mitaguchi or demanded, like Ubu, a complex, entirely unspoken standard of behavior. All Kit wanted was to be kept away from his family for a while.

She'd have to hide Twelve, she thought. And maybe Ubu would never know.

The inner hatch slid open. Beautiful Maria wore a red vest trimmed with silver lace and a pair of grey pipestem trousers that looked as if they'd come from the closet of an onstation accountant. The contrast was meant to be surprising, and it brought a grin to Kit's face as he unsealed his helmet and began to wrestle with his suit's hard plastic shoulder harness.

Maria gave a chuckle as she stepped forward to help him. "Hi," she said. Her smile was cheerful. He could smell the odor of her hair and breath, feel the warmth of her skin. He wondered whether he should kiss her or not. She didn't offer, so neither did he.

He hooked his feet under a pair of straps made for the purpose and let her haul the harness maneuvering unit over his head. He unclipped the harness hardware leads, unsealed the bottom part of the suit, then hauled himself out of the bulky trousers. The top half of the suit was next.

Maria snugged each element of the suit in an elastic net. Then she stepped back and looked at him as he tugged his t-shirt down from around his armpits.

"You've lost mass," she said.

"Gained," he said. "Mostly muscle. Marco's had me doing all the repair and heavy hauling."

Her look softened. "My fault?"

A flash of resentment cracked through him. "On account of you, yes," he said. With more anger than he'd intended.

Damn. He was supposed to be charming, not make her angry.

"Sorry." She smiled guiltily. "*Real* sorry."

"Forget it."

She started to say something more, but the idea faded from her eyes and she turned easily in air. "Let's go to the lounge," she said.

Maria levered herself through the hatch with both arms, then waited for him to leave the lock before closing the hatch and sealing it. He drifted ahead for the moment, turned down the trunk housing that led to the centrifuge, kicked out past the auxiliary control room.

"What's that smell?" he asked.

"Smell?" Maria's voice was loud.

"Smells funny in here."

"Oh." There was a pause. "Ubu was painting something in auxcontrol."

"Huh. Smells like an animal or something."

"When have you ever smelled a real animal?"

"My mother kept cockatoos."

She chuckled. "I don't think birds count."

"Okay. I suppose dogs and cats don't count, either. So in that case I haven't ever smelled an animal."

Good, he thought. He'd put her at ease again. He was going to have to watch those bursts of hostility. Even his brothers had learned to be wary of him when cracks of anger began to glow in him like lava welling through the misting methane surface of a cold moon.

As Kit went down the ladder into the centrifuge, he tried to remember their first meeting. Something he'd done then, he thought, had made him attractive to her. He wished he could remember what it was. He could feel tension turning his shoulders to iron.

He stepped downspin along worn pale green carpeting to the upper lounge, sat on the sofa. It was lunchtime for her, and she offered him something to eat and drink; he accepted and called it supper. She handed him a bulb of Lark and dropped food from the warmer on a plate, then filled her own and sat in one of the side chairs.

Kit took a few bites of cashew chicken, then looked up at her. Was it stupid to start so soon? He really couldn't think of anything else to say.

"I've been hearing a lot about you."

"Heard what?" Her pale hands danced in a gesture of dismissal. He felt a deep vibration inside him, a thrumming bass chord of memory; he had forgotten those extravagant hand gestures.

"About your arrival here." Choosing his words carefully. "And how you—got over your problems."

"Not you, too." Maria shook her head. "We're not talking about any of that stuff." She looked up at him, gave a throaty laugh. "I've had lots of questions. From the press, from the Navy, from every shooter onstation."

"I'm curious."

"Don't start." The warning tone was clear.

"Okay."

"I'm not going to say anything to a man whose uncle keeps files on everybody." Laughing.

Kit laughed, too. Suddenly this was funny. He was on board *Runaway* to seduce this femme, get her into the rack and fuck the information clean out of her brain; and here she was on to him from the start. This wasn't going to work: Marco's idea was the stupidest he'd ever heard.

"Won't mention it again," Kit said.

"I'd be grateful if you didn't."

Kit felt his tension fade. He didn't care about this any more. In another few days he'd go back to greasing bearings, and Marco was welcome. He looked up at Maria.

"So what *else* have you been doing for the last six months?"

A bubble of laughter burst from Maria's throat. She put down her plate and kicked her heels up. Kit had the impression she hadn't laughed in a while.

"Haven't done anything," she said. "How about you?"

"Greased bearings. Rerouted power cables. Worked auto-loaders. Strapped a lot of cargo." He shrugged. "That sort of sums it up."

Her eyes sparkled. "Tell me about it."

Kit told her. He threw in stories about his family: his Aunt Sandy, who slipped him food when the others weren't looking; Marco scheming alone in his room, under his yellow light, the mirrored espresso machine his only company; Ridge, strutting and flexing his pecs in front of some downside girls on Salvador Station, only to have a half dozen of their brothers beat him silly. The words came easily, without calculation. Maria listened with bright attention. The cat ghosted into the room, sniffed Kit warily, found his lap acceptable. The meal was finished, put aside. She charged his bulb with another round of Lark.

He stopped for a second, looked at her. "Could I touch you?" he asked. "I'd sort of like to—I dunno." He shrugged.

Maria's eyes appraised him. "Not yet," she said. "I'm just a little—" Her hands fluttered like his mother's white cockatoos. "I'm not sure if I need someone touching me right now."

Suddenly he knew why they'd seemed so easy before. They'd just been a pair of junior shooters then, meeting by chance, spending a few hours between Nows. Now Maria had a secret, Kit was a spy, and both had a history together.

He smiled at her. "You *will* let me know when you're ready, right?"

"I'll make it good and clear."

He stayed another pair of hours before Maria had something to do. Kit told her he'd be free the next few days, kicked out toward the airlock. She helped him into his suit, pressed her lips to his before sealing the helmet.

He tasted promise. He was going to enjoy this as long as he could before Marco lost patience and decided to have him doing double-shift maintenance again.

"Well, boy?" Marco met him at *Abrazo*'s airlock. The red light above the inner hatch guttered in the old man's deep eyes.

"Nothing yet. She doesn't want to talk about it."

"Not be doing this for my own amusement, boy."

Kit wrestled with his shoulder harness, pulled it over his head. His own inner laughter at this pointless melodrama was a secret warmth deep inside him. "I'll do what I have to do," he said. Maybe that would sound positive enough for the old man to leave him alone for a while.

Marco glowered at him. "Listen, boy. This is serious. The contract with PDK is due for renewal in less than three years. Every time we renegotiate we lose some of our margin. *That contract's been keeping us alive, boy!*" Marco's voice was a shout. Kit looked at him in amazement. Marco's middle finger trembled as it pointed at Kit. *"The family's gotta live!"*

"Okay," said Kit. He looked at the pointing finger, the red light gleaming off the yellow, horned nail. "I know." Marco said it often enough, practically every breakfast, lunch, and dinner.

"You don't know shit. You think this is some kind of fucking game."

"I'll do what I have to do."

"You say it. Do you mean it?" There was a gleam of saliva on Marco's lower lip. Kit watched it as he tried to work out what was happening here. He had never heard the old man talk this way before.

"We're *dying* here," Marco said. Spots on his sallow skin flushed bright red from anger. "I looked at the figures and I *know*. The PDK contract has been supporting us for years, but that's because till now places like Angelica weren't big enough to support Hiline commerce. Now they're growing and soon we won't be needed." He pushed closer to Kit, took him by the vac suit collar. Kit could smell the garlic on the man's breath, see the desperation in Marco's eyes.

"I'm not doing this for me." Marco's voice beat on Kit's ears. "I don't give a fuck any more. I'm gonna die soon anyway. But the *family*, boy, we gotta keep it alive. I been trying to impress this fact on you young assholes, but it never seems to come through clear. We've got eighty-one people on five ships, and in another few years none of us will be there any more. The whole apparatus is gonna come unraveled. I'd have Ridge *beat* this fact into your head, if I thought it would do any fucking good. But Ridge doesn't understand it himself, and it wouldn't work anyway, not with you. So what do I have to do to get it through to you that we're *dying?*"

The last word was a scream. Spittle rained against Kit's face.

Marco's momentum faltered as he looked into Kit's startled, terrified eyes. He hung there for a moment, attached to Kit by his collar, and then his old leer returned. "Hope you got in her pants anyway, boy," he said. "Bet she's got a young, tight pussy. Been years since I had one myself."

Marco pushed Kit gently backward in the lock, used the momentum to drift through the hatch. Marco turned and kicked off without another word.

Kit drifted against the closed outside hatch. His heart hammered like a riveting gun.

Marco was *serious* about this survival stuff. Kit had just always thought it was part of the man's hatefulness, part of the background. He'd never thought Marco really cared about anything.

Eighty-one people on five ships, he thought. And they're dying.

Kit visited Beautiful Maria again the next day, ate vat-grown huachinango in pico de gallo sauce, drank with it some of Ubu's toasty home-brewed beer.

Eighty-one people, he thought, and remembered Marco screaming as if he were in pain.

There was a tone from the comm panel and Kit jumped as if he'd been stung. Maria told the system to answer. A neutral machine voice came on.

"Mr. C. C. Mahadaji calling from his office. Request permission to encode transmission using Cypher 17."

"Stand by," Maria said. Maria gave Kit an exasperated look. "Sorry, but it's the lawyer. He and Ubu and I are doing some negotiations. I need to be alone, okay?"

"No problem. I'll put the dishes away."

"Would you? Thanks."

Kit scooped up the plates, left the room, and closed the screen behind him. Dimly he heard Maria's voice answering the phone.

He stepped between scarred corridor walls until he came to the kitchen. He put the dishes in the washer, then straightened, listening to the ship.

Eighty-one people, he thought. And these two have already made a fortune.

Kit moved down the corridor to the ladder, looked up and down. The lower-level control cage was visible from the bottom of this ladder; he wouldn't even hear Maria coming, and this would be the first place she'd look.

He went up, to auxiliary control.

The cold touch of your dream, whispered the song in Twelve's mind, *the colder wind of your soul.*

Since hearing the old dolores ballad a few days before, Twelve had been unable to get it out of his thoughts. He couldn't say why, but somehow the words stirred him. Yet a literal reading of the lyrics made little sense, and the lyrics furthermore possessed problematical subject matter.

Dream? he thought. Soul?

His definitions were inadequate.

This was the sort of thing he needed to ask a human about; but he'd asked Ubu and Maria about lyrics before, and the answers hadn't been very helpful.

He drifted in the empty room.

Yes, he thought. No.

He was being drawn into the human mind. Experiencing the cold, comfortless touch of the human dream, the demanding presence of their gods.

His mind had been contaminated.

On his return to Beloved, he should report himself unfit to live.

He wished he could play the synthesizer, hear the comforting tones of Beloved's drumbeats. But Beautiful Maria had informed him that there was a visitor on board *Runaway* who should not know of Twelve's presence, and that Twelve should lock himself in auxiliary control and do nothing to cause attention to himself.

And suddenly there was a tug on the screen that led to the trunk corridor outside. Alarm crashed in Twelve.

There was another tug on the screen. "Hello?" A strange human voice.

Terrifying thoughts sped through Twelve's brain. Perhaps he would be carried off, like Kirstie in the hype, for his genetics.

"Anyone there?"

Twelve could see the flimsy screen lock moving up and down as the human outside tested it. If the weightless human outside got some leverage, Twelve knew, he would wrench the screen open easily.

He needed to do something fast. Human words hurled themselves through his mind.

"Who is it?" He spoke loudly, in Ubu's voice.

"Oh." Twelve received the impression of surprise. "Sorry, bossrider. This is Kit de Suarez. I didn't know anyone was here."

"I'm busy now. I cannot talk. Please go away."

"Yes. Sorry, bossrider. I was just looking around."

"*Goodbye!*" Twelve produced the sound at such volume that his voder buzzed heavily under the strain. Twelve's hearts raced as he listened in the silence, hoping he hadn't given himself away by his loss of control.

There was no more noise from the corridor. The lock suffered no more strain.

It wasn't until after he calmed down that he remembered the name of the intruder. De Suarez.

The human god had warned him about that name.

Renewed alarm rang through his mind. He would have to tell Ubu and Maria about the intrusion as soon as the intruders left the ship.

But the human god had told him to keep the information to himself. Twelve thought for a long time about that.

He decided to find out more before he came to a decision.

A tsunami of fear flooded through Kit de Suarez as he bounced down the ladder. He'd given himself away.

Still, he now knew there was something going on in the auxcontrol. Ubu was performing some task behind the locked screen. Maybe he was plotting a return course beyond the Edge, to *Runaway*'s next pickup from the lost human settlement. Or maybe Ubu had an artifact hidden there—an odd-smelling artifact, at that—that would give some clue as to where *Runaway* had been.

Maybe Ubu was just playing with his new parrot.

Gravity sang in Kit's inner ear. He stepped off the ladder onto the pad on the bottom, then walked downspin to the second-level lounge.

Maria's voice still alternated with voices from the comm. Kit couldn't make out the words. He waited outside the door, trying to come up with a plausible story for why he had been found trying to get into the auxiliary control room. Nothing came to mind.

The conversation inside ended. Beautiful Maria slid open the screen, gave Kit an apologetic smile. "You should have taken your beer," she said.

He forced a smile. "I'll have some now, then."

"Sorry. Ubu and I are getting into some heavy trading with—" She paused for a moment, a smile touching her lips lightly, then resumed. "With someone. We're trying to nail down a contract."

"I wasn't even going to ask." He recharged his bulb and sat down on the sofa.

"Sorry. Things got paranoid a while back. Someone tried to break in. We had to install lots of security equipment."

"Who?" Kit looked up at her in surprise.

"We don't know." Maria sat down on the sofa next to him. Warm hair brushed his upper arm. She looked at his serious expression and laughed. "Don't worry," she said. "It wasn't Marco. Your ship hadn't got here yet."

"That's not what I was thinking."

"What were you thinking, then?"

He looked at her, chose his words carefully. Know exactly why you're doing this, he thought.

"I was thinking," he said, "you could get hurt."

"Oh." Maria looked down. A faint flush rose on her translucent cheeks. "Thank you." She took one of his hands and kissed it. A hot electric current seemed to lick Kit's nerves. "That was a nice thought."

He leaned close and kissed her. Maria turned to him, lips parting, her breath warm on his cheek. Know exactly, he thought, why you're doing this.

Eighty-one people.

The comm rang again. Maria giggled from around his tongue, then turned away.

"It's *not* a good day, Kit," she said.

He sat on the couch, defeated. Ubu would tell Maria of his reconnaissance expedition, and that would be that.

The call was from the lawyer again. She turned to him. "Can you come back tomorrow?"

"Yes. Of course."

She'd cancel, he thought as he rose to his feet.

But for some reason she didn't.

"Shooter Maria, I wonder if it is safe to remain in auxcontrol with visitors on the ship. Visitors usually enter through the dorsal lock and must travel past through the auxiliary control room to enter the centrifuge."

The sizer beat out a thoughtful pattern. Maria's face folded in a way that Twelve was learning to think of as thoughtful. "I see your point. We were trying to keep you out of gravity as much as possible."

"I have been strengthened for gravity. I have visited the centrifuge several times." Twelve dreaded the experience, the painful breathing and the load on his muscles, but the truth of the human god's warning had been borne out, and he needed a place to hide from any strangers while he gave further thought to what the god had told him.

"Yes. And you can't stay in auxcontrol once the Lahore people start retrofitting our new AI." Maria's face folded again. She shifted one of her feet for another in the castoff bar on top of the pilot's acceleration couch. "I'll put you in one of the spare cabins on the second level. No one's lived in it for years. You'll just have to be very quiet."

"Thank you, Shooter Maria."

"There will be another visitor tomorrow. I'll help you move."

"May I ask his name?"

Beautiful Maria seemed surprised by the question. "Kit de Suarez," he said. "A member of a rider family."

"And the nature of his visit?"

"We're friends."

"Do you and his family have commerce together?"

"Ah. No. We're sort of rivals. It's just me and Kit who like each other." Her eyebrows neared one another. "Why do you ask?"

"I wish to learn about humans."

Once, Twelve thought, he would have been appalled by the idea that people from different clans could have the intense affinity the humans called friendship. Now it no longer seemed to bother him.

She accepted that and the conversation drifted on to other subjects. As usual, Maria's assistance was minimal in regard to his problem with the dolores lyrics. "It's *poetry*," she said. "You're not supposed to read it literally. You're just supposed to *feel* it."

Feel it, Twelve thought. By which Maria meant exercise of gestalt and intuition.

The horrifying fact, for Twelve, was that he *was* beginning to have such intuitions. Proof, as far as Beloved would be concerned, of his own contamination.

And of the need for his obliteration, as soon as he reported his disease to Beloved.

This time the meal was a rice dish, filled with meat and vegetables, a red pepper sauce over all. The peppers warmed Kit as he made love to Beautiful Maria afterward, spiced her kiss, her breath. He was faintly amazed at the fact he was allowed aboard *Runaway* at all, that she made no mention of his visit to auxiliary control.

He felt weirdly blessed. For a while he could pretend he was here because it was his idea, because he wanted to immerse himself in Maria, in her presence, her laughter . . . and then memory would come, a simulacrum of Marco's voice in his own mind. *She used you.* Then, *the family's gotta live!* And there he could feel a catch in his own happiness, a break in the steady throb of his pleasure.

He had forgotten, Kit thought, why he was doing this. Or maybe he just needed to find another reason.

Kit reached out a foot, the narrow metal rack swaying with the shift of weight, and snagged his forcebulb carefully between first and second toes. He raised the bulb from the floor, brought it nearer, took it in his hand, fired warm Lark into his mouth.

Appease the demon, he thought.

Beautiful Maria followed his balancing act with her placid dark eyes. She was lying partly under him, and it would have been too much trouble to disentangle himself from her.

"You *have* got stronger," Beautiful Maria said. "I noticed."

"I'm still growing." He offered her the bulb. "Not like you."

She took some Lark. He could hear it fizz in her mouth. He lowered himself to her, rested his head on her knobbed white shoulder.

"You remember," he said, "back on Angel Station, you mentioned the possibility of an apprenticeship program? I think I could work it now. Marco doesn't want to see me any more. He'd be glad to let me go."

He wasn't entirely certain what he was after. Marco would approve the scheme, he knew, just to find out where *Runaway* was bound.

Still, he knew he hadn't asked the question entirely for Marco.

Maria's slow heart beat four times, the sound plain in Kit's ear. Then she sighed and took his hand.

"We can't do it, Kit," she said. "Not for a long time."

"Yeah." Suddenly he was angry. "You and Ubu are so paranoid."

Maria stiffened. Her answer came fast and sharp. "We wouldn't have to be paranoid if it weren't for people like Marco."

Kit bit back his resentment. He emptied his lungs, took a long breath. "Sorry," he said. "It was just . . . a fantasy I'd like to come true."

She ruffled his hair. "Maybe it will. Who knows? Gonna have to expand our operation at some point. Just not now."

Eighty-one people, Kit thought. He kissed her perfect cheek. Inside him, without a sound, without a protest, the fantasy died.

He lowered the bulb to the mattress and, as if by accident, touched the trigger. Lark foamed over Maria's cheek and hair. She gave a yelp and came upright, almost pushing him off the rack.

"Sorry," he said.

A moment later Maria stepped into the shower to wash her hair. His sense of unbelievable luck returned as Kit watched her roll shut the cubicle door. Water began to drum against the door and Kit rolled out of the rack and jumped for the ladder.

The auxcontrol screen was open. Other than an odd smell, Kit could detect nothing unusual. He was going to get away with this. He hooked his knees under the nav board and called up *Runaway*'s log.

Cold surprise brushed the back of Kit's neck as he saw that a huge chunk of the log had been erased. Tampering with logs was illegal—a ship's records were considered public property rather than property of the shipowner, and could not be altered. Kit could conceivably get Ubu and Maria in trouble by reporting the missing files, but that wouldn't help De Suarez Expressways.

So much, he thought, for luck. Maybe Maria was careless about letting him wander around the ship because there wasn't anything for him to find.

He looked numbly at the nav board and wondered if he could get into some other record—find a private journal, a copy of *Runaway*'s contract with its supplier, something like that . . . His fingers touched the keyboard, called up a list of files. He scanned down the list, the filenames a meaningless blur, and then another idea took him.

His fingers answered without conscious thought. It all happened so fast that Kit didn't even develop suspense over the outcome.

He called up the navigation plots of the last set of shoots. An awed shiver of triumph rose in him as he saw them all displayed, everything he needed, logged and plotted. These were the working plots made before feeding the final result into the shooting computer, and apparently *Runaway*'s computer automatically saved them. Ubu and Maria had forgotten about them entirely and had never so much as slugged them under a password.

He paged back through the plots, trying to memorize as much as possible, then realized that all he had to discover was the point where the return series of shoots originated. He flipped backward through the file until he saw the four-dimensional gravity well of a Population I star alongside a series of smaller planetary wells. The star had a neat label, a number followed by a name.

Santos 448.

He flipped back further into time just to make certain, found the outward-bound point of origin at Angel Station. He cut the power to the nav board and kicked out for the exit.

An unusual feeling welled through him, danced like a magnetic storm in his head. Power, he thought, it's power. He had never had power before.

He raced back to Maria's cabin, caught her just as she was stepping out of the shower, picked her up in his arms, and, while laughter bubbled in her throat, swung Maria in a furious, awkward dance—she was taller—then carried her to the rack. Her giggling protests were disregarded.

He knew who had the power now, and who didn't.

Now it was time for his, Kit's, fantasy.

CHAPTER
18

MARCO'S EYES WERE BLACK HOLES IN JAUNDICED FLESH. BEHIND HIM, below the bloodied Jesus, the espresso machine hissed like a viper. Kit, standing in the resumed gravity of Marco's office, felt the power ripple through his body.

"I found it," he said.

Marco's smile twisted in the yellow overhead light. "I figured you would, boy. You'll do well with that charm of yours."

"Don't think charm had much to do with it, bossrider." Kit looked at the old man and smiled. Power ran through him like a current through glassware. He found he was reluctant to give it up. "You remember our deal? I transfer to the *Familia*, become a shooter."

Marco waved an impatient hand, a skeleton dismissal. "Yeah. I remember. You ever known me to go back on a deal once I make it?"

Kit didn't answer that. He cocked his head back, smiled. Relished the power.

"Santos 448," he said.

Marco's expression hardened. He turned to his computer,

banished to limbo whatever he was working on, called up the star catalog. "Main sequence star," Marcos read, "believed to possess planets, either gas giants, protostars, or a dark companion." He called up nav files, and a black holographic cube appeared, dusted with stars and silver trails of data. "Nearest Edge system is Angelica. You figure Santos is where the lost settlement is?"

"I don't know what's there. I only know that's where *Runaway* went."

Marco turned to Kit. "We're blowing station in twenty-four hours. I want you to alert everyone. If they're not on board, I want you to find them and give them the news."

Kit looked at him in surprise. "We have the PDK shipment to load and deliver to Masquerade."

"I'll hire another ship to do it—there are enough trampers stuck here looking for cargo. *Andiron*'ll probably move our shipment in exchange for docking charges." Marco scowled. "Lose some money, there. Maybe win everything."

"About me," said Kit.

Marco pushed his chair back on its rails and stood. Holographic stars gleamed off the silver crucifix he wore on a tight thong around his neck.

"What about you, boy?"

"The transfer to *Familia*. Will I wait here or ship off with the tramper?"

"You're staying with us for right now."

Kit straightened in surprise and looked down into the old man's face. He might have known.

"We had a deal."

"Deal's still good, boy. But we're gonna race to Santos 448 and I want to use every shooter we can. On our way back we'll drop you off at Angel Station or somewhere else on *Familia*'s run."

"You mean I get to boss a shoot?" Not believing it.

"Piss." Marco glared. "We'll give you a shoot somewhere in the middle of the run where you won't put us too far off schedule if you glitch." He jabbed his middle finger in Kit's direction. "Now get the fuck out of here and let the others know we're gonna blow!"

Kit staggered for the nearest comm unit. He wasn't sure

whether to believe Marco or not. Behind him he was aware of Marco shambling out of his office, heading for the blue-painted cabin that had been converted to a shrine to Our Lady.

He spent a lot of time there, Kit knew. Striking deals with God, Kit had always assumed, using the Virgin as his agent, beads and candles in exchange for commerce.

A sudden awareness brushed his spine like the touch of a decompression wave. Perhaps, Kit thought, Marco spent his time asking for forgiveness.

The thought chilled his triumph. He didn't want to think of Marco as anything that real, that complex.

Didn't want to think of him as anything but enemy.

"Some kind of new priority shipment. Marco didn't tell me what it is. Maybe we're carrying some of the stuff *Runaway* brought onstation."

Soft-footed regret crept through Maria's heart. She looked at Kit's transmission, seeing the new hardness in his look, his eyes.

"Anyway, we're blowing station tomorrow. So I won't have time to see you." He hesitated. The hardness eased for a moment. "See you next Now."

End of transmission. Beautiful Maria gazed at the cursor that danced in the upper left of the empty screen, considered running the message again, decided against it. She pressed the ERASE button. The command cage creaked as she left the comm board.

Kit had changed. Become more adult, more decisive . . . also more de Suarez. What in him had been unfocused resentment was now finely honed anger; the feelings that had once been open were now tightly controlled. When he'd mentioned the apprenticeship she'd had the feeling the question hadn't been asked so much out of desire to escape as an intention to close off some door of his past, answer a question that in his own mind had been left too long without a solution.

Survival, she knew. Kit had adapted to the de Suarez way of life. Practical, ruthless, masculine, all the attributes Marco demanded. Kit wasn't Ridge and thankfully would never be, but he'd adopted enough traits to blend in with the others.

Perhaps, she thought, in some ways, he'd even changed for the better.

While *Abrazo* undocked and burned away from Bezel Station, *Runaway* left Bezel's proximity and moved to the Kompanie shipyards, where the century-old Torvald AI that monitored and manipulated its singularity was replaced temporarily by an onstation unit jacked into the hull. The old computer would be torn out of *Runaway*'s insides and replaced by the new Lahore.

The whole business was a security nightmare. There were techs all over the ship. Ubu had to hire guards to make sure they didn't wander where they might find Twelve, and in the meantime who watched the guards? Finally Ubu decided to keep Twelve in one of the unused cabins on level two of the fuge and post a pair of guards in the hallway outside with instructions to keep everyone out of *any* of the cabins. Twelve remained inside, the lights turned off so no one would see a glow beneath the door screen, listening to music through a pair of headphones that Ubu had altered so they could both sit atop his head and feed the sound directly into his vocoder.

The replacement of the AI, rerouting of cables, and checking of systems took six days. On the seventh, *Runaway* moved back to Bezel, docked with Modular Unit One, and began filling Hold A with the other Lahore AIs that had been assembled over the last month on the planet below. Twelve went back to weightlessness and auxcontrol with expressions of relief.

Hearing the distant hum of autoloaders through the skeleton of the ship, Ubu sat in the shooter's chair and loaded the new Lahore software. The business of taming singularities hadn't changed much in a hundred years, nor had the technology. The Lahore's improvements weren't a leap in advance of the Torvald, more like a cautious quarter-step. Ubu had only decided to swap out the Torvald because it seemed silly to be shipping a better class of AI to Beloved than one he owned himself.

The Lahore representative was a station-bred man, dark-skinned, mustached, with gold-rimmed spectacles worn over eyes whose vision was perfectly adequate—the specs were just a fashion accessory. The best the man offered was an improved visualization of the shoot.

"The data will be better realized," he'd said. "You'll get a clearer view of the black hole, a better look at any developing perturbations. When things get moving, you may start getting too *much* information—you may overload."

"We'll see," Ubu said, skeptical.

Now he sat in the shooter's couch and let the stim antennae array themselves around his head. He punched up a simulation, a simple four light-year jump from point to point in deep space, no nearby heavy bodies to complicate things, and was startled when the stim singularity appeared hard-edged and solid in his mind, its color not black but a devouring nullity, wailing the song of dying matter, the event horizon surrounded by a bright silver halo like a polished and perfect thumbnail . . . Ubu had the unsettling conviction that the thing was *real*, not the hazy simulation he was used to, the edges of the Now blurred by the fact the computer couldn't quite keep up with the flow of data, but a real singularity burning in his head, drawing him into its crushing and lethal embrace.

He made his run, the Now filling his skull. If the old Torvald had provided the crashing, thudding sensation of riding a broken atmosphere craft to the frozen core of a gas giant, the Lahore offered the sense of being inside the fast-homer bullet of a gauss gun, a smooth and total acceleration to superliminal speed. The Now was perfectly realized and overwhelming, almost too intense to bear, like the subjective recording of a very fast sports event projected at three times normal speed. Ubu wanted to close his eyes and flinch away, but there was no way to close his eyes to a hallucination projected into his brain.

The constant acceleration was smooth, the visualization perfect until the very end, when the Lahore's macroatoms were unable to keep up with the black hole's perturbations. Even then there was only a slight hazing around the singularity, a refracting of its halo, before the Now dissolved into whitehole.

The stim antennae withdrew. Ubu opened his eyes, realizing the tech had been right. The experience was too overwhelming. The visualization was so real that it distracted Ubu from the job that needed doing. His heart was pounding, his nerves felt like they'd been clawed by an animal. His score showed he'd missed his target by almost two tenths of a light-year.

Red shift to blue shift, he thought.

Blue Seven would be too much a move in the other direction, he thought. He charged a chak with Blue Ten. Relax the nerves, leave the mind rational.

Much better. The Blue Ten dulled slightly the bright hard edges of the simulation, let him withdraw slightly from the experience. His score increased by a factor of almost ten.

He called up harder and harder simulations. When he finally gave up, he noticed he'd been at it for nine hours straight. And his score was only marginally better than his average score with the old Torvald. The technology hadn't changed much, or his scores, but what changes there were had made it easier on the shooter.

Ubu left the command cage and found some food, beans and green chile on a flour chapati, in the galley. Beautiful Maria was lying on the couch in the upper lounge, weary with a day of supervising the loading and strapping down of the cargo. She was still dressed in the grey coveralls she wore on the loading dock.

Loading was finished. All that remained before *Runaway* blew station was for Mahadaji to finish his negotiations with Portfire A.G. concerning the Group's purchase of the next shipment. A richer one this time, since Ubu had purchased on Bezel several valuable compounds that he didn't normally carry on the ship, and at least some of which Beloved was sure to be capable of synthesizing.

"How'd the stims go?" Maria trailed a weary hand out of the couch, stirred the nap of the dark grey carpet.

Ubu smiled. "Interesting."

"I'll try it before we leave."

"We could make some record times once we get used to it."

He pulled down the table from the wall and ate his dinner. Beer and the Blue Ten made him drowsy.

He went to bed. For once he didn't feel like partying onstation.

When Ubu woke he woke hungry. He headed for the galley and ran into Beautiful Maria in the corridor. She looked wrung out. Her hair hung in damp strands over her face, and there were dark sweat stains under the arms of her coveralls.

"I tried the Lahore," she said.

"All night?"

"It's too much. I shoot by instinct, but my instincts get overpowered when the visualization's that good."

"Did you try Blue Ten?"

"Tried *everything*. I'm gonna have to reprogram that little licecatcher. I don't *need* that kind of clarity."

"Work on a backup, for God's sake. I don't want you messing with the core—"

She gave him a look. "What do you think I am, shooter man? A fucking amateur?"

"Yeah, well . . ."

"I'm just gonna mess with the stim subroutines anyway. Not the core programming."

"Whatever. It's your shoot, Maria."

She trailed away to her cabin. Undirected energy bubbled up Ubu's spine. He went to the comm station and called Mahadaji. The attorney had just been about to call him—the new contract was ready. Portfire would be buying the pharmaceuticals, as before, but didn't want them delivered to Bezel. *Runaway* had flooded the local market. Bezel Station was too big, too busy, and too many rumors had already been started. Portfire A.G. wanted the next shipment delivered out on the Edge, to Angelica.

"Fine," Ubu said. "It's sorta out of our way, though." The occasional lie, he thought, never hurt. He wouldn't mind visiting Angel Station again, he knew. Hire some shooter muscle, visit the Monte Carlo, follow Jamison home from work and see whether it was possible to knock her bright red lipstick askew.

They made an appointment for another long lunch at the Klub to be followed by the signing of the next contract. He had four hours before he was due at the Klub, but he didn't want to visit Port Town and start a party he'd have to leave. He also didn't trust Mahadaji entirely, didn't want to show up high to an important meeting. Mahadaji, with his endless rounds of drinks and his water pipe, was going to make him high enough at lunch.

Soon, he thought, he'd be on his way back to Maria the Fair. He thought of Beloved, and her drumbeats rang inside him. He headed up and downspin to the lounge, contemplated watching a hype, decided against it. Tales of galactic exploration and the discovery of aliens seemed pale against the real thing, and it was too early in the day for hype's other staple of sex, war, and violence.

Beloved's rhythms rattled in his heart. He opened the music locker and rolled out the sizer, programmed it for one of Beloved's more complex rhythms, and let the sound bang off the green metal walls.

The pattern was complex, compelling, but Ubu's interest fell away completely when he realized it was just going to repeat forever. Even so, Ubu thought, this could be the start of something more satisfying.

Ubu began playing with the paired keyboards, not trying to put a melody over the rhythm pattern, just find a combination of sound and structure that somehow called to his mind the textures of Beloved's ship, its dark walnut-shaped hull, oval corridors like corroded arteries burrowing through her body, the eerie blue light though which her unearthly creatures danced in the weightless air . . .

He came up with an atonal chord that brought Beloved's scent sharp in his nostrils, the thick humid air heavy with long-chain organics, but his efforts otherwise fell short. Annoyance flickered through him. Without taking a lot of time to manipulate the settings, he just couldn't bend the notes properly on the keyboard. His old problem. He got the Q-body guitar and audolin out of the locker and arranged the guitar in his two lower arms, the audolin in the upper pair. Beloved's drumbeats continued their thunder. With his right hand Ubu stroked the bow over the audolin's metal strings.

A blue chromatic rang through Ubu's head. His left hand touched the buttons that manipulated the bridge, altered tone and timbre. The azure rainbow narrowed, centered on the precise blue-white light cast by Beloved's fluorescents.

Ubu found other sounds, other correspondences. Beloved's ship assembled itself in his mind. Maybe one in every five hundred million humans shared his particular brand of synaesthesia and would find in the chords the same spectrum of correspondences, but Ubu didn't care. The colors seemed to burn with the fire of their own internal truth.

He began to work with the elements, assemble them into a design. What resulted was far too abrasive to be called a melody, but it had structure and pattern and a driving force courtesy of Beloved's solid backbeat. Setting the last piece into place, he looked up and saw that he was scheduled to be in the the Pan-Development Klub in twenty minutes.

He grinned. His left lower hand had lost sensation in the fingertips: it had been too long since he played the guitar. Lucky his fingers weren't bleeding. Ubu recorded the last version of his creation, stood, stretched, told the machine to play it again, loudly, while he went to his cabin and donned some new clothes.

Beloved beat in his pulse. For a moment he paused, trying to recall through the perfect aural memory just what his appointment was about.

Portfire, he thought. Right.

Aches rolled dully in ligaments stressed by gravity. Twelve prescribed himself silence, weightlessness, a grateful end to the torments of human passion. He drifted in auxcontrol, thankful that his tenure aboard *Runaway* would soon end. Even at rest his mind buzzed with human words, human concepts . . . human garbage. Beloved sang distantly in his blood. He tried to concentrate on Beloved's rhythm, Beloved's comfort.

Suddenly his mind snapped to attention. Beloved's song continued. Twelve looked at the synthesizer, saw that it was shut off. His palps tingled. He swam to one of the acceleration couches, seized its castoff bar, felt his fingertips resonate to Beloved's distant thunder. Her faint drumbeat was ringing in the structure of the ship. Twelve's hearts surged.

He pushed off, entered the trunk corridor, kicked out, and moved to the centrifuge hub. Beloved's pulsing was louder, but other sounds were layered on top of it.

A pang of resignation touched Twelve as he realized the sound was coming from the lower levels of the centrifuge, that he would have to endure gravity once more. He climbed aboard the open cargo elevator and touched the controls. With a faint metallic whine the platform began to sink.

Beloved's drum thudded clearly in the air as soon as he left the hub. The air grew heavy in his lungs. His insides felt as if they were turning inside out.

He would never get used to this.

His hearts seemed to seize to a stop as the elevator jerked to a halt. His bowels felt heavy as lead. He stepped carefully from the elevator to the scratchy green surface of the deck and only then realized he was not listening to Beloved's song alone. Other sounds had been joined to it.

White-hot anger scorched his nerves. Blasphemy! he thought. Beloved's message had been polluted with human accretions. Twelve accelerated, rage overcoming the caution he employed when moving in gravity. He took the lounge door too fast, at too wide a line; he caromed off the doorframe and staggered into the room, waving angry fists like clubs.

Think carefully, said Beloved's rhythm. *Think carefully, then act.*

The room was deserted. The sounds were coming from a synthesizer. Twelve's anger throbbed uselessly in his veins.

Think carefully, Beloved instructed. *If you think carefully your actions will be correct.*

Beloved's instruction was nonviolent. Under its influence Twelve's anger began to subside. He looked at the sizer, heard the human cacophony winding in and around Beloved's patterns, wondered what it meant.

Think carefully.

There was a sound in the corridor outside. Twelve spun in place, his fists still clubbed, and saw Ubu walking into the lounge. Ubu looked at Twelve, smiled, and reached for the synthesizer controls. He turned off the noise.

Beloved's thunder faded. Twelve felt very alone.

He gestured toward the synthesizer. "Was it you who did this, reverend bossrider?"

"Yeah." Ubu was in a hurry to get somewhere, was putting things in his pockets. "I thought I'd make a piece of music around Beloved's drumbeats. I used sounds that remind me of Beloved."

"The sounds do not have anything to do with Beloved's message."

Ubu's shoulders rippled. "That's not how my mind is wired. That's not how I think of things. I just wanted to call Beloved to my mind, and I used the sounds that worked for me."

Confusion eddied in Twelve's mind. "Are there words to this song?"

"No." Ubu was looking for something in a drawer. "I'm not a lyricist."

Desperation wailed in Twelve. He had to make himself understood, and there was only one thing about which he was certain. "You must not use ladino rhythm!" he cried. "You must not!"

Ubu stopped hunting in the drawer. He was clearly surprised. "Why not, Twelve?" he asked.

"You must not interrupt Beloved's message. Ladino breaks the rhythm, despoils the content. It would be blasphemy."

"I see." Ubu appeared to consider this. "Very well, Twelve," he said. "I won't make any ladino tunes. Thank you."

The bossrider found what he was looking for, put it in a vest pocket, and hurried away. Twelve waited disconsolately in the lounge, gravity tugging at his entrails. Eventually he went back to auxiliary control, each step propelled by despair.

Beloved, he thought, was doomed.

Ubu had taken Beloved's sacred rhythm and used it for his own purposes, overlaid the drumbeats with his own music, his own inner song. Beloved would meet the same fate: the humans would use her as they would, despoil her divinity to fulfill their own tainted designs, scroll their polluting thoughts in the perfect spaces of her mind.

The only possible remedy was to urge Beloved to disassociate herself from the humans, destroy them if possible. And that, he thought, she would not do. They were too valuable to her purposes.

Twelve programmed his own synthesizer to rap out one of Beloved's most restful, encouraging patterns. It altered his mood only slightly.

Maxim, the white cat, appeared in the door, then cast off toward him. Twelve caught him in his arms. The cat settled itself against his chest and made a low buzzing sound.

Maxim had never approached Twelve before.

Twelve imitated the actions of the humans when Maxim came

to them, stroked the cat's back, scratched under his chin with his inner fingers. The buzzing noise grew louder. A desolate pleasure, alien to his former reality, touched his mind.

Twelve understood that the cat was pleased with Twelve's behavior, was offering itself and this buzzing as a reward. Twelve had done something correct in its estimation.

As he stroked the cat aimlessly, this thought comforted him not at all.

Runaway blew station a few hours later, after Ubu returned with a copy of the new Portfire contract and a credit counter with his advance payment in his pocket. Following a three-hour burn that took them well out of Bezel's gravity well, Ubu bossed *Runaway* through three shoots in a row, pausing between each only long enough for the navigation comp to get an accurate position check and for Ubu to plot the next leap. After Ubu grew tired, Beautiful Maria bossed the next shoot, but she hadn't yet modified the Lahore software to her satisfaction and her accuracy was far off her usual standard. Disgusted, she rose from the shooter's couch and stalked without a word to her cabin. Ubu waited till the position report came in, plotted the next shoot, then shut down the boards and left the cage.

He checked on the passenger, found Twelve drifting in the control room to a slow beat from the synthesizer. After exchanging civilities he left the centrifuge hub. There was a light on in Maria's cabin. He tapped on the screen, then opened. Maria was bent over her computer deck, working with the Lahore software. She hadn't noticed him. He left her to her work.

Ubu, the drug still drifting idly through his veins, hit the rack and slept for hours. His dreams were filled with Beloved, her baroque servants dancing to the rhythm of her drumbeats, all bathed in her blue alien light. He awoke with her heavy scent sharp in his nostrils.

His mind felt clear, his body relaxed. The energy that had flamed through him the last weeks had ebbed. He was content to be alone again in the cosmos with only Maria and *Runaway*.

And Beloved, he thought. And Beloved.

He looked in on Maria, found her asleep in her rack, her pale body asprawl in the darkness. He closed the screen and headed to the lounge, where his instruments waited. He called up another of Beloved's rhythms, the slow one Twelve had been meditating to, and played tentative chord structures to himself. Beloved's reality rose bright in his mind, a white-hot sun rounding the horizon of an eclipsing moon.

Hours passed. The composition was longer this time, much more deliberate. Beloved's vessel assembled itself in Ubu's vision. As he finished, the alien vessel, fading from Ubu's present, wrote itself into some ineradicable corner of his mind.

Ubu found Beautiful Maria making herself breakfast in the galley. "Getting along with the Lahore?" he asked.

"I'm doing better in the simulations." She filled a bulb with alljuice. "After I wake up a bit, I'd like to boss the next shoot."

"Fine." He watched her pour egg-and-milk mixture into a hot pan. A hushed sizzling sound began.

"Hey," Ubu said. "I've been thinking about Beloved."

"Beloved's a lot like me," Ubu said. He'd been talking throughout Maria's breakfast, bouncing up and down on the scuffed galley floor as she ate off the small fold-down table. "She doesn't forget things. Her perceptions have gotta be as peculiar as mine. Maybe she's what I'll be in a couple thousand years."

"You're mobile, shooter man," Maria said. "She's not." She chewed the last warm bit of smoked ferenc. Little bones crunched beneath her molars.

Get Ubu away from other people, she thought, and he was almost easy to live with.

"Beloved experiences everything through remotes. Her servants."

"But there have to be errors in transcription from the minds of her remotes to her own. She doesn't get the real picture." She pointed her alljuice bulb at him. "Besides, she doesn't get the news realtime."

"She could if she had the right remotes." He began bouncing up and down again while Maria watched in amusement. "Hey, we can sell Beloved hardware that could allow her remotes to feed her realtime experience. Holographic transmission, with an interface to allow Beloved to read it. And we can replace a lot of her servants with robots that we can sell her." He jumped up again and clapped one set of hands over his head. "Make ourselves a fortune, there."

"*Another* fortune, you mean."

He grinned. "Yeah. Exactly what I meant." He bounded up and down once more. "I want to meet Beloved face-to-face. Think she'll allow that?"

"I doubt there'll be much to see." Maria thought about it a moment and chuckled. "Big sacks of biomass? Rooms full of brain tissue? Green goo?" She laughed and pointed at Ubu. "You can float up to her and explain to her how the both of you are so alike."

Ubu grudged a smile. She hadn't seen him smile in a long time. "Okay," he said. "So I got enthusiastic."

"Just don't do it again."

"Be so. Promise. No more enthusiasm."

Maria put her dish in the washer and refilled her alljuice bulb. She looked at Ubu and a sudden warm affection washed through her. She put her arm around his waist and grinned up at him. "Shall I con us out of here?"

He kissed her. "When you're ready."

"I'll empty my bladder. You go tell Twelve we're gonna start shooting."

She went to the drug locker for Blue Ten and met Ubu in the shooter's cage. Getting the Lahore's software up was a matter of seconds, but getting herself into the proper mental state took longer. Maria was nervous, and the Lahore's feel was just so *different*.

The reduction in intensity she'd programmed into the Lahore seemed to work. There was less distracting her from the Now, from her own witch's comprehension of the subatomic universe. She felt her awareness reaching out, touching the singularity, the magnetic fields that kept it confined. On that level, at any rate, the Lahore improved her perception.

The singularity was cooperative, threw few obstacles in her path. She rode the Now for hours, far past the point at which she would normally leap out of the simulation and let the computer whitehole on its own.

She was right on target, missing her ideal objective by only a few tens of thousands of kilometers. The positioning software produced their coordinates in a matter of minutes—*Runaway* had been out here before and the computer had many more referents than it had during their previous blind jumps. As soon as the position report arrived, Ubu exchanged couches with Maria, plotted the next shoot, and bossed the ride. They alternated a series of shoots, moving almost wordlessly from one to the other, in synchrony with both each other and the Now. At the end of the series *Runaway* was one jump from its rendezvous with Beloved and both were too tired to be confident of shooting to Maria the Fair with any accuracy.

Babbling their praise of the Lahore, they shut down the cage and drifted to the galley, where they munched cold cuts and hot peppers from the fridge. The Now still danced in Maria's head, electrons ringing in her mind like bells.

They slept tangled in Beautiful Maria's rack, and on waking made love.

Surprising, Ubu thought, how good it had been. After weeks of living apart, standing watch-and-watch aboard *Runaway* without their lives really connecting, he and Maria had stepped into their old relationship with barely a moment of transition.

He'd thought he'd lost her. He had certainly tried hard enough.

Things change, she'd said.

Maybe some things didn't.

It didn't seem right, somehow, that everything had been so easy. He wondered what could have made the difference. That they were rich? That they shared humanity's greatest secret? That they'd fooled *everybody?*

Beautiful Maria lay on her rack, stretched on her stomach. He had separated her hair into three thick bundles. One hand held each and the fourth was used to hold the growing braid in place as he advanced the thick coil down the length of Maria's knobbed spine.

"I've turned some of Beloved's drumming into music," Ubu said. "*My* kind of music, that is."

"I'd like to hear it. Play me some later."

"It might be more than you can take."

"I *like* your music. Some of it anyway."

"The only person who liked it was Pop."

"Pop," chuckling, "had a bad ear."

Hands worked plaits steadily, silken warmth passed smoothly

through palms. "Pop hasn't put in an appearance lately," Ubu said. "Guess he's been lecturing the uninhabited parts of the ship."

Through his thighs he could feel her stiffen. "Didn't I tell you?" Maria's voice was muffled by her pillow.

"Tell me?"

"I glitched him out of the computer."

Ubu's hands stopped moving. A stunning sense of loss beat in his heart.

"I put him in a file." Maria spoke quickly, turning to look at him over her shoulder. "We can call him up whenever we want. It's just that—" She gave a sigh. "He's not randomized any more. That's the difference."

"He wanted to be free." Indeterminate emotions bounded in Ubu's senses. He couldn't say what they were. He tried to touch them, give them definition. "He wanted things . . . the way he had them."

Maria looked at him. There was a shrill note in her voice. "I couldn't stand it any more, okay? I *just . . . couldn't . . . take it.*"

He was surprised by her vehemence. "Okay," he said.

"It was too much seeing him all the time. Seeing him fall apart all over again."

"*Okay!*" Ubu clamped back on his rising anger. He didn't know yet whether he wanted to be angry or not. "Okay," he said again. "Jesus Rice, I said it was all right."

"Sorry."

She turned her face to the pillow. Ubu saw the braid had come partway undone. His fingers worked automatically to complete the work. When he was done, Maria rolled over, kissed him, and, tossing her braid, scooped up some clothes and danced toward the galley.

Ubu headed for the shower and tried to decide how he felt about Pasco being caged. Maybe he should be happy. He hadn't managed to summon much happiness by the time he locked down the centrifuge, got in the shooter's cage, and watched Beautiful Maria boss the shoot that placed them a mere day and a half's burn from Maria the Fair.

The comm board lit up almost at once, even before Ubu had a chance to trigger his own greetings to Beloved. Ubu watched in astonishment as letters tracked across the display:

ABRAZO SUGGESTS TO CLAN LUSTRE THE FOL-
LOWING: SEVEN HUNDRED TONNES PER AI, A DELIV-
ERY EVERY HUNDRED HUMAN DAYS, CLAN LUSTRE
TO ASSEMBLE A CHEMICAL FACTORY IN ORBIT
AROUND A NEARBY STAR OF OUR CHOICE.

"Marco's here," Ubu said. He looked at Beautiful Maria in numb surprise. "Marco's followed us."

In her eyes he read not surprise, not fear, but growing comprehension.

CHAPTER
19

"STAND BY FOR TWO GEES." ADRENALINE DROVE THROUGH UBU'S veins like a ferrous charge through a mass driver. His words were almost a scream. He tracked his couch to the pilot's station, hit the heavy-acceleration alarm. The positioning software had already given him a heading for Maria the Fair; that was all he needed. Any necessary course corrections could be added later. Ubu triggered the reaction drive.

Acceleration slammed him in the kidneys. The command cage shrieked as it swung on its gimbals. Struts quaked and moaned. *Runaway* was lightly loaded and velocity built quickly. More positioning data came in, giving the planet's course and velocity.

"My fault," Maria said. Her voice was stricken.

"Not now." Ubu's rage was a hot magnesium light scorching his mind. Two hands tapped separate keyboards as he simultaneously fed the computer a course correction and sent his greetings to Beloved. A third hand worked on the nav board, trying to get an idea of where *Abrazo*'s signal was coming from.

Gravity piled weights on Ubu's chest. He fought it, struggled to keep his arms raised to the keyboards. He could feel gravity peeling his lids back from his eyes.

LUXURIANT AND EXPANSIVE GREETINGS, BOSSRIDER UBU ROY. Beloved's reply. WE HAVE BEEN SPEAKING TO OTHER HUMANS.

Ubu's eyes flickered to another display. *Runaway*'s sensors had spotted *Abrazo*'s plasma jet, plotted its course and trajectory. *Abrazo* was three days out from Maria the Fair at its current single-gee acceleration. Thanks to Maria and the new Lahore, *Runaway* would rendezvous with Beloved's ship before *Abrazo* could come close.

"My fault," said Maria.

A tremor ran along *Runaway*'s frame. Ubu's eyes blurred for a moment. His fingers kept tapping keys.

I HOPE CLAN LUSTRE HAS NOT BEEN DISTURBED BY UNINVITED INTRUDERS.

His heart beat trip-hammer time while Ubu waited for a reply. When it came he could feel waves of anger and determination coursing along his nerves.

CLAN LUSTRE HAS FOUND OUR DISCUSSIONS WITH CLAN DE SUAREZ PROFITABLE. WE HOPE YOU WILL JOIN OUR CONCLAVE.

And, a moment later, a video message from *Abrazo*: a close-up of Marco's ancient, leering, unshaven face.

"Bossrider Ubu Roy," he said. "I wonder if you can guess how I got here." He let that sink in for a moment. "I'm ready to talk," he said, "whenever you are."

Gravity smothered Beautiful Maria like a rug, tore tears of sorrow from the corners of her eyes. *Runaway*'s engine was a constant rumble in her ears, a tremor in her spine. "Kit was on the ship," Maria said. "I let him on. Twice. No, three times. Somehow he must have found out about Santos 448."

"Jesus Rice. A de Suarez. How could you . . ." Ubu's voice trailed away in incomprehension. "How could you *do* it?"

"I wiped the log. There was no record of where we were. I was with him every minute."

"There was *Twelve*. He could have seen Twelve."

"Twelve would have told us."

"Maybe not."

Maria contemplated the shadowy thought of some dark, strange conspiracy between Twelve and the de Suarezes. A protest wailed in the burning cavity of her heart. "He *used* me!"

"Payback."

"Shit. That bastard."

Somehow, despite her words, anger had failed her. Maybe she couldn't yet believe in the reality of all this. Maybe, she thought, she just couldn't blame Kit.

"I'm gonna talk to Twelve." She swung a keyboard out of the couch's armrest, slotted it into place across her lap. She called Twelve and explained the situation.

"A ship from Clan de Suarez is here?" Twelve's voice had crackling, whining overtones that bespoke the double-gee strain. "I am profoundly disturbed, Shooter Maria."

"You didn't speak with Kit de Suarez at any time?"

"No, Shooter Maria." There was a hesitation. "He attempted to enter the auxiliary control section when I was here, but I used Bossrider Ubu's voice and told him to stay out."

"Fuck. Thank you, Twelve."

She turned off the intercom. Anger came at last. "That *bastard*," she said, and this time meant it.

Ubu was still tapping course currections into the nav comp. As if they were blunt instruments, his fingers made furious jabs at the keys. "He knew something was here," he said. "The question is, what did he find?"

"A backup of the log?"

"Isn't one."

"Not that we know about."

Ubu clenched his teeth. "If *we* don't know about it, he's not going to."

"You didn't write anything down? Leave it where he could find it?"

"I don't write *anything* down. I just put it in the—Jesus Rice."

Ubu's fist, twice its normal weight, slammed into the padded armrest. His other arms were already calling up nav files.

A threedee grid appeared, courses and data tracking across

night. "My fucking shooting plots. Look at this. The computer saved them automatically."

"You didn't erase?"

"I forgot."

Renewed anger roared like a furnace in Maria. "You had me erase the fucking *log*, commit a fucking *felony*, and you didn't—"

"They were just working plots. I didn't even remember them."

"Jesus Rice."

They fell silent for a long moment. Slowly, gravity drained Beautiful Maria's anger. She grudged every lost drop of it.

"I fucked up," Ubu said. "I fucked up *again*." Fists crashed on couch arms.

Maria closed her eyes and battled for breath. Electrons wrote faint tracks across her retinas. *Runaway*'s acceleration rattled her teeth.

Ubu's voice was low, his words determined, spoken through clenched teeth.

"I'll give Beloved a better deal. That's what I'll have to do."

"Ubu Roy." The sound of Marco's voice brought bright sparkles of angry light dancing in Ubu's head, the taste of oil and unsweetened lemon to his tongue. "Better stop trying to underbid me. We're just cutting our own profit margin, competing this way. And I'll win anyway."

"Piss off, licehead." Ubu didn't bother to broadcast his answer. He hadn't answered any of Marco's communications.

Every time Ubu had transmitted an offer to Beloved, she'd repeated its essentials to *Abrazo*. Shortly thereafter Marco transmitted a counteroffer, one Ubu couldn't beat except by cutting *Runaway*'s profit percentage again.

Marco, after countering *Runaway*'s first offer, had been busy with his transmitter. He had offered to make *Runaway* a part of De Suarez Expressways, at least for purposes of trade with Beloved, granting *Runaway* equal status with the five de Suarez ships. Control of the combined outfit would remain with Marco, as would scheduling.

All Marco wanted to do was keep Ubu from telling the Multi-Pollies about the aliens until Marco was ready.

The two-gee acceleration was sapping Ubu, draining his anger, his mental energy. He was out of ideas.

Marco was right, damn him. Bidding against *Abrazo* was suicidal.

Fucked up again. The thought rebounded in his skull.

Ubu looked at the nav board, saw that *Runaway* was a few hours from its deceleration point, and decided to end the acceleration early. He sounded the zero-gee warning and stopped feeding matter to the singularity.

His heart was loud in the sudden silence. His grateful body drifted free in the harness. Weariness throbbed through him.

Maria threw aside her webbing and kicked off out of the cage toward the toilet.

Ubu drifted in the opposite direction, to the sick bay. The medicine locker opened to his thumbprint. He took out the vial of Blue Eighteen and looked at it for a long moment. His mouth went dry.

Nightmare memories flashed through him—Beloved's sudden violence, the half glimpse of armored, purposeful soldiers, the long poison-tipped barb that coiled toward him in an eyeblink.

He remembered that the attack hadn't been Beloved's idea.

He put the vial away, closed the white enamel locker door with its flaking red cross.

Not yet, he thought. Not yet.

"Most assuredly, Shooter Maria, Clan Lustre will honor its previous commitments. You shall have your shipment."

"And afterward?"

"I cannot say, respected shooter. Our agreement covered only this next shipment."

Twelve's body was a mass of aches. During the acceleration burn he had felt as if he were drowning.

His mind staggered in weary circles. Clan de Suarez here? The human god had warned him explicitly that they were not to be trusted.

He had to give this information to Beloved as soon as possible.

One of Maria's feet was hooked to the castoff bar atop one of the acceleration couches; her body eddied slowly to her left and right like a ribbon swaying in a slow current. "The de Suarezes are treacherous," Maria said. "They are also very aggressive. We can cite numerous examples of both characteristics. With *Runaway*, we have dealt with Clan Lustre as a single ship negotiating with a single ship. The de Suarezes are larger. Beloved may be overwhelmed."

Alarm rang in Twelve. "We do not speak of a military attack?" he asked quickly.

"No. Simply that Beloved, after a time, may find their demands difficult to resist."

"I will inform Beloved. It would be best if this were accomplished soon."

Resignation rose in him. He knew he was condemning himself to a high-gee deceleration burn.

Fucked up again. Again again again. The words rang wearily in Ubu's head as he and Maria helped Twelve climb into his ill-shaped vac suit.

Last chance, Ubu thought. If Twelve couldn't persuade Beloved to deal exclusively with *Runaway*, he'd have to surrender to Marco.

Or, the idea flashed, use the Blue Eighteen.

Reflex horror drove the thought away.

"Thank you, good shooters," Twelve said. There was a tinny resonance in his voice that showed his weariness. The long deceleration burn had ended only a few hours ago.

Twelve sealed himself into his suit. Beautiful Maria handed him his keyboard transmitter. He began to type.

"I thank you, reverend Bossrider Ubu Roy, for this opportunity to journey with you. I wish you all good fortune."

"You are very welcome, Volitional Twelve," Ubu said. "I hope we'll have the opportunity to travel again."

He and Maria floated from the airlock and watched as the inner hatch swung shut, as the lights over the door went from green to red, then green again.

Blue Eighteen, Ubu thought.

"I have a plan," he said.

Maria looked at him. "So do I."

Maybe the same plan, Ubu thought. He didn't want to give voice to it now.

"We'll talk about it later," he said. "If we need to."

"Fine."

"Who's gonna supervise the first shift of loading?"

"Your shoot," Maria shrugged. The small motion sent her body drifting slowly toward one passage wall. Ubu sighed.

"I will," he said. "Get some sleep."

Ubu went to the medicine locker and took two capsules of Red Nine to give him the energy to get through the work.

He tried not to look at the vial of Blue Eighteen.

Twelve stiffened as bliss struck him with the force of a hammer. *Glory glory glory*, he chanted, his mind filled with stunned awe. Never had he been separated from Beloved for so long; never had the ecstasy of fusion been so powerful.

Twelve had sensed prosperity and happiness from the moment he had seen Beloved's ship silhouetted against the gas giant's blue-green mass. The unsightly magnetic grapples were gone, and new sensor arrays studded the ship's surface. Light gleamed from the polished wings of two dozen new atmosphere craft that were carried on the ship's flanks. Once Twelve entered, a bright-orange sentient named General Volitional Twenty, ruddy frame glowing with youth and health, met him at the airlock to help him remove his vac suit. Improved nonvolitionals leaped from the walls to give Twelve's skin a welcome and thorough cleaning. Beloved's tympani beat out rhythms that summoned him to her presence, and with his hearts pounding in resonant answer he made his way along a short corridor to his old umbilicus. Several soldiers, their armored bodies molded around their weapons, hung motionless in one darkened room. Beloved had grown them there, in the sealed-off section.

Twelve stiffened as he passed another room. Though a tympanum covered the door, his palps could nevertheless detect the scent of a dissolution chamber. Had it been prepared for him?

You have done well, Beloved sang. Neuronic drills quested for his centers of memory. *You have brought other humans, rivals to* Runaway. *We will take great advantage of this*.

A wave of distant fear rippled through Twelve. He was too stunned by Beloved's outpouring of pleasure to give voice to it, but Beloved detected the hesitation in his reaction. Twelve's ecstasy dimmed to the point where he was able to assemble his thoughts.

All glory is to Beloved, he said. *There is danger. Do not take my memory. This-individual's thought has been polluted.* Sadness whimpered through his mind at the realization that he may have just triggered his own death. *This-individual did not bring Clan de Suarez to this place. Their arrival was their own doing. Perhaps an evil god prompted them.*

Through the umbilicus he sensed the awesome, deliberate movement of Beloved's limitless thought. Terror danced in his veins. Would she order his immediate dissolution?

I need further information, Beloved said. *You will report to me, in full, of all you have seen.*

Twelve hung in fusion for hours. Nourishment was brought by Volitional Twenty, who hovered before him and regurgitated food into his mouth.

I will be more cautious in My dealings with Clan de Suarez, said Beloved. *Still there is too much advantage to be gained from the human rivalry for Me to disregard it altogether.*

Beloved, this-individual urges caution. The human god—

Pain resounded in Twelve's mind. He quailed before a wall of stunning agony. *Do not presume to offer Me advice,* Beloved said. *Your thought has been contaminated; you recognize this yourself.*

Glory, Twelve said fervently. *Glory glory glory.*

The pain eased slowly. Beloved's instructions echoed in his skull.

You have at least fulfilled part of your mission, in that you have learned to vocalize human sounds. This knowledge will be transferred to Myself, and then to My servant Volitional Twenty.

Glory to Beloved, he said, resigned. Twenty, Twelve knew, would supersede him. After that, he would meet dissolution as a threat to the purity of Beloved's sacred thought.

Anaesthetic pleasure poured into Twelve's mind. It did not overwhelm his sadness but served to make it only more poignant. Beloved's umbilicus pulsed as it injected Twelve's linguistic centers with carefully shaped polyribonucleotides that began to copy his human speech ability. Twelve could feel his heart speeding in order to provide enough fuel to his mind so that this activity could be performed efficiently. He heard Beloved speaking through his own voice, ordering Twenty to fuse with her through another of the umbilici.

The transfer went quietly at first. Twenty's voder began making tentative human sounds, then a few words. "Bosssssssrider," said the orange volitional, and then his right arm flailed. "Bossrider!" he yelped. "Bossrider, bossrider!" He kicked out with his right foot. Spittle flew from his palps. His right side thrashed, but his left side seemed paralyzed.

Twelve, his mind dizzy with pleasure and sadness, watched in surprise as Twenty stiffened, then went slack at the end of his umbilicus.

Twelve's pleasure dimmed. Beloved's voice rang in his head. *Twenty has gone into shock. You will watch him.*

Yes, Beloved.

If he awakens soon, you will inquire as to the source of his distress.

Yes, Beloved.

I had been assured that his type was most flexible and adaptable. My disappointment shall be transmitted to Others. Perhaps this type will be devalued.

The sense of Beloved's presence withdrew from his mind, although the umbilicus did not detach itself. Twelve had the impression that Beloved's attention was busy elsewhere.

Twenty's palps flickered faintly with respiration, but otherwise he did not move. Twelve waited, trembling with fear, with anticipation. *Die*, he thought as he gazed at Twenty, *die die die*. If Twenty died, perhaps Twelve might live.

Hours passed. Twelve found himself needing to excrete but dared not detach himself from the umbilicus. He voided and let the nonvolitionals clean up first the mess, then himself.

He looked up in sudden fear as soldiers filled the doorway. Black and businesslike, they swarmed inside. Many arms appeared from their carapaces to seize Twenty. The umbilicus withdrew. Carrying Twenty's inert form, they left without a word.

Suddenly Beloved's presence returned to his mind. *Glory, glory,* Twelve chanted.

Twenty's dissolution has been ordered.

Glory to Beloved.

I will attempt to grow other volitionals, both of your type and his. The necessary information concerning humans will be fed to them gradually as they mature. Perhaps the shock will not be so great.

Glory to Beloved. Success to her plan. Hope fluttered desperately in his hearts.

I desire more information, Twelve.

This-individual is Beloved's servant. After the information, then, would come his dissolution. Unless, he thought desperately, he had the information Beloved desired.

We have detected communication between Runaway *and the Clan de Suarez ship. We are unable to translate these communications. Can you offer any suggestions?*

Perhaps the transmission is holographic, Beloved. We would need to have a holographic receiver.

Have you discovered how to construct one?

Twelve's hope foundered. *Alas, Beloved.*

Have you returned with technical knowledge of human AIs?

Worse and worse, Twelve thought. From one pit of ignorance to another. *This-individual knows only their appearance and some of the techniques of operation.*

Volitionals operating under My supervision disassembled one of Runaway's *computers. It appears to be composed of a crude analog of neural circuitry which achieves its power by virtue of speedier calculation. Some of the elements of its operation were discovered, but not the principles behind some of its critical components.*

Glory.

We discovered what appear to be components that permit an electronic signal to move at a speed faster than light.

Surprise rose in Twelve. *This-individual understood the speed of light to be an absolute limit for electromagnetic spectra.*

This was My belief also.

Twelve was stunned. Beloved had admitted to an error in her fundamental comprehension of the universe. The implications were too disturbing to contemplate.

Glory, glory, he stammered.

Beloved disdained reply to the disturbance she surely perceived through her neural connection.

Other components transmit electricity without resistance. These have been analyzed and their elements noted, but the secret of their manufacture is not evident from a mere list of their components. The acquisition of this technology should be your greatest priority in conducting future negotiations.

Terror and hope warred in Twelve. *This-individual is to continue as your voice?* he queried.

It is My desire. You have the greater experience.

Glory to Beloved. Never had the ritual answer been more heartfelt.

Your mind has been contaminated by human thought. I wish to correct some of your errors.

Yes, Beloved.

You mistook the nature of the hype you observed. The god was a dramatic device, not a literal truth.

This-individual does not comprehend, Beloved.

Your comprehension is not necessary to My purpose, Volitional Twelve. I am familiar enough with dramas to recognize their tropes. You need only know that no human gods should concern you.

Yes, Beloved. Still puzzled. *Glory to Beloved.*

The god who appeared to you was probably a trick by the humans, who wished to warn you away from their enemies.

Yes, Beloved. Twelve's mind swam. Beloved was familiar with drama?

You will await My further instruction. Maintain yourself in the meantime.

Beloved's umbilicus withdrew. Twelve hung alone in the room, unhappiness gnawing at his bones. *Beloved understands drama,* he thought. He felt vaguely betrayed at Beloved's revelation of a life beyond his own knowledge, a life in which, presumably with the other independent intelligences, she participated in drama and other royal pleasures which she did not deign to share with her servants, even the most devoted of them.

At least she had spared his life, even if her action had been the result of an accident with another of her servants. He still had an opportunity to prove his worth, to make certain that Beloved still required his services.

To make himself as invaluable as possible.

Ubu's hope was dying.

Twelve had been aboard Beloved's ship for three days without contacting *Runaway*. The last container had been loaded into *Runaway's* hold. The final Lahore AI had been delivered to Beloved. *Abrazo*, advancing at its more sedate pace, was nearing rendezvous with Beloved and *Runaway*. There had been no word from Beloved, although presumably she had taken note of the fact the two human ships had ceased to bid against one another.

When Beloved's answer came, Ubu knew what it would be. He and Maria sat in the command cage and watched the holographic letters rise from the comm display, the statement that Clan Lustre was accepting the latest offer from De Suarez Expressways.

Dumb hopelessness filled Ubu's heart. His rage had long ago burned itself out. *Fucked up again*, he thought. *Just like every time before. Just like Pasco. Finally had the big score and lost it.*

I urge Beloved to reconsider, he typed. A pointless exercise, but one that seemed necessary. He pushed Transmit and looked at Beautiful Maria.

White incisors were clamped on her upper lip. Cold fury filled her wide eyes. "That bastard," she said.

A distant surprise stirred in Ubu.

Beautiful Maria looked at him. "I'm not gonna let 'em *do* this!" Bright color blossomed on her pale cheeks, like shellfire falling on snow. "Tell me your plan," she said. "I'll tell you mine."

Glory to Beloved. With trembling and obeisance, this-individual begs a favor.

You may ask, General Volitional Twelve. Beloved's reply was cool. It was not her policy to encourage initiative among her servants.

If this-individual is to continue negotiations with the humans, this-individual would find it valuable to know the worth of that for which he is negotiating. This-individual begs to discover the results of Clan Lustre's negotiations with other clans.

Beloved's thought rolled onward for a long moment. *Your request has merit*, she concluded.

There was a pause during which Twelve could sense Beloved's neurons shifting in his head, invading the sight and vocoder centers of his brain.

And suddenly experience crashed in on him and his awareness dissolved into a roiling onslaught of immediate sensation. Twelve's nerves flamed as his perceptions expanded at superliminal velocity—suddenly he was enormous, a vast body floating through nothingness, sensory information pouring in from organs that studded his resinous skin. He felt the caress of radiation on his exterior, the turbulent flow of heat from the side of the body nearest the sun to the side in shadow. His bones were rippled by gravity, compacted by acceleration. Living in his heart was the ship's burning singularity, roaring like an angry beast inside the magnetic bottle that held it prisoner. Data flowed past. Calculations were performed too rapidly for Twelve to follow. And somewhere *outside* his mind was *something else*, the one thing in the universe that seemed outside his own ken, a feature cold, alien, and troubling.

Twelve realized that he was experiencing the ship from the perspective of Beloved's pilot, body and mind fused with ship sensors. He was aware of the pilot's mind straining to overcome its limits, burning oxygen and nutrients furiously as it tried to process data swiftly, exactly, with greater and greater precision. He felt the pilot's frustration as his hands tried to keep up with the data churning through his brain—and Twelve realized that the pilot was feeding the data into the human computer, that the strange object so peculiarly *outside* the pilot's perception was the AI that would guide the singularity shoot.

Then the pilot's mind relaxed. The last bit of data had been fed into the computer. Twelve experienced the depression of the pilot's sensation, his growing sense of loss—Twelve intuited that the pilot normally went beyond this point, that he controlled the singularity right up to the instant when the data blurred past at too great a speed for his mind to keep pace.

Displays flickered on the human computer, more data, all in human script. The pilot was baffled at its speed.

And then, suddenly, the universe contracted. Through external sensors Twelve could see the stars' radiation refracting in strange ways, spraying bright rainbows across his mind; and then the whole universe collapsed and, in an instant, rebuilt itself.

More data flowed in from the sensors. The pilot's blood pressure declined as the processing function of his mind was reduced. His consciousness was turned toward discovering the ship's precise new location.

When the last coordinate rolled into place, Twelve felt a staggering hammerblow of surprise. The human AI had far outperformed the pilot even on his best day.

The pilot began again, readying himself and the computer for the next shoot. Dimly, beneath the throbbing of the pilot's hearts, the flow of blood and data, Twelve sensed the pilot's shock and terror, the growing understanding that he and his entire kind had been superseded, made obsolete by a single, inexpensive device obtained from an incomprehensible source.

Sorrow filled Twelve's hearts. The pilot's world had changed far beyond his ken. He had participated in his own obsolescence, and done so by use of a medium that even his own universe-encompassing powers of perception found incomprehensible.

Perhaps, Twelve thought, he and the other general volitionals would be next to feel supersession as the result of trade with the humans.

The pilot's mind faded from Twelve's consciousness and another memory slotted neatly into place. He wore this new personality with greater ease, with a heightened body awareness and a familiar sense of movement through space . . . He realized that he was experiencing the memory of another general volitional, one of his own body type.

A white alien corridor loomed around him. Foreign odors nagged at his palps, odors not from his own clan. Sentients and near-sentients flooded the space around him. Strange rhythms beat at his vocoder, echoed from the corridor's pale walls.

The point of view shifted from the corridor to a smaller room as Beloved's general volitional moved through a doorway. Behind, rear eyes confirmed that a drumhead membrane slid over the oval doorway behind, assuring privacy. The membrane hummed faintly in resonance with throbbing outside.

Inside was a general volitional, blueblack in color, with a pair of arms affixed to his lower torso and a long pair of whiplike tentacles sprouting from just below his head. He was connected to an umbilicus. Beloved's volitional offered a respectful salutation.

"Clan Lustre gives respectful greetings to the Potent Clan. This-individual is Volitional Twenty-six."

Twenty-six! thought Twelve in surprise. He had known no such sentient on board Home. Volitional Twenty-six must have been grown as a replacement while Twelve was sealed off in his corridor.

The blue-black sentient rippled his tentacles in a barely civil greeting. "This-individual is Potent Volitional 3281. Please state your business with the Potent Clan."

The Potent Clan, Twelve knew, lived up to its name: it owned several hundred planets, moons, and planetoids, the orbital stations that exploited their resources, and the ships that trafficked between them. Twelve now guessed the location of this dialogue: Potent 5367, a giant station in the center of a gas cloud charged with protostars. The station was owned by the Potent Clan but used by clans of all sizes and descriptions in their efforts to mine the valuable proto-systems.

Volitional Twenty-six stiffened in a formal declamatory stance. "Clan Lustre wishes an informative broadcast on the station information service, announcing that Clan Lustre now offers for sale a method that allows a ship to travel up to ten light-years with a necessary correction of less than one thousandth of one percent."

Volitional 3281's whip-arms rippled to wavelike movements that reached the tips, then rebounded. "Clan Lustre offers for sale a new-model pilot?" he queried.

"This-individual did not make that statement," said Twenty-six. "Shall this-individual repeat Clan Lustre's desired announcement?"

"This-individual's memory is not faulty." 3281's stance stiffened. His whips coiled toward his body and he hung motionless for a moment, during which 3281 apparently communicated with his governing entity. "The figures you-individual claim are absurd," he said. "No pilot is capable of guaranteeing such results."

"This-individual has never spoken of a *pilot*." Twenty-six's tone was sharp. "Neither is Clan Lustre accustomed to having its veracity questioned. If the Potent Clan does not believe the capabilities inherent in Clan Lustre's offer, the Potent Clan does not have to purchase them. Other clans shall bid, however, and if the Potent Clan cannot guarantee deliveries as efficient as those of its rivals, then the Potent Clan will have only itself to blame."

Twelve's hearts thrilled as Twenty-six spun and kicked off for the entrance. The tympani-membrane did not withdraw in time and Twenty-six contemptuously yanked it aside before propelling himself out into the pounding corridor.

Glory, Twelve thought. Pride glowed in him.

The offer went out on the station communications net. Inquiries followed. Twenty-six negotiated cautiously, refusing to give more than hints of what he was actually selling. The first computers sold were offered entirely on speculation—*if* they performed as advertised, Beloved would be guaranteed a share of the profits from any cargoes. But Beloved insisted on long-term contracts—demanding shares of profits for decades—and the skeptical bidders made their offers, figuring they had nothing really to lose. And, once it became clear that bids were actually being offered, and that the quantities of computers were limited, the bidding grew in volume, intensity, and profitability. One of Clan Diamond's ships, equipped with the computer, made a brief shoot outsystem and back and reported the AI performed as advertised. Panic promptly set in. The dozens of clans that did business on Potent 5367 made ridiculous offers—sending gifts to Beloved of genetic material, newly grown hardware, offering credit, cargoes, even ship hulls—and all simply to get Beloved's *attention*. Beloved chose among the bids with care and made a fortune.

Elation danced through Twelve's veins as the images rolled through his mind. Beloved was dealing as an equal with the Potent Clan, with Clan Tattoo, with Clan Sapphire and Clan Starwind . . . Clans so mighty that formerly they would have barely acknowledged Beloved's existence. The AIs could guarantee a clan's competitiveness, or another's extinction. Their manufacture and components were a secret that could be kept for years, perhaps for decades. And during that time Beloved's profits would be increasing as demand grew.

Glory to Beloved, Twelve chanted joyfully.

And then another series of memories swarmed into him.

Though the memories were brief and simple, Twelve was overwhelmed as to their scope, detail, and intensity: it was as if he had suddenly become aware of an entire dimension of existence that had somehow escaped his attention. Twelve realized, awe pouring into him, that the memories were Beloved's.

The memories concerned the preparation of a brood chamber, the metabolic changes necessary to assemble the long, long chains of Beloved's genetic components all in one location, all coiled in a single cell.

Beloved was going to reproduce. Children were being created, readied to occupy new ships that would trade across the gulf of space with the humans.

A glow of happiness settled in Twelve. Things, he realized, could only get better.

Marco looked weary, as if he'd been awake for a long time. "Ubu Roy," he said. A jaded enmity sparkled in reddened eyes. "I wonder why you didn't call before."

"Had no business with you till now."

"Be none now, Ubu Roy."

Ubu felt cold energy whirling in his mind. *I know something you don't, old man,* he thought. *That gives me power.*

"You made an offer, bossrider," Ubu said.

Marco scratched his grizzled chin with knobbed fingers. "The situation's changed, Ubu Roy. You be wanting a piece of this action now, you get it under different conditions."

Ubu looked at him. "Don't see any reason for alterations," he said.

Casual contempt touched Marco's features lightly, as if Ubu wasn't worth the effort of a real sneer. "Clan Lustre accepted my last offer," Marco said, "and I don't need you any more. But since I don't want you interfering with my operation, I'll make you a part of it. But you don't have a sixth any more, you have a twelfth. And a de Suarez comes aboard *Runaway* to make sure you do as you're told."

"Eat shit, Marco."

Marco stared at him. "Be all you're getting, Ubu Roy."

"If that's your best offer, *Runaway*'ll shoot straight to Angel Station and tell the Navy and the Multi-Pollies exactly what's going down out here. We've got recordings of the negotiations and they'll believe us."

Marco snorted. "Too late. We'll have our exclusive contract. The Multi-Pollies'll have to deal with us."

Ubu grinned. "What you gonna do with your cargo, old man? What you gonna do when I start telling the Navy about contamination from alien life-forms? They'll *embargo* your ass, Marco. Maybe you'll get out of quarantine eventually, but in the meantime your ships are gonna be hanging in space unable to move cargo."

"So you say." This time Marco went to the trouble of a real sneer.

"Clan Lustre isn't gonna wait around while you get your ships out of quarantine, they're gonna want to deal with *someone*. And Clan Lustre isn't the only alien clan. So while you're sitting in quarantine with no money coming in, I'll be investing my profit from the first shipment while I negotiate with a Hiline company to go looking for aliens. We know the right general direction, and we'll find 'em now we know they're there. You'll be frozen out, Marco. And while you're stuck in quarantine I'll be waving at you from my new yacht and grinning."

Marco stared at him stonily. "What you be wanting, Ubu Roy?"

"We'll abide by any prices you negotiate. *Runaway* sets its own schedules. We want a sixth of the total action, including any new deals cut with Clan Lustre. Any ships I build or buy come into the arrangement on equal shares with any de Suarez ships."

"That all, Ubu Roy?"

Ubu smiled at him. "Just a fair share, Marco. That's all."

Marco lifted a chak to his nose, fired twice. Thought for a moment. Finally he nodded. "Okay, Ubu. You're smarter than I thought."

"It's my licehead sister that fucked up. Not me."

Marco gave a skeptical grunt. "Neither of you fuck up again, we get along fine, Ubu Roy."

Ubu switched off. *I know something you don't,* he thought.

He rose from the couch and bounced toward the ladder. After the heavy-gee burn, he'd set the centrifuge to six tenths of a gee in order to give stressed ligaments a chance to repair themselves; his movement was a half dance, a lofty skip. He went easily up the ladder and began drifting to his cabin.

Beautiful Maria stepped from the galley. A forcebulb was in her hand. She stopped, shook her hair back, looked at him.

"Just talked to Marco," he said. "We're in business." He planted his feet on the carpet's scratchy surface and thought of Kitten, the smell of burning, the way her tear reservoir had stained the pillow.

Maria nodded. "Good."

Ubu's upper right fist hooked out, caught Maria high on the cheek. She went down, the bulb bounding on the deck. The force of the blow and the light gravity bounced Ubu a few inches to his rear.

He looked down at Maria, his heart hammering. She was crouched on the deck, her hand raised to her cheek. Her hair covered her face and kept him from seeing her expression.

Ubu's nerves twisted like wires. He reached down, helped her rise.

And hit her again.

Twelve, in his vac suit, hung in the airlock, his arms and legs braced outward to prop himself against its walls. His helmet was pushed back, his forward eyes peering out from beneath its seal.

"I am pleased to see you, Volitional Twelve," Ubu said.

"I am honored to be aboard *Runaway* once more, reverend bossrider."

"I hope you will convey my compliments to Beloved."

"It will be my pleasure to do so, Bossrider Ubu Roy."

Beloved had at last consented to allow Twelve a personal visit, allowing *Runaway* to set up its delivery schedule without De Suarez Expressways finding out by listening on an open radio channel.

Ubu ghosted into the lock entrance. "Would you like me to help you remove your vac suit, Twelve?"

"My apologies, reverend bossrider, but I will not be here long. I would not wish to put you to the trouble."

Ubu's heart sank. He frowned and looked at Twelve. "I understood Beloved wished to negotiate a delivery schedule."

"That is so, Bossrider Ubu Roy. But she regrets she cannot

conduct negotiations at present. Clan de Suarez wishes to conduct deliveries at another star system, and which star has not been decided."

"If I don't know the star, I can't make deliveries."

"It is my understanding, reverend bossrider, that Clan de Suarez will inform you of the schedule when it is concluded."

Anger warmed Ubu's nerves. His fists clenched in fury. "That would give Clan de Suarez control over *Runaway's* deliveries," he said. "That would give Clan de Suarez a monopoly over trade with Beloved. Beloved can't want this."

"I but follow Beloved's instruction in this matter, bossrider."

"It isn't to her advantage."

"I am Beloved's unworthy voice, Bossrider Ubu Roy."

Ubu stared at Twelve, fury burning inside him. Marco had guaranteed him his own delivery schedule, and then gone behind his back with Beloved to make sure *Runaway* had no control.

"Very well, Volitional Twelve," Ubu said. "I trust you will convey my sentiments to Beloved."

"That shall be my pleasure, bossrider."

Ubu pushed back from the lock entrance, let the inner door slide down. The red light above the lock reflected off his hands, turned them red, like blood. Blue Eighteen, he thought.

Madness.

The fuge, building slowly to one gee, gave a tremor. One of the ceiling natural-light fluorescents blinked out. Ubu glanced upward in irritation.

Marco gazed at him hollow-eyed, a hologram skull. "We know you had a visit from one of Clan Lustre's people. I don't think that's good for business."

Ubu looked into the hollow eyes and grinned. "And I know you want to make your deliveries to Clan Lustre in another system, so you can maintain control over the schedule. I'm a part of that schedule, Marco. I wanna see it. Who do you think I am, my stupid sister?"

"You'll see the schedule when it's finished."

"Then I'll talk to Clan Lustre's people anytime I want."

Marco's unshaven chin gave a contemptuous jerk. "I don't think you're taking this business as seriously as you should, Ubu Roy."

"I think I'm taking it as seriously as my one-sixth share requires, Marco de Suarez."

Marco gave a scowl. The expression only made Ubu want to laugh.

Abrazo ended transmission without a word.

Ubu's cold amusement drained away a few minutes later as he read a transmission from *Abrazo* to Beloved, asking that Clan Lustre send a personal representative to conclude the final details of the contract.

Fury filled him. He left the command cage and paced angrily along the centrifuge, driving his bare heels into the worn green carpet as he passed the machine shop and the food storage area and all the empty cabins that were once filled with Pasco's family. He ended up back at the command cage. The dancing lights on the comm board showed that intercepted transmissions were still being read. He didn't want to see them and went up the ladder quickly. Cooking smells drifted toward him and he stepped into the galley.

Maria looked up at him. She was making dumplings. Ubu's vitals twisted as he saw the split lip, the purple bruise on the eye. His fists clenched.

"Marco's asking for a private meeting with Twelve," Ubu said. "Shit."

"We're gonna lose it unless we do something."

Rage burned in him. His heart boomed Beloved's war song.

Ubu hit her twice more, sickened by the way her head jerked back with each punch, the way she stood and took the strikes, her hands at her sides.

He couldn't look at her any more and found himself staring at the counter, seeing the half-readied dinner, dough the pale color of Marco's flesh, Maria's nail marks on the sealed edge of each completed dumpling.

Hot bile rose in his throat. He turned and fled out into the fuge. Once there, all he could do was run in a circle.

CHAPTER
20

"YOUNGER BROTHER." THE SOUND OF RIDGE'S VOICE MADE KIT JUMP as it came from the concealed speakers behind him. Even disembodied, Kit's cousin was always sneaking up on him.

"Bossrider wants you. His office. Savvy?"

Kit looked across the wardroom table at Juan and shrugged. Juan gave his playtable polarizer a twist and Kit looked down into the ebon surface: an array of threedee ships filled the blackness, plasm flowing from their engines. Trey through six. "Short squadron," Juan said.

Kit twisted his polarizer knob and let Juan see his array. Suns glowed in the depths of the table, surrounded by planets that moved in their orbits. "Cluster," said Kit.

"Shit."

"You shouldn't have redoubled, Elder Brother. You knew I bid eighteen last round."

"Shit. Chinga tu madre."

Kit touched a symbol on the display that added Juan's losses to his account, then stood and left the shooters' lounge. The screen automatically snicked closed behind him.

The lock was keyed to his print now. He'd bossed his first shoot on the way to Santos 448. It hadn't been the best shoot of the trip, but it hadn't been the worst, either. He was proud of it.

Marco even called Kit by his name now.

Marco's office door was closed, which was unusual. Usually Marco liked to keep it open so that he could keep an ear on what was happening in the ship.

Kit scratched at the door. "It's me, bossrider."

"Come in, shooter man."

He pushed the screen open and stepped inside. His heart staggered. "Hi," he said. The greeting was pure reflex.

Beautiful Maria looked up at him. She was sitting on the edge of Marco's workstation couch, her long legs hanging over the side. Bruises mottled her face. "I've run away," she said.

Kit folded a chair down from the wall and sat in it. Flexing his lipless smile, Marco looked from Kit to Maria and back. "She wants to stay with us," he said. "What do you think of that?"

"I want to stay with *you*," Maria blurted. Her dark eyes stared at Kit, and Kit's nerves went hot.

There was a silence filled briefly by the hiss of Marco's espresso bulb. The bossrider sat on the edge of his desk, knobbed feet dangling, wearing only his crucifix and a pair of blue trunks. His gaze settled on Kit.

"What do you think of that, Kit?" he asked.

Kit found his voice. Anger and horror churned in his belly as he looked at Maria's face. "What happened?" he asked.

"Ubu blames me for . . . the way things have gone. He's been hitting me. I couldn't take it any more."

"So you wanna join Clan de Suarez," Marco said. "Kindly, lovable Clan de Suarez. Known for our compassion by all human-ity."

Beautiful Maria's glance flashed to Marco. Kit could see a muscle in her jaw twitching. "I can earn my way," she said. "I'm a shooter. A *great* shooter. And I can deal with the aliens, better than anyone, probably. And you're gonna be expanding anyway, right? Need more shooters if you're gonna have more ships."

"Got it all thought out, don't you, girl?"

"Be so. Haven't had much else to think about."

"Guess not." There was another pause. Marco looked at Kit again. "I haven't heard from you, shooter man. You want this femme or not?"

Kit's eyes hadn't left Maria. His blood surged hot, then cold. He felt a weird sense of unreality, as if this was some improbable fantasy, or a preposterous joke. Life couldn't really be like this.

"Yes," he said.

Color bloomed high in Maria's cheeks, shading the space between the bruises. She looked down at her lap.

"Thank you," she said.

A giddy sense of blessedness rose in Kit. He had made a deal with Marco, with his personal demon, sacrificing Maria in return for becoming a shooter, leaving *Abrazo* behind—and now he was going to have Maria back in his life, just as if he'd never used her, never surrendered her.

"Shooter man says yes," Marco said. "But bossrider hasn't said anything."

Kit looked up at Marco in sudden fury. "I can choose," he said. "I can choose who—"

Marco looked at him, his mouth twisting. "Shut the fuck up, Kit."

Kit's anger froze. His words caught in his throat.

"Good," Marco said. He turned back to Beautiful Maria. "Wanna know what Ubu's up to, shooter femme," he said. "Wanna know what's going on in his head."

Maria shrugged. "Hard to say."

"You think he's gonna stick to our agreement?"

Maria flashed him a look. "Only if you make him."

Marco leaned back on his desk and took a slow swallow of espresso. "We can hear him on the radio trying to negotiate with Clan Lustre. Trying to work out a fast delivery schedule, independent of ours."

"Be stupid not to," Maria said. "Beloved—Clan Lustre can

synthesize the drugs faster than any of our ships can possibly deliver them and return. If he piles up a lot of cash right now he can insulate himself against whatever happens next."

"You think he can shuttle *Runaway* back and forth without your help?"

Beautiful Maria seemed to think for a moment. Her lips twitched in the beginnings of a smile. "Won't be easy for him," she said.

Marco leaned closer to her. "You think he'll hire help?"

"Could be. He's got options on two singularities. Gonna have to hire help anyway, when the new ships get built."

Marco scowled, obviously not liking that idea. He thought for a moment, rubbing his nose with a finger.

"Of course," Maria said, "he's just lost half his profits."

Marco's eyes widened. "Half?"

"We inherited equally from Pasco. We each own fifty percent of the ship."

Marco considered this. "Why's Ubu the bossrider, then?"

"He wanted it. I didn't. And he's older, a little."

"What's Beloved?" he said. "You started to say something about Beloved."

Maria gave a surprised smile. "You don't know?"

"Know what, Pasco's Maria?"

She blinked. "That's right. You don't know anything about them. I forgot all about that." She took a deep breath. "Beloved's their . . . bossrider, I guess. Their governing intelligence. Beloved's what her servants call her. I don't know what she calls herself." Her cut lips twitched in a smile. "Clan Lustre, maybe."

"Go on, shooter femme."

"The aliens aren't like us. They're really only one person, one thing. One idea. The others are just . . . like robots, almost. They don't even have names." She gave an amazed laugh, shook her hair back. "You don't even know what they *look* like, do you? What did you think you were going to find here, when you came?"

"We expected to find people," Kit said. "A lost habitat, maybe. Or something that had been set up on the sly."

Marco was looking at him. Suddenly he was aware of how loud his voice had been.

Maria was nodding. "A reasonable idea, I guess. Everyone *knows* there aren't any aliens."

Marco turned his attention to Maria, studied her for a long moment. He leaned close to her.

"You part of some kind of plan, Maria?" Kit was surprised at the soft, friendly tone in his voice. "You here as part of some scheme of Ubu's?"

Maria seemed nervous at the question. She hesitated for a moment, then stared up at Marco. "Could be, Marco," she said quietly. "Nothing I'm gonna say will change your mind, if that's what you think."

Marco didn't say anything, just leaned closer and looked at her for a long time. Maria stared back, her expression defiant. Her color rose, then fell away.

Kit realized he'd been holding his breath. He let it out slowly, then breathed in.

Marco nodded. "If Kit wants you, you can stay. The both of you'll transfer to *Familia* after this next run."

"Thank you, bossrider," Maria said. Politely.

Kit's mind swam. He'd felt as if he'd been falling down a long, dark, nightmare tunnel, then struck nothing but soft cushions at the bottom.

"There's a room just upspin of here," Marco said to Maria. Behind him, the espresso machine gave a long gurgling hiss. "Painted blue. A shrine. Wait there for Kit. I want to talk to him."

"Yes, bossrider." Beautiful Maria rose quietly from Marco's chair and stepped toward the door. Her hand dropped on Kit's shoulder, gave it an encouraging squeeze. Kit looked up at her and gave her a faint smile. The screen slid shut behind him.

Marco dropped off his desk and sat in his own chair. He slid the chair forward on its tracks, turned it to face Kit.

"Congratulations," he said. "You've come a long way in the last few months."

"Thank you, bossrider."

"I wouldn't start thinking you're irresistible if I were you," Marco said. "I think she's still working for Ubu. I think she's here to spy on us. So don't think it was your pretty brown eyes that brought her here."

Kit stared at him. Marco cackled.

"Don't be so fucking surprised, shooter man. I bet Maria's trying the same thing on you that you tried on her. I'm gonna try to negotiate a secret delivery schedule with Clan Lustre, and Ubu's gonna want to know it." He gave a grating laugh. "He probably still figures he can take it all away from me. I don't know how. Probably a delusion." He looked at Kit. "Ubu should have demanded half the business, not a sixth, right? The fact he didn't makes me think he's planning something."

"If you think that," Kit said, his thoughts whirling. "If you think that," starting again, "why'd you let her on board?"

Marco shrugged. "Maybe I'm wrong. Could be she *is* here because she's desperate, or because she's so charmed by you it hasn't caught her attention that you fucked her over." He cackled again. "Of course I figure it'll never hurt us to have someone on our ship with command of half *Runaway*'s profits. If she's really mad at Ubu, we can encourage her to file a lawsuit against him to get control of *Runaway*. Keep him so busy fighting in court he won't have time to plot against us."

He shook his head, then gave Kit a sharp look. "It's better to have her here where we can watch her. She's half Ubu's brainpower. Maybe the better half."

Kit's spirits fell. He was beginning to see where Marco was heading. "You want me to spy on her, right? My own femme."

Marco grinned at him. "You don't have to. She's on *our ship*, for Rice sake. There are nineteen people on board—we'll know where she is every minute. The thing is just to keep her from spying or doing any sabotage. So, as of this hour, every critical bit of information is going under new passwords. All our shooter files, our operating system, our nav files, our contracts. And Beautiful Maria gets frozen out of all of them. We don't give her the new passwords, we don't let her near the comm equipment or key her into the shooter's lounge or let her boss a shoot on the trip back to Angel. We don't even let her into the command cage. Nothing."

"Marco. She's gonna want something to do."

"There's maintenance. Cooking. That sort of thing."

"Shooters don't do that."

"Not on our ship, maybe. But she's used to it. She must have done all those chores back on *Runaway.*" Marco gave a dry laugh. "It'll all give her more time for romance, shooter man. Think about the good side of it."

Kit just looked at him. "Who's going to tell her, bossrider?"

Marco eased himself down from his desk, turned to his terminal. His voice was a mumble. He'd already lost interest.

"Nobody else better qualified than her man, shooter."

Anger had hummed in her for days, a constant background whitenoise hiss atop which spun her other thoughts, like skaters on ice. The anger had become a permanent presence, a foundation for reality. Now the hum increased in volume, became an urgent roar in her mind.

"Sorry," Kit said. He stood in front of her in a stance of helplessness. "It's what the bossrider wants."

"Is he gonna have people follow me around?" Beautiful Maria asked. "Lock me in my room third shift?"

Kit tossed up his hands. "I don't have anything to do with this." He stepped forward, took her arms. "After this run, we transfer to another ship. Things will be more normal then."

Maria's anger growled in her ears. She spun away from Kit, wrenched herself free. "Marco thinks everyone's like him," she said.

Kit said nothing. Presumably he couldn't argue that one.

Fury wailed in her bones. She took a long breath.

The shrine's blue color reminded her of the blue-white light on Beloved's ship. The room was small, with benches, little colored lanterns, the statue of a pale-skinned woman in a blue gown.

"This is your church, huh?" she said.

"Marco's, mainly. Most of the rest of us aren't regular observers." Kit sounded relieved that the conversation had moved onto neutral territory.

Maria walked down the aisle, looked at the statue more closely. Pointed stars shone on the woman's gown. "Why do they call them stars," she said, "when they've got all those points on them?"

"I never thought about it."

"Religious people aren't very smart."

"Tell that to Marco."

Beautiful Maria thought about that. "Yeah," she said. "Okay. Point taken."

"Show you our room?"

She turned toward him. "Sure."

Maria followed him out of the shrine. As she stepped into the corridor a wave of vertigo swept over her, an eddy of pure panic. She was alone here, in a strange place, Marco had isolated her, and *Runaway* was no longer an option. She'd never been so thoroughly cut off from her home before.

Her heart hammered. A whirlwind shrieked through her mind. Somehow she kept her feet moving as she followed Kit down the corridor. She kept her eyes focused deliberately on his back. She saw that he'd had a haircut recently, that his short nape hair came to a central downward point between the two strong tendons at the back of his neck. Her fear abated. Kit stopped, reached out, opened the door.

Maria's anger boiled up again. She looked at Kit's open, smiling face with purest hatred.

"Here we are," he said.

You bastard, she thought.

CHAPTER

21

I'D FUCK EVERY DE SUAREZ ON THE SHIP IF IT'D GET US THOSE
coordinates.

Beautiful Maria's voice rang suspended in Ubu's mind, every
inflection perfect, each word sharpened by anger, burned with acid.
He remembered his fists striking her, knuckles jarring on bone.

Hatred was no justification for this. Even if Maria wanted it.
Even if it was her idea.

He paced the centrifuge. Maxim rode on his shoulders, claws
lightly pricking the flesh.

Fucked up again.

A tremor passed through him. In the name of hatred, he'd just
turned pimp.

The walls were decorated with a complex pattern of pornography
and holo pictures of hype-people. Michiko Tanaka, dressed in chain
mesh, her eyes heavy with mascara and her lips painted white,
grinned as she straddled the bloody corpse of a villain; next to her was
a smiling blond girl with freckles on her nose and semen on her face.
Phil Mendoza brandished a laser rifle from amid a constellation of

aroused nipples, perky buttocks, moist vulvas, and bizarre tattoos. Kit seemed embarassed about it all, but Beautiful Maria found the sight improbably funny.

Juan de Suarez was packing all his bathroom stuff into a blue plastic collapsible box. His clothes filled only one small collapsible; his pills, vitamins, tooth cleaner, cologne, cosmetic, and hair pomade filled another box just as large.

He didn't claim any of the artwork.

Kit and Beautiful Maria watched, trying to stay out of his way, Kit on his rack, Maria moving from place to place. "Everybody's sure surprised," Juan said. "I think you're both real lucky."

This was the third or fourth time he'd said it. Maria and Kit had given up replying.

Juan stacked one box on top of another, then bent and picked up both. "Guess I'll leave you guys alone." He looked at Maria enviously. "Have fun. Just don't play Kit at spirals."

He left, slid shut the door behind him. Maria looked at Kit.

"Spirals?" she said.

"When I got keyed into the shooters' lounge I found out there's always a lot of gambling going on. We bet against our shares of the next run. Most of the other shooters are big plungers." Kit gave a shrug. "They really don't know how to play. Anyone with half a brain can beat them."

"I've always been good at games of chance," Maria said.

"Too bad they won't let you into the lounge."

There was a long, cold moment of silence. "Yes," Maria said. "Too bad."

"It's not my fault." Quickly. "I didn't make any of these decisions."

"I know."

"When we get on board *Familia*, things'll be normal." Kit gave an uneasy laugh. "And we'll probably have lots of money. It looks like the shares I've been winning are going to be worth a lot."

The thought rang through Maria, clear as a bell, that maybe she ought to be nice to him for a change. She took her bag of clothes and slid it under Kit's rack, then sat next to him. He took her hand and she couldn't stop herself from stiffening.

"Sorry," she said. She took a breath, tried to relax. "The last guy to touch me did it with his fists."

She could feel Kit's sudden flare of anger, the spring-steel tension running through his limbs at the thought of violence to her. Suddenly it was all too much—her anger, his, her sharp sense of aloneness. She shook her head slowly.

"Would it be too much to ask you to leave me alone for a couple hours? I'm just—I've had a bad day."

"Sure. Okay."

Maria smiled at him and squeezed his hand. "Thanks."

She kissed him and he stood, looking at her with troubled eyes. She could read his concern and confusion, an uncertain disappointment.

"Thank you," she said. "I'll make it up to you, okay?"

Beautiful Maria watched him close the screen. Relief dizzied her.

She flopped back on Kit's rack and closed her eyes. Her cheekbone ached where Ubu had hit her; her neck was stiff with whiplash. The pillow smelled faintly of Kit. Another reminder that she was alone here, no one but de Suarezes on board.

Maria reached out with her mind, tried to touch the electron world. She could feel it faintly, a gentle web of mutable energy that surrounded her and the ship. The sensation was warm, familiar. The only familiar thing in this place.

She rose, reached for her bag, stepped to where the desk folded into the wall. She pulled it and the terminal out of the wall, tracked a chair to it. She took a chak of Red Nine from the bag, fired it twice, and turned on Kit's computer terminal.

Passwords, she thought. *I'll show them passwords.*

The electron world rose and took her in its arms.

Sweat gleamed on Beautiful Maria's body after an hour's furious work on the de Suarez system. Red Nine made her hyperconscious of her body, of every ache and itch and discomfort. She swallowed some Blue Seven, folded the desk back into the wall, and headed for the shower.

She'd glitched her way through file after file, found and examined the preliminary agreement with Beloved. *Abrazo's* main computer was an old Kanto, and it took some time to get used to it, but once she had she'd leaped like a dancing spark through the comm system and arranged for any further communication with Ubu or Beloved to be dumped into an accounting program full of old data that, she assumed, had only been kept for tax purposes, and which no one had looked at in years.

That was all she could do now, just prepare for the moment when she got the right data. Red Nine screamed at her to do more—murder, pillage, assassinate, run through the de Suarez system in a fiery particle storm of destruction. The electron world tugged at her, trying to rise in her mind and pull her out of her wired skin.

She took a shower instead. The shower cubicle featured a mural of three naked holograph girls with sinewy moned bodies and painted prepubescent faces. Maria cackled in surprise as they solemnly fondled one another when Maria moved from one point of view to another. She turned the taps and water bounded from her flesh, each impact a bullet strike. She stood in the shower for a long time, then turned off the water and switched on the blowers, letting them blast her dry until her long hair licked around her body like flame.

The Blue Seven was beginning to dull Red Nine's keen edge. Maria left the shower and tried to comb her hair out, but impatience made her toss the comb back in her bag. She ate another Blue Seven, pulled down the terminal again, and called up the game file. She played two fast games of NovaWar, stars exploding on the holo display like patterned retinal flashes, and then the Blue Seven began to drag at her reflexes.

A sharp pain stabbed her kidneys and she used the toilet. Hype aliens, armor and yellow eyes, threatened her from the toilet door. The electron world caressed her like a slow-motion dream, no longer urgent or demanding. It occurred to her that she was exhausted, that she'd been running for days on little but nerves, pain, and anger. She put away the terminal and dropped into bed, then turned the lights off so she wouldn't have to look at any more naked women. Patterned radiation danced in her mind. She closed her eyes and slipped away.

When Kit quietly slid into the rack, she at first had difficulty distinguishing him from the gentle touch of the other world. She laughed when she discovered his reality. The brush of his lips and hands raised a storm of bright photons in their wake.

Passion, anger, and hatred had all drained away on a warm river of Blue Seven. What remained was texture: the touch of skin, rustle of sheets, hiss of breath, all touched by the spectral rainbow shimmer of electricity. All components of Maria's perception, an embracing totality of sensation . . . it might be possible to build an entire universe from this, she thought, construct a benign creation from which rivalry and mercilessness and anger, all Marco's weapons, had been excluded, the new universe built out of mental perceptions in the same way the cascade of the Big Bang might have started with a single virtual particle.

But virtual particles never last—at some point the universe blinks and the particles disappear, and so Maria's universe was compelled to vanish once reality took notice. The whole creation disappeared, folded into itself until it went away, into the bleakness of an unsettled stomach, stabbing pain behind the eyes, a bright, razor-edged, and merciless morning . . .

Maria pushed her breakfast tray away. "I wish you'd think about it again," Kit said.

"I have." Breakfast chiles burned in her stomach. Pain throbbed in her neck with every skip of her heart. She rubbed her stiff neck. "I'm not welcome anywhere in the ship. So why leave the room?"

"There are only a few places you can't go," Kit said.

"I can go to the galley," she said. "Great. I'm allowed to cook for everybody if I want to, I'm just not allowed to do my job."

"Everyone would like to meet you."

"I meet them on my own turf, or everyone can go to hell."

Kit turned away, took a few resentful steps. Maria propped herself in the rack and reached for her comb. Her hair had knotted impossibly overnight. She worked at it for a few furious moments.

Kit reached for the tray. "I'll take this back to the galley."

He stepped to the door. She remembered, at the last minute, to look up and say thanks before he slid the door shut behind him.

"I am pleased to see you, Volitional Twelve."

"I am honored to be aboard *Runaway* once more, reverend bossrider."

"I hope you will convey my compliments to Beloved."

"It will be my pleasure to do so, Bossrider Ubu Roy."

Ubu helped Twelve out of his vac suit, then led him to auxiliary control. The room was shut down now, cage empty, the boards dead. A sad place. Ubu remembered Pasco here, drifting and weeping while the drugs increased their slow, certain grip on his throat. Pasco's holograph ghost had been contained, but now Ubu had begun to feel spectral himself, a lonely remnant haunting the empty ship, abandoned or forgotten by all who knew him.

Ubu touched a castoff bar, spun slowly to face Twelve. "I'm glad that Clan Lustre requested this meeting."

"Clan Lustre will not forget that *Runaway* is our oldest human acquaintance."

Maybe, Ubu thought, he'd get separate deliveries, after all.

"*Runaway* will always consider Clan Lustre a treasured friend," he said.

"Beloved hopes that Clan Lustre and *Runaway* may be of service to one another. Perhaps we may assist one another irrespective of the agreement between Clan Lustre and Clan de Suarez."

"Glory to Beloved," Ubu said. Glee filled him. Was Beloved preparing to stab Marco in the back?

"Glory to Beloved," Twelve answered.

"*Runaway* hopes always to be of service to its friends."

"Glory to *Runaway*." Politely.

"Glory."

Twelve drifted for a moment, his body turned so as to regard Ubu with three of his eyes.

"Clan Lustre would like to purchase knowledge from *Runaway*. Knowledge, bossrider, rather than hardware."

"I understand." Ubu's mind spun. "What knowledge does Clan Lustre desire?"

"Beloved would like to learn the technical skills to produce certain items contained within human artificial intelligences."

I just bet Beloved would, Ubu thought.

"May I ask the items in which Beloved is interested?" Ubu figured he already knew.

"Clan Lustre wishes the ability to produce resistance-free wiring and circuits."

That's one, Ubu thought. "Very good," he said.

Twelve stiffened. His limbs trembled. "Does this mean you know this secret, bossrider?"

"It is . . . obtainable, Volitional Twelve."

"We wish also to obtain knowledge to produce the electric switches that transmit a signal at superliminal velocity."

That's two, thought Ubu. Triumph surged through him. Maybe he had something to fight Marco with, after all.

Macroatomic switches and superconducting glassware circuits. With them Beloved could build her own AIs.

And Ubu had the knowledge in *Runaway*'s own databanks. None of this was a secret among humans. For that matter Ubu could design and build his own macroatoms in *Runaway*'s clean boxes.

"Clan Lustre asks a great deal," said Ubu.

"Beloved hopes the deal would be profitable for all concerned," Twelve said. "For each ability, Beloved would offer twelve cargoes filled with whatever Bossrider Ubu desires, provided that it is within Beloved's power to create it. This arrangement would be independent of any arrangement made with Clan de Suarez."

"I regret that *Runaway* could not part with either technology for less than twenty cargoes," Ubu said.

The bargaining was pure reflex. Ubu couldn't tell whether he wanted to work this deal or not.

Beloved had played it wonderfully, Ubu thought. She had threatened to let Marco control the delivery schedule and limit *Runaway*'s action, then offered Ubu this way out. He could make a fortune and undercut Marco at the same time.

One thing was certain. If he sold the knowledge, any further trading with the aliens would be wrecked. Artificial intelligence was humanity's edge, the thing Beloved wanted most.

A cold thrill hummed in Ubu's nerves as he realized he didn't need to make any decision now, that he could destroy Marco at any time. Wait, he thought. Find out the delivery schedule. Wait till Marco overextends. Wreck him then.

"Does the reverend bossrider have this information available now?" Twelve asked.

"The information will not be available until I have visited human society at least once more." Which would give him a breathing space. He'd see how Maria did aboard *Abrazo*.

Or maybe Ubu could wreck Marco in some other way. He'd have to give it time.

"Does Bossrider Ubu Roy wish to conclude an agreement at this time?"

Ubu smiled. "With all respect to Beloved and Clan Lustre, it may not be possible to discover this information. I wish to acquire it before I conclude any agreement with Clan Lustre."

"As the reverend bossrider wishes."

"Please thank Beloved for her considering *Runaway* in this matter."

"I am honored to be the emissary between your greatness and hers."

Ubu drifted in the dead control room, his mind on fire. If only Beloved had made this offer before, he knew, he wouldn't have let Maria sacrifice herself.

Glory to Beloved.

Was the bossrider intrigued?

In this-individual's best judgment, he was.

Was the bossrider telling the truth when he said he did not possess this knowledge? Or was this a bargaining ploy?

Glory to Beloved, this-individual cannot say. Perhaps so.

Has the bossrider inquired concerning the schedule for delivery of this knowledge?

Glory to Beloved, he did not.

There was a moment's pause. *The bossrider has a limited comprehension of consequence.*

This lack of response in the bossrider was, perhaps, a stratagem.

Twelve offered the thought cautiously. Why, he wondered, did he feel an impulse to defend Bossrider Ubu's intelligence?

Perhaps. Twelve received the impression that Beloved did not rate this theory highly.

General Volitional Twelve, you will next visit the ship of Clan de Suarez. I wish you to confirm that control of the human delivery schedule is entirely in the hands of Bossrider Marco.

This-individual is honored to be of service to his Beloved. Correctly.

You doubt the wisdom of My strategy?

Chill fear entered Twelve's mind. Beloved had divined his mind, but to doubt Beloved's wisdom was appalling blasphemy. His answer was carefully phrased.

Clan de Suarez has shown itself ruthless and opportunistic. This-individual wonders at the consequences of giving them sole control of our commerce.

Beloved's reply was curt. *If Clan Lustre receives the primary human technologies, I will have no need of Clan de Suarez.*

Glory to Beloved, that is so. But there are many things not yet understood concerning the humans.

I understand all that is necessary for Me to understand. From Beloved's mind, Twelve felt a stab of hostility. Fear possessed him.

Glory to Beloved, he babbled. *Glory glory glory.*

Beloved's consciousness withdrew from Twelve, though the umbilicus itself did not withdraw. Twelve could still discern, at a distance, the awesome workings of her many-tiered mind.

A cold, unwelcome thought lodged in his brain, and he squirmed involuntarily at the discomfort it caused him. He understood Beloved's decision, and his own instinctive opposition to it; and he knew it had entirely to do with the difference in their natures.

Since opening communication with the humans, Beloved had been taking one appalling risk after another—she had dared, at the peril of contamination, to open her mind to human language and thought, even though it had driven many of her servants mad; she had dared open trade with an alien species who might use their knowledge of Beloved and her capabilities in an attack upon her; she had dared to parlay alien, incompletely understood technologies among other independent intelligences of her species, risking the spreading of any contamination; and finally, without being able to fully comprehend the consequences or the natures of the parties involved, Beloved now dared to play one human faction against another in a gamble aimed at acquiring their most valuable resource.

Beloved had dared all these things, and Twelve, in his own mind, could not encompass or comprehend such daring. Beloved, Twelve realized, had absolute confidence in her own omnipotence, her own ability to understand and control the consequences of her actions. Twelve, her servant, possessed nothing of the sort.

On an instinctive level, Beloved understood such individuals as Marco de Suarez. Marco behaved as Beloved would have behaved, or at any rate as Beloved liked to think of herself as behaving— decisively, ruthlessly, opportunistically. His ship was organized on a strictly hierarchic level, with Marco at the top, taking all the risks, making all the decisions. The others were perceived as instruments of his will.

Runaway, by contrast, was anarchic and, from Beloved's point of view, quite hopeless. Ubu possessed little of Marco's authority, his crew dared to contradict him publicly without fear of death or reprimand, and Clan de Suarez had somehow stolen his greatest secret. Beloved would instinctively avoid such a chaotic, incomprehensible clan as Ubu's, and ally with the strength and certainty of Clan de Suarez. Ubu would be used as an instrument to transfer the technology Beloved desired, undermine the other humans' position; otherwise he would be discarded.

Twelve, though, could understand such humans as Ubu and Beautiful Maria better than could Beloved. He understood their lack of strength, their confusion, the way they were victimized by stronger humans. Twelve understood their essential helplessness. He was helpless himself, a tool of Beloved's. That was the consequence of his nature.

Ubu, too, would become Beloved's tool. That was Beloved's intention.

And Twelve, because of his nature, would make it come about.

"Bossrider wants to see you."

"Bossrider can fucking well come here, then."

Kit stared at her. At first his surprise was too great for any other feeling to work its way to his face. But then Beautiful Maria saw a series of emotions roll to the surface: shock, fear, a growing look of foreboding. What, he had to wonder, has he got himself into? She almost felt sorry for him.

The bastard.

He licked his lips. "I don't think . . ."

"If Marco wants anything, he can come here. Till I get another place to work, this room's gonna be my office."

He took a breath, let it out. "Okay," he said. "I'll tell him."

Maria grinned at him. "Thanks," she said.

She could see tension bracing his shoulders as he left. Amusement rose in her as she saw how Kit was walking—without realizing it, he was nearly on tiptoe, as if maybe he wouldn't annoy anyone if he was careful not to make any noise.

Maria leaned back on the rack, her supple spine touching the wall, and crossed her legs on the mattress. Disconnected sexuality patterned on the wall before her like a jigsaw puzzle composed of flesh.

Some spy, she thought. She'd seen how female spies behaved in the hypes, how Michiko Tanaka slid into an assignment on an aura of glamour and seduction, ruthless sexuality and cold cunning. Maybe if Maria had any smarts she'd play it that way herself—charm Marco into being careless, tease Kit into being her accomplice, have the entire *Abrazo* in thrall.

Fat chance.

She wasn't a trained spy, she wasn't living in a hype, and she was far too angry to be able to hide it for long. She'd have to use the anger somehow, win herself moments of being alone so that she could do what she needed.

The door slid open. Maria's rage burst into flame at the sight of Marco's skeletal body, grey skin, bulbous knees and elbows, sunken chest. He was dressed only in a faded grey g-string and the cross he wore around his neck. His hollow eyes were fixed on hers, not friendly, not hostile. Kit hovered over his shoulder.

"Kit said you weren't feeling well," he said.

"He was being tactful," Maria said. "I'm feeling fine. I'm just not leaving my office here till I'm allowed to travel freely on the ship."

Marco shambled to one of the chairs, folded it down from the wall, and sat. He looked at her again, considered. "That's nothing to me, shooter femme," he said. "So long as it's understood you're a part of this ship now, that you give me what I want when I need you, you can stay in the closet for all I care."

"So long as it's *my* closet, bossrider."

Kit looked like he was praying for invisibility.

"I come to ask you about Clan Lustre," Marco said. "They're sending an emissary, and I want to find out about him. If he even *is* a him."

"My office," said Maria, "is always open to you."

Excitement buzzed in her mind. Negotiations had to be coming to a close, then. The information she wanted might be in the de Suarez computer within a few hours. "Do you know which emissary is being sent?"

"The emissary is General Volitional Twelve. If that's a name and not some kind of designation."

"It's both," Maria said. "A general volitional is a species designed for the kind of tasks that need both intelligence and mobility."

"I noticed they communicate in the twenty-one-centimeter range. At 1427.9 megahertz. That's almost one of the water holes, but not quite. Do you know why?"

Beautiful Maria looked at him in surprise. "Not be knowing what you mean, bossrider."

Marco looked impatient. "Water holes. One of the frequencies of water. Hundreds of years ago, when people were looking for alien civilizations, they listened on the water frequencies, because that seemed an obvious place to look."

"We never knew that, bossrider. We broadcast to them on a whole spectrum of frequencies, and that was the one they answered on."

"Thought it might be important. Thought it might mean they think like us."

"They don't think like us at all, bossrider."

"Then it doesn't matter anyway." Marco leaned forward, his

expression intent. "This Volitional Twelve's gonna be visiting us. Does he need anything special? So he'd be comfortable?"

"He can breathe our air. If he needs food, he'll bring it. He can stand gravity, though he's not used to it and would be more comfortable weightless."

Marco's face twitched. "It might be to our advantage to take him into the centrifuge, then," he said. "Tire him out."

Poor Twelve, she thought. "Beloved still has to approve any deal," she said. "The advantage would be temporary at best."

"Can I see Beloved, then? Can't she come and do her own negotiating?"

Maria grinned. "Beloved is either built into their ship or has grown to fill large parts of it. I don't think she's gonna come calling anytime soon. And I don't think she'd allow a human anywhere near her. We might contaminate her in some way." She gave Marco a look. "You want me to join you in these talks? I might be able to help you."

"I conduct my own negotiations." Marco's answer was final. "I just want you to tell me everything you know about this Beloved, shooter femme."

Maria felt the anger flushing her skin. She fought it down, shrugged as if she didn't care, as if Marco's hollow eyes hadn't seen it all. "I'll tell you what I know. It isn't much."

The interview lasted two hours.

Beautiful Maria's mind reeled after her questioning. The bossrider had been incredibly thorough.

Kit stayed after Marco left. He and Maria talked afterward, mainly about the aliens. After a while Maria's well of knowledge, already drained by Marco, ran completely dry. They worked at finding something else to talk about and found it hard going. Finally, after Maria heard the distant sound of airlock pumps ticking through the hull of the ship, she suggested Kit might head for the shooters' lounge and play some spirals. He took the suggestion gratefully.

She dropped the desk and terminal out of the wall, locked the door behind her, and called up some Evel Krupp striff. She took the chak of Red Nine in case she needed it, propped it on the desk near her hand. She got into the Kanto's main directory, saw that there was a file open on the terminal in Marco's office, and glitched into it without trouble.

From above the terminal, a black-skinned woman with heavy breasts regarded her gravely from between parted knees.

A holographic image leaped into view as voices rattled from the terminal's speaker. Maria's heart jumped as she saw that Marco was recording his meeting with Twelve. The meeting was in the office, under full gravity—Poor Twelve, Maria thought. Marco wasn't the type to give up an advantage, however slight. Her fingers tapped keys as she arranged for the record to dump the recording into her dummy accounting file and bent closer, put her ear to the speaker to hear the negotiations over Evel Krupp's furious guitar attack.

"We should be ninety standard human days in and out," Marco said. "Possibly under. Shortly after that Clan de Suarez will have three ships coming in with the first three deliveries."

Where? Maria almost shouted the question.

"During that time," Twelve said, "Clan Lustre will set up a chemical factory somewhere in the Montoya 81 System."

Maria could feel her elation explode, scattering burning bits of triumph through her body. Montoya 81! She repeated the star-catalog number in a fierce whisper. All she had to do was get the news to Ubu.

She let the rest of the negotiation record itself while she went in search of the files that governed the communications units. All she had to do was commandeer a directional antenna, pulse a short coded message to *Runaway* that would be understandable to Ubu but not to Beloved should she overhear, and make sure to wipe the record of it afterward.

Simple enough, she figured, but she worked at it for hours. *Abrazo* was an ancient ship, almost two centuries old. The Kanto had been built into the ship during its construction, but the comm hardware was some kind of Stone Age gear that had been scavenged from a ship even older. The comm software was unusual, written in an old assembly language she wasn't entirely familiar with, and through which she had to navigate by instinct. Odd security features had been added at random throughout the text and almost seemed designed especially to frustrate someone with Maria's particular abilities. By the time she finally cracked the program her nerves were cranked on repeated doses of Red Nine, and she had difficulty calming down enough to comprehend the programs that worked the antennae. She couldn't get the servomotors that tracked the directional antennae to work at all, and then realized that in order to be trained on *Runaway* they had to be keyed into their target through the data in the nav displays. To her fury, she discovered she couldn't get the navigation displays up without setting off lights on the nav board. She was trying to work out some way of bypassing that system when there was a knock on the door.

Frustration howled in her skull. Maria turned off the terminal and slammed it into its slot in the wall. "Maria?" A soft female voice called from the corridor.

Beautiful Maria flung open the door and discovered a small wiry woman with four arms and greying blond hair. She was Kit's Aunt Sandy, the aunt who used to sneak Kit food when he was in disgrace, now come to say hello. She had brought a recycled plastic box full of macaroons. There was no choice but to ask her in.

They talked for half an hour in a disconnected, jangled fashion. The drug was still coursing through Maria's veins and her responses to the woman's conversation were frantic, loud, and inappropriate. The electron world wove patterns through the air, distracting her. Maria couldn't manage to eat an entire macaroon: for some reason her swallow response wasn't working properly.

Eventually Aunt Sandy left. Beautiful Maria suspected she hadn't made a good impression.

Maria jumped back to her work. A crashing headache began to throb in her skull. White flashes danced in her vision in time to the furious striff music. After another few doses of Red Nine, Maria managed to bypass the displays on the nav board, but she still couldn't get the antenna servomotors to function. She called up some ship power schematics and discovered that power to the servomotors had to be manually switched on from the comm board, and that except for the one antenna that was pointed at Beloved's ship, all had been switched off. Maria could move or create single electrons; her talent couldn't move something the size of a manual switch. And she couldn't use the one powered antenna, because its altered tracking would be obvious to anyone overseeing the comm board.

Maria shrieked in frustration. The fragile desk shuddered as she slammed her fists down on it. All that was required was one burst of nine characters, taking no more than a fraction of a second to transmit, and the Paleolithic communications apparatus on the old ship had made it impossible.

All she could do was hammer out a short line of programming that would automatically aim an antenna and fire her message if one of the antennas was turned on. Maybe no one would notice such a brief message.

The chances of someone turning on an antenna in this system weren't very great.

She turned off the terminal in fury, slammed it into the wall so hard that a metal rivet on one of the polycarbon hinges popped across the room. Maria stood, frustration running through her, and found herself staring into the improbably pink three-dimensional vagina of the spread-legged black woman. She dug in one of the drawers under the rack, found a heavy clasp knife that would serve adequately as a scraper, and working with manic, gleeful energy, began to deface every piece of pornography she could find.

Kit walked in after twenty minutes, carrying Maria's dinner on a tray. He froze by the door, staring at the savaged faces and bodies on the walls, the thick white curls of torn plastic that littered the compartment and revealed occasional glimpses of holographic flesh. Beautiful Maria saw his expression and was helpless to stop an explosion of laughter that eventually left her kicking helplessly on the rack, clutching her aching sides.

When she recovered, Maria pointed to Aunt Sandy's box. "Wanna macaroon?" she asked. Kit just looked at her. Maria couldn't stop herself, and burst again into shrieking laughter.

"I thank you for coming aboard *Runaway*."

"All credit is Beloved's."

Ubu, in the airlock, had just tugged off Twelve's helmet. He was now looking straight at the top of Twelve's head, and from their positions surrounding Twelve's voder, the alien's four eyes gazed straight back at him. I've got *used* to this, Ubu thought. The experience didn't strike him as odd, not in the least.

"I have been considering the subject of our last conversation," Ubu said.

"Have you agreed to sell us the information, Bossrider Ubu Roy?"

Twelve was rotating slightly in the airlock with the momentum imparted by the last wrench of the helmet. His eyes stayed fixed on Ubu.

"I may if I can get it," Ubu said. The slowly rotating eyes stared at him. "What occurred to me," he said, "was that, if I locate the information you want, I can't get it to you. Not unless I know your location."

"This star will suffice," Twelve said. "Beloved will pilot her ship here from time to time. Once you deliver the information, deliveries will commence immediately."

Ubu's fists clenched as heat flashed through his veins. Jesus Rice, he thought. Beloved was playing this brilliantly, allowing Marco to cut Ubu out of the regular delivery schedule, making him desperate enough to go behind Marco's back to sell the knowledge that would give her the upper hand in further commerce.

"The transfer would be more convenient if I knew where to find your ship," Ubu said.

"I am but Beloved's servant." Simply.

There was no possible answer to that.

The Red Nine was still glitching Beautiful Maria's swallow reflex. Kit tried to talk to her while she hacked at the food on her plate, but he wasn't much more successful at communication than Aunt Sandy. When he took the tray away he didn't come back. Maria went back to the terminal, called up the file of the meeting between Marco and Twelve. Maybe it would give her ideas.

Twelve, she found, had accepted the draft contract in an earlier meeting, but both sides had proposed minor changes. The final, altered agreement would have to be approved by Beloved, and there would be another meeting at thirteen hundred tomorrow.

Plans flashed through Maria's mind in jagged lightning streaks. She picked two of the best, considered her options, called up a schematic of *Abrazo*, and made preparations.

There was nothing left to do. She took some painkillers and Blue Seven, then spent some time rattling around the Kanto's files. A lot of the programming was ancient, designed to run equipment that had been replaced decades ago. One of the oldest files was the game file, and she saw it was running spirals in the shooters' lounge. She decided to watch. There were, she saw, four players, Juan, Ridge, Kit, and someone using the handle of Dancer.

Maria laughed as she remembered Ridge calling her a whore back on Angel Station. Glitches crackled from her fingertips. She started by giving Ridge a series of good arrays, each better than the last; but in each case she gave one of the others something greater. Ridge doubled, lost heavily, redoubled, lost again. "Now who's a loser, asshole?" Maria cackled. Ridge plunged again and again, stubbornly declining to give up. Finally his account dropped to zero. Maria hoped he'd lost the proceeds from the next fifty cargoes.

Ridge was replaced by two others. Maria gave Kit a few good hands, but she knew hardly anyone else in the game and lost interest in the outcome. The Blue Seven was beginning to swim through her veins. Maria folded the desk away, showered, staggered through the cardboard shavings to bed. She drowsed, lost track of time.

Bright light burned through her eyelids. She opened her eyes, saw Kit standing by the door looking at the mess. "I thought you've have cleaned this up," he said. She rolled away from the light and pulled the covers over her head.

"Hey," Kit said, his voice louder. "Wake up. Be trying to talk, here."

"Turn down the lights."

The white blaze faded. Kit sat heavily on the mattress. The bed swung on its gimbals.

Beautiful Maria turned over and blinked at him. She could smell beer on his breath.

"I want this shit cleaned up," Kit said.

"Tomorrow." Maria yawned, stretched.

"Jesus Rice, it's lucky Marco hasn't seen it. Here one day, you make a mess out of my room."

"*Our* room." Annoyance rang in her mind. "*Our* room." Kit kept talking as if he hadn't heard.

"You're antagonizing everybody. You won't act like a part of the crew."

"I'm *not* a part of the crew. I'm not allowed to be."

"You need to learn how to behave around my people." Kit stood up and stalked angrily around the cabin, kicking bits of plastic out of the way.

Maria gave up. It didn't seem worth the effort of fighting her way through the fog of Blue Seven.

"I'm sorry," she said.

"Jesus Rice." Kit sounded as if he was trying to keep the edge on his anger.

"Sorry about everything, Kit," she said.

"Eighty-one people," he said. "Five ships." As if that explained anything.

Kit showered, dried, climbed into the rack. He put his arm around her.

"I love you," he said.

Sorry about that, too, she thought.

"I just want to be happy with you," Kit said. He kissed her cheek.

"Be sorry about the pictures," she said. "I just didn't want to look at them any more."

"Most of them were Juan's anyway."

She gave a little laugh. "Which ones were yours?"

He tensed as if he was trying to decide whether or not to be angry. "Guess," he said after a while. He pulled her to him and kissed her hard.

Very de Suarez, Maria thought.

This would be all right, though. As long as the Blue Heaven held out.

Scarred walls, a swaying bed, light that drilled straight into the skull through expressway eye sockets. Children screamed and laughed in the corridor outside, each sound a slap on the ear. Beautiful Maria needed a jolt of Red Seven just to get herself out of bed. Pain stabbed her joints; she required fifteen minutes' stretching before she was able to move without stiffened muscles clawing at her limbs.

She put on a jumpsuit and cleaned the litter off the floor while Kit was off at breakfast, then ate ravenously after he returned with her tray. "Marco told everyone to get the ship ready for lockdown and high gee," Kit said. "We might be shooting out of here today."

"Can't happen too soon for me," Maria said.

She reached for the box of macaroons. Breakfast hadn't been nearly enough.

They decided to call up a hype and Maria watched *Terror Squadron* for the fourth or fifth time. Nerves and Red Seven made her fidget. Kit gave up holding her hand after noticing how much it was sweating. After lunch, Kit had duty snugging things down. Beautiful Maria got ready to make her move.

She tied her hair back, dumped her belongings out of her shoulder pack, then fired up some Red Nine and listened to the dopplered highway song of neurotransmitters multiplying along the byways of her nerves. She pulled the terminal keyboard from the desk and stuck it in the bag. Maria hitched the bag behind her back, stepped to the door, slid it a few centimeters open, listened. Her pulse boomed so loudly in her ears it was hard for her to hear anything outside.

Feet raced down the corridor and she jumped back as if she'd been struck. It was one of the kids, giving a strange off-key crooning sound as he ran. The sound touched some chemical resonance in Maria, shuddered up and down her cranked nerves like the scream of chalk on slate. Maria ground her teeth. The sounds faded downspin, and Maria put her ear to the doorframe again. Voices came to her, a conversation about last night's spirals game. "Shitty fucking luck." Ridge's voice. "You should have seen the plays I was getting."

"I heard you didn't do so well." The answer was noncommittal.

Maria bit back a laugh. The conversation went on. Red Nine urged Maria to run, scream, attack. She slid the door open a little more and peered out.

The voices were coming from an open compartment door, downspin of her, between her and the main control cage.

So much for slipping into the cage without being noticed and switching on an antenna. She was going to have to do this the hard way.

Maria looked left and right, then stepped into the corridor and walked quickly upspin. A ladder took her up to the centrifuge hub.

Long fluorescent tubes lit the white weightless polymer-walled corridor, the forward part rolling slowly as the big centrifuge rotated around it. Maria kicked off gently from a pad crisscrossed with orange tape and drifted out of the hub, into the stationary corridor behind. Distant voices sounded from ahead. Maria reached out, caught a castoff bar, stopped her progress.

The voices continued, barely louder. There was a ladder stretching the length of the corridor, for use when *Abrazo* was under acceleration and the move into the centrifuge would become a march uphill. Maria began to move along the ladder, hand over hand from one step to another.

The voices came clearer. Maria held her breath as she realized one of them was Marco's. "As soon as that fucker gets clear of the torch," he said, "I want max acceleration out of this gravity hole. Be wasting enough time out here."

"Yo, bossrider." Aunt Sandy's voice. "Just give the word. I've already got the software up and running."

The voices were coming from auxcontrol, then. Aunt Sandy was going to boss the shoot from there rather than the cage in the centrifuge.

Darkness flooded Beautiful Maria's vision as panic rattled in her pulse. She took deliberate breaths, cleared her mind. She pulled herself slowly along till she came to the open door, then moved crabwise along the walls till she came to the space between the doorframe and the corridor, a distance of about twenty centimeters. Maria couldn't hope to keep her whole body, that and the shoulder bag, entirely out of view; she could only hope none of the people in the control room were looking directly out the door when she drifted past it. She tensed, dug her toes into the plastic surface of a wall cushion, and pushed off.

"Have we got an estimated ETA for *Familia*'s arrival at Angel?"

The voice, male, was new, louder than the others, maybe floating right by the door. Maria barely stopped herself from screaming, from flailing and trying to halt herself right in the yellow spill of light from the doorway.

She ghosted past, fear beating time in her skull. Aunt Sandy's voice answered the question, but Maria's staggering mind couldn't understand the words, comprehended only the tone of voice, which was normal.

No one had seen. Relief rattled in Maria's throat. Sweat stung her eyes.

She drifted on till she passed the corridor that led to the trunk airlock. Two doors beyond was the paint locker. Maria found a paint sprayer, slapped in a compressed-air cartridge, and charged the sprayer with pale green paint. A drawer yielded up a paint scraper and a pair of heavy gloves.

Across the corridor was the ship's safe, hidden behind a heavy steel fireproof door covered with flaking red paint. Maria touched the door's controls. Hydraulics hissed, and she stepped inside.

Backups of the ship's primary software were locked behind metal doors, protected here from radiation. Everything flammable was stored here as well: standardized drums of solvent locked onto cross-braced tubular racks of white metal, further secured with elastic safety nets. Boxes of real paper stood high on racks, some of it so old Maria could smell the musty scent of its decay. There was some paint here also, though most of the paint on the ship was of the powdery, nonflammable type. Sensors and nozzles of greenish bronze stood ready to identify and suppress any outbreak of fire. Maria touched the interior control, and the heavy door slid shut.

Maria pulled the terminal deck from her shoulder bag. Ship schematics had shown her that there was an access jack here, in case the primary software had to be reloaded. She looked behind one of the drums, reached back, plugged the terminal into the jack, and powered it up.

Time to wait. She reached into the pocket of her jumpsuit and brought out a couple of Aunt Sandy's macaroons.

Beautiful Maria returned her attention to the keyboard as soon as she heard the airlock pumps begin to tick over. In another few minutes she was eavesdropping on the conversation between Twelve and Marco.

The contract had been finalized; the brief meeting consisted of elaborate greetings and congratulations offered by two parties, plus the formal printing of two copies of the agreement. Within a matter of minutes, Marco and Twelve were on their way back to the airlock.

Beautiful Maria touched a key. The down rippled on her arms at the eerie sound that blasted from beyond the steel door, an unforgettable electronic screech. A collision warning.

Maria had programmed *Abrazo*'s radar to detect an oncoming swarm of small asteroids.

Beautiful Maria was thrown into a rack as automatic collision-avoidance programs went into effect and the ship began to alter course. Solvent sloshed in the drums. Maria fought against the sudden acceleration, shoved herself off the rack, secured the terminal in one of the safety nets. She hit the door control and the steel door rolled open.

Outside the screeching was louder. *Abrazo* shuddered to another alteration in course. Maria stuck her head out of the door and saw Marco diving along the corridor toward auxiliary control, slamming into the padded walls with each burst of acceleration. The corridor was shorter now: a heavy steel-alloy collision seal had slammed into place where the corridor met the centrifuge compartment.

Marco threw himself into auxcontrol. Maria pushed off, darted around the corner, saw Twelve ahead, wearing only the lower half of his vac suit, arms and legs flung wide as he tried to react to the surges in acceleration. A collision alarm wailed in time to the howling Red Nine in Maria's blood as she bounced along the corridor.

Twelve's voder gave a loud buzz as he tried to shout over the sound of the alarm. "I am surprised to see you here, Shooter Beautiful Maria."

"I am here conducting negotiations," Maria shouted, "and I thought I would pay my respects to yourself and Beloved." She grinned as *Abrazo* began an attitude change. "I seem to have picked the wrong time."

Abrazo fired its engine again. Maria and Twelve clutched at castoff bars for support. "What is the difficulty?" Twelve asked.

"I don't know." Maria looked at Twelve and took a long breath. If this didn't work, the whole point of the exercise was lost. "I was hoping to ask you for a favor, Volitional Twelve." Maria reached into a pocket of her jumpsuit, pulled out a plastic data counter. Red Nine made her teeth chatter as she spoke. "Could you deliver this to *Runaway* on your return to Beloved's vessel?"

Twelve took the counter with the delicate inner fingers of one hand. "What does it contain, Shooter Maria?"

"Data from some of *Abrazo's* sensors. They're more sensitive than ours in some ways."

She grinned tautly at Twelve while her heart quietly sank. This whole story, she realized, was impossibly lame. It must have been the Red Nine that made her think she'd actually get away with any of this. Even Twelve couldn't be this naive.

Twelve took the counter. "I am pleased to be of service to *Runaway*," he said.

Relief and astonishment filled Maria. "Thank you, Volitional Twelve," she said. "I'm sure Bossrider Ubu will be grateful." She looked over her shoulder. "I should assist in this emergency. Glory to Beloved."

"Glory."

Maria made a staggering flight back to the paint locker, closed the heavy steel door, reached for her terminal deck. She tapped in a piece of code, and new asteroids ceased to appear on *Abrazo's* screens. There were a few final bursts of acceleration as the remaining phantoms were avoided, and then the howling alarms fell silent.

A sudden wave of despair rolled through her. Twelve, she knew, was going to give the counter to Marco. She would be discovered and locked in a bare room for the rest of the trip.

Some slower, gentle acceleration ensued as *Abrazo* regained its matching orbit with Beloved's ship. Pumps ticked in the hull as the airlock cycled to permit Twelve to leave. Maybe, she thought, she'd somehow gotten away with it. Maria waited for another few minutes, then stuffed the terminal deck, the paint gun, her scraper and gloves in her sack.

The door slid open and she looked out. There was no one in the corridor, and the door into auxcontrol was closed. She pushed off. An acceleration alarm sounded, a high, ringing bell.

The centrifuge was shut, having been braked and locked down during the emergency. Maria kicked off and drifted down to the second level, then ghosted swiftly down the residential block till she came to her door.

Kit was inside, floating in the center of the room. Red Nine made her laugh in surprise. Kit looked up.

"Where've you been?"

Maria reached into her bag, pulled out the sprayer. "I thought I'd do the walls," she said. "Got stuck in the paint locker when alarms started ringing." She looked at him. "What happened?"

"Buncha asteroids on collision course for the planet. Million-to-one shot we were in their way." He gave her an uncertain smile. "I'm glad you've decided to go out."

"I haven't." Laughing. "Nobody saw me."

Kit seemed disappointed. The bells rang again, the signal to prepare for acceleration. Kit reached for the intercom button, touched it. "Kit and Beautiful Maria are ready," he said.

Maria hopped into the top rack, the one Juan had used, and webbed herself in.

The bells rang again. Red Nine rumbled up and down Maria's spine.

Maria felt the kick from behind as *Abrazo* fired its engines. The sleeping racks swung to new attitudes. Gravity began to close its fingers on Maria's throat.

The electron world dizzied her, bathed her in soft color.

Maria began to laugh. She could hardly wait for what was going to happen next.

CHAPTER

22

EVEN IN A GRAVITY-FREE ENVIRONMENT, THE THIN PLASTIC DATA counter seemed an implacable weight. As the outer hatch slid soundlessly open, Twelve seemed to feel the counter pressing against his skin even through the ballooning suit. His mind whirled with questions and possibilities as he pushed himself out into the darkness.

The counter represented some kind of scheme, obviously, but whose, and to what end? At the sight of Beautiful Maria aboard the Clan de Suarez ship, Twelve's surprise had been total. Beloved's entire strategy was based on manipulating the antagonism between the two human clans, on keeping them apart. Was Beautiful Maria's presence evidence of some collusion between the two human clans, a plot aimed at Beloved?

And in that case, what was in the data counter? If Maria was conspiring with Clan de Suarez, she should be able to carry her own messages to *Runaway*.

Possibly, he thought, Maria had been restricted by Clan de Suarez in some way. Maybe their negotiations hadn't prospered, and Maria had been taken captive.

But that didn't make sense, either. If she was a prisoner, how had she got free in order to give the block to Twelve?

Possibly the emergency aboard *Abrazo* had something to do with it. Perhaps she had arranged it somehow.

Another thought rang in his mind. Possibly there was nothing in the counter at all. Perhaps this whole bizarre incident was nothing but a test of Twelve and his Beloved, a trial of their goodwill and intentions. If so, *Runaway* and Clan de Suarez were both a party to it.

Twelve's mind swam, his thoughts unstrung. He could make nothing of this.

He could see Home plainly, silhouetted against the dark green of the planet below. *Runaway* gleamed like a captured star just on the planet's lumined rim.

Twelve set a course halfway between the two. He deliberately gave himself a slow rate of speed.

Twelve remembered *Bloodbath in Building Four*. Possibly Maria had been inserted as an agent into Clan de Suarez, much in the same unspecified way that Ahmad had been inserted into Kirstie's clan in the hype. Maybe Clan de Suarez didn't *realize* Beautiful Maria wasn't one of their own. Perhaps he should alert them, give Marco the counter . . .

No, he thought. Marco de Suarez knew precisely who Maria was. If she was there at all, it was with his knowledge and permission.

It was all too confusing. He should consult Beloved, he knew. Perhaps Beloved understood enough to make sense of this.

He knew that Beloved would be alarmed by the possibilities inherent in this curious communication. Doubtless she would take the data counter and use her computer to try and read it. Perhaps she would succeed.

In any case, Twelve was certain, the data would never arrive aboard *Runaway*. Beloved's policy depended on keeping the humans isolated and confused. She would not aid in any covert attempt at communication, particularly when its manner so hinted of conspiracy.

But Twelve was a volitional. He could act without instruction, so long as he did not violate any of Beloved's stated policy.

Without entirely understanding why, Twelve adjusted his trajectory.

Heading for the artificial star that gleamed on the edge of the planet's disk.

The electron world settled over Beautiful Maria like a brilliantly patterned blanket. She was barely aware of the moment when the acceleration ceased, when *Abrazo* began to drift toward its shootpoint. Instead she concentrated on the data that sang through her nerves, the software that calculated the ship's position and kept track of *Abrazo*'s relationship to the hypothetical spot, light-years away, that would be the aiming point for the shoot.

She'd asked Kit to call up *Smuggler's Road*, with Phil Mendoza, for the duration of the acceleration. Watching it kept him occupied and conversation to a minimum.

A warning gong sounded. Sixty seconds to shoot. Maria took the inhaler and fired more Red Nine.

She was aware of a sudden increase in data flow, test programs coming up, safety checks being made. Electrons flowed through macroatomic switches, leaping fractional seconds ahead in time. Giving a picture of the singularity as it would be in the fragmentary future.

Shoot. Beautiful Maria had never been wired this far into the electron world without the benefit of stim antennae, without control of the magnetic pathways by which the singularity was permitted to devour the ship that contained it, and that's why she needed the Red Nine, something she never needed when she was using a direct interface . . . *Abrazo*'s Kanto was an old machine, but new circuitry had been jacked into it for tide riding, and its acuity was as good as *Runaway*'s old Torvald. Maria tried to reach out for sensation, for certainty, and the electron world opened its floodgates and poured in a hot river through her veins. She could sense the burning, all-devouring heart of the singularity; and she was simultaneously aware of its status an infinitesimal fraction of a second in the future, its existence stepped ahead by the long chains of macroatoms. Her awareness reached out for the singularity-that-would-be, touched it, enhanced a developing perturbation. *Abrazo* staggered on its course, corrected, swung back to optimal. Maria gave a laugh. She'd never done this before, deliberately thrown a shoot off course instead of smoothing the ride.

Maria experimented with the singularity, accelerating its perturbations, rippling its tides, exaggerating its minute flares, bringing chaos out of the black hole and into *Abrazo*'s macroatomic reality. Aunt Sandy's conning began to grow erratic—things were speeding up for her, everything was growing critical, and *Abrazo* staggered wildly as Aunt Sandy altered the shape of the singularity's magnetic bottle in order to compensate. Soon, Beautiful Maria knew, she'd lose it entirely, give the shoot up to the computer.

Maria threw an electronic storm at Aunt Sandy, flares, gravity perturbations, sudden bursts of electromagnetic radiation. *Abrazo* spun madly as it was drawn into the black hole, wildly off course. Incoming radiation skewed, formed electric rainbows. Gravity rolled through the ship in long, inexorable waves.

Whitehole.

Laughter rose in Beautiful Maria's throat. She rolled off the rack, drifted into the holographic image of the hype. Laser fire burned around her. She pointed at an armored figure. "Bang!" A woman screamed, blood streaking her faceplate. Death exploded around her. Electrons danced in her brain. Her sinuses felt as if they were fluorescing. *Abrazo*, she knew, was off optimum by an absurd figure, by light-years.

She was suddenly aware of Kit staring at her, an appalled expression on his face.

Maria kicked and laughed and let the holocaust rain down.

The airlock light on the status board went from red to green. *Montoya 81*, Ubu thought. The star's name sang in his mind. Maria's scheme had worked.

They'd have everything again. Marco had stolen Ubu's trade with the aliens; now Ubu would steal it back.

Montoya 81. About eight light-years away; with the new Lahore he could do it in three jumps, in a few subjective hours.

Ubu headed for the command cage to plot his course.

This-individual trembles in the knowledge that he has displeased his Beloved.

Beautiful Maria was obviously engaged in conspiracy. You were not obliged to assist her.

This-individual thought it best to do as asked and then inform you. This-individual did not wish to cause Maria offense without clear cause.

Instead, you have caused offense to Me.

Terror racked Twelve's body as he sensed the trend of Beloved's thought. His palps could taste only the scent of his own fear.

Dissolution, he knew, was only a moment away.

But somehow, with impossible, glacial slowness, the moment moved quietly past.

Beautiful Maria learned later that *Abrazo* was four point two light-years off optimum, probably the worst shoot that anyone aboard had ever experienced. As soon as the navigation software read out the ship's position—and then read it out again, because no one believed it the first time—Marco ordered another shoot.

Maria was ready, and burst into laughter at the sound of the one-minute warning. She drove a foot through Phil Mendoza's stoic face, kicked off from the wall of the compartment, tumbled, kicked again, rebounded. "Maria . . ." Kit said. Maria kept bouncing back and forth like a photon caught in an energy pump, the electrons ringing in her head like bells.

The shot commenced. Beautiful Maria danced weightlessly through it, playing tag with the holograms, twisting and cannoning her body in time to the pulse of electrons. Whoever was conning this shoot didn't approach Aunt Sandy's ability to recover from a surprise—the new shooter's instincts were to accelerate and try to power into optimum by force. If his gambling style was anything to judge his shooting by, maybe it was Ridge on the con this time. The ride ended up in a nearly lateral direction from optimum, hardly any progress at all.

Beautiful Maria cast herself into the rack again, clutched at the webbing. Electrons crawled like waves of insects up her spine. Sweat beaded her face, her neck. The bell rang for gravity and the centrifuge began its low, shuddering startup.

Maria giggled. No more shooting today! She swayed as she

lowered herself off the rack and stepped into the bathroom for some capsules of Blue Heaven. "Maria," Kit said. His voice seemed to come from far away. "What are you doing?"

"Taking a shower."

"I mean, what are you *doing?*"

She turned, gave him a wired grin. "Having fun," she said.

Maria stayed in the shower a long time while the water rolled on her skin like bounding electrons. When she came out, she untied her hair and danced slowly around the compartment, moving to the fading rhythm of streaming particles. Circling her as she spun were torn smiles, breasts, vaginas. Kit watched her from the rack, his face expressionless. She danced over to him, reached out a hand, touched his face. He jerked away.

Kit rose, opened the cabin door, left without a word. Maria bobbed to the door, closed it behind him.

A thought struck her mind like a stray neutrino touching matter, a ghost transfer of energy. *She could hurt Kit.* She had the power. Her dancing faltered, and she looked at the closed door.

Good for me, she thought. Though for some reason she did not rejoice.

The electron storm took her, and in the gathering gravity she began to dance.

Bells woke her, the warning for weightlessness. Beautiful Maria groped her way out of the lower rack, reached for her bag, stumbled to the bathroom through swirls of Blue Heaven. Two jolts of Red Nine brought her sharply to attention.

She stepped outside. Kit was blinking in the upper rack. Maybe, Maria thought, they weren't sleeping together any more.

"What's happening?" she asked.

"The last two shots were way off optimal. They thought there might be a hardware problem in the computer or in the electromagnet governors." The bell rang again. The centrifuge trembled faintly as brakes were applied. Kit shrugged. "Guess they got it fixed."

"Right," Maria said happily. She hopped back into the rack, hooked her toes through the webbing, fired another pair of rockets. Burning warmth flooded her upper throat.

"Not again," Kit said.

"Not what again?"

"Not the fucking drugs again. Jesus Rice. When I came back from the lounge you were passed out."

"I was asleep."

"You were in a goddamn coma."

Beautiful Maria reached up, hooked her fingers around the tubular frame of Kit's rack, and pulled. In the decreasing gravity both racks swung toward each other. Maria poked her head above the level of Kit's mattress and looked at him.

"I don't have anything else to do, Kit. I'm not allowed to be crew, so I'm gonna party."

"You're not even enjoying it. It's like—something you're making yourself do."

She grinned at him. "I'm having a great time. Really. You have no idea." Red Nine tickled laughter from her throat. "You can party with me, Kit."

He turned away, drew the webbing over himself. Maria dropped back to her rack, fired another pair of rockets.

The next de Suarez shooter was pretty good. Maria only put him a little over three light-years off optimum.

Ubu knew he'd have months to waste: he took his time jumping to the Montoya star. He detoured to an old red main-sequence star, Kitsune 71, and found no planets, though there were enough orbiting chunks of matter to serve his purpose. After two days' search he found a twenty-kilometer-long asteroid on his radars, moved *Runaway* into matching orbit, then brought his ship into a cautious, gentle rendezvous, the ship's electromagnetic grapples locking him into place on the asteroid's nickel-iron surface. Later, hovering above the ship in a vac suit, Ubu watched while the autoloaders pitched every one of Beloved's containers out onto the corrugated surface of the rock. The giant red sun hung above the asteroid's short horizon like a cold ruby, scarcely warming Ubu's unshaded flank. The long standardized containers, the color of old blood, bounced and skidded in the asteroid's light gravity, kicking up pebbles shiny with nickel and quartz. None of the containers had enough velocity to escape the asteroid or go into orbit: they bounced along for a while, then arranged themselves in sprawling piles. Probably a few sprang leaks.

Ubu would come back and pick the cargo up later, or send someone. He put a solar-powered radio beacon on the rock so that whoever returned for the cargo wouldn't spend too much time trying to find the right asteroid, then Ubu degrappled, accelerated away, and loaded the shooting software.

He made Montoya 81 in three easy shoots, ending about three AU from the sun. The system had once had seven planets: now it had five and two asteroid belts. Ubu had no way of knowing where in the system Beloved would appear, but just because he might as well go somewhere he put *Runaway* into an easy glide toward the largest of the survivors, a medium-sized gas giant striped, almost invisibly, in cool grey and near-black violet, a dark marble sphere rolling on ebony. The largest planet made as good a rendezvous as any.

Now all Ubu had to do was wait.

"Bossrider."

"Shooter Maria." Marco's baleful yellow eyes stared out of red-rimmed sockets. Fatigue lay heavily on his drawn face.

There was good reason for Marco's weariness. After the third shoot, *Abrazo* had drifted in deep space for over two days. The hardware had been checked again, and the shooting and positioning software had been gone over with extreme care. In the end Marco decided to erase everything and load the software over again from the primary molecular data store kept in the steel-walled safe.

Three shoots followed. Each had been a catastrophe, and now *Abrazo* drifted again.

"Shooter Maria," Marco said again. His voice was loud in the small compartment. "I wonder if you understand our problem."

"Your riders haven't been hitting the mark." Beautiful Maria picked at a scab of pale green paint on one hand. When she hadn't been glitching the shots, she'd been scraping porn off the walls and repainting.

"Maybe something's keeping them from hitting optimum," Marco said. "You got any idea what that might be?"

Maria shrugged and scratched at the green paint. "Maybe your singularity's got indigestion."

"We've looked at the spectra. The black hole's only acting up during shoots."

"A software problem." Maria flipflopped her paint-stained hand. "A hardware problem." She finally looked up from her hand, gazed at Marco. "Why you asking me? I've been in this compartment the whole time."

"Funny coincidence. You come aboard, our shooting's turned bad. And then there was that asteroid storm—our radar saw it, but *Runaway*'s didn't, and neither did Clan Lustre's. We took evasive action and they didn't."

"I don't see how I can cause an asteroid storm *and* a bunch of bad shoots."

"There's access to the computer from this compartment."

Maria gave a burst of laughter. "Kit's been with me during the shoots. Ask him. I haven't been anywhere near the terminal during a shoot. Most of the time we've been watching hype."

"You could have brought something aboard. Loaded a program into the core that would have glitched the ride software."

Maria stared at him. "I *could* have. I didn't." Marco was going to have to get a lot more imaginative before she'd have to start lying to him directly. "Besides, I thought you dumped the software and loaded it again from the original media."

"You could have reloaded your sabotage software, too." Marco leaned in close to her. Maria looked at the grey wattles under his arms.

"I'm gonna deactivate the terminal in here," Marco said.

"I won't be able to get any hypes or games."

"You won't be able to mess with our database, either. If you like, I can get you hard copy. Books, that kind of thing." His mouth twitched. "Another thing. I don't want you leaving this compartment. That shouldn't be a hardship since you're not leaving anyway."

Beautiful Maria stared into his red eyes, anger twitching in her nerves. This was all so fucking useless, she thought: there was no way that stopping her from entertaining herself was going to put *Abrazo* back on schedule.

"I wanna have something to *do*, bossrider."

Marco only smiled. "Just think about getting us to Angel Station in a real short time. That's your assignment. That's all you gotta do."

Runaway was filled with silence, a slab-sided floating island inhabited only by Ubu and a white cat, two insignificant bits of organic debris rattling in a giant metal box. Ubu made repairs, assembled new gadgets, called up one of the new hypes he'd purchased at Bezel. An hour into the story, he found himself grinding his teeth as the holo figures went on with their business, scheming, fucking, or dying with equal dedication to the dictates of formula. Ubu left the hype on infinite repeat and left the room for another aimless circumnavigation of the centrifuge.

Ubu paced, waiting for something to happen as the ship rolled around him. Nothing did.

Even the ship's ghost had gone.

He didn't want to think about Maria. He couldn't forget the way his knuckles grated against her cheekbone, the flowering of bruises on her translucent skin, the compression wave of shock that had swept along his nerves at the discovery of his own capacity for brutality.

Necessary to the plan, she said. She had to be convincing when she asked for shelter.

Hit me while I'm not expecting it, she said. I don't want to have to know when it's coming.

Ubu's teeth grated as he fought a brief, sharp battle against memory. Memory won.

Pimp, he told himself. You're a pimp. Sold your sister to the de Suarezes for two words: Montoya 81. How do you forget *that?*

Ubu went back to the lounge. The hype continued, but Ubu had lost track of the plot entirely. A holographic man's buttocks jogged as he fucked a placid, lightly frowning, moon-faced woman. There was something in her calm that reminded Ubu of Maria. Ubu's nerves burned to ash.

Ubu turned on his heel and stalked out again. Maxim, sensing something wrong with his behavior, scuttled ahead down the corridor, his furry white tail waving like a warning flag. Ubu paused, wondered where to go. He looked down at his hands and discovered that his nails had gouged precise crescents in his palms.

He'd never been alone before. Never for more than a few hours at a time.

Ubu wondered how Beloved managed it, alone for months at a time with nothing but her biological robots for company.

He dropped down a ladder to the lower shooter's lounge, called up the computer directory. There it was, a file called "Pasco," occupying a stupefying amount of computer memory. He wondered how Pasco had managed to hide it all before.

Ubu braced himself, told the file to run.

His father appeared, and told Ubu about his day.

After confiscating Beautiful Maria's terminal, Marco dumped the core program again and reloaded from the data store. The next jump was a success only by comparison with the others: *Abrazo* succeeded in lurching about three light-years in more or less the optimum direction. Marco decided that would have to do: he initiated a long daisy chain of shoots, one after another, a different rider bossing each.

The whole sequence took hours and achieved about a ten light-year advance toward Angel Station. Maria was thankful she didn't have to do anything complex—to control a shoot she'd need a stim set, but to throw a ride off optimum all she needed was the drug. She was crazy with Red Nine by the end of the series—talking nonstop, jumping around the compartment, laughing and shrieking, obsessively trying to drive a comb through her knotted hair. Kit couldn't stand it and left after a few hours, returning only to bring trays of food that she couldn't bring herself to eat.

After the series ended, the Blue Seven put Maria out for fifteen hours, a rocklike sleep in which the subatomic world never fully faded, just danced through her dreaming mind, a ballet of streaming, blazing particles locked in intricate patterns . . . The electron world itself woke her, the patterns changing to somehow let Beautiful Maria see that the shooting software had been called up again. Without even opening her eyes she hung an arm outside the rack and groped for the chak of Red Nine.

The new series of shoots was more brutal than the last. Beautiful Maria spent the last few hours strapped on the toilet, her mind burning with visions of the electron world while her body trembled to the repeated doses of the drugs.

She went to sleep afterward, the electron world shining in her mind. At some point she awoke, found her way to an abandoned tray of food, ate every scrap, and returned to the rack.

At this rate, *Abrazo* might make Angelica System after another pair of series.

"Today we made a profit," Pasco said. He was addressing an empty corner of the lounge. "The profit almost makes up for the slight losses on our last three runs." He sighed. "In order to pay the fees in Truchas I had to take a contract that wasn't very good. Multiple deliveries. I dunno—" Pasco shook his head. "I thought it was gonna be a better contract than it turned out to be."

Ubu watched his father and wondered why he seemed different. Even though the holo image was only a few feet away, Pasco seemed smaller, less significant—distant, as if viewed through the wrong end of a telescope.

There was no pain, Ubu realized suddenly. That was the difference, no edge of sorrow slicing through him like a sword. Now there was just sadness, and even the sadness was distant.

Had time done this? Ubu wondered. It had been months since Pasco had last appeared to freshen the wounds.

"I have a plan," Pasco said. His plump fingers, held in front of his chest, wove congratulatory knots into one another. "If I can get some credit I can buy outright a shipment of nitrogen-fixing conifers here on Decatur. I know they're on demand on the Edge out on Trincheras or Masquerade. We can make quite a profit if we sell them on our own account."

Surprise rose in Ubu as a diamond-perfect memory scrolled across his mind. He remembered what had come of Pasco's scheme, the shoot to Trincheras to discover that the settlements had grown their own terraforming trees in massive gene tanks, each tree genetically adapted to Trincheras' alkaline soil, and that Pasco's own trees were useless—and Masquerade, where *Runaway* had next jumped, had been almost as bad. The conifers were dumped at a dead loss.

In outline, Pasco's plans for the conifers was the same scheme as Ubu's purchase of the mining equipment for Dig Angel. Somehow Ubu hadn't remembered. Why, he wondered, hadn't he recalled this before? He, Ubu, with the mind that never forgot anything?

Pasco spoke on, nattering about how well Ubu and Maria had handled some of their first shoots, their promise as tide riders. Pasco seemed unreal to Ubu, like a puppet carved in the shape of his father.

Ubu stared at the figure, not listening. Why hadn't he remembered?

A cold hand touched his neck. Something, he thought, had kept him from remembering. Something had wanted him to repeat Pasco's mistakes.

Ubu reached for the keyboard, cut Pasco off in midsentence. The holographic figure hovered there, perfect as if preserved in crystal.

Ubu looked at the file name on the comp screen: Pasco. The diary of a man who never finished anything. Who schemed, and implemented, and lost interest, and never finished, and never won. And who recorded it all, programmed himself as a ghost, so that his children would see it all happen again, again, again . . .

Programmed, Ubu thought. An armored claw clasped his heart and squeezed. Tears stung his eyes.

Ubu had done nothing but lose. Repeated Pasco's mistake on the Dig Angel contract, lurched into the Monte Carlo scheme without doing proper groundwork, staggered into jail and out, blown station into the emptiness beyond the human sphere . . . By pure chance he'd found something wonderful, something that would solve his problems, and he'd failed with that as well, given it all away to Marco. A stupid move that involved another strange piece of forgetfulness, failing to remember that the navigation comp automatically saved its plots.

Marco thought Ubu was a loser, had said as much. And Marco was right.

Pasco's image burned in midair, a shrunken icon, turned by Ubu's sudden tears to a brightness, a star. Ubu choked and turned away. He had mourned Pasco by imitating him, by trying to complete the pattern, failure echoed by failure, loss by loss. Pasco had never taught him anything but that.

Ubu stood, stepped through Pasco's image and out into the centrifuge. Time, he thought, to learn from someone else.

Beloved's forceful drumbeat rolled through *Runaway*'s empty corridors. Ubu's fingers bent the strings of the audolin so that the metal bow brought a discordant yowl from the speakers, a scream that stirred the hairs on Ubu's neck.

In his mind, fleshy petals uncoiled, offered Beloved's chemical analyzer. Ubu's fingers carefully bent the G string a little more.

There, he thought. Precisely that weirdness.

He was constructing Beloved in his mind, measure after measure. He had been doing it for days.

Ubu had hours of music now, all invoking Beloved. He was calling her to Montoya 81, calling her into his mind and thoughts.

He needed to remind himself of everything he knew about Beloved, of her ways and thought, of how she did business.

He needed to learn from her.

Beloved was alone, had been for years, perhaps centuries. Down on her luck, or else she wouldn't have been prospecting in unknown territory. Though she and her species understood singularity mechanics, their methods of travel weren't as efficient as humanity's. Their ease in controlling their own biochemistry had led them away from human-style technology, from machinery, and this approach had penalized them when they became a starfaring culture. Because they were so much less efficient, their interstellar trade economy therefore had to be more fragile, less dependent on commerce. New habitats and settlements, not to mention ships themselves, had to be more self-sufficient than were those of humans, because the ability to move supplies on schedule was not as great.

But Beloved *was* more self-sufficient. She could create engineered life-forms with far more ease than humans, and she and her ship composed together a chemical factory that could refine raw material into complex chemical and organic forms . . . she could probably survive for decades on her own.

So why was she in such trouble?

Ubu's bow skittered speculatively over the strings, colors brightening in his mind. Beloved's ship, like *Runaway*, was a transport; but transport between stars in Beloved's sphere was more risky, the economies more delicate. The economy on which Beloved depended could have crashed, or could have become choked with competitors. Maybe Clan Lustre, alone, couldn't compete against larger, better-organized clans.

Ubu knew well enough how that felt.

He hesitated for a moment, then struck a different chord. He shouldn't judge Clan Lustre by his own situation. Things might be entirely different. He was assuming too much.

Maybe there had been a war. Beloved carried soldiers on her ship, primed for combat, and that said something important about the level of competition among her species. By contrast, *Runaway* didn't have so much as a handgun aboard, and the human interstellar Navy was composed primarily of exploration and search-and-rescue teams. There was strife on human planets, civil conflicts and the like, but no one had fought a battle in space in two centuries. The Navy and interstellar codes were strong enough to assure that—besides, there wasn't any point. Human settlements were so far apart in terms of time and distance that interstellar war was completely impractical. What did people that far apart have to fight about?

War or not, for whatever reason, Beloved needed humanity, needed human technology badly enough to risk the mind pollution that Twelve had been so wary of. It could be assumed that humanity was Beloved's edge in dealing with her peers. She needed human technology in order to keep that edge.

What would she do to keep it? Ubu wondered. How much would she compel herself to believe?

He had to know. And so he built, chord on chord, his mental image. Surrounded himself with Beloved, with her patterns.

When the time came, he would out-Beloved Beloved.

"I've been thinking about luck, Little Brother." A pair of heavy hands dropped onto Kit's shoulders from behind.

Kit frowned down at his array. Should he double or cut his losses?

He cut, as Randy and Fidel had done earlier. Juan, the only player left in the game, gave a tight smile and collected his winnings.

"Luck, Little Brother. Remember?" Ridge's fingers burrowed

under Kit's collarbones like blunt drills. Kit clenched his teeth. He could smell the beer on Ridge's breath.

"What about luck?" Kit said.

"Ever noticed," Ridge said, "how when you get lucky everybody else starts losing?"

"I wasn't lucky just now."

"Maybe that means good news for the rest of us." Ridge circled around the table, gesturing with his bulb of beer. He'd lost so much gambling that Marco had forbidden him the table for the next several runs. That gave him little else to do but watch hype and drink.

"Little Brother gets lucky in the games, and the rest of us lose," Ridge said. "Little Brother gets lucky with some femme, and suddenly we can't shoot anywhere near optimum."

Kit looked at Juan. "Another round?"

"I'm winning for a change. Sure."

A new array flickered into existence in the table's polarized surface. Two pair, Kit saw. He'd discard the lowest, hope for something better.

Ridge had finished his circumnavigation of the table. One hand thumped on Kit's shoulders again.

"We were talking, Little Brother."

"You were doing all the talking, Ridge. I was playing spirals."

"I thought you might have something to say about all these coincidences," Ridge said. "I figured you might have some comment on luck and how to get lucky."

Hot anger stormed through Kit's nerves. He turned in his chair, knocked Ridge's hand away.

"People make their own luck," he said.

Ridge clenched his teeth. "Your cunt's glitching us," he said. "My question is, are you gonna do anything about it, or shall I?"

Hate glowed in Kit like a fusion torch. "You won't do anything, Ridge," he said. "Because if you fuck with someone else's femme, Marco's gonna have you cleaning out the shitters for the next fifty years."

"Better tell her, Little Brother. Tell her I might pay her a visit."

"Hey," Fidel said. "Are we on the table or what?"

"Yeah." Kit turned his back on the older shooter. "Yeah, I'm on the table."

"I'm in for three," Juan said.

"Call."

"*Playing.*" Ridge's voice rang in the room. "You liceheads keep playing. And some bitch is fucking with our shoots."

The bell rang, the lockdown warning. Juan groaned. "Just when I was starting to win."

"Play this last," said Fidel.

"Huh," Juan said. "Fidel's got a good array, I bet."

"Liceheads," said Ridge. "Bunch of liceheads." He stalked to the door, turned, pointed a finger at Kit. "Straighten out that bitch of yours, Kit. Or someone will." He left, the door hissing shut behind him.

Little quantum packets of anger were running up and down Kit's spine and he couldn't pay much attention to the game, but his second array was unbeatable and he won anyway. The others groaned, then shrugged, then fell silent. As Kit left the table he could feel their eyes on him. Maybe they were thinking this was an omen for the next series.

If Kit wins, Ridge said, everyone else loses. Shit.

He was in the second shift of shooters and wasn't on call immediately, so he headed for his compartment. Gravity fell in little lurches as the centrifuge braked, Kit's stomach dropping away each time. As he arrived at his compartment door he could feel sudden tension knotting his shoulders.

He hadn't thought it would get this bad.

He opened the door and saw Beautiful Maria sitting in the upper rack, wearing a navy-blue halter and trunks, her long sleek legs kicking aimlessly over the side as the rack swung beneath her. Her eyes were fever-bright; there were spots of color high on her cheeks. She was chewing gum like a machine. The knot of tension between Kit's shoulders began to tighten.

"You're high again," he said.

She gave a machine-gun laugh. "Hi to you, too," she said.

The smell of fresh paint stung Kit's nostrils. He closed the door behind him. His stomach dropped away as the centrifuge braked again. Maria popped her gum and kicked out with both feet. The rack swung forward about fifty degrees, dropped back slowly. She drew her feet up onto the rack and turned toward him.

With her abrupt movements, tangled shroud of hair, and intent expression, Maria looked like an unearthly animal perched on a rock, her glittering gaze fastened on anything that moved.

Kit's mouth was dry. Ridge calls this *getting lucky*, he thought. He shook his head. "I can't talk to you like this."

Maria's mouth twitched. Maybe it was a smile that came and went so fast that Kit couldn't catch the full effect. "I don't know how much there is to talk about," she said.

"Us. We could talk about us."

"Talk. You start." Maria pressed her bare feet against the tubular frame of the rack, then clamped her hands on the frame on either side of her ankles. She began to push, rock the frame back and forth on its gimbals.

"Talk," Kit repeated. "What's the point? You're not listening."

"I listen good, Kit." The rack swung violently upward, hesitated at the summit, then fell back. Beautiful Maria gave a ferocious metallic giggle. Despair fell on Kit like a cold drizzle from a broken condenser.

"I don't want it to be like this," he said. "I want us to spend some time together."

"We're together now." The rack swung up again, hesitated, fell over backward for a full 360-degree spin.

"I can't talk to you when you're high," Kit said. The rack kept spinning, its speed increasing as gravity fell away. Maria's hair rippled out behind her like a cloak. "You're not . . . a person I want to talk to."

"Then don't talk." Simple enough logic.

Maria let go of the rack and gave a yell as it flung her across the compartment. She absorbed the impact against the wall with palms and feet, then dropped easily to the floor in maybe one-sixth gee. She turned to him. "Ever do that when you were a kid?"

"Yeah." She looked as if she was going to jump back onto the rack and he reached out, snatched her wrist. Frustration roared in him. "*Why are you doing this?*" he shouted.

Maria's eyes snapped to her wrist, then to Kit's face. Like an animal, he thought again.

"It's something I need to do," she said.

"This isn't you. You're not like this."

"We haven't spent that much time together. You don't know what I'm like, Kit."

She snatched her arm back and jumped across the room, landed in the rack and swung to face him.

"People are saying you glitched us," Kit said.

She gave a low laugh. The rack began to swing again. "How am I doing it? I'm a fucking prisoner with nothing to do." Her laugh increased in pitch. "What am I, a witch or something?"

"Ridge has been threatening you, Maria. I don't know how many people agree with him."

She flung her arms out and braced against the walls, stopping the rack's motion. Her expression was a mask of taut fury. "Let the groundlice bastard come, then," she said. She made claws of her hands. A tremor of fear shuddered up Kit's spine. "I'll rip his throat out," Maria spat. "Just let him try something. He'll regret it for the rest of his fucking life." She threw her head back and laughed. "It won't happen, though. I control fifty percent of *Runaway* and its profits. Marco's not gonna forget that. He won't let anybody bother me."

"Ridge might not ask Marco's opinion."

"Huh." Contemptuously.

He said nothing, just looked at her.

"You used me, Kit," she said. Her voice was light, almost singsong. "You used me to get the rendezvous coordinates."

Kit's skin went hot. "I didn't—" His tongue was thick. "I didn't have a lot of choice. Marco didn't give me one."

"Maybe." She gave a laugh. "Maybe I didn't have any choices, either. Maybe I needed to get a ride to Angel Station, and the only way to get it was to play on your sympathy."

He clenched his teeth. "Be true?"

She giggled. The humanity was gone. "Be true," she taunted, "you didn't have any choices back on Bezel?"

He didn't have an answer. He turned and folded a chair out of the wall and sat.

Beautiful Maria began to rock the rack once more, got it rolling over again and again like a miniature centrifuge. The shoot began. Kit tried not to watch Maria as she spun around in the rack, waved her arms, kicked, shouted, laughed, beat the mattress with her fists.

"I'm a witch, Kit!" Gleefully. "I'm a witch!"

Kit didn't say anything. He was looking at his store of hope as he had looked at his spirals array, counting his score, trying to decide what play to make. Cut, he thought, or double?

Cut, Kit thought. As if the choice hadn't really been made for him.

The shoot went four light-years in the wrong direction.

Cut, he kept thinking. Cut. Cut. Cut.

Halfway through the series, Kit left to boss his shoot. Out of a distant, lingering sympathy, Beautiful Maria didn't give him quite as hard a ride as the others.

She slept for twelve hours afterward, the electron world an immediate presence in her dreaming mind. Kit woke her, shaking her shoulder. A forcebulb thudded to the pillow next to her. "Coffee," Kit said. "Espresso."

"Thanks."

"Breakfast on the table."

Maria rubbed her eyes. "Thanks, shooter man."

She heard the door slide shut. He'd already left.

Maria devoured her breakfast. Charged particles seemed to dance on her plate, shoot from the tines of her fork when it wasn't directly in her gaze.

She looked at the floating lime-green numbers of the holographic chronometer that glowed above the folded-away desk. How long till the next shoot? The last series had hammered a third of the way to Angel, not as well as expected. The next would have to begin soon.

Caffeine began to clear away the slow-moving sludge in her veins. Awareness fluttered around her mind in the tentative manner of a brand-new butterfly.

Kit came into the compartment, slid the door shut behind him. Beautiful Maria smiled at him, stretched.

"When I got in, you were passed out again," he said.

Maria's skin prickled. She dropped her smile. "There's not much to do around here but sleep," she said.

Kit stepped across the room and dropped into a chair. His movements seemed overprecise. He'd been drinking, she assumed, or was otherwise high.

"Marco's decided the next shoots are going to be the last," he said. "We're gonna keep on shooting till we make Angelica System."

Maria slumped back against the newly painted compartment wall as sudden weariness sapped all the energy she had carefully gathered since waking. This had all been going on too long.

"When?" she asked.

"They're going through the software again. Trying to find out what's glitching us." He shrugged. "When they give up . . ."

"Yeah." Beautiful Maria closed her eyes and let the weariness caress her with its warmth. The electron world wove its embroidery around her mind.

"I give up, too," Kit said.

Something in his tone made her open her eyes. Magnetic fields glimmered in the periphery of her vision. Now, she thought, she knew why he needed the drinks.

"I give up," Kit said again. "I can't live with you. Don't even want to any more."

She looked at him through the dim gauze of the electron world. I've hurt him, she thought, and I hardly even noticed.

The thought seemed lighter than a feather.

"I'm sorry."

"I just wanted to tell you when you were sober."

"Too much history," Maria said. "We've used each other too much."

"Maybe that's it." Kit looked as if he wanted to say something else, but didn't quite know how to say it.

There was a change in Maria's perception, in the patterns that wove around her. *Abrazo* was loading the shooting software again. Maria reached for the chak under her pillow, brought it up.

"Do you have to do that now?" Kit said. His voice was sharp.

Maria looked at him. "Yes. I have to."

There was a pair of hisses, a brief nasal coolness. Then the flash of fire in the veins, the sudden focus of awareness.

Kit stood up. He looked as if he'd just been hit over the head and was trying to remember what it was he was doing a moment ago. "No use talking, then," he said. "And I don't see any point in telling anyone else, right? Not their business. So I'll keep on sleeping here."

"Okay." Maria could feel a grin beginning to twitch its way across her face. This is *serious*, she thought, and fought the grin down.

"I talked to Marco about the threats Ridge was making. The bossrider said he'd talk to him. So you'll be okay."

Maria looked up at him, recalled that Kit, if left to himself, would never have been her enemy, that he didn't have to do this. "Thank you," she said. "That was kind."

"See you later maybe."

"Yeah. Next Now."

The door closed. The shoot began.

And it was the next Now already.

In many ways the last series was easier than any. The number of shoots was greater, but by now Beautiful Maria was as locked into the electron world as if her mind had been built of macroatoms. Heavy doses of Red Nine weren't necessary, just enough to keep her mind cranked to the point where she could feel the bright touch of the electron flow, keep her mind aware and on edge.

Abrazo jumped to Angelica along a path as jagged as a bolt of particle lightning. The last shoot in the series put the ship ten weeks from Angel Station, given one gee acceleration and deceleration. That was too far from Marco's point of view: by the end of that ten weeks he was already due at Montoya 81.

Maria gave a laugh when she perceived that Marco had decided to try another jump, from one point into the Angelica system to another. The scope of error with a small shoot was almost as great as it was with a large one.

Abrazo leaped across the system and ended up almost twelve weeks away from its goal, farther than when it had started.

Marco surrendered. Bells sounded to warn of acceleration. Marco had decreed one point two gee to get to Angel a little faster.

Three months with nothing to do, Maria thought. Maybe Marco would let her have her terminal back.

Ubu swam in a sea of Beloved, resonated to her heartbeat, to the chords that assembled Beloved in his senses. When the alarms rang that indicated another ship shooting insystem, Ubu made his way to the comm board.

Beloved was relatively close, he saw. If both ships accelerated and decelerated at one gee, they could rendezvous in about ten days.

Think carefully, then act. Beloved's drums seemed to offer him a message. *If you think carefully, your actions will be correct.*

Ubu began tapping keys.

Runaway *sends respectful greetings to Clan Lustre*, Ubu sent. Runaway *is pleased to inform Beloved of the destruction of* Abrazo *and Clan de Suarez.* Runaway *hopes to forge a new and profitable relationship with Clan Lustre, free of interference from rival clans.*

He laughed as he hit the Send button. The readiness within him began to unfold.

CHAPTER 23

RESINOUS TETHERS, DISSOLVING, FILLED THE CHAMBER WITH A WET, sticky rain. Beloved's drums flogged the air, calling for readiness. Twelve's body cleansed itself internally, prepared for duty. Blood poured through the fat, nourishing umbilicus into his body.

Twelve's palps flickered out, tasting the heavy resinous scent, tasting also an enzyme meant only for him, an urgent summons tagged with his chemical name. *Come to Beloved.* His hearts surged at the summons. With half-awakened limbs, Twelve began to flail against his restraints.

His vision slowly cleared. At a great remove, as always, he was aware of pain, but the pain was buffered by Beloved's specialized analgesics and did not impair him.

Nutrient liquid shot from his mouth as his lungs convulsively emptied, then inflated with air. The umbilicus fell away. Beloved's improved nonvolitionals began to clean his flesh with their grating tongues. Twelve wrenched out of his restraints and drifted free into the room till he could contact a wall and push toward the exit.

One of his legs had not awakened yet and wouldn't obey

him—his first jump went wide of the door. No matter: he could compensate. He used his arms to navigate between the awakening soldiers and navigators and make his way to the exit; he pulled away the tympanum and thrust his way down the corridor. Beloved's drumbeat was more urgent here and Twelve made haste, Beloved's summons driving him to furious exertion. Half a dozen nonvolitionals, busy cleaning, crawled over his body as he swam into the fusion chamber and allowed Beloved's umbilicus to connect with his mind.

At once the urgency of Beloved's rhythm moderated. *Think carefully*, Beloved urged, *think carefully, and be of service.*

All glory to Beloved. How may this-individual serve his Beloved?

His last service, upon Beloved's return to Potent 5367, had been everything he had hoped. Prices for the last shipment of AIs had reached preposterous heights, particularly after it had been announced that these were improved models. Already a fleet of ships was building, each to be inhabited by one of Beloved's children. Half a dozen singularities had been purchased, as had many servants, some of them latest-model research volitionals intended to work on the mysteries of creating artificial intelligence.

Beloved's tympani rattled for attention.

We have reached the rendezvous star where I anticipated meeting Clan de Suarez. Clan de Suarez is not present, but instead I find Runaway.

Chill dread rolled through Twelve. *Glory to Beloved*, he replied. *How can this be?* He feared he already knew the answer.

Bossrider Ubu Roy informs Me that Shooter Beautiful Maria had been placed aboard Abrazo *for the purpose of destroying it, and Clan de Suarez with it.*

Twelve hung in shock from the umbilicus, his worst fears realized. His mind stumbled dazedly over the new information.

Beloved, this-individual is surprised.

I must evaluate this data, Volitional Twelve. I need to know whether Bossrider Ubu speaks the truth.

Twelve hesitated. Through the umbilical connection he could sense alarm in Beloved, the knowledge that all her schemes might have come apart. Her mind seemed fragmented, each division working frantically on different parts of a larger, yet-unrealized whole.

This-individual can only guess, Beloved, Twelve said. *This-individual can reason only from the data presented in* Bloodbath in Building Four, *which is a hype that in itself is only a kind of lie.*

Your best judgment is required in this matter.

As presented in the hype, the humans have the ability to place their people within the structure of enemy clans. These humans then act in the best interests of their clans, and their behavior may include violence or sabotage.

In your judgment, is it likely that Beautiful Maria was so placed within the structure of Clan de Suarez?

It is not inconsistent, cautiously, *with what they have permitted this-individual to learn of their behavior.*

Twelve sensed Beloved's dissatisfaction with this answer. *Bossrider Ubu,* she sent, *has invited Me to remain in this system for a length of time necessary to confirm that Abrazo will not appear. He appears to make this offer with perfect confidence.*

Beloved of course may wait. Twelve offered this carefully, not wanting to presume to give Beloved advice.

Bossrider Marco was expected here before now.

Delays are proverbial in navigation. He may arrive at any moment.

There is evidence that all is as Bossrider Ubu claims. You were aboard the de Suarez ship at the last rendezvous when it began a violent series of evasive maneuvers. Shooter Maria was likewise present.

Bossrider Marco said that Abrazo *was avoiding an asteroid storm.*

We detected no asteroid storm. Runaway likewise made no evasive maneuvers. Could it be that Beautiful Maria had seized control of Abrazo *in order to take advantage of the confusion so as to give you a message for Bossrider Ubu?*

Twelve made the reluctant concession. *That is possible, Beloved.* His hands and feet trembled in terror.

If Shooter Maria could control the de Suarez ship in such a manner, she could likewise seize control of it to destroy it.

Glory, Beloved. This-individual can but praise your reasoning.

Suddenly Twelve sensed the fragments of Beloved's mind assembling itself into a vast, awesome, and implacable whole. *You have aided this plot against My interest*, Beloved transmitted. Twelve thrashed in terror as he sensed Beloved's resolution, as Beloved's drill-tipped neurons made further penetrations of his mind. *You have been contaminated by human thought and sympathy. You are dangerous. Your use is at an end. You will destroy yourself immediately.*

Glory glory glory. Beloved was making a mistake—give him another few moments and he could explain why. But Twelve had only time to chant a few words of praise before Beloved's chemical onslaught struck at his brain and all rational thought dissolved. In an instant he felt his will shatter beneath an overwhelming conviction of his own worthlessness. Even though he knew the emotion had been planted within him, the experience was nevertheless genuine, an overwhelming, bitter surge of despair. A wail of hopelessness burbled from him. Beloved had declared him void. He knew himself unworthy. Alkaline tears beaded from his pores as his flesh contracted in an involuntary spasm of self-loathing.

The umbilicus withdrew, but not fast enough to satisfy Twelve's impulse to self-destruction. Frustrated by his inability to annihilate himself instantly, he clawed at himself with his inner fingers, drawing blood. The umbilicus finally withdrew, and he kicked and launched himself for the exit. He could feel the nonvolitionals abandoning him, leaping out into the light, their reaction triggered by the bitter taste of his weeping skin.

Clawed hands seized him. Beloved had sent several of her soldiers to hasten his end. "Thank you, brothers," he tried to say as the soldiers' arms pinioned him, but his voder was paralyzed. Still he was grateful as the fighters drew him down the blue-lit corridor.

The tympanum covering the dissolution chamber was torn aside. Twelve's palps were stung by the scent of decay, that and a heavy odor of complex enzymes. The soldiers flung Twelve into the darkened chamber.

In a tangle of limbs Twelve struck the far wall. The moist, fleshy lining of the chamber squelched as it absorbed the impact. A furious, despairing rage consumed him. His light had failed, he had become contaminated, all that he was should be destroyed. He pressed himself against the moist, greedy flesh of the wall, exposing as much of his body surface as possible to its destructive enzymes. The wall held him in place. The tympanum behind him drew shut, and he was left alone in darkness.

His skin, where exposed to the wall, began to tingle, then experience sharp jabs of pain. Ecstatically, Twelve welcomed the sign that his dissolution was near. His only joy remained in his own annihilation. His dismay was that it could not be accomplished instantly.

The pain increased, spreading like fire along his limbs, his trunk. Beloved had no further use for him, no reason to buffer the agony as she had when he was awakened from transit-sleep. The enzymes of the chamber were dissolving his flesh, breaking him down into amino-acid chains that might be safely recycled. The process would take many hours.

Gradually the agonizing self-hatred ebbed as Twelve metabolized Beloved's final chemical attack. Unending pain lanced through his mind. He tried to flail away from the wall, but the sticky flesh had already encircled his limbs with tough, fast-growing filaments. He tried to scream, but no sound resulted—Beloved had neatly severed the links between his brain and voder. He realized that Beloved would not wish the echoing sound of his screams distracting her other servants.

There was an ebbing of the pain as many of Twelve's nerve endings were consumed. The enzymes were pausing in their work, summoning reserves before working deeper into the muscle tissue. Thoughts reassembled in his mind, the thoughts that, had they been expressed, might have saved his life.

Anguish tore at him. Beloved, he thought. You may have just destroyed yourself along with me.

She had fallen victim to a human scheme. The details hardly mattered, whether *Runaway* and Clan de Suarez were working in concert, whether Maria had really destroyed *Abrazo*, whether any of Ubu's scenario was really true or not—the crucial fact was that Beloved's attempt to seize control of her situation had failed. The humans now had the upper hand.

The opportunity to take control might come again, but if it did Beloved would probably miss it. Her pattern was too limited.

Twelve had not entirely understood his decision to aid Beautiful Maria and Ubu, had only felt an obscure rightness in the act. Likewise he had instinctively opposed Beloved's scheme to deal with Clan de Suarez and cut off *Runaway*'s trade. Beloved had assumed these attitudes to be the result of human contamination, and she was right. Twelve, her servant, had been polluted by human contact.

What Beloved failed to realize was that she required servants who had been so polluted. She needed servants who could instinctively recognize human schemes, who could warn her away from actions that might worsen her situation. Her own icy rationality was not flexible enough to deal with the human threat.

She needed Twelve. She had thrown him away. Now she was more vulnerable than ever.

Twelve shuddered as a new wave of enzymes began assaulting his frame, burning deeper into his flesh, reaching new nerve endings with their chemical claws. *Beloved!* he thought. *I can still save you!* And then his thoughts were swept away by a blazing wave of hot, retching agony.

This time there was no respite.

Think, ordered Beloved's drums. *Think carefully, and all will be well.*

I understand your music, Ubu thought, *and I understand you.*

A hot river of triumph burned through his veins. Beloved's answer glowed above the comm board. She had agreed to his terms.

The ships would shoot to another star, Santos 439, eight light-years distant, which would be used in future for all face-to-face meetings and exchanges of cargo. It was there that Beloved would build her chemical factory and warehouse. Montoya 81 and Santos 448 would be declared off limits to both parties. To seal the agreement *Runaway* would receive one full cargo, the pharmaceuticals intended for *Abrazo*, which Beloved had been synthesizing and storing in resinous containers since she left Santos 448.

Ubu had presented Beloved with a version of reality, and compelled Beloved to believe it. He hadn't made a single false move, betrayed a single weakness.

He had encompassed Beloved in his mind, imprisoned her in a structure of his own making.

Beloved hadn't even questioned his insistence on abandoning the sites of previous meetings. Ubu had been worried about that point—he knew Marco would show up at Montoya 81 eventually, and if he and Beloved were to meet again under uncontrolled circumstances, Ubu's agreements could unravel—but Beloved hadn't balked.

She hadn't dared. Ubu had been right: Clan Lustre needed the trade with *Runaway* more than *Runaway* needed Beloved.

The leap to Santos 439 took only a few subjective hours. The two ships ended their final shoots within two weeks of one another, Beloved within two days of a candy-striped red-and-white gas giant, one lacking only a little more mass to become a sun in its own right. Ubu suggested Beloved begin assembling her chemical factory in orbit, and *Runaway* would join her there. Beloved agreed.

Ubu spent the transit time with Beloved's drumbeats thundering in his ears, his chord structures bringing her existence swimming into his senses. He had presented her with a reality she didn't dare deny; now he needed to present her with a future she couldn't live without.

A future in which her servants would expand trade, build ships for humans, assemble habitations and worlds . . . where human AIs would manage her new empire, as well as help it to expand across the sphere occupied by her own species . . . where humanity and Beloved's servants would interpenetrate, spiral into one another until they were no longer discernible as separate species . . .

He would have to make this future live in Beloved's mind as Beloved now lived in his. Beloved had to need it as much as Ubu did.

And Beloved had to be prevented from noticing that, buried within this vision, it would be humans who would manage the data, keep the books, maintain control of the relationship.

The structure Ubu created had to keep her from observing this. For that he needed more concrete knowledge of her.

He needed to know if he was right, if his chords and experimentations had built a true picture of Beloved.

He had to see her. In person.

The candy-striped protostar grew nearer. Ubu sat in the upper lounge, surrounded by instruments, speakers, computers programmed for notation and recording. Dizzy with the music of Beloved, he played till his fingers bled.

Bossrider Ubu desires to meet Beloved, he sent. *Beloved may take whatever precautions she deems necessary for her own protection.*

Dry-mouthed with anticipation, he licked his lips. Tambors rattled in his head.

The answer, affirmative, printed itself above the comm board in holographic letters the color of molten gold.

There were conditions. Ubu would go through decontamination before he left *Runaway* and would stay in his vac suit throughout. Beloved would have her guards present.

The conditions didn't matter, Ubu knew. The fact of the meeting did.

Beloved thundered in his blood as Ubu left *Runaway* and hung outside, plotting his course. The huge protostar dazzled his eyes with its brilliant scarlet and white bands. Beloved's ship rolled atop the giant's equator, its black silhouette surrounded by the bright atmosphere craft that were plundering the giant's moons for raw material.

Beloved's ship had changed its outline. A shiny bubble grew from one cargo bay—a delicate-looking resinous lattice, gleaming silver in the bright sun, that would become the framework for Beloved's station. Nonvolitionals, some very large, crawled gracefully over the silver fretwork, augmenting the frame with thin, strength-enhancing layers of exudate. Eventually the station would be larger than Beloved, filled with factories and living quarters and cargo bays, would feed itself raw material from the protostar's moons and manufacture the elements of *Runaway*'s commerce.

Beloved's airlock beckoned with its flashing strobes. Ubu's hand touched the joystick of his maneuver pack and he fired himself like a bullet, a bullet aimed at Beloved's heart.

When the airlock cycled and the inner door clattered open—whatever system Beloved used to draw up the hatch, it was still noisy—Ubu saw the dark form of a volitional hovering outside. Somehow he knew at once that it wasn't Twelve.

"Glory to Beloved," Ubu said. A rapid drumbeat pattered over his voice. "I am Bossrider Ubu Roy." His voice was fed into speakers he'd clipped to his helmet. He wondered for a moment if he should have used the old system of holographic translation, whether this new volitional understood his speech.

"Glory to *Runaway*. I am General Volitional Twenty-six. It is an honor to apprehend the form of Ubu Roy."

The words were perfectly articulated, the voice alto, pitched to carry over Beloved's drumbeat.

"Pleased to meet you," Ubu said. "I expected Volitional Twelve."

"General Volitional Twelve is no longer living. Please follow me, Bossrider Ubu Roy."

Surprise lurched through Ubu's mind as he guided himself through the hatchway. He wondered if he should ask how Twelve had died, or why.

Natural deaths, he thought, *are not common here. Beloved, therefore, had Twelve killed.*

Because he helped us? Ubu wondered. *Because his mind was polluted? Because Beloved's plans didn't work out, and one of her servants had to serve as scapegoat before she could accept any new arrangement?*

Maybe, Ubu thought as he swept down the corridor, braked, pivoted, and followed Twenty-six down a new, wide tunnel, *maybe Twelve was killed just to keep me off balance.*

Ubu's mind hardened. He wasn't going to let Beloved throw him.

Twenty-six regarded Ubu from his rear set of mild brown eyes. Tympani of all size lined the corridor's irregular walls. Drumbeats high and low beat the air, each rapping out a different pattern, the totality becoming ever more complex.

A large gap appeared in one wall, unsealed by a tympanum. Blue light poured through the gap, intense as a carbon arc. Ubu dialed up the polarity of his helmet visor. Twenty-six caught the edge of the gap with one hand, checked momentum, pulled himself through. Ubu braked with his handset. Drumbeats rattled through his helmet, throbbed in his pulse. Air vents hissed below his chin.

The room was large, maybe ten meters across. A strong wind

tugged at Ubu as he entered, and he countered it with careful spurts of his jets. Shiny bodies limned by the intense light, black soldiers were braced against the walls by strutlike limbs, taloned, armored, carrying mother-of-pearl firearms that seemed as much exudate as their helmets and shells. The rest of the room at first seemed to be cluttered with random organic debris . . . tympani, lighting strips, long banks of pale whiplike flagella, each several meters long, that flailed against air, throbbing pumps like disconnected animal hearts, each half Ubu's size, bound in place with strips of pale sinew and connected to one another by long flexible conduits of crossgrained arterial tissue. Multilegged nonvolitionals, types Ubu hadn't seen before, crawled like swarms of scavenging insects through it all, busily performing tasks of uncertain purpose. There were tympani everywhere, of all sizes, and the drumbeats were incredibly complex, layered, impossible to follow. Though Ubu couldn't feel it in his vac suit, he knew the room was incredibly humid—everything, the nonvolitionals, Twenty-six, the soldiers, was covered with a precipitate dew, and droplets flew like shooting stars in the path of the strong cold wind.

Beloved, Ubu thought. Everything in the room was Beloved. And this room was only a part of her.

His mind spun. Beloved throbbed in his pulse with greater complexity than he had ever heard. His music had never encompassed this, he knew. He had never thought of Beloved as being this alive.

"Greetings, Bossrider Ubu Roy. Welcome to Myself."

The voice was a resonant tenor, issuing simultaneously from several of the tympani in the room.

Ubu swung in the wind, lost in the gusting breeze. He performed the corrections necessary to remain in place, and the ease and familiarity of the motions helped calm him. An organic body this large had to generate enormous heat, he thought. The cold wind carried excess heat away. That was why Beloved's ship was black, because black bodies radiate heat as efficiently as they absorb it.

The thought gave him confidence. I am in charge here, he told himself. Beloved has permitted me to come here because I am dictating her reality.

The layered drumbeats hammered at him. Dimly, he began to

follow some of the patterns. He realized that the black soldiers, overwhelmed by the nearness of their Beloved and the immediacy of her drumming, were moving their free limbs, their fingers and toes, in time to one of the patterns.

The nonvolitionals on the floor were moving to another pattern. The flagella to yet another.

Beloved's pattern encompassed all her creatures.

Twenty-six, he saw, had hooked one set of toes around a wall extrusion that looked a lot like a castoff bar. Ubu maneuvered himself next to Twenty-six and thrust one boot through the bar. He could feel the resin stretching, taking the strain as he swayed in the wind, then steadied at a different angle. He looked again at the array that was Beloved, saw everything alive, everything in motion. He would understand this, Ubu thought, he would encompass its existence.

Chords rang in his mind, building the structure he needed. He blinked sweat from his eyes.

"Glory to Beloved," he said.

He told her what he wanted her to know.

CHAPTER
24

"NEXT NOW, SHOOTER MAN."

Kit shook his head. "Goodbye, Maria."

Beautiful Maria watched as Kit turned and kicked off across Angelica's lowgrav docks, heading for his father's ship. A palpable sadness lodged in Maria's throat, warring with the delight that flooded her body at the light gravity after *Abrazo*'s ten weeks of heavy gee.

Maria kicked off and flew above the deck. Wind lofted her hair. The electron world danced in her mind. Suddenly her heart surged, and the sadness was gone.

Her body sang with joy as it skimmed over the grey polymerized deck, bounding up the dock levels to the lowgrav habitations. She rented a hotel room in the hub, a place used mainly by mutantos. She would stay in light gravity for a few days, give rest to her weary joints.

Heading to her room, Maria followed a pair of mutanto kids down the hexagonal-section corridor. One of the boys had short-cropped hair that came to a little point in back. The feature reminded her of Kit.

She wondered about the joy she felt, whether it was inappropriate. Whether the way she'd made Kit unhappy meant she wasn't a nice person any more.

The ten weeks of one point two gee hadn't been as bad as it could have been. Since it didn't matter any longer, Marco let Beautiful Maria have her terminal back. She watched hours of hype, played games, occasionally used the terminal to play spirals with people she hadn't ever met. She was careful not to cheat, and more or less broke even.

Not cheating was hard. The electron world never seemed far away, always danced on the periphery of her mind. If she closed her eyes, she could see fields patterned like phosphors on the back of her lids. With a wave of her arm she could alter it, change the flow.

Kit kept her company and brought her meals, but didn't have a lot to say to her. His presence kept loneliness from overwhelming her, and that was all, at this point, she wanted.

The high gees weighed everyone down, took the urgency out of everything.

Through Kit, she was aware of Marco's ordering the *Familia* to remain at Angel, to give its regularly scheduled cargo to a tramper. She also knew that Marco was trying frantically to buy every high-powered computer he could lay his hands on. There wouldn't be enough for a full shipment, she knew, not in the Angelica System. *Abrazo* would have to move on, maybe to Bezel. Marco would shift to *Familia* and head for his rendezvous at Montoya 81 with what would only serve as a down payment to Beloved.

Too late, Maria knew. She'd given Ubu months in which to cut a new deal with Beloved. Marco had at least to suspect that.

Marco played on despite the losing game. Experts on Angel Station were set to work on *Abrazo*'s computer problems and offered no answer. They could only suggest that *Abrazo*'s backup software was the source of the problem. They suggested Marco reload the software from backups held in Angel's antiradiation safe.

Marco came to Maria's room the last day out of Angel. The high gees had drained him; his steps were uncertain, his skin sallow.

His deep eyes were shot with blood.

"Bossrider," Maria said.

"Shooter." Marco's hand trembled as he pulled down a chair. Beautiful Maria waited for him to sit.

"You may have won," Marco said.

She shrugged. Weeks of high gees made most things seem unimportant.

"Just remember how much trouble we can make for you," Marco said. "Ubu threatened me once. With informing the Multi-Pollies, with quarantine, with all sorts of things. I can do the same to you."

Maria sighed. "If you want to send a message to Ubu, bossrider, send him one. Don't talk to me."

He stared at her. Maria could see the pulse struggling in his throat.

"I don't want you on any of my ships. Not until I regain contact with the aliens."

She managed a weary smile. "You still think I'm sabotaging you somehow?"

"If my ships have no trouble shooting when you're off them, we'll know. I'm putting you up in a hotel on Angel till *Familia* comes back. If you want to keep on living with Kit, you can go aboard then."

She looked at him. "I can afford my own hotel room."

Marco rose, swayed, almost fell back into the chair. "So much the better," he said, his voice a whisper, and walked carefully away.

Maria realized later that Marco had been trying to negotiate his surrender. He wanted *Runaway* to buy him off. She'd just been too tired to notice.

She didn't see him again.

The high gees had tired her more than she thought: after her first burst of exuberant flight she spent most of the first two days in a zero-gee sleeping bag, the rest of the time eating. The electron world soothed her, performed a sleepy dance in her mind. Her spine made cracking sounds every time she stretched or turned her head. Eventually she made her way to the Bahía and ordered a bulb of pomegranate juice. Chattering mutantos—shooters, systers, miners —bounded around her in the bar's pale rose light, their lower elbows tucked into their upper armpits. One group was strapped to the same table, their heads together, nursing the few drinks they could afford, their heads nodding to a melancholy dolores ballad. Maria overheard that their ship had just been confiscated for debt: the shooter family would be broken up as they sought work elsewhere, and the ship would be broken up as well, the singularity sold to a Hiliner.

She could buy their ship, Maria thought, and give it back to them. Buy this bar and everyone in it. Maybe the whole station.

She and Ubu were operating on the scale of a small Hiliner company now, well out of the depth of anyone here. The relative prosperity of De Suarez Expressways had been enough to set Marco's clan apart from other shooters—Ubu and Maria already were standing on assets amounting to several times Marco's worth. In a few years, with proper exploitation of their relationship with Beloved, they could be wealthier than anyone now alive.

Cut off, Maria thought, from this entirely. From everything they'd ever known.

Maybe the shooter culture would be dead by then, crushed under Consolidation and Hiliner pressure like a mutanto under high gees. All these people might be adrift or working for the outfits that had destroyed their way of life.

Mutantos floated around her in rose-colored light, their genetics as specialized as many of Beloved's servants, their minds free of Beloved's chemical controls, Beloved's indoctrination.

The juice stung Maria's tongue. She didn't want to lose this.

Maybe, she thought then, maybe she didn't have to.

They'd won. The deal with Beloved had been struck. Beautiful Maria could tell simply from the cold, triumphant, ice-chip intensity in Ubu's eyes. He floated in holographic miniature in Maria's hotel room, his four arms spread like those of a Hindu god. *Runaway* was eight days out, had just completed its shoot into Angelica System.

Music throbbed through the holographic link, Beloved's thundering beat mixed with a succession of choppy, eerie chords. A cold hand touched Maria's neck at the sounds.

"Is Marco listening?" Ubu's first question.

"*Abrazo* and *Familia* blew station four weeks ago. There are no de Suarezes in Angelica that I know of, but this link is not completely secure. You know that." They had bought elaborate scrambling equipment on Bezel, but Maria hadn't dared take any of it aboard Marco's ship.

Ubu rotated slowly during the seconds it took Maria's answer to return to him. Beloved's tympani boomed distorted from the inadequate hotel speakers, Ubu's layered chords repeating themselves in complex mathematical sequence. Ubu waited for the answer, then nodded.

"Everything worked out like we thought. Contact the Portfire reps and see if they want our next couple shipments."

"I'll do that."

"Are you all right? Did things . . . work out . . . on *Abrazo?*" The questions came on the heels of Ubu's first statement, without waiting for Maria's reply. There was a sudden haunted tension in Ubu's expression.

Maria thought about all those weeks in the little room, the electron world dancing in her mind. Twelve lurching in the corridor as *Abrazo* accelerated away from imaginary asteroids. Kit's face, the way his expression evolved as he taught himself not to feel. *Goodbye, Maria.*

"It was . . ." She hesitated. "Tense now and again. But they treated me okay."

Strain seemed to fade from Ubu's face. "Good," he mumbled.

"We need to talk."

"In eight days. Face-to-face. Once I dock."

"Good." The time lag still overlapping their speech. "I just needed to know how you were." He licked his lips. There was still a hint of tension lurking in the set of his eyes, the shadowed columns of his neck. "We've got to work out what happens next."

"I've been thinking that." Maria gave a hesitant smile. "I think I've got a plan."

"So have I."

For a long moment they just looked at each other. "We have a *lot* to talk about," Ubu said.

"Next Now, shooter man."

"Next Now."

The image vanished. Maria's mind danced, flew, fluttered, pirouetted into the future.

By the time *Runaway* jumped into the Angelica System, Beautiful Maria had been onstation four weeks, making plans. After a few days in near-zero gee, she'd moved to the outer rim of the wheel, a two-room suite in a Fringe hotel, and spent half of each day under the alpha trodes, her mind absorbing the contents of one fastlearn unit after another.

Economics, law, history. Her skull filled with an ordered schema of disconnected facts. She would have to provide a connecting framework herself. She, Maria thought, and Ubu.

Within minutes of *Runaway*'s docking—Ubu had paid extra to put himself at the head of the unloading queue—Beloved's identical resinous containers began rolling out of the autoloaders. The personnel tube hadn't even been connected yet, so Maria waited, bouncing lightly on tiptoe as a river of containers came pouring out of *Runaway*'s cargo bay, Beloved's product flowing endlessly into humanity.

After the light above the lock went green, Maria ghosted up the accordion-walled tube toward *Runaway*. As she cycled through the scarred ship's lock she felt ebbing from her a tension she hadn't known she'd possessed. Familiar electron patterns began to sing in her mind. She was home again.

As the inner hatch began to roll up, Beloved's scrambled time signatures began to cascade from the other side. Maria stiffened. This was not a part of her comfortable memories.

Ubu waited on the other side. He hesitated, then came forward and took her in his four strong arms.

Ubu talked nonstop for hours, first while cooking dinner and then while sitting with Beautiful Maria in the lower lounge. She sat on the old sofa and listened to Ubu run on about his negotiations, his visit to Beloved, his plans for their future. Expanded trade, items tailored for one another's markets, the slow convergence and mutual absorption of humanity and Belovedkind . . . Maria listened to it all, sitting with white Maxim purring in her arms, but insisted after a while that Ubu shut off Beloved's music. Without the drumbeat, his thoughts seemed a little more disconnected. Maria found that disturbing.

"I've been teaching myself to think like Beloved," he said. "We need that."

"Just so you don't try to *become* her."

He gave her a look. "We need that, too."

Maria straightened in alarm. Maxim shifted uncomfortably in her arms. "Not be liking that, shooter man."

Ubu shrugged. "I'm halfway there already," he said. "Her brain is maybe a hundred times larger than mine, but my memory is better."

"Your memory is what makes you unique."

His face tautened. "Twelve is dead. Beloved had him killed."

Chimes of sadness seemed to sound softly in Maria, the vibrations ringing in her nerves. Twelve was another one she'd used, another who had paid for it. "We did it to him," she said.

Ubu's fingers tapped nervous rhythms against his bare chest. "He was contaminated. That's the point. He had too much human in him, and that frightened Beloved. She killed him, and I think that was her big mistake." Ubu glanced toward the ceiling. "I've got a new volitional this time, Twenty-six. Same model, different number. He doesn't ask questions. He doesn't move around. He just sits there in auxcontrol and listens to Beloved's patterns on the sizer. Beloved doesn't *want* him to find out anything about us, not unless he gets lucky and stumbles across something that will give Beloved the advantage." He grinned. "I'm not making those kinds of mistakes any more. That's why I've beaten her. Because I've got Beloved in my head, and she won't put us in hers." He gave an ironic smile. "But I'm contaminated now. Beloved's a part of me, and I can't get rid of her. Her responses are going to be a part of mine forever."

"That doesn't make you her." Insistently.

"It makes me better, I think." He flexed his heavy shoulders thoughtfully. "I'll be the one of us to deal with Beloved and her species. I'm good at that, I've proved it." He looked at Maria and gave a rueful grin. "You're the one who's going to have to cope with humans and keep our own species off our backs. I think I've shown that I'm not good at that kind of thing."

"You're . . ." An ache burned in Maria's throat. "You're really all right, you know. You don't have to become an alien just because—"

Ubu shook his head. "Become an alien? That's not the plan." He gave a brittle laugh. "That's almost trivial. I'm going to be something better. Something better than a human, too. I'm going to be . . ." He laughed again. "I'm going to be *everything*, Maria. Beloved is already a part of my mind, and she's the most alive thing I've ever seen. If I can manage to live long enough, I'll swallow Beloved, humanity, every perception, every potential. I won't ever stop being me, Maria. I'll just be everything else, too."

She looked at him, tears stinging her eyes. She bent over Maxim and pressed her cheek to his fur, feeling his warm comfort against her skin. "Stop it," she said. "I just want to come *home*."

Ubu was silent for a while. He moved toward her, reached to touch her shoulder. "I'm sorry," he said. "I didn't realize." He took a breath. "I've done it again, haven't I?"

"No." Maria wanted to scream.

"I've just been out too long. I need to decompress." He squeezed her shoulder. "Is there anyone we know onstation? Maybe we can meet some friends."

It was Ubu I wanted to meet, Maria thought. "I don't know who's here," she said. "I've been staying in my hotel and working."

"We can find out."

She gave a sigh. "Yeah," she said.

"We've got to change, Maria." Ubu's voice was kind. "All Pop ever did was show us how to fail. If we don't change, we'll be nothing."

Maxim shifted uncomfortably in Maria's lap. Her tears were making his fur wet. "I don't want to use people any more," she said.

Ubu didn't offer a reply. His thoughts, she knew, were elsewhere.

The Fringe was shorter than it had been, losing space as its collective economic power waned. More people seemed packed into a smaller amount of footage. Ubu and Beautiful Maria moved from bar to bar, listened to music, shared drinks with some people they knew. Ubu was reserved, took small bursts of Sharps from his bulb, listened to the clamor of the Sanchez family band. Maria was surprised—Ubu was usually a lot more determined to have a good time after a long series of shoots.

Clan Sanchez finished their set. It seemed like a good moment to leave. Maria followed Ubu out into a twilight metal street filled with the scents of cooking and humanity. Music roared out of open doorways and stung Maria's ears. She imagined it all turned eerie, the music lurching to Beloved's beat, Ubu's chord structures, the shooters and systers and tourists all members of Beloved's species, new-model general volitionals marching to alien rhythm . . .

Maria shivered.

Ubu paused, lower hands in pockets. Ahead on the rising slope was brightness, the polished white surface laid down by the encroaching Hiliners. The potbellied Laughing God beckoned outside his casino. Ubu looked at Maria.

"Shall we invade?" he said.

"Last time we got the shit beat out of us."

He laughed. "Let them be trying it now."

They stepped across the invisible line onto the razor-thin insets of white marble. "Gotta live in this world now," Ubu said. "Gotta learn it. Move in it. Then own it." He looked at her. "That's how I see things."

"And the Fringe?"

Ubu looked at his bare feet as they paced along the cool mottled stone. The holographic Laughing God chortled and waved its arms as they passed it to starboard. "We can't help the Fringe," he said.

"No. Wrong. We can."

He stopped walking and faced her. His lower hands were still in his pockets. People in grey jackets and striped trousers passed by, gave them suspicious looks. "I don't want to fight any more battles we're gonna lose," he said. "I haven't got the heart for it any more."

"We can't do everything by ourselves," Maria said. "We're building ships and somebody's got to fly them. Somebody's got to sell our product. Somebody's got to do the work of developing these new designs you want to sell everyone."

Ubu nodded. "I thought of that. We could put shooters to work, sure. But they'd be our *employees*. It wouldn't save their way of life. Be like any other Hiliner outfit hiring them."

"I've been thinking about that. We don't have to put them on any kind of payroll. We can hire them as *crews*, as *ships*. Make them part of an association."

Ubu turned and began to move again. The Monte Carlo sprawled for two hundred meters on their left, its façade a shimmering holographic aurora. Autocars moved past on whining electric motors, taking gamblers to and from their hotels.

"We create the association," Maria urged. "We can each take twenty-six percent of it, so we can retain control. But the rest—the shooters can buy in. Pay for their shares out of profits. We can cut out the Hiliners entirely."

"Let me think about it for a minute."

"I want it, Ubu." Desperately. "I want to save our people."

Ubu plunged on, head down, then was brought up short by a blaring horn. An electric car whined by, driven by a white-haired male groundling in a long-sleeved blue suit. Sitting next to him, a hand on his thigh, was a tall moned black-skinned woman with diamonds implanted on her shoulder and breasts. Her face was a cool, expressionless mask.

Maria's heart lurched into her throat as she recognized Colette. Who had lost everything when Beautiful Maria broke the bank. The first person Maria had used, and it hadn't even done Maria any good.

The car moved on, its occupants not bothering to look at the pair of ragged shooters.

Colette had survived, Maria thought. Survived, she thought with a hysterical laugh, the same way Maria had.

Ubu marched on, not seeing. Maria ran to catch up. "I want the association," she said. "I want it in position to help the people we've used. Because if we don't help them, we've used those people for nothing. We're no better than Marco."

"Be not sure."

"I've turned whore. You've turned pimp. And it's just so we can make a big score?"

Ubu almost stopped, his shoulders hunching as if he was ducking a blow. He hesitated, then started walking again. Maria almost had to run to keep up.

"I've done a lot of checking. A voluntary association is perfectly legal. We can attach practically any conditions we want to membership, short of slavery." She gave a breathy laugh. "And I think we could probably work that into it, too, somehow."

To their left, a cascade of water fell from the wheel's tented roof, arched in a brilliant spotlit polychrome line across the open space below as the station rotated out from under it, then fell with a continuous rippling splash into a deep lapis-lined fountain set in the street. It hadn't been here when they were last onstation. Ubu marched past it without seeing.

"I want some kind of structure in place when the Multi-Pollies finally figure out what we're doing," he said. "We want to be emplaced, a part of the power structure. So that they can't afford to cut us out."

"Shooters can distribute our product everywhere," Maria said. "We can be in place. Most of them can just move stuff. They don't even have to know where we're getting it. And we can keep them alive that way."

Ubu said nothing. Pastel holographic adverts scanned past, were reflected in white marble. Here, outside the twenty-four-hour traffic of the Fringe and despite the brightness of the lighting, it was early morning. Hotel lights beckoned from above arched doors. Outside the immediate bustle of the Monte Carlo and the other casinos, there were few people on the street. Robots moved about the surface, polishing the laminated marble.

She thought about Colette's face, the hardness there that masked her need for the game, for the Monte Carlo and the Laughing God and the other casinos. The same hardness she'd seen growing in Kit, the hardness that came when you knew how people were going to use you, when maybe you didn't care any more.

"We've got to trust somebody, sooner or later," Ubu said.

"We can try to control those in the know. Make sure that, on joining, they're not allowed contact outside their ships. Major penalties for anyone who blows the secret, like expulsion from the association. And we could also spread false rumors about where we're getting the stuff."

Ubu looked at her with amusement. "Rumors like what?"

"Kit told me something. He told me what Marco thought we'd found when we were back on Bezel, when he didn't know about Beloved. He thought we'd found this settlement of shooters who had gone off beyond the Edge when Consolidation came in, that they'd built their own civilization out there. And they'd been manufacturing compounds and maybe a few other things so generic that they couldn't really be traced, and dealing secretly for the stuff they couldn't make themselves. Marco thought we'd found them by accident, and they'd bought us off with this big cargo."

Ubu laughed. "Guess it fit all the facts he knew."

"We can tell a few people, in confidence, that that's what's been going on. And we can tell others that we're working secretly for different Hiline companies. And everyone will settle for the explanation they like best, at least for a while. We can tell our *own* people that."

Ahead, just beyond the Lucky Counter casino, the white reflective marble came to an end. The twilight Fringe yawned ahead, heralded by the thudding of distant music. Ubu slowed.

"Funny," said Beautiful Maria. "We can make Marco's fantasy come true."

"We've still got to buy him off somehow."

"Offer him membership in the association."

Ubu gave her a warning look. "If you say so."

"I think we should."

"Because if you don't want to, fuck him. If he mistreated you in any way, we don't have to deal with him at all. We'll deny anything he claims and we'll buy off everyone around him and if he makes trouble we can buy out his contract with PDK and put his whole licehead family out of work."

Maria looked at him, at the taut anger in his face, the anger burning in his eyes. "We need him," she said. "He's smart. He's discreet."

"Shit." The muscles worked in Ubu's heavy shoulders, over his cheekbones. Finally he sighed. "I pimped you to him. I don't wanna be reminded of that."

She stepped up close and put her arms around him. "It was my shoot," she said. "My plan."

"I shouldn't have let you."

"Funny thing about Marco," Maria said. Ubu's four hands stroked her hair. "He invented this fantasy about shooters who went off on their own, who helped each other and formed their own settlement and got around Consolidation. He could think of it, but he wouldn't do it himself. He didn't believe in it. We're gonna have to believe in it for him."

"It's up to you. You're the one who can deal with people."

She looked into his pale eyes, saw Beloved there, Twelve, the inhuman pattern that had become a part of him as the electron world had become a part of her, the pattern in Ubu that, somehow, she would have to find some way to cherish.

"We'll be okay," she said. Hoping she believed it.

CHAPTER
25

THERE WAS *FAMILIA*'S BEACON, AND THERE *ABRAZO*'S, ABOUT twenty degrees apart with the colossal burning radio cloud of Montoya 81 between them. They were moving toward a rendezvous with one another and still hanging on, still waiting for Beloved.

Ubu could taste Blue Ten on the back of his throat. In his mind he could detect a residual mental coolness, aftereffect of the drug.

He tracked his couch from the shooters' station to the comm unit. It would take his message about half an hour to reach *Abrazo*, then half an hour for a signal to return. By that time he figured the Blue Ten would have worn off.

The other ships would have detected his incoming burst of radiation. Marco and the others would be sitting over the comm boards, waiting for a message from Beloved.

He put on a headset, tested the mic, then sent out his beacon and ID. He followed this radio punch to *Familia*'s solar plexus with a personal message, delivered with his face creased by the sunniest of smiles.

"Bossrider de Suarez," he said, "I wonder if you can guess how I got here?"

Ubu's music was bouncing from the laminate walls of the fuge as Ubu sat under the alpha trodes. He saw the comm board lights go on, waited for the full message to read itself into memory, then turned off the music and triggered the message.

Marco was sitting in a darkened room, with one yellow overhead light that made him look like death. The taut muscles of his neck stood out like ramparts on his thin shoulders. Jesus Rice was a bloody mess on the wall behind, a posture echoed by the crucifix around Marco's neck. The two of them together looked like some kind of depressing religious allegory.

"Doesn't matter how you found out," Marco said. "You and me got a contract, bossrider. You get a sixth. Nothing more."

Gotta admire that Marco, Ubu thought. The man goes down fighting.

Marco's voice grated on. "I could tie you up in court for years, Pasco's Ubu. I could get the Multi-Pollies to embargo you. Remember all that."

Ubu took off the trodes and put on the headset. His mind felt clear and perfect as a pool of distilled water. He pressed Transmit.

"One sixth of zip is zip," he said. "Your contract with Clan Lustre was broken when you didn't show up on time—there's a clause about timely deliveries, remember? That makes our own contract a big zero.

"Don't make me laugh about tying me up in court, either. What you gonna pay the lawyers with when I buy out your contract with PDK?" Ubu gave his sunny smile again. One of Beloved's primary patterns, 5-5-5-3-3, rolled through his mind.

Marco, he thought, was going to become a part of him. Just like Beloved.

"Don't worry, bossrider," he said. "I haven't left you out of any new arrangements. I'm gonna send you a contract. It'll supersede our old arrangement. Read it, then send me your signature and print. The moment I get it, I'll tell you where to pick up your first delivery."

Ubu triggered the comm board to send a burst including the

text of the contract, then ended his transmission and lay back under the trodes again. He called up more music.

He wished the time lag wasn't so long and that he could watch Marco's face when the message came in.

The cacophony of his music burned on, building worlds in his mind.

There was that religious allegory again, Jesus swooning over Marco's bony shoulder. Marco looked a little more relaxed this time, the muscles of his throat and bony shoulders not quite as rigid. Death, Ubu thought, taking a vacation.

"Hell of a document, Pasco's Ubu," he said. "Be a fine mind at work, here."

It's gonna give you a living for the rest of your miserable life, Ubu thought.

"Could quibble about my percentage. Maybe thirty percent of the profits would be more reasonable. Could bitch about the schedule." He gave a mirthless grin. "But why bother? Shit, you're being generous. The least I can do is respond in kind." His eyes narrowed. He stabbed at Ubu with a middle finger. "I got files, bossrider. Files on a lot of people. I got a lot of data I've been saving for the right time. Anyone gives you grief, I can maybe deal with it." Marco showed teeth: Ubu couldn't be certain whether it was a smile or a snarl. "I got a lot of stuff on the Kompanie. Enough to make them our friends. I'll send it to you." By now, Marco was smiling. "Maybe you'll figure out how useful I can be."

He leaned forward, touched something off camera that transmitted the contract and the data to *Runaway*, then leaned back in his chair. His eyes burned in their deep sockets, perhaps with amusement. "I realize you can't tell me now," he said. "But someday I wanna know how it was done. Okay?"

End of transmission.

Ubu felt the hair on his neck and arms prickle, as if he were being attacked. Marco had surrendered, but somehow it didn't feel much like a surrender.

He was trying to find a place as Ubu's hatchetman.

Ubu looked at the data Marco had sent him, a long list of who was paying off whom, places, dates, and figures, and he nodded. If he ever needed to manipulate the local Kompanie managers, he could do it. He wondered how much more of this stuff Marco had, on how many people.

Marco would be useful, as long as Ubu kept him on a short leash.

Who, or what, Ubu wondered, was next? Bright-colored harmonic structures floated, as yet unassembled, in his mind.

He touched the Transmit button.

"There is an asteroid orbiting Kitsune 71," he said, "with twenty-eight thousand tonnes of pharmaceuticals on it. The beacon transmits at twenty-one centimeters. There's a Portfire rep waiting at Angel Station for the delivery. Beautiful Maria is there. You can work out a schedule with her." He grinned. "Next Now, bossrider."

He ended his transmission, then tracked his couch back to the shooter's board. Time to get out of here, back to Santos 439 and Beloved's station.

A universe of music hammered at him. He nodded absently to the beat as he set up his shoot.

This was only the beginning.

CHAPTER
26

KING UBU DOCKED AT ANGEL'S COM AT EIGHTEEN HUNDRED, NINE hours after the yacht's pinpoint arrival, only a few hundred kilometers off optimal, in Angel System. The station, expanded over the last few years from its original wheel shape to a half-kilometer-long cylinder, was still growing. A bright skeletal gossamer, dotted with nonvolitionals, latticed one end of the cylinder and marked the first step in a further expansion.

By eighteen-ten Ubu Roy was onstation, had met briefly with his official reception committee from the Angelica Senate, then taken a private shuttle to the station's original rim. Within another few minutes he stepped into the Monte Carlo Casino, where his sister, who had disembarked from the *Maria the Fair* three days before, had rented the entire second floor.

Beautiful Maria, webbed in the electron world, kept informed of Ubu's progress via a receiver implanted in her mastoid, and watched Ubu's entrance on the casino security monitors. His feet and massive torso were bare. He wore only black trousers. Ubu was surrounded by a rotating screen of bodyguards, grey near-volitionals cased in armor, four-legged, clawed, bristling with sensors and weapons. On the surface of each was the bright monogram, a scrolled *U* linked with a scrolled *M*. The code for the insignia had been scribed in their genetics.

Ubu stepped onto a private elevator, rose to the second level. Maria's own bodyguards buzzed reverently from their voders as he passed. In a moment he was at the door of their suite.

Beautiful Maria put down her crystal bulb of pomegranate juice and turned to the door. Her silver bracelets, old gifts from Ubu, chimed as they rang against one another. The electron world buzzed discordantly in her head; she turned off the mastoid receiver and diminished the other world's volume. Her heartbeat quickened. She hadn't seen Ubu in a little over two years.

The door rised open, and Ubu stepped into the doorway. Cyphered voderings from his bodyguards nattered in from the hall. Black alloy ornaments with cool silver-and-chrome-yellow scrollwork dangled from Ubu's ears and brushed his bare shoulders. The patterns, Maria knew, signified something to him, some peculiar synaesthesiac pattern he saw when listening to his music, or when thinking about something important. Possibly the texture of the jewelry, the slick pattern of the alloy and the looped, rolling grains of pigment, meant something as well.

Ubu's expression was alert, focused, his attention on her. What was he seeing? she wondered.

Every time she met him, Ubu was a little further removed from the brother she remembered. He had too much in his head now to ever be *just Ubu* again.

It was her self-appointed work to keep Ubu human. Thus far she was succeeding maybe half the time.

Maria stepped to him, put her arms around him, kissed him. The embrace of his lower arms almost drove the wind from her. Part of him, then, still cared.

He looked at her. Measuring. "You've cut your hair."

She shook her head. "I cut it short over a year ago. Now I'm growing it back."

Maria took his hand, drew him into the room. Maria's two white cats—clones of Maxim—appeared from under furniture and began tracing figures around his ankles. "It's been too long since we've talked," she said.

"Angel's changed." He bent to say hello to the cats.

"Doubled in size since you were last here. We lease almost all the new area."

"We're doing well." A flat declaration. She raised an eyebrow.

"Clan Potent?"

"Absorbed."

She nodded. "That should bring the Multi-Pollies into line."

He gave a thin smile. "The Potent entity signed a separate treaty with us. Beloved's not in the picture. I expect she'll protest."

"Let her."

"Are the ministers here yet?"

"Expected in a few days."

"So." His shoulders rippled. "We have time to relax, a little."

"A drink? Something to eat?"

"Sharps for starters. It's the middle of the night for me."

For most of the last two years Ubu had been on Lustre Station at Santos 439, dealing with the question of competetive alien AI. Clan Potent had been pouring resources into developing their own macroatoms, their own glassware and software. Ubu had let them begin marketing, then swamped them with his own new line. His new shooting computers had the advantage of a stim antenna system that gave Ubu's customers the advantage of state-of-the-art visualization during the shoot, equivalent to what humans had enjoyed for decades but something that had as yet eluded the alien competition. Ubu's new stims were only useful with a new-type volitional navigator purchased from Beloved.

The competition had been blown out of existence, scattered into burning nothingness like matter stripped by a singularity. Clan Potent had been forced to come to terms—surrendering not to Beloved, but to Clan Runaway.

Since trade with Beloved had become public knowledge, Beautiful Maria spent almost all her time on *Maria the Fair*, her yacht-cum-office complex, dashing from one Edge station to another to quell an endless series of crises. The massive and expanding trade had propagated through the human sphere as a wave front, picking up entire economies and smashing them. Consolidation had been paralyzed, then reduced, and now almost abolished; the Multi-Pollies had been forced to unleash shooter entrepreneurial talent in the hope of creating Edge economies that could compete successfully with the onslaught of wealth pouring in from the point of alien contact.

For Maria, crouched beneath the curl of that massive, irresistible wave, it had all been a wild careening ride, almost as immediate as diving into the Now. And she had concerned herself with things that were not strictly her business. Just as she had made it her job to keep Ubu human, she had likewise assigned herself the task of trying to minimize the human damage resulting from the shattering blows of the new trade. She had acquired broken companies recklessly, often against the advice of her consultants, always against the threat of expanding too fast. Always a new flood of wealth had justified her extravagance.

Not any more, though. The reckless binge of acquisition had to end. Clan Runaway had become too important: anything that threatened to destabilize it became a threat to the entire human economy. Now Maria would have to concentrate on solidifying the empire she had, almost willy-nilly, acquired.

She filled a small bulb with Sharps, then picked up her own crystal bulb of juice. Ubu fired one round and then glanced over the suite, juggling the bulb from one lower hand to the other. Maria could feel the electron world from the floor below, from the casino, a constant presence pressing upward, like a scratchy carpet on the feet.

Ubu looked at her. "How safe is it to talk here?"

"Very." Her free hand traced invisible electric patterns in the air. "I would know if there was anything listening."

"The Multi-Pollies." He scowled. "Never thought I would be negotiating with them as equals."

"We're not." She smiled, touched her bulb to his. Crystal rang. "We're their superiors." She fired a round of pomegranate juice. "We know what's happening next. They don't have a clue. They hope to hell we're going to tell them the answer."

"And in exchange they give us a monopoly."

"They legitimize the one we already have. Other than our

association, there's no trade over the Edge now but a few Fringe humans trading with some fairly desperate clans on the other side. Nothing large-scale, not since Marco took Clan Diamond and Biagra-Exeter down."

"Fringe humans dealing with desperate clans." A thoughtful smile. "Us, once."

"The Multi-Pollies service the people in the Core, and in the Core they want security. No more of the chaos we started." She looked at him. "They think we can control it."

Ubu gave a laugh.

"If they give us the monopoly, they think things will stabilize."

There was a refined little hiss as Ubu fired another round of Sharps. "Let 'em think it," he said.

"The Kompanie went down," Maria said. "Ten days ago."

"I got the newsfax."

"It was not unexpected. We're picking up the pieces." She remembered the mirrored golden doors of the Pan-Development Klub, the particolored birds that floated over the transparent roof. The solidity and assurance that had never been real. A chord of sadness hummed through her.

Marco's old files had come in handy. Too many people in the Kompanie's power structure had, thanks to the files, been working in Clan Runaway's interest.

"We're hurting a lot of people, Ubu," she said.

His look was impatient. "These are the same people who once cut us off without a thought."

"Some of them."

"People should be aware of things." Angrily. Ubu shook his head. "Can't be helped anyway."

"Probably not." Her sadness was a distant concern. She had done what she could, riding that colossal wave, but it had long been out of her, or anyone's control.

Ubu shook his head. "Giving us a monopoly. *Enforcing* it at their own expense. From now on, our competition can be put in *prison*." He fired Sharps, then gave her an amused glance. "Be awful stupid, these people, Maria."

"Yeah. I'm beginning to think so."

"So maybe we're not just lucky, huh?"

She reached out, touched one arm. "Maybe not." They shared a smile. Maybe, she thought, this would be okay.

"Wanna see the casino?" she asked.

"Yeah." He grinned. "Maybe win some money."

"I'll tell our guards." She triggered the mastoid radio. Electron awareness flooded her skull.

As, surrounded by silent and bristling guards, they stepped on the moveway that would take them onto the casino floor, the relaxed music played over the casino loudspeakers was replaced by one of Ubu's compositions. Dense, layered, atonal, still based on Beloved's patterns but more involved now than ever, Ubu's music had evolved, growing infinitely more complex and far less comprehensible. They both heard it and laughed.

"I saw a newsfax article a few months ago," Maria said. "This musicologist person who claims to understand your music."

"I saw it, too. Guy doesn't know shit."

"That was certainly my impression."

The electron flow danced brightly in Maria's perceptions as the casino floor grew nearer. She could pick out the burning pattern of individual tables, individual games. Her hands danced electron patterns; Ubu's bracelets chimed.

"I went through here on a stroll yesterday," she said. "I was glitching the games at random, letting people win big. Nobody said anything. The house paid off."

"Be knowing we'll buy their casino out from under them if they make us angry."

Beautiful Maria gave a laugh. "We may *already* own a large part of it, you know. We're so big it's getting hard to keep track."

"Another hundred years," Ubu said, meaning it, "we'll own everything. Everything that matters anyway."

People on the casino floor were clustering, staring upward. The moveway was intended for grand descents, and took its time. Ubu gave her a look.

"The fax mentioned you in connection with someone named Fargo."

She turned to him, acknowledged the appraisal in his eyes. "We're connected, yes," she said.

"Is he here?"

She smiled, took one arm. "I didn't take him along. This meeting is for business and politics. And family."

His fingers twined around hers. "I'm glad."

"Fargo's an old shooter. He understands these things."

Somewhere in Maria's mind, a small, continual anxiety diminished. Humanity was assured, at least for the present.

People clustered about the moveway. "Ubu!" they shouted. "Ubu!"

Half these people were Clan Runaway employees, and the others were dependent on its trade. Maria had been given her grand reception three days ago. Now it was Ubu's turn.

Ubu raised a couple arms, smiled. The chant deepened, grew, began to harmonize with Ubu's music.

"*Ubu! Ubu! Ubu!*"

"You know," Ubu said, "this reminds me of something."

"*Ubu! Ubu! Ubu!*"

"What's that, shooter man?"

His lips twitched in amusement. "Doesn't matter."

The near-volitional bodyguards cleared a path at the base of the moveway. Ubu and Maria stepped onto the floor of the casino.

All night long they moved from table to table, and never stopped winning.